TRAI[GROUND

Book one of
Girls of Summer

by Kate Christie

SECOND GROWTH

Second Growth Books
Seattle, WA

Printed in the United States of America on acid-free paper
First published 2016

Cover Design: Kate Christie

ISBN: 0-9853677-3-3
ISBN-13: 978-0-9853677-3-2

DEDICATION

To the kids and the not-so-young who still think of themselves as damaged. You're not. We're not. We are *fierce*.

CHAPTER ONE
~JULY 2003~

"I'll be right back," Jamie called through the closed bathroom door.

The doorknob rattled and her mother poked her head out. "What did you say?"

"I'm going out to grab some Gatorade."

"Oh." She ran a hand over her hair, still damp from the shower. "Give me a minute. A walk sounds nice."

Seriously? Jamie offered what she hoped was a neutral look. "7-Eleven is a block away, and I have my phone. Okay?"

Her mom hesitated, glancing toward the sunlit window at the opposite end of the hotel room before returning her gaze to Jamie's. "Fine. But be careful. And come straight back."

"I will. See you later."

As she ducked into the corridor, Jamie released a long breath. The act was sometimes difficult to maintain, especially on a night like tonight—the last night of the tournament. Only a few teams remained, mostly ones with early flights the following morning. Her own team had piled into SUVs and Subaru wagons shortly after their last game and started north up the five, headed back to the Bay Area. They would have been home tonight, too, if Jamie's mom hadn't scheduled a meeting at a gallery in San Diego the following morning.

She jogged down the hotel hallway, tying her sweatshirt around her waist as she went. At least her mother hadn't noticed she was overdressed for a one-block stroll. Otherwise her plan might have failed before she even left the room.

As she bypassed the elevator and reached the stairwell door, she caught sight of a girl in a purple T-shirt and faded jeans in the vending alcove on the opposite side of the corridor. She looked familiar, and Jamie cycled through the past few days. Her T-shirt had a husky on it, so Washington. That was it— the Shoreline club. Jamie's team had knocked the Seattle side out of contention the day before.

As if feeling the weight of her stare, the girl glanced up and smiled. "Hey."

Jamie nodded at her. "Hey."

"Apparently the ice machine's out of ice."

"There's another one in the lobby. I can show you if you want." She held the stairwell door open.

"Cool." The girl followed her down the stairs. "I'm Emma."

"Jamie. You're from Seattle, aren't you?"

"Yeah. NorCal, right?"

"Right." They reached the first floor and Jamie led the way down a side hall. "Nice game yesterday."

Emma made a face. "No, it wasn't. You guys are really good, though."

"Thanks. If it helps, you were the best player on your team."

Emma smiled at her again, dimple flashing as she brushed back a few strands of honey-blonde hair that had escaped the omnipresent soccer girl ponytail. "I'm a center back. No one notices me usually."

Jamie doubted that, but she let the comment slide.

The ground floor machine had plenty of ice, and Jamie

lingered while the other girl filled her bucket.

"Why are you still here?" she asked over the sound of crashing ice.

"My dad has a work thing. What about you?"

"Same, only I'm with my mom."

As they headed back to the lobby together, Jamie slowed her gait. After four days of round-the-clock teammate bonding, she'd been looking forward to a few hours to herself. Now somehow the idea of being alone wasn't quite as tempting as it had been when she hatched her escape plan.

"I'm on my way out for a walk," she said, watching Emma out of the corner of her eye. "Would you maybe, I don't know, want to come with me?"

As soon as the words were out, she held her breath. Why had she even asked? It wasn't like they could actually be friends. They might be in the same ODP region, but that didn't mean their paths would ever cross again.

Emma stopped beside her in the lobby. "Where are you going?"

"There's a park on the water about a mile from here. I thought I'd watch the sunset."

"Alone?" Her brow creased adorably.

"Well, yeah. Although I told my mom I was going to 7-Eleven." She wasn't sure why she admitted that last part. Something about the other girl—her clear, gray-green eyes maybe, or her lips that turned up at the corners even when she wasn't smiling—invited confidence. She seemed like someone Jamie would be friends with, assuming she didn't live a thousand miles away.

Emma squinted toward the main entrance. "I guess I could use a walk. Let me go tell my dad."

"Awesome. But, um, maybe don't mention the park?"

She glanced back at Jamie, eyes still narrowed. "You're not

planning anything that would get us in trouble, right? No drugs, no spray paint, no secret gang affiliation?"

Jamie laughed at the image of herself as a tagger looking to leave her mark on the Del Mar country club scene. "Not a chance."

Emma's dimple flashed again. "In that case, give me a few minutes."

As she waited, Jamie replayed the previous day's game in her mind. If not for Emma's steady play at back, the score would likely have been higher. As it was, Jamie's team had only won by one—a goal set up by a corner kick she'd placed on a teammate's head just outside the six. According to Pete, her club coach, Jamie was an assist magnet. While other players might have a nose for scoring, she preferred to work behind the scenes. Honestly, there was less pressure on the person who set up a scoring opportunity than on the player who found herself in front of the goal with only the keeper to beat.

After five minutes and no Emma, she started to wonder if the other girl had changed her mind. It was possible she only seemed nice and was actually one of those pretty, shallow girls who typically wouldn't give someone who looked like her the time of day. Even Jamie's high school, fairly chill as far as public schools went, had them in droves.

She was about to bail when Emma appeared in the lobby, a sweatshirt looped over her shoulders. "Sorry about that," she said as she reached Jamie. "Ready?"

They set out along the main road, stopping briefly at the convenience store to pick up snacks and sports drinks. Then they resumed their trek, chatting about family, school, and soccer as they walked the short distance to the beach, the evening sun setting slowly in the distance. It was easy to talk to Emma, and soon Jamie knew quite a bit about her companion: She was about to start her senior year of high school; her parents were still married, though they had come close to divorce a year earlier; she had a thirteen-year-old brother who was more into skateboards and online gaming than organized sports; she was a member of the under-17 national team; and she had already verbally committed to play soccer at University of North Carolina.

"The national team *and* UNC?" Jamie shook her head. "I thought you said people don't usually notice you."

"Just wait. In another year your house will look like a college recruiting office exploded in it, too."

"Even if it doesn't, my sister and I are double legacy at Cal, and they have a decent women's program."

"Both of your parents went to Cal?"

"That's where they met. They've been together forever, but they still act all sappy." She shook her head, remembering how her mother had called and talked to her father for half an hour before bed every night since they'd arrived.

"You must be smart if you can get in there."

"Smarter than I look, you mean?"

Emma laughed. "I didn't say that."

"You didn't have to." Jamie smiled a little. She liked being responsible for the other girl's laugh. "What do your parents do?"

"My mom's a pediatric nurse and my father is a peds surgeon. What about yours?"

"Dad's a software engineer and Mom's day job is in graphic design."

"Day job?"

"She's a textile artist, but it doesn't pay as well as the tech industry." She started describing her mother's work, mostly dioramas and quilts made from reclaimed materials like vintage fabrics, books, photographs, and maps. Emma nodded and asked questions in the right places as if she was genuinely interested.

Hmm. Not a shallow, mean girl after all, apparently.

By the time they reached the park, the sun was barely hovering over the horizon. Jamie led the way along a bluff overlooking the ocean, and they sat down on a bench with their chips and Gatorade and watched in comfortable silence as the hazy, orange ball slipped over the horizon, bathing feathery clouds in pink and gold. Just as the sun disappeared into the sea, Jamie's cell phone rang.

She read the name on the screen and hesitated. Then she hit the call button. "Hi, Mom."

"Where are you? I thought you would be back by now."

"Sorry. I ran into a friend from another team and we're heading back to watch TV in her room. If that's okay?"

There was silence at the other end. Meanwhile, at this end, Emma was frowning. Jamie could understand why the other girl might not want to lie for someone she had just met, but she couldn't spend another night trapped in that room. She needed motion, fresh air, the company of someone who wasn't watching her every move. Television wasn't enough to distract her from the images waiting to flood her brain as soon as the lights went out. At home she could take a puff of weed and read herself to sleep by flashlight if she needed to, but here neither tactic was possible, not when she and her mother were sharing a room.

Probably she should have told her mom the truth from the start, but she hadn't wanted her to worry any more than she already did. Besides, talking was overrated.

"Which friend?" her mother finally asked. "And what room will you be in?"

"Emma from Seattle, and she's in room number...?"

"265."

"265," Jamie finished, flashing Emma a grateful smile.

"I guess that'll be okay, then," her mother said slowly. "But be back by eleven, and keep your phone on."

"I will. See you later." She hung up and turned down the

ringer before tucking the phone back in her pocket. *Whew*. At least she had won herself a few hours of freedom.

"Did she believe you?" Emma asked.

"I don't know. I haven't exactly given her much reason to lately."

"What do you mean? Why not?"

Jamie looked at her, noting how the fading light played across her face.

"What?" Emma asked, returning her gaze.

"Do you always ask people to share deep, dark secrets the night you meet them?"

She seemed to consider the question seriously. "No, I don't think so. But I usually don't run away with girls I meet at the ice machine, either."

"Fair enough," Jamie said, and shivered a little as the ocean breeze kicked up around them. The next thing she knew, Emma's hands were at her waist undoing the knotted sleeves of her sweatshirt and tugging it out from under her. Jamie froze, swallowing hard at the intimate contact.

"Good thing I'm here, though," Emma said lightly. "You clearly need someone to look after you."

Jamie pulled her warm-up over her head, staring out at the darkening ocean as Emma slipped into her own sweatshirt. How had a girl she didn't know figured out something that Jamie's friends at home hadn't yet glommed onto? It had been three months since spring break, and yet barely a day passed that she didn't find herself sliding backward in some fashion. Every time she thought she was moving on, something happened to bring the fear flooding back. This weekend had been worse than most. Surf Cup was the first tournament she'd traveled to since Europe. And while Southern California and the Rhône-Alpes region of France had little in common, soccer tournaments were soccer tournaments and hotels were hotels.

"I think the sun has pretty much set," Emma commented.

"Do you want to head back?"

"Not really. Do you?"

"No." Emma scooted closer. "As long as you block the wind, that is."

"Deal."

Jamie leaned into her, amazed that a stranger could make her feel so safe. Her initial impression of Emma had been spot on. She was a good person. Cute, too, but that didn't seem nearly as important. Sighing, Jamie slid a little lower on the bench and watched waves crash on the beach below them.

\#

Emma didn't usually lie. After what had happened with her father, she detested dishonesty. But when the girl from Northern California invited her on a walk and then asked her not to let on where they were going, she knew there was more to the story. Maybe it was the shadows under her blue eyes, or the way her smile didn't quite seem genuine, but Emma kept the girl's secret as she told her father she was headed out on a snack run and then back to a friend's room to watch a movie. Unlike Jamie's mother, her dad didn't ask for details. He only told her to take her phone and have a good time, barely even glancing up from his laptop.

Now as she and Jamie sat huddled together on the bench, the ocean crashing below them and color fading from the sky, she was glad she'd listened to her gut. Jamie was shivering beside her, but Emma was fairly certain it wasn't from the cool air off the ocean. She didn't stop to think that they didn't really know each other. She didn't stop to wonder if Jamie might not want to be touched. She simply slipped her arm through the other girl's and tugged her closer, tightening her grip as Jamie glanced at her, startled.

"I'm cold," she said, even though the temperature was warmer than what she was used to. "Is this okay?"

After a moment, she felt Jamie relax against her. "Yeah,"

she said, and cleared her throat. "I mean, it's the least I can do, after dragging you out here and whatnot."

Emma hid a smile at the toughness Jamie was trying to project. She had noticed her during the game, of course. So had half the girls on her team. She had overheard the gay ones talking about her later: her baby dyke swagger, her light eyes and short, dark hair, her confident smile. Jamie was hot, no doubt about it. But that wasn't why Emma had accepted her invitation to check out the sunset. Back at the hotel, Jamie had looked lost somehow, and Emma had a genetic predisposition to try to help anyone in pain.

They sat in silence for a while, watching light fade from the world until the ocean and the sky were almost the same color. Then Emma asked how Jamie had started playing soccer, and little by little, life returned to the other girl's face and voice. She clearly loved the game as much as Emma did. She was describing her first AYSO experience when Emma's phone buzzed.

"Sorry," she said, checking the screen. She frowned a little and hit ignore. Why was he calling again? It wasn't like five days away was even that long.

"Everything okay?" Jamie asked.

"Fine."

"Guy troubles?" When Emma glanced at her quickly, she shrugged. "Sorry. Didn't mean to pry."

"No, that's okay. I just didn't think you would want to talk about that kind of thing."

"Why not?" Jamie looked at her, head tilted in apparent confusion.

"Oh. No, I mean, it's, you know…" And then she noticed Jamie's grin. Finally, a real smile.

"You mean because I'm gay."

"Are you? I never would have guessed."

At that, Jamie let out a belly laugh that temporarily drowned out the sound of the ocean. Emma smiled back, pleased she had managed to coax such a response from someone who had seemed close to tears a few minutes before. *My work here is done*, she told herself, and then wondered at the pang the thought elicited.

"Do you want to talk about it, though?" Jamie asked. "My friends say I'm a pretty good listener."

"I don't know." She shrugged. "I think maybe I'm not good girlfriend material."

"But you're so, I don't know, conscientious."

"How would you know? You just met me."

"I watched you play yesterday," Jamie said, her voice only half-teasing, "and now here you are looking after me, remember?"

"Maybe I haven't met the right guy, then."

"Or girl."

Emma smiled a little. "Right."

"How old are you, anyway?"

"I'll be seventeen in October. You?"

"Sixteen. In January."

"That's like six months away," Emma pointed out.

"I know, but fifteen sounds so young."

"You don't seem that young to me."

"Thanks. I think." Her eyes seemed to darken as she glanced out over the ocean.

Emma watched her profile for a moment, and then she leaned once again into Jamie's side. She wasn't usually this touchy-feely with someone she had just met, but the wind off the water really was chilly. "Tell me more kiddie soccer league stories. They're my favorite."

"You're weird, you know that?" But there was a hint of a smile back in her voice.

The minutes slipped away and the night deepened around them as they talked about school, family, and, of course, soccer. Early on they discovered they had both been at the 1999 World Cup final match at the Rose Bowl, and each considered it one of the best days of her life. They were both also hoping to attend a World Cup match in the fall when the US hosted the tournament for the second time in a row, but neither was sure their soccer or school schedules would cooperate. Though Jamie didn't mention a hope to someday play at the top level, Emma felt certain they were on the same page when it came to a future career in soccer as they talked coaches and team dynamics and protein diets, training schedules and game tape and the challenge of choosing between club and prep teams.

"You're one of those girls who has a catchphrase, aren't you?" Jamie asked, long after the sky had darkened and the nearly full moon had begun to rise through the filmy clouds overhead. "Let me guess—it has something to do with a positive attitude. Am I right?"

Emma was glad the light from the nearby lamppost wasn't bright enough to reveal her pink cheeks. "No comment," she said, and stood up, stretching. "And on that note…"

Jamie rose beside her, arching her back. "Damn, I must be out of shape."

"Or it could be you played five games in four days," Emma pointed out.

"Six, actually."

"That's right, you guys made it to the finals, didn't you? Sorry you didn't win."

"How did you know that?"

"I stayed for the game. It was either that or hang out watching my father work on his laptop."

"Sounds thrilling."

"Doesn't it? I'm actually lucky I ran you into you tonight.

This was a much better way to spend the last night at Surf Cup."

"I completely agree." Jamie glanced at her watch. "I should probably get back before my mom kills me, though."

They gathered up the remains of their snacks, and then Jamie held out her arm, her voice teasing as she asked, "May I walk you home, miss?"

"Why yes, you may." Emma linked her arm through Jamie's, wondering at her own almost giddy response to Jamie's flirty tone. Jamie might be hot, but Emma had a boyfriend. Besides, even though she had thought about kissing a girl—quite a bit, actually—she had yet to do so in real life. Somehow the shadows in Jamie's eyes told her that tonight was not the time to start, no matter how much she might be tempted. And here on this bluff, far from her everyday life, she was tempted. A cute girl smiling into her eyes, a beautiful sunset over the ocean, the moon rising through gently swaying palm trees—it all added up to one of the more romantic moments of her life.

But she wasn't here for romance, she reminded herself as they retraced their earlier steps. She was here for the chance to continue to develop her game, which would help her get to the next level—the under-19s, then the under-23s, and then, eventually, if she was lucky, the senior national team. That was her goal, and nothing else was nearly as important.

She almost stumbled when Jamie paused on the paved walkway, her eyes fixed on the property that abutted the park. It was lit up against the night sky, and through gaps in the fence they could see a pool, hot tub, and wisteria-lined deck on one side of the massive house, a manicured lawn extending toward the cliff on the other.

"Can you imagine living like that?" Jamie asked, wrinkling her nose.

"No," Emma admitted. "Even if I had that kind of money, I wouldn't spend it on a house."

"What would you spend it on?"

"I don't know. Probably medicine for third world countries, or education reform or animal protection. No one needs that much stuff."

Jamie was smiling again. "See? I knew you were the conscientious type."

"Whatever." Emma tugged her back onto the trail. "Let's get you back before you turn into a pumpkin."

They returned to the lamp-lit main road, arms still linked, chatting easily as they passed in and out of the shadows. A little past the halfway point, an approaching car slowed and a guy leaned out the window.

"Muff divers!" he shouted, pairing the insult with a crude gesture.

Beside her Emma felt Jamie stiffen, and she quickly held her back as she made a move toward the car. "Let it go. They're jackasses. Not even worth it."

After a moment, Jamie gave in and kept walking. The car speeded up again and roared away, and Emma let out a breath of relief. *What the hell?* Guys could be such assholes. Usually she thanked the gods she had been born in the US instead of some tiny country where women weren't even allowed to go to school, let alone play soccer. And yet, that kind of crap happened here, too.

They walked on separately, the narrow space between them somehow huge now. Jamie's brow was furrowed, and it seemed like she had retreated into the remote place inside her own mind that Emma had temporarily lured her from.

"I'm sorry," Emma said, trying to move closer on the sidewalk.

Jamie maintained the buffer between them. "Why are you sorry?"

"Because that's probably not the first time something like that has happened to you."

"Yeah, well, probably won't be the last time, either."

"Seriously, that sucks."

"Sticks and stones," Jamie muttered, her voice as dark as the look that flickered and faded across her face.

Emma wasn't sure what to say, so she remained quiet as she walked along the suddenly perilous-seeming street, Jamie pacing coolly beside her.

When the hotel was within sight, Emma stopped and said, "Give me your phone."

"What?" Jamie looked over at her, blinking as if she'd gazed too long into a bright light.

"Give me your phone."

"Um, okay."

"Add yourself to mine too, okay?"

Nodding, Jamie took the phone and started to peck at the extended keyboard. Emma went to work on Jamie's flip phone, typing in her full name, both her cell and home numbers, and her email address. As she saved the info, an alert popped up on Jamie's screen: four missed calls from "Mom." That couldn't be good.

"I had fun tonight," she said, checking her phone surreptitiously as they traded back. Jamie Maxwell. That explained why she'd heard Jamie's teammates calling her "Max."

"So did I." Jamie started walking again, a ghost of a smile flitting across her lips. "You're okay—for a Washingtonian."

"You're not so bad yourself, Miss California."

"Hate to tell you, but I'm not exactly the beauty pageant type."

"If you were, you would totally win." Emma winced a little. Flirting with the cute gay girl was not cool, especially when she'd ignored a call from her boyfriend while hanging out with the girl in question.

Fortunately, Jamie took her comment as a joke. "Because fauxhawks and painter's pants are the stuff of beauty queen legends."

They were still smiling at the image when they entered the hotel lobby, eyes on each other. Before the door had even closed, a middle-aged woman in a flowing skirt and Birkenstocks was rushing toward them. Without thinking, Emma stepped forward so that she was slightly in front of Jamie, but the woman only brushed past her and grabbed Jamie's shoulders.

"Where have you been? Why didn't you answer your phone? Do you know how worried I was?"

"Mom, we're fine. It's barely eleven."

Emma smiled and held out her hand. "Hi. You must be Jamie's mom. I'm Emma."

The woman reluctantly released Jamie to shake Emma's hand. "Yes, your father and I have been getting acquainted," she said, her voice cool.

For the first time, Emma noticed her father standing in the background. His shirt was untucked and his thick hair disheveled, and he did not look pleased.

"I'm sorry I kidnapped Jamie," Emma continued, her eyes back on the other girl's mother. "We were going to come back to watch TV, but I really wanted to see the sunset and then we lost track of time. It was my fault, really."

"See?" her father put in, coming to stand beside her. "It was just a misunderstanding. I'm sure they were being careful. Weren't you, girls?" His hand on her shoulder was a little heavy, and Emma glanced up at him. No, he did not look pleased at all.

"Yes, sir," Jamie mumbled.

"Good," he said, and started to steer Emma toward the elevator bank. "And now, I think it's time to call it a night."

Jamie and her mother followed, and they all rode up to the

second floor together in awkward silence. Beside her, Emma could feel the unhappiness rolling off Jamie in waves. She didn't want the night to end like this. She wanted to tell Jamie's mother to go easy on her, but judging from the way she'd reacted to their disappearing act, the woman was well-acquainted with the shadows in her daughter's eyes. Emma, on the other hand, had only known Jamie for a matter of hours. And yet, she didn't feel like a stranger.

Their rooms lay at opposite ends of the hotel. When they got off the elevator, Jamie waved a little and said, "See you, Emma."

"Bye, Jamie," she replied. Then she and her father headed in one direction while Jamie and her mother went the other.

Emma stalked along the corridor. This was ridiculous. They weren't children. They may not be adults, either, but they should at least be able to speak to each other without their parents' interference.

"Hang on," Emma said to her father, and jogged back toward the elevator. "Hey!"

Jamie turned, smiling a little as she moved to meet her halfway. "Hey yourself."

"Thanks for keeping me company tonight," Emma said softly. "Give me a call sometime, okay? I want to hear how your fall season goes."

"Really?"

"Really."

"Okay, then. I will."

"Good." Emma hesitated, and then she reached out and pulled Jamie toward her for a hug. "Take it easy on yourself, Max. Got it?"

"Got it," Jamie murmured, her breath warm on Emma's neck. Then she pulled away and gave her a cocky grin. "Good luck finding the right guy. Or girl."

Emma rolled her eyes. "Call me," she said over her shoulder

as she walked away.

"I will. See you."

"Later."

Her father was frowning when she caught back up, his slightly lined brow furrowed.

"What?" she asked as they continued down the hall.

"We both know that little excursion was not your idea."

"Whatever," she said, feigning boredom.

"I'm serious, Emma." He held their room door open for her. "I don't want you hanging around with someone like that. You don't need that kind of trouble."

Emma swallowed against the slow burn his words evoked. He didn't know Jamie. She may be troubled, but she wasn't trouble. Or was it that she didn't look or dress the way he thought a girl should?

"Really? Huh. I think I forgot how much you care about what I need."

He sighed, and when he spoke again, his voice sounded tired. "What's that supposed to mean?"

"You know exactly what it means. You've barely been around the past few years, let alone paid attention to what I do. You wouldn't even have come along this weekend if it wasn't for your stupid conference."

He shook his head and walked toward the door that connected their rooms. "I'm sorry you think that. The truth is, I came with you because I thought it would give us some quality time together. Apparently I was wrong, once again."

She watched the door swing shut behind him. It wasn't fair. He was the parent, and yet he was always the one who walked away. She and her brother had been grasping at him for so long that she couldn't remember what it had been like before he'd begun perfecting his vanishing act. Except that wasn't entirely true. It was just too painful to remember the man he had once been before his work had taken him away from them. From her.

Her mind cycling from the walk with Jamie to her father and back again, she got ready for bed and sat propped against the hotel bed pillows, trying to concentrate on the novel she'd brought along. Normally reading calmed her, but tonight the words left barely any impression. She was about to give up when her phone buzzed. *Whoops.* She hadn't thought about Josh even once since the park.

But it wasn't Josh. Emma smiled as she read Jamie's text: "Wanted to say thanks for taking the blame back there. I'm not grounded, so props to you for that minor miracle."

"No problem," Emma typed back. "What are friends for, right?"

"Friends, huh?"

"I'm in if you are, California girl."

"Sounds good to me. Good night, Blake."

"Good night."

Emma set her phone on the bedside table and clicked off the lamp. Jamie had used her soccer nickname, short for Blakeley, her last name. Apparently she had been paying attention during the game yesterday. Was it strange that they had connected in such a short time? But no, the same thing had happened with a handful of the girls at the inaugural U-17 national team camp the previous fall. Within the first few days together, it had seemed like she knew those girls better than some of the kids she'd grown up with. Each subsequent time they'd been called up for training or a match, it was like they hadn't been apart for long, even though months might have passed. Maybe it was that they were more alike than they were different. Back at home, there weren't that many girls who lived for soccer the way she did. But on her club team and even more so on the youth national team, they all shared the desire to be the best at the sport they loved most.

As she lay alone in her hotel room, she wondered if she and Jamie would ever play on the same team. It seemed like a longshot, but Emma had a saying: "Plan like you'll live forever; live like you'll die tomorrow." As long as they both kept working hard and managed to stay injury-free—always a big if when you played competitively year round—it could happen.

See, not a word about keeping a positive attitude, she congratulated herself, remembering the way Jamie had teased her about being the kind of person who would have a catchphrase. At least there was that.

CHAPTER TWO

"Jamie, Emma's on the phone," her mother called from the kitchen.

Ignoring her older sister's raised eyebrows, Jamie grabbed the receiver from the coffee table and stepped outside onto the back patio. It was September, her favorite month of the year, and the early evening air was warm and dry.

"Hola," she said as she headed for the hammock strung between a pair of beech trees.

"Hola, *chiquita*. How was your game?" Emma asked.

"Awesome. We won by two."

Jamie was a couple of weeks into fall travel league with her club team based in the East Bay burbs, which meant carpooling with various SF and Oakland teammates half an hour to practice twice a week. She also had a game each weekend somewhere within a two-hour radius of home.

"Did you get on the board?" Emma asked.

"One assist. What about you? You guys were at home, right?"

"Yeah. We crushed our crosstown rivals."

Unlike California, where girls' prep soccer was a winter

sport, Washington schools offered girls' soccer in the fall. Emma's squad was currently ranked second in the state of Washington in their division, and Emma had been named a pre-season Parade All American for the second year in a row. So much for not being noticed.

After a brief comparison of game notes, they moved on to Saturday night plans. Both of their school teams were planning to get together. In a matter of hours, alcohol and other recreational substances would be flowing freely at whoever's house was parent-free that night.

"Are you taking Josh?" Jamie asked.

"Not exactly. I, um, might have broken up with him last night."

"Might have?"

"No. I did."

"Finally. I can't believe it took you that long."

"Happy now?"

Jamie rolled her eyes even though Emma couldn't see her. "The better question is, are you?"

"I think so. I mean, it'll be hard to see him every day at school, but it's kind of a relief, to be honest. He was always giving me those puppy dog eyes. Now I don't have to feel guilty for forgetting our three-month anniversary, or some other supposedly major moment that somehow slipped my radar."

"Are you sure you weren't the guy in that relationship?"

"Ha ha. What about you? Did you talk to that girl in your Spanish class? What's her name?"

"Faith. And no, not yet."

"What are you waiting for?"

"Honestly? I think I have plenty to worry about right now without adding dating drama. It's hard enough juggling classes and my high school team and club stuff. Not to mention driver's ed."

Emma was quiet for a moment, and Jamie wondered if she would press her for the real reason she was dodging her latest girl crush. But she didn't, a fact that Jamie appreciated more than Emma knew. Someday, if they stayed friends, she would probably tell her about France. But not yet. She still wasn't entirely sure how to talk about it to herself, despite the therapist she'd been seeing for the past five months.

"Driving is fun," Emma said finally. "If you can skateboard, then something with brakes and air bags will seem easy."

They talked about Emma's little brother's new skateboard, and then the conversation swung back to soccer, as it always did. With their fall seasons in full swing, there was endless fodder on that front. Plus the English Premier League (EPL) season had just started up again with Champions League soon to follow, and World Cup group play was set to begin this very weekend. US Soccer, the official governing body for the sport in America, recommended that youth players watch as much quality game film as possible, and Emma and Jamie were only too happy to comply. Over the summer they had discovered they could spend hours on the phone watching the matches they'd taped off satellite television. This involved staking out the TV at a prearranged time, calling each other up, and hitting play at the exact same moment. Jamie's sister thought they were crazy, but Emma said their behavior was normal given their shared aspiration to one day play at the highest level.

It had been two months since Surf Cup, and barely a day went by without a text, email, or phone call. Jamie's Berkeley friends kept teasing her about her girlfriend up in Seattle, but it wasn't like that. She and Emma had things in common that none of her other friends cared about. Like the Food Network—sometimes they made plans to watch cooking shows together instead of game tape. But that was their secret. Not even their parents knew about their shared obsession with Giada De Laurentiis, the star of *Everyday Italian*.

"Do you still want to watch the games tomorrow?" Emma asked.

"Of course," Jamie replied, swinging the hammock slightly. The following day boasted not only an early season match-up between Arsenal and Manchester United but the first match for the US women at the World Cup. The first-round games for the American side were all on the East Coast while the semis would be in Portland and the finals in Los Angeles. Jamie wasn't going to be able to attend any games, thanks to school and soccer, but Emma was going to Portland for the semis.

"The women are going to kick Sweden's ass, but your boys are going down!"

"They are not," Jamie said, though she knew there was a good chance Manchester United would carry the day at Old Trafford. "I still don't understand how you can root for Man U. It's like being a Yankees fan."

"We can't all be champions of the underdog."

"Why not?"

"Because we can't. Anyway, what do you think about watching both games live?" Emma asked.

"The guys kick off at seven."

"And?"

"And it's my only day off all week? I was planning to get up for the women."

"Aw, come on," Emma cajoled. "It'll make the time before the US game go so much faster. Pleeease? Think of it as an early birthday present."

"Your birthday is like a month away."

"Duh, that's why I said early."

"Fine," Jamie grumbled. "I'll set my stupid alarm. But you're not getting anything else for your birthday."

"Right." Emma snorted.

"Excuse me?"

"You know you can't resist sending me stuff, dork."

"I think you overestimate your charm, nerd."

"No, I just know how much you like giving presents."

That was true. Jamie had sent Emma two care packages so far, one for a national team tournament in Texas and another to mark the start of her senior year. In fact, Emma's birthday CD was already burned and waiting to be mailed.

They chatted for a little while longer, and then Jamie's sister Meg poked her head outside to tell her it was time to set the table for dinner.

"Have fun tonight," Jamie said.

"You too. Talk to you tomorrow?"

"Bright and early."

"Cool. See you…"

"…Later."

They always hung up the same way. If it was late, they wished each other sweet dreams, and if it was earlier, like now, one would start their standard farewell phrase and the other would finish it. Jamie couldn't remember exactly how the tradition had started, but it had become habit by now.

"How's Emma?" her mother asked as Jamie entered the kitchen, humming the chorus from Avril Lavigne's "Mobile," one of the songs she'd put on Emma's birthday CD.

"Great. They won their game, too."

"Good for them," her mother said politely. She attended most of Jamie's games, but unlike her husband, she wasn't exactly a sports fan.

As they set out napkins and silverware, Meg asked, "What did your long distance girlfriend have to say?"

"She's not my girlfriend."

"Are you sure about that?"

"I am capable of being friends with a straight girl.

Homophobic much?"

Meg shook her head. "Don't play the homophobia card just because you don't like what I'm saying. You have to admit, you talk to her more than you do any of your other friends. I bet you already have a plan to talk to her tomorrow, don't you?"

"Well, yeah. There are two games on so we had to make a plan."

"You *had* to?" Meg enquired as their father walked in, open laptop in hand.

"Yes, we *had* to. The World Cup starts tomorrow."

"No wonder she hangs out with you. No one else she knows could possibly be as much of a soccer junkie." A newly minted senior herself, Meg had wondered aloud more than once why Emma would want to bother with a lowly sophomore.

"You say that like it's a bad thing," Jamie commented.

"Last time I checked, addiction is pretty much always a bad thing."

"Meg, leave your sister alone," their mother said, "and Tim, you know the rule. No computers at the table."

He glanced up, glasses sliding down his nose, and offered an apologetic smile. "Sorry, honey. I wanted to show Jamie something. It won't take long." He set the laptop on the sideboard and waved her over. "I think I found the shirt you were looking for, kiddo."

"Really?" She stood next to him, gazing at the web page open to eBay. "Is the back blank?"

"According to the images. Take a look."

"Can't this wait until after dinner?" her mother asked.

"It's an online auction," he replied, "so no. What do you think, Jamie?"

She touched his arm. "It's perfect. Thanks, Dad."

"You're welcome, sweetheart," he said, and started typing.

A few hours later, Jamie sat outside on her friend Ari's patio, nursing the same mostly full wine cooler she'd held all night. Since France, she couldn't bring herself to drink beer. Even the smell was enough to turn her stomach. Inside the house, the party was going on without her. There were more guys than she remembered from past team parties, and more weed, too. The cloud inside had been a bit much, as had been the coupling off of her teammates with male soccer players she barely recognized after a summer spent traveling for club tournaments and the Olympic Development Program. Girls didn't change all that much over such a short period of time, but guys were different. Their faces, torsos, voices, even their hair was constantly evolving now that they were all in high school.

The lyrics from "Mobile," her current favorite song, came back to her again. Everything really was changing around her, and she felt like a mobile, spun out of control by feelings she couldn't always name. How much of it was France, and how much a normal part of being a teenager? Not that she would ever know. What had happened couldn't be taken back. The images began to replay in her head, as they still occasionally did when she paused in one place too long, and she shook her head, hoping motion would help.

Lights from the pool area blurred in her vision. This property was unreal. Ari's father was a venture capitalist, her mother a partner at a corporate law firm in the city. Their house in the affluent Claremont Hills neighborhood was a "modern monstrosity," according to Jamie's mother—all concrete and glass panels that seemed destined to rain death upon the house's occupants when the next major earthquake struck.

As she watched, two guys and a girl wandered out of the

house and made their way to the pool, where they wrestled around until, predictably, all three ended up in the water, laughing and shrieking. It was warm out, but it wasn't that warm.

Pulling her phone from her pocket, she texted Emma: "How's your party? Mine's not quite my style…"

She waited a few minutes, but no answer. Maybe Emma was coupling off even now, taking advantage of her newly single status. No doubt there were guys lined up waiting for a chance to hook up with her. After all, she was cute, smart, and a nationally ranked soccer player headed to the opposite coast to play for a storied athletics program. Some of the biggest names in American women's soccer had graduated from UNC. Personally, Jamie couldn't imagine moving to the East Coast for college, but then California offered significantly more opportunity than Washington as far as collegiate soccer programs went.

Still restless, she texted her sister: "Where are you?"

A minute later her phone lit up: "Becky's."

"Can you come get me? Please?"

"Of course. When and where?"

"Ari's. Is now okay?"

"Be there in fifteen, James."

"You rock."

Jamie set aside her unfinished wine cooler and made her way around the side of the house to the front porch. She was lucky to have Meg as a sister. Some of her friends had older brothers and sisters who picked on them or, almost as bad, pretended they didn't exist. But even before France, Meg had looked out for her. Since Jamie had given their parents permission to tell her what had happened in Lyon, Meg had been even more attentive. They had a deal that if Jamie was ever someplace that made her uncomfortable for any reason, Meg would find a way to come pick her up, no questions asked.

Ten minutes later, Becky's ancient Datsun chugged to a stop in front of Ari's house.

"Hey, loser," Becky said as Jamie slid into the back seat.

Meg smacked her best friend in the back of the head. "My little sister is not a loser. She is awesome. For a sophomore. Right, James?"

"Whatever you say." She fastened her seat belt. "Thanks for rescuing me, guys."

"You're welcome." Becky winked at her in the rearview mirror as she pulled her beater car away from the curb and guided it downhill toward the city.

"You okay, kiddo?" Meg asked, watching her from the front seat.

"Fine. Wasn't in the mood for the ultra-hetero make-out session, though. What were you guys up to?"

"Working on a song. It's almost done."

"Awesome. Can't wait to hear it."

"Actually, you could pay us back," Becky put in. "You're good with computers, right?"

"Sure."

"We were wondering if there's a way to record electric piano tracks directly to my Mac."

"I don't see why not, depending on what kind of line out the piano has. Let me take a look and talk to Dad. I bet there's something out there that would even score the music for you."

"I told you she's not a loser."

"Yeah, yeah, your sibling bond is the envy of us all."

Meg glanced back and smiled at Jamie. "No lie, homey."

Jamie nodded. "True dat, yo."

Becky huffed. "Stop with the white girl appropriation of Black English! Otherwise I'm going to make you both get out and walk."

"Touchy, much?" Meg said. "You k.
calling you an Oreo is not our fault."

"Oreo?" Jamie echoed.

"You know, black on the outside, white or.

"What does that make him then? Double st

The two girls in the front seat cracked up. B   , , younger
brother had never been thin, but since joining the middle
school football team the previous year he had bulked up
substantially.

"Nice one, sis." Meg held up her hand for a high five. "But
all this talk of cookies is making me hungry. Who's up for ice
cream?"

"I am!" the other two called out in unison.

They parked downtown and walked to Ben & Jerry's. The
line was out the door on this, a warm Saturday evening, but
they didn't mind. Becky and Meg sang their new song for
Jamie, she told them about her game in Central Valley strip-
mall hell, and they all agreed that the crowd at Ari's was way
too fast.

"Julie Hanford was totally snorting coke in the downstairs
bathroom," Jamie told them as they paid for their ice cream
cones.

"I don't ever want to hear about you doing anything like
that," Meg said, staring at her.

"As if. Hard drugs and soccer do not mix, in case you hadn't
noticed."

"Good," her sister said, and tugged her closer for a second.
"Make sure you remember that."

"Yes, Mom," Jamie said, rolling her eyes.

They took their cones to go and walked around downtown
Berkeley, taking in the sights. College kids and Silicon Valley
yuppies mingled with tourists, hippies, and Rastafarians on this
warm weekend night, and every once in a while the scent of

drifted past. Jamie loved people-watching in her hometown. San Francisco was fun to explore and only a short BART ride away, but to her mind, you couldn't beat Berkeley.

Jamie's curfew was earlier than Meg's, but the older girl didn't complain as they finished their cones and headed home to Elmwood. When Becky grumbled about babysitting sophomores, Meg gave her a look that Jamie recognized as their mother's infamous no-sass-allowed stare. All at once, she could see her sister a few years down the road with kids of her own. And she wondered—would that be her someday, too? Being queer meant she wasn't automatically expected to pine after the white picket fence and two and a half kids. Which was just as well—at the moment, she couldn't imagine going on a date with anyone, let alone settling down and starting a family. When you're working on surviving, it's hard to picture a future where you might be responsible for the lives of others.

Becky dropped them in front of their house and tooted her little car's horn as she drove off. They headed up the front walkway together, Meg's arm around Jamie's shoulders.

"I'm glad you called, kiddo."

"Me, too." Jamie rested her cheek against her sister's ponytail. "But you know, I *am* taller than you. Maybe you should stop calling me kiddo."

"Perish the thought!" Meg flicked her shoulder.

"Ow." Jamie rubbed the spot, laughing as they climbed the front porch stairs.

"Oh, did I hurt the big, strong jock?"

"You're such a bully."

Their parents were in the living room reading as they walked in. Or their mom was reading, anyway. Their father had his laptop perched on a wooden lap desk and was typing away as usual. He looked up and smiled when he saw them.

"Hi, girls. Did you have a nice night?"

Meg nodded. "Ice cream and songwriting—what more

could anyone ask?"

Their mom was frowning at Jamie. "I thought you were playing mini-golf with the soccer team."

She shrugged, toying with the zipper on her hoodie. "We got done early so Meg and Becky came to get me."

"Thanks, sweetie," their dad said, his eyes on Meg.

"No problem. What are big sisters for?"

There was a brief silence in the room, and Jamie could almost hear the thought circulating: Big sisters looked out for little sisters, the same way friends were supposed to watch out for friends. Chocolate ice cream and lime-flavored wine cooler rumbled in her stomach, and she swallowed back an alcohol-infused burp. Nothing a little weed couldn't fix.

"Anyway," she said, and headed for the stairs, "I have to be up early to watch soccer with Emma. Good night."

"Good night," her family echoed.

She would have bet good money they were going to discuss her emotional state the second she was out of earshot. Sure enough, as she creaked about the second floor of their 1920s Craftsman, she heard the low murmur of voices below. She could have eavesdropped through one of the heating grates in the hall floor, but honestly, she wasn't sure she wanted to know what they were saying.

Her evening routine took only a couple of minutes—the perks of being a tomboy. Brush her teeth, rinse her face, smooth down her hat-head, and voila. Dressed in boxers and an old YMCA soccer shirt, she slid between her sheets and reached for the incense in her bedside table. Once it was lit, she removed the drawer's false back and pulled out the pipe and baggie her buddy Blair had given her. Working methodically, she lit the previous evening's bowl and inhaled, closing her eyes as the hot smoke coiled into her lungs. The effects were almost immediate. She exhaled slowly and felt her shoulders relax, her face soften, even the tight knot in her stomach ease. Smiling a little, she set the pipe aside to cool down. Thank the gods for medicinal marijuana.

She was closing the drawer a little while later when her phone's alert sounded. Her smile widened as she read Emma's text: "Sorry, forgot my phone was on silent! Are you still awake?"

"I'm up," she typed back.

"Party here was lame too. Left with Dani and Sian and rented a movie. You?"

"Went for ice cream with my sister and Becky."

"Ooh, even better! Jealous…"

"Next time I see you, I'll take you out for a cone. Or are you a cup person?"

"Cone all the way, and you're on. Now go to bed. You have to be up early."

"So do you. Go USA!"

"Go USA!!!!! Sweet dreams."

"Sweet dreams to you too."

Jamie turned off her phone and lay back in bed, staring up at the glow-in-the-dark constellations she and her father had hung on the ceiling years before. Why did she feel closer to a girl she'd only met two months earlier than to the classmates she'd known since kindergarten? Maybe it was that she'd met Emma after France. She couldn't see how Jamie had changed, not the way her Berkeley friends could. And here she'd thought coming out the previous year would be the hardest thing she'd have to face.

She closed her eyes and tried to slow her breathing. Emma was right. They had to be up early. As the usual flood of memories tried to hijack her brain, she took a calming breath and reminded herself that she was safe; memories couldn't actually hurt her. To distract her mind, she mentally listed the twenty women on the US World Cup squad, including college and pro teams. Then she tried to remember Arsenal's starting line-up, overall record, and current standing in the first division of the EPL. When that was done, she was still awake, so she pictured Emma in her house in Seattle. Emma had emailed a few photos, and while the house was nothing like Ari's, it was significantly posher than Jamie's. The view out over the water toward islands and mountains was incredible, and Jamie wondered if she would ever see it in person.

Wondered, too, if this friendship could possibly last when their lives were so different. Emma was leaving for college in less than a year. When she was in North Carolina, would they keep emailing and texting? Would they still get up early on weekend days to watch TV together? Somehow she doubted it. But she would take what she could get for now. Her friendship with Emma made her feel calm, normal even. It gave her hope that someday she would be able to fall asleep without medicinal assistance.

Small goals, she reminded herself. It was always best to start small.

#

The day before she turned seventeen, Emma received a phone call from the manager of the under-19 national team. There was a training camp scheduled for the third week of November at US Soccer headquarters in Los Angeles. Was she interested in attending?

"Yes," she said quickly, even though the timing wasn't ideal. Mid-November marked the end of her high school season. If they made it to states, she risked missing part of the tournament, possibly even her last ever high school game(s). But this was the next step on the road to—she hoped—playing for the senior side. She couldn't say no. She didn't want to, anyway, even if it meant possibly letting down the girls she'd played soccer with her entire life.

As soon as she hung up the land line, she grabbed her cell phone. It was a Sunday, and for once no one else was home. Her father was away on one of his many work-related trips, and her mother had taken her brother, Tyler, to a skate park to work on his middle school science fair project, which apparently involved measuring the effects of speed on the distance and height of his favorite skateboarding trick. Leave it to Ty to find a way to combine science with his love of skateboarding.

"Hey. Call me!" she texted. Less than a minute later her cell rang. She picked up, laughing. "Okay, that was fast even for you."

"You better not have opened your presents early," Jamie said.

"Pres*ents*? As in, plural?"

"Apparently you didn't or you would know that. What's up? I thought we weren't going to talk until tomorrow after the family thing?"

Emma's father was planning to fly home from Nevada—or was it Oklahoma?—in time to whisk them all off to a fancy birthday dinner in downtown Seattle. She would believe it when she saw it. Although maybe that wasn't entirely fair. He had been trying much harder recently, and Ty at least had forgiven him for any past transgressions.

"I couldn't wait for tomorrow," she told Jamie. "Dude, I got called up to the under-19 team camp next month in LA! Can you freaking believe it?"

"Of course I can," Jamie exclaimed, her voice nearly as excited. "I told you, you are one badass soccer player. When's camp?"

Emma shared the little she knew. More details would arrive via a formal letter of invitation sometime in the next few days.

"I can't believe it's happening!" she added. "I mean, I've worked really hard, but so have a thousand other girls our age, you know?" As soon as the words left her lips, she realized that one of those thousands was on the other end of the telephone line.

"Well, I'm not surprised," Jamie declared, and Emma could hear the smile in her voice. "You're totally going to show those SoCal biatches how it's done."

One of the things they'd bonded over was the annoying supremacy of Southern California teams. No matter how far their own club teams went, they inevitably encountered and usually lost to a team from SoCal populated with taller and stronger than average players who tugged on jerseys and threw elbows and kicked you when you were on the ground. They were the quintessential mean girls—except that they could play soccer better than almost anyone else.

Unsurprisingly, the junior national program had significant representation from LA and its environs.

"Anyway, what are you up to?" Emma asked, sitting down on the tan corduroy rocker in the living room. Their house was situated at the top of a bluff above Spring Beach, and three wide picture windows offered an expansive view of Puget Sound, Bainbridge Island and, on a clear day, the snow-capped Olympic Mountains.

"Homework. Did I tell you my chemistry teacher pulled me aside the other day and told me she thought I was one of her most talented students?"

"No way. That's awesome."

"I don't know," Jamie said. "I kind of think chemistry is mostly memorization, and I've always been good at that."

"She probably knows what she's talking about. Didn't you say she's your favorite teacher?"

"Yeah. She's really funny and smart, and she wears these kickass shoes and these really cute glasses..."

"Sounds like someone has a crush," Emma teased.

"Ew! She's like twenty years older than us!"

"Ooh, so mid-thirties? Sounds hot." She could almost hear Jamie's blush over the phone line.

"She's straight and married. Get your mind out of the

gutter, Blake."

"Not everyone who's married is straight."

"I think my gaydar would have pinged by now."

Emma paused. This would be the perfect time to tell Jamie about her own—flexibility, as she liked to think of it. When she'd started having crushes on girls in junior high, she had assumed it was a passing stage. But the crushes didn't stop. If anything, they'd only grown stronger. She still liked guys, and she still saw herself settling down with one. Despite the roller coaster of her parents' marriage, she'd always wanted kids; a man seemed like a necessary part of her future. And yet, she couldn't pretend that girls didn't fascinate her—the way they smelled, the softness of their skin, the ease with which they shared their feelings. Most of the boys she knew got stuck on the surface of things, as if it didn't matter what was going on underneath.

"Earth to Emma. Are you still there?"

"I'm here," she said, and let the moment pass.

They talked about schoolwork and soccer, team dinners and gossip. A girl on Jamie's team was pregnant and keeping the baby even though her boyfriend didn't want to. As a result, she wouldn't be able to finish out the season.

"I can't believe she was so careless," Jamie said. "It's 2003, and there's a Planned Parenthood only a few miles from our school."

"At least you've never had to worry about that, right?" Emma commented. Another advantage to dating girls.

It was Jamie's turn to go radio silent. Emma looked at her cell screen, but the timer kept ticking away. Maybe the call had dropped at the other end? Then Jamie's voice returned, sounding strangely far away.

"Right. Good thing."

Something about her tone took Emma back to the night they'd met, when Jamie had stared out at the ocean looking like she might cry. Weird. All Emma had said was that she'd never had to worry about getting pregnant. Jamie had told her she'd never had a boyfriend, so why would that upset her? Unless— Emma stopped the thought. Clearly she'd seen too many Lifetime movies, heard too many cautionary tales about teenaged girls.

But still… "Are you okay?" she asked softly.

"Totally."

But neither of them spoke, and Emma couldn't stop thinking about what might have happened to the girl she could hear breathing over the phone line.

"Anyway," Jamie said at last, "I should probably get back to my homework."

"Yeah, I should go, too."

She didn't really want to hang up, but she also didn't know what else to say. Jamie was open in so many ways but not about this—whatever "this" was. What had she called her issues with her mom the night they met? A deep, dark secret? Apparently she preferred to keep it that way.

"Congratulations again," Jamie said. "I'm really happy for you, Em."

"Thanks, Jamie. I'll call you tomorrow, okay? I don't want to open presents without you. Not that being on the phone is the same."

"My dad says a company in Belgium is working on software that will let people connect through video chat. Wouldn't that be cool?"

"Heck yeah. Keep me posted."

When they finally ended the call a little while later, Emma stood up to pace the living room. Lucy, the family's aging black lab, thumped her tail against the couch each time Emma reached one end of the Oriental rug and spun on her heel to start back.

She talked to herself as she paced. "I can't ask her straight out, can I? I mean, what's the etiquette here? 'From things you have said—and haven't said, really—I'm wondering if there's something you want to tell me…' But that's stupid. If she wanted to tell me, she would have. Or what if she's waiting for me to ask? Aargh!"

Suddenly she flung herself onto the couch and leaned into Lucy, resting her cheek on the old dog's warm fur. Lucy's tail thumped again and she reached out a paw. Obediently Emma rubbed her belly. Why did life have to be so complicated? When she was younger, everything had seemed so easy. Her parents had loved her and Ty and each other, and she had loved soccer and school and sunny summer mornings, and someday she would grow up and play soccer all over the world before settling down and having a family of her own. But then she had become a teenager and her parents had seemed to stop loving each other, at least for a time, and now Ty was becoming a teenaged boy—*bleh*—and while soccer was definitely looking up, she wasn't sure anymore who she was or what she wanted.

If she wasn't girlfriend material, if she cared more about soccer than anything else, then how would she ever manage the family bit? Who wanted a wife or mother who was never around? That role seemed reserved for men. Look at her own parents. Her father's career had taken off eight years earlier when he'd developed a surgical technique that simplified the treatment of complex airway disorders in pediatric patients. His technique had saved the lives of thousands of children, and he traveled the country and world consulting on difficult cases and teaching his technique to other surgeons. Her mother's career, meanwhile, had always come second. For one thing, her job was here in Seattle. She was the one who kept the household running, who made sure Emma and her brother did their homework and got to lessons, practice, and games on time.

Speaking of being on time… She glanced at her watch. It was almost five, which meant she had to get going. Dani and Sian, her two closest friends on the soccer team, were taking her out for a pre-birthday dinner. *Good*, she thought, rising to her feet. A night out with the girls was exactly what she needed to take her out of her own head.

An hour later she was seated at a table in a sushi bar in the International District, munching edamame and mixing wasabi and soy in a dipping dish. She had dressed up in a red scoop-necked shirt and striped jersey skirt, pairing them with flats that wouldn't hurt her feet if they decided to take an after-dinner walk. Her friends were similarly clad in comfortable skirts and light make-up and were currently discussing the rumor they had heard that Justin Tate, captain of the boys' soccer team and newly single, was planning to ask Emma out.

"You guys would be like soccer royalty," Sian said, her cheeks flushed from the walk up the hill to the restaurant. She was in shape, but her fair skin colored at the slightest exertion. After every practice and game her entire body was pink and shiny, a fact she bemoaned regularly.

"High school royalty," Dani corrected, her olive skin blush-free as usual.

"Whatever. Do you like him?" Sian gazed at Emma expectantly.

"I don't know. Even if I did, I just broke up with Josh. I'm not ready to date yet."

"That was like a month ago," Dani said, "and it was your call."

"Well, I'm not sure I have time, then. I got a call from US Soccer today. They want me to go to an under-19 camp in LA next month."

"Oh my god!" Sian squealed.

"No fucking way." Dani shook her head, smiling.

"I know, right? I hoped I would make it to the next level, but I wasn't sure it would happen."

Dani rolled her eyes. "Oh, please, Miss Modest. You started almost every match for the seventeens."

"Yeah, and you made a bunch of all-tournament teams with them, didn't you?" Sian asked. "You had to know it was only a matter of time before the nineteens called."

Emma shrugged. Nothing was guaranteed when it game to the national team pool. Coaches and scouts were human, and their decisions were unpredictable and subject to change.

"Wait." Dani frowned. "Next month? When exactly is this camp?"

"That's the thing…" She stopped, grateful for the reprieve as their server delivered several trays overflowing with colorful rolls and plates of nigiri sushi. They divvied up the food and dug in, Dani's question momentarily on hold as they oohed and ahhed over the melt-in-your-mouth quality of the fish.

Finally Sian circled the conversation back around. "When do you have to go?"

Emma tapped her chopsticks on her plate. "November fifteenth through the twenty-second."

"But that's during states!"

"I know. I'm really sorry, guys."

Lips pursed, Dani nodded slowly. "I guess you've gotta do what you gotta do."

"You know I don't want to miss the end of the season, but this is the next step. If I do okay, it's on to the under-23s. And if I do well there…"

"You could get called up to the senior team," Dani finished for her. "We get it, don't we, Siani?"

"Yeah, sure," Sian mumbled, and took a sip of ice water.

"It's just shitty timing," Dani added, her eyes on Emma's.

"The shittiest," she agreed.

They were quiet for a few minutes while they continued to demolish their sushi. Japanese food was Emma's absolute favorite. Did Chapel Hill even have sushi restaurants? And if they did exist, would they be any good? Somehow she hadn't managed to ask that question when she'd visited campus the previous spring. Occasionally she wondered if she was making the right decision to move three thousand miles away from home, but UNC was a perennial national championship favorite—in fact, they'd won it two out of the last four years and were expected to win again this season—as well as a feeder school for the national team. More UNC graduates had participated in the national pool than any other school in the country. As soon as the coach had made it clear he wanted her, her decision had been made. She would be crazy to turn down the opportunity.

After they'd gotten some food in their systems, the other girls seemed to recover enough to ask about her plans for the next day. She filled them in on her father's promise to take the family out to Canlis, a landmark restaurant situated at the south end of the Aurora Bridge. Then she paused, wondering if she should tell them about Jamie. But why shouldn't she? They knew she had gotten close with "Surf Cup Girl," as they called her.

"And then when we get home," she finished, "I'm going to call Jamie and open the package she sent." She popped a piece of salmon nigiri in her mouth and chewed slowly, enjoying the taste sensation as her friends exchanged a look. She swallowed the bite and regarded them across the table. "What? If you have something to say, spit it out."

"It's nothing." Dani fiddled with her chopsticks. "Except, I don't know, you've been talking about this girl a lot lately."

"So? We're friends."

Sian elbowed Dani, who said, "Are you sure that's all you are? Tamara pointed her out in some of the Surf Cup photos, and I totally remember her now. She's cute, if you like that sort of thing."

Emma stared at her. "You were looking for pictures of her?"

"No. Tamara happened to point her out, that's all."

"Okay," Emma said, leaning away from the table. "Well, you're right, she is cute. And smart, and nice, and a good soccer player, and we're friends. Not sure how else to say it, and frankly, I'm a little pissed I have to."

"Sorry," Sian offered immediately.

"Well, I for one am glad you're not lezzing out on us," Dani said. "Not that there's anything wrong with that. I just didn't believe what people were saying."

"Wait. People have been talking about me being gay?"

Since when did being friends with a lesbian automatically make you one? Not that the gossip was that far off base. Or maybe it was. God, did she really have to figure it out right this second? Why couldn't people mind their own freaking business?

"Some of Josh's friends are saying you broke up with him because of Surf Cup Girl," Sian explained. "I think because of the timing."

"That, and wounded male pride," Dani added.

"I broke up with Josh because I thought he was a douchebag, and this conversation only confirms it."

"Um, duh," Dani said. "Took you long enough to figure that one out."

"Jamie said almost the same thing. You guys would really like her. Assuming you could get past the *lezzing out* thing." And she stared hard at Dani.

"Don't get your panties all in a bunch. You know I don't have anything against the gays."

"Then maybe don't call them 'the gays?'" Emma shook her head, trying not to smile.

Dani smirked. "See? I can always make you laugh."

Emma threw an edamame shell at her. "Sometimes I think being born in New Jersey ruined you for life."

"Hey, don't be taking pot shots at my family," Dani said in

a heavy Jersey accent. "Otherwise my boys might have to come over and teach you some respect." She stuck out her bottom lip and held up a fist.

Emma wanted to stay annoyed at Dani, but she couldn't keep a straight face at the sight of her best friend channeling Tony Soprano. Friends since kindergarten, they had always had each other's backs. When Emma's parents were separated the previous year, Dani had been there for her, lending a shoulder and doling out tissues as needed. The year before that, when one of Dani's brothers had caused a car accident that had seriously injured a young boy, Emma had stuck by her despite the stares and whispers that followed them through the school halls. Now, as seniors, they had realized their childhood dream of captaining their high school team together.

An all-state striker, Dani was headed to UCLA on scholarship next fall, so soon enough they would be living on opposite coasts. But Emma couldn't imagine not being friends with her. Dani knew her better than anyone. And yet, she didn't know that the rumors about Emma's sexuality weren't entirely unfounded. No one did.

That was going to have to change, Emma told herself as she drove home that evening. They had gone for a sunset walk at Alki Beach in West Seattle, throwing rocks into the water and talking about soccer and families and boys and how impossibly fast their senior year seemed to be moving. Despite several chances to come clean, Emma had kept her secret to herself. She didn't want to risk losing her closest friends over something that may or may not ever happen. What was the point? She thought of Jamie, who had come out to her family and friends when she was thirteen and to everyone else— teachers, classmates, aunts, uncles, cousins—a year later. Emma couldn't even imagine the courage that whole process must have taken.

Then again, maybe coming out was easier for someone like Jamie. No one would look at her and think, "Wow, that chick looks totally straight." But that was exactly what people saw when they looked at Emma. To be honest, it was what she saw when she looked in the mirror, too. How could she be attracted to girls? She simply didn't look like the type. That was partly why she kept waiting for it to pass—life would be so much simpler if she'd only ever thought that way about guys.

Her mother was in the living room when she got home, curled up on the couch with a book, Lucy asleep beside her. She glanced up and smiled when Emma wandered in.

"Hi, sweetheart. How was dinner?"

"Fine." Emma walked over to the couch and squeezed between the dog and her mother, leaning her head on her mom's shoulder. She smelled familiar, of vanilla soap and lemon ginger tea.

"You sure about that?" her mom asked as she set the book aside and slipped an arm around her shoulders.

"Not really." For a moment, she thought about telling her mom. But then she pushed the idea away. Why traumatize her parents when she hadn't figured things out yet for herself?

"And here I thought you would be on cloud nine."

"What do you mean?"

"US Soccer came up on caller ID. I assume you have news to share?"

She filled her mom in on the call, as well as Dani and Sian's—and her own, of course—disappointment at the timing.

"Ah, I see," her mother said, pulling her reading glasses off and setting them on top of her book. "You have to choose between your past and your future, and that's rarely a stress-free task."

Except that Emma hadn't stressed over the decision at all. She didn't bother correcting her mother, though. The fact that she had thrown her high school team's post-season under the bus without hesitation was not one of her prouder moments. But she was only being pragmatic, which as an American of

Scandinavian descent—her mother had grown up in Minnesota, land of ten thousand lakes and a million or so Swedes—was her birthright.

"Is that why you're not celebrating the call-up, or is something else bothering you?"

"Something else," she admitted, and leaned her head on her mother's shoulder again.

"Do you want to talk about it?" Her hand ran soothingly over Emma's hair.

"If you don't mind." But she wasn't sure how to broach the topic of her conversation with Jamie. The farther she got from the call, the more she wondered if she wasn't reading into things. What if she was wrong? Then again, what if she wasn't? "It's about Jamie, actually."

The hand on her hair froze. "I see," her mom said slowly. "I have to admit, your father and I did wonder."

Emma glanced at her. *What...?* But then she realized and pulled away, frowning. "Not that. God, Mom, we're just friends."

She held up a hand. "I'm sorry. You seem very close with this girl, and when you mentioned she was gay, the thought did enter our minds."

You and everyone else. Emma shook her head. "Jamie being gay is not the issue."

Her mom took her hand and gave it an encouraging squeeze. "What is, then?"

Haltingly, she told her what she knew and what she only thought she knew. Her mom listened closely, her face growing more and more serious as Emma described their assorted interactions.

"I already know she's never had a boyfriend, and she's been out since she was thirteen, so unless she hooked up with a guy at a ridiculously young age, which I totally doubt, then that would mean...it would mean she must have been..." She trailed off, looking at her mother.

"Are you saying you think she could have been assaulted?"

Emma nodded, swallowing against the knot in her throat. The idea of some strange man doing terrible things to sweet, funny Jamie made her want to go out and slam a soccer ball against the garage door as hard as she could. Or what if it wasn't a stranger? What if it was someone she still had to see regularly, like a coach or a teacher or even a relative?

"From what you've said, it does sound possible." Her mother tightened her grip on her hand as Emma exhaled noisily. "I'm so sorry, sweetie. I had hoped you wouldn't ever have to deal with something like this, especially not in such a close friend."

"What do I do, though? Should I ask her about it or do I wait until she brings it up?"

"It's up to you, sweetie. You could bring it up or you could wait for her to raise the topic herself. Either way, the main thing is to let her know that you care about her and that you're there for her."

Emma rubbed a hand over her eyes. "I really don't want to do or say the wrong thing."

Her mother slipped an arm around her shoulders. "I have some material at the office you can read to prepare for if and when she tells you. Would you like to look through it together?"

"That would be great," Emma said.

Her mother kissed her forehead. "You're a good person and a great friend, you know that?"

"I really care about her."

"I know you do."

They were quiet for a few minutes, their eyes on the ferry and barge lights blinking between the mainland and the island. Then Emma said, "Life is going to keep getting more complicated from here on out, isn't it?"

Her mother nodded. "It is. And with your big heart, I'm afraid you're going to feel like it's your job to protect the people you care about. But the fact is, you can't save anyone else, honey. The only person who can do that for Jamie is Jamie. If and when she's ready, she'll let you in."

"What if she isn't ever ready?"

"I doubt that will be the case. From what you've said, it sounds like she has a very close, loving family. They'll help her through it. Assuming they know?"

"Um, yeah." Emma remembered the panicked look in Jamie's mother's eyes when they'd returned five minutes late to the hotel in Del Mar. "I'm almost positive."

"Hopefully they've got her in counseling. Research shows that the sooner a rape victim begins to heal, the better their long-term chances are at overcoming depression, self-hatred, and everything else that comes with sexual assault."

Emma's throat tightened again. *Rape victim, depression, sexual assault*—her mom sounded so detached. This was Jamie they were talking about, the first person Emma talked to most mornings, the last person she talked to at night. Jamie, who listened quietly and somehow always knew the right thing to say.

"Ah, geez." Her mother squeezed her tighter. "I didn't mean to go all clinical on you, sweetie. I know you're worried about your friend, and I'm here for you, okay? It's important that you have support through all of this, too."

"Thanks, Mom." Emma kissed her mother's cheek. "You know you're pretty great too, right?"

Her mother shook her head. "When did you get so grown up?"

"I am a senior, Mom, remember?"

"How could I forget?"

Her mother's smile was lopsided, and Emma was pretty sure she knew why. Even though her parents understood her dream to go to UNC and supported her decision a hundred percent, it would be difficult to watch her go so far away when most of their friends' children were headed to U-Dub or Western, Whitman or Reed. Pacific Northwest kids typically stayed closer to home. They didn't pick schools that were thousands of miles away.

"I'll be home for holidays," she reminded her mother, "and summers, too. It's not like I'll be gone forever."

"I know, sweetheart. Don't worry about us old folks. You worry about you."

They talked a little longer, and then Emma jogged up the stairs in the center of the house, one hand on the wooden railing that lined the wall. They had moved to this house when she was ten, and by now she knew every creaky stair and floorboard like the back of her hand. It was hard to imagine that there were other houses, dorm rooms, apartments that she would grow to know equally as well. Hard to imagine that anyplace else would ever feel like home.

But for now, home still meant her cream-walled room and her window overlooking the Sound, her parents and brother down the hall, the wind off the water carrying with it the scent of salt and seaweed. Her heart was still here, although that wasn't entirely true anymore. Part of it was eight hundred miles away in another city on a bay with a girl who was broken but trying her best not to be. Emma hoped Jamie would give her a chance to help in any way she could. Because even though she understood rationally that she couldn't save anyone who didn't want to be saved, that didn't keep her from wanting to try.

CHAPTER THREE

"Happy Thanksgiving! It's eighty and sunny here," Jamie texted. "How about Seattle?"

Emma's reply came right away. "Funny. As in looking, not hardy-har-har."

"Someone's bitter."

"Damn straight."

"Um…." Jamie typed.

"You're hilarious but I have to go peel like a thousand potatoes."

"Huh. Didn't realize there were any Amish this far west."

"Again with the humor. Check your email. I sent you something. Ciao for now."

"Ciao."

Jamie set her phone on the coffee table in her aunt and uncle's den. Beside her, her younger cousin played Super Mario on his Gameboy while on the other couch her father and his brother, a slightly older, markedly yuppier version of himself, were drinking microbrews and discussing the Trojan horse that hackers had tried to slip into the latest version of Linux. On television, the Dolphins were trouncing the Cowboys, which probably made most non-Texan Americans happy. And really, were Texans even American? Hadn't they been threatening to secede from the Union pretty much since day one?

She managed to deflect her curiosity for all of three minutes before jogging upstairs to knock on her older cousin's bedroom door.

"Come in!"

"Hey." Jamie ducked into the very large, very pink bedroom.

Nikki turned away from her dressing table and held her cell phone away from her ear. "Is it time to come down already?"

"No, I was hoping I could check my email."

Her cousin, who was a year ahead in school and a thousand times girlier than her or Meg, waved her manicured hand at the Mac on her desk. Then she went right back to her phone conversation, which appeared to revolve around a boy with a tattoo in a certain hard-to-see area.

Like Jamie's dad, Nikki's father was a tech geek, though he worked in the public relations field rather than in software. The Mac purred to life and quickly connected to the Internet, and soon Jamie was opening the promised email attachment. The photo showed Emma posing with her back to the camera and her arms raised to show off her muscles as she smiled over her shoulder at the viewfinder. She was wearing the shirt Jamie had ordered on eBay and sent her for her birthday—a Man U jersey with her last name and soccer number embroidered on it.

"Awesome," Jamie said out loud, laughing. The jersey looked good on her. Then again, everything looked good on Emma. Not that she would have told her as much. Didn't want the straight girl to think she was hitting on her.

Being friends with a straight girl could be a challenge, in Jamie's experience. The girls at school either treated her like she was a freak or, alternately, batted their eyelashes and felt her biceps, giggling as if she was just another guy to worship them. Emma hadn't behaved like that at all, which was another thing Jamie appreciated about her. She didn't worry that at some point Emma would pout and ask her why she hadn't tried to put the moves on her.

Honestly, Jamie couldn't imagine putting the moves on anyone. The thought of touching someone or being touched herself, even by a girl she found attractive, made her stomach flip, and not in a good way. Shoshanna, her therapist, said this reaction would pass eventually, but Jamie would believe it when she saw it. Fortunately, her parents had a rule that she wasn't allowed to date until she was sixteen, which took the pressure off. For now, she would continue on as she always had, hanging out with teammates who accepted her for who she was or with guy friends who treated her like one of them. Her skating buddies talked a good game, and she joined in. But when it came to actually hooking up with a girl, she still got the jitters every time she thought about it.

She hit reply on the email and sent Emma a rambling message about her aunt and uncle's house in Pasadena. The back yard was large enough to easily fit a pool, gazebo, hot tub, outdoor kitchen, and flower garden that her Aunt Mary maintained herself. Nikki and Todd, who was thirteen, bemoaned the fact that they had to work in the garden for at least an hour every weekend. But what did they expect with a mom who worked as a curator at The Huntington?

At the end of the email, she paused and then wrote, "BTW, I've been meaning to ask you. Any interest in visiting Berkeley over Christmas break? Assuming you don't have to jet off again for the national team, that is. My parents said it would be okay. I would offer to come up there but they won't let me. While that may seem lame, they have their reasons, which I actually thought we might talk about if you come to California."

She paused to reread what she'd written, and then deleted the last two sentences. While she wanted to tell Emma about France, she didn't want to commit to doing so. What if their friendship was better from a distance? What if they finally saw each other again and didn't have anything to say? Honestly, she couldn't imagine such a scenario, but if Christmas was the right time to have the big talk, she would know it. Shoshanna had encouraged her to tell Emma if she felt ready. Apparently opening up about her experiences to someone she trusted was a signal that she was on the path to healing.

Nikki turned off her phone and stood up. "Are you almost done? I need to get on there."

"Oh, yeah, give me a sec."

She typed the rest of the note quickly: "Anyway, let me know what you think. I'm off school December twentieth through January seventh, and we have family visiting until the twenty-eighth. Anytime between the twenty-ninth and the seventh works at our end. Thanks again for the awesome photo. Happy Turkey Day!! Love, Jamie."

With Nikki standing behind her, she hit send and logged out of her email account. As she closed the browser window, it suddenly occurred to her how she'd signed off—*love*? That was a first. She chewed her lip. She had meant it as a friend, of course. Emma wouldn't read into it, would she?

"Jamie?"

She glanced up into her cousin's expectant face. "Sorry," she said, and rose.

"Your girlfriend is really pretty. Does she play soccer, too?"

"Yeah, but she's not my girlfriend. My parents won't let me date yet."

Nikki rolled her eyes. "Mine tried that whole not-dating-until-we-decide-you're-old-enough thing, too. There are ways around it if you want to be with someone enough."

"Well, Emma and I are only friends."

"Okay," Nikki said, but Jamie could hear the doubt in her voice.

Was it so hard to believe that a lesbian could be friends with a straight girl? *Geez.* It wasn't like she was actually a guy, even if people mistook her for one occasionally. She could keep it in her pants as well as the next teenaged girl. Probably better, given what Shoshanna referred to as her "intimacy issues."

As she jogged back downstairs to resume the sacred Thanksgiving tradition of heckling the Cowboys, she released a breath. Why was it that when you didn't want to have sex, it was all anyone wanted to talk about? Or maybe she was reaching the age where it was all anyone talked about regardless.

Damn. She missed being a kid already, and she wasn't quite sixteen.

On her way to the den, she detoured to the large kitchen where her mother and Aunt Mary were seated at the slate-tiled bar enjoying wine and brie. The scent of roast turkey filled the air while the sound of the dishwasher echoed rhythmically off rustic walls and exposed wooden beams. Tall windows afforded a view of the pool where she could see Meg reclining in a lounger, soaking up the early winter sunshine. Much as she ripped on Southern California—the rivalry was a regional requirement—Jamie had to admit that this kind of warmth in late November was not the worst thing ever.

"Hola, *chiquitas*," she said to the sisters-in-law seated with heads close together.

They paused mid-sentence, and Jamie stopped in the middle of the room, taking in her mother's red eyes and her aunt's forced smile.

"Hi, honey," her mother said quickly, sitting up straighter.

Maybe it wasn't what it seemed and they hadn't in fact been talking about her. Even if they had, she didn't have to deal with it. She could simply grab a soda and duck out.

"Dinner is still an hour or so away," Aunt Mary said, her cheerful tone a little bit off.

"I just came in to get a Sprite."

"Oh. Right."

Even in middle age, her aunt maintained a slender figure. Her skin was smooth—the luck of the Asians, she liked to say—and her hair was as black as it had ever been, her eyes as bright. Now those eyes settled on Jamie's face only briefly before skittering away, and Jamie felt her chest tighten. She knew. Her aunt knew, and she couldn't even look at her.

Jamie stared at her mother. "Did you tell her?"

"I'm sorry," she said, her voice low. "I needed—"

"*You* needed? Seriously, Mom? I can't believe you."

She turned and walked out, bouncing on the balls of her feet as she strode across the Spanish tile entryway. It wasn't fair. It wasn't even her mom's story to share. Before she could formulate a plan, she burst out the front door and down the walk. She couldn't stay here. She couldn't look into their concerned faces and read the pity in their eyes. It only reminded her that she would never be—*could* never be—the same.

"Jamie! Wait," her father called after her.

But she pretended she hadn't heard. Leaving her aunt and uncle's house behind, she began to run along the sidewalk, heading toward the nearby foothills. Her legs were tired from her morning swim but loose, and she ran at an LSD pace— long slow distance. She didn't push it. Her coaches would kill her if she tore something in an angsty attempt to escape family drama. There was always something at the holidays, wasn't there? She just wasn't accustomed to being at the center of the ruckus.

Her phone rang, the ring tune—Darth Vader's theme song, a joke between them—signaling an incoming call from her dad. She silenced the ringer and ran slowly on through the hot afternoon, belatedly remembering her goal for invading the kitchen in the first place. Dang it, she was thirsty, and she didn't have any money for a convenience store run. Looked like she would have to tuck her tail between her legs and go back sooner rather than later.

Reluctantly she slowed to a walk, turned and started back the way she had come, crossing the street when she saw a schoolyard with a giant evergreen oak shading part of the playground. On a whim, she ducked through the staggered chain link gate and found a seat among the tree's gnarled roots. Then she leaned back against the rough trunk, lifted her chin, and gazed up into the dense canopy.

Her therapist wasn't going to like hearing that she ran. Or it wasn't that she wouldn't like it. She would ask her to think about why she had run and what she might have done differently. Jamie could practically hear Shoshanna's slightly nasal voice: "Clearly you gave in to your brain's fight or flight reaction to the conversation. But let's look at what might have prompted that response. Why specifically do you think you felt the need to flee?"

After more than six months of seeing Shoshanna once a week, the therapist's voice had begun to appear at the back of her mind whenever she had to face something traumatic or even merely uncomfortable. While she probably wouldn't have admitted it except under severe duress, Jamie had discovered she liked having that internal guide to help her figure out how to rein in the fear that never seemed far away. France had left her unable to rely on her own reactions or judgment, but Shoshanna's blend of realism and practicality made sense. It didn't hurt that she specialized in cases like Jamie's. She knew what she was doing, and it was a relief, honestly, for Jamie to let go and trust in Shoshanna's counsel.

Not that she'd been eager to do so in the beginning. At her first session Jamie had sat silently, arms folded across her chest, one leg bouncing uncontrollably, her gaze fixed on the paisley pattern in the dark green carpeting. Everything about the therapist's office was comfortable and soothing, from the overstuffed couch she was sitting on to the muted abstract art on the almond-colored walls. And yet she felt the opposite of soothed. She didn't want to be there. She didn't want to talk about what had happened because that would mean she would have to willingly conjure the memories. And right then, only a few weeks out, she wasn't prepared for that.

"It didn't really happen," she'd told herself almost daily. She didn't believe her own attempts at pretense, of course. She wasn't totally crazy. But the "what if it hadn't happened?" fantasy provided a temporary respite from the "Oh my god it happened it happened it happened it really happened" panic that washed over her the moment she awoke and ambushed her regularly throughout the day. Except when she was playing soccer—on the field, she was so laser-focused on the game that nothing could intrude, not even her panic about what she was sure must be the utter destruction of any chance at a normal life.

That first day, though, Shoshanna didn't let her sit in silence. She talked a little about a therapeutic approach called cognitive behavioral therapy (CBT), and then turned the conversation to Jamie and what she might be hoping to gain from working together. When Jamie answered her initial questions with monosyllabic responses, Shoshanna set her notepad down and removed her reading glasses.

"I get the feeling you don't really want to be here."

Jamie shrugged. If her parents hadn't told her she couldn't play ODP or Surf Cup that summer unless she talked to Shoshanna, she wouldn't have agreed to come.

"I get that a lot, especially from people your age. Let me guess: One of your parents thinks you're not as happy as you used to be, so they dragged you in to see me hoping I would 'fix' you, without understanding that mood changes in teenagers go with the territory of hormonal shifts and a maturing cerebral cortex."

Jamie was tempted to agree and hightail it out of there, but not only was the therapist's assessment inaccurate, it pointed toward a fact she found difficult to believe. "Are you trying to say my mother didn't tell you why they're sending me here?"

"She may have wanted to, but I don't believe in knowing things about my clients that they haven't chosen to share. Just because you're not an adult yet doesn't mean you don't deserve a say in what happens to you."

For some reason, this simple statement brought tears to Jamie's eyes. Only the crying wasn't really a mystery. The notion that she should have a say in what happened to her wasn't an easy one to swallow right then, not when she was sitting in this stranger's office precisely because she'd done something that had resulted in another person gaining control over her body, her emotions, her life.

Shoshanna had set a box of tissues within her reach. "I'm guessing you're not here about a little moodiness, are you?"

Jamie shook her head and pressed the tissue against her face, biting her lip as hard as she could to try to hold in the sobs. If she started crying, she wasn't sure she would be able to stop.

"I'm sorry, Jamie," Shoshanna said. "I can see you're hurting. Right now it probably feels like if you start crying, you'll never stop. I would imagine, too, that you're having trouble sleeping, and that you're struggling with fear and with being close to other people. Does this sound familiar?"

Jamie nodded, lowering the tissue. Tears still squeezed out of her eyes, but she didn't feel like she couldn't breathe anymore.

"I've been doing this for a long time," the therapist said. "I've worked with too many young women—and young men, too—who have felt the way you do now. But the good news is, I've helped quite a few of them move through the darkness you're struggling with now, whatever its cause, and out the other side to a stronger, healthier place. I would like the opportunity to try to help you, but you have to want that help. The only promise I can offer is that it won't be easy. There's no magic bullet here, no guarantees. I can offer guidance, but you have to be willing to do the work yourself."

This sounded like something one of her coaches would have said. In fact, she was pretty sure she'd heard almost the exact same speech about learning technical skills and performing optimally on the soccer field. Maybe that was why she found herself meeting Shoshanna's eyes and nodding one more time.

"Okay," she said, and the tears stopped, as if they'd been waiting for her to figure out that running away from what had happened was only going to get her more lost.

Now, sitting beneath the California oak a few blocks from her aunt and uncle's house, she closed her eyes and tried to focus on her breathing the way Shoshanna had taught her. She recited her mantra inwardly, trying to make her emotions match: "May I be filled with loving kindness; may I be well; may I be peaceful and at ease; may I be happy." Shoshanna said that this meditation fit the "fake it 'til you make it" model, and Jamie found that it usually helped whenever she freaked out. As she recited the words "loving kindness," she pictured her mother. Nothing about this was easy for her, either. She had been asleep in the hotel in Lyon when it happened, and Jamie had overheard her telling her dad that she should have been more attentive; that if she had been a better parent, none of this would have happened. Jamie didn't think that was true, but her mom did.

With the word "well," she imagined physical strength and well-being flowing outward from her heart and lungs and through the rest of her body. At "peaceful and at ease," she relaxed her shoulders and paid even closer attention to the breath entering and leaving her body. And at "happy," she smiled and thought of a particularly good memory—the moment the previous month when Emma had opened the birthday box containing her Man U jersey and squealed so loudly that Jamie almost dropped the phone.

She went through the mantra five times, and by the end she was still thirsty but otherwise okay. The shakiness was gone, the anger had vanished, and what she wanted most—other than a glass of water—was to tell her mother she was sorry.

With one last pat to the rough tree bark, she rose and headed back to her aunt and uncle's house. A block away, she pulled her phone out and found Shoshanna's mobile number.

"Happy Thanksgiving," she texted. "And thanks to you it will be here. I used the kindness mantra to get rid of lizard brain. See you next week."

As she neared the house, she could see her mother and father sitting out on the front steps, waiting for her. Her steps slowed, and butterflies flitted about her belly. The clarity that meditation brought on was awesome while she was alone, but facing other people after she had messed up yet again was always more difficult than it had seemed in her head.

"Hey," she said, nodding at her parents as they rose. "Sorry I took off. I needed some space."

"I'm the one who's sorry," her mother said. "I should never have done that without talking to you first. It wasn't planned. It just happened, but that doesn't excuse it."

Jamie reached out and touched her mother's arm hesitantly. "I get why you needed to talk to her, I really do. But I think you're right. If you could talk to me first, that would feel better. Is that okay?"

"Absolutely," her mother said, nodding quickly.

Jamie could tell it was killing her not to crush her in one of her famous hugs. She took a breath and stepped closer, slipping her arms around her mother's waist. "Cool," she said as she felt her mom's arms wrap carefully around her. And then her dad was there, too, and she was tucked between them like when she was a little kid, and it didn't feel nearly as claustrophobic as she would have expected. In fact, she felt downright safe standing there in the warm sunshine with her parents holding her gingerly, as if she might break if they held on too tightly. Honestly, she'd been a little worried about that herself.

"Happy Thanksgiving," her dad said.

"Happy Thanksgiving," Jamie and her mom echoed.

Then she pushed out from between them. "I am so freaking thirsty right now I could drink an entire cooler of Gatorade," she announced, not meeting their eyes.

"Well, let's get you something to drink then," her mother said.

Jamie moved up the steps ahead of her parents. "Sounds like a plan."

#

Emma read through the email one more time, grinning. She had been trying to think of a way to subtly invite herself to California, but now she wouldn't have to.

"I'm in," she wrote back. "I'll check Expedia and keep you posted. Can't wait! Love, Emma."

She stared at the screen for a long moment, and then as she heard her mother's voice calling from the kitchen, hit send and left the den. *Love?* Whatever. It wasn't like either of them meant anything by it.

"There you are," her mother said. She pushed a stray strand of brown-blonde hair away from her face, flushed from cooking assorted Thanksgiving dishes. Despite the gravy and cranberries splattered across her apron, she looked happy. What a difference from Thanksgiving a year earlier when Emma's father had visited from his hotel room and the atmosphere more closely approximated that of a funeral than a holiday. He had moved back in by Christmas, but for Emma the damage was done. No matter how committed both her parents claimed to be to their marriage, she couldn't help wondering when he would leave them again.

She smiled at her mother and danced across the kitchen in time to the music playing on the Bose radio on the counter. "May I have this dance?" she asked, grabbing her mom's hand and spinning her around.

The older woman let herself be twirled about the kitchen as Mariah Carey crooned what she really wanted for Christmas. When the music stopped and an advertisement came on, they both collapsed against the butcher block island, laughing.

"What's gotten into you?" her mom asked, touching her cheek with a flour-dusted finger.

"Nothing. I'm happy."

"Well, good. Your father and Ty should be back soon with your grandmother. In the meantime, those potatoes are not going to peel themselves."

"I'm on it." Emma reached for an apron. There would be plenty of time later to talk her parents into letting her visit Jamie. For now, the trip to California was only for her.

The fall had been crazy—soccer season had gone so quickly, and then, right when they were set to advance to state quarters, she'd had to leave for training camp. She'd actually cried on the flight to LA, not that she ever would have admitted that fact. The first day had been rough, too. She was the only U-17er at first, training with mostly college players from all over the country who had clearly known each other a while, and she had lain awake in her hotel bed that night wondering why she had ever thought she could do this.

But the following morning one of her U-17 teammates, Jess from Boston, had shown up, and then more high school seniors had arrived and things had started to improve. Two players from UNC were already on the team, and when they found out Jess and Emma would be Tar Heels the following year, their demeanor shifted. Soon Emma found herself part of a tight foursome at meals, during warm-up, and for what little free-time they had. By the time she got home, she couldn't wait to graduate and get started on what she now thought of as her "real life" at UNC.

One of the hardest things about the week-long camp, other than missing the final two games of her high school career (Dani left her a voicemail letting her know they'd lost the state semi-final match), had been being out of touch with Jamie. With double sessions every day—fitness in the morning and technical training in the afternoon—meals with the team, and mandatory study sessions each night so that they didn't fall behind on schoolwork, she barely had time to talk to her parents, let alone Jamie. As soon as she got home, she sat down and wrote a long email to her, describing the camp experience, the surreal quality of being done with high school soccer, and the excitement of hanging out in LA with her future college teammates. The U-19 World Cup was slated for the following November in Thailand. It was still a ways off, but in a private conference the coach had told her she had a good shot at making the squad if she stayed healthy and kept up the good work.

"I missed you, though," she'd written at the end. She couldn't help but wonder if the trip to LA was a taste of what life would be like once she graduated from high school and left home: a whirlwind of activity and studying with girls she liked, some maybe a bit too much. One of the UNC players, Tori, a sophomore goalkeeper, had been undeniably cute in a tomboyish way. Emma had felt Tori's eyes on her and couldn't deny that the thought of seeing her again made her palms sweat. She wanted to tell Jamie about Tori, wanted to hear if she thought kissing a teammate was as bad an idea as Emma thought it probably was. But that wasn't a conversation to have on the phone, not after she'd let it go unsaid for this long.

New Year's, she promised herself, trying not to scrape her fingers with the potato peeler. If all went well, she and Jamie would ring in 2004 together and she would come out to someone for the first time in her life. That meant she better know what to call herself by then.

The door from the garage opened and her brother walked in, his REI raincoat and beat-up baseball cap damp with rain.

"Burr, dude," he said, and went straight for the sliced carrots, jamming two into his mouth at once.

Emma threw a potato peel at him. "Gross. Wash your hands, idjit."

He grinned and came at her, holding out his hands threateningly. Since spring he had grown an ungodly amount. Looked like she wouldn't be the big sister much longer.

"Tyler Dean Blakeley," their mother scolded. "No boots in the house. It's only been the rule your entire life."

"Sorry, Mom," he said, turning back to the garage just as their father appeared in the doorway, his mother's arm looped through his.

Emma watched as her grandmother tottered into the room, peering around fearfully. Her dad had warned her, but Emma was still thrown by the changes in the elderly woman. With soccer and classes like AP Biology and Calculus kicking her butt, she hadn't spent much time with her grandmother in the past couple of months. Now she wished she'd tried harder to carve out the time.

When her grandmother's gaze fell on her, the tiny gray-haired woman beamed, fear suddenly driven out by joy. She held out her arms and said, "Come give me some sugar, sugar," as she'd always done. Emma scooted over and wrapped her arms around the old lady, careful not to squeeze too tightly. She felt even frailer than last time.

When she pulled back, her grandmother touched her cheek. "You are so lovely, Elizabeth."

For a moment, Emma faltered. But then she smiled again and said, "Thank you. So are you."

"Oh, now I know you're making things up. But aren't you sweet."

Emma's mother stepped forward. "Hello, Janelle. Happy Thanksgiving. Can I get you a glass of sparkling grape juice?"

"Sparkling what?" The older woman's brow creased. "What is that? I don't know what that is."

Emma's parents exchanged a look, and then her father said,

"Why don't we get you situated in the living room, Mom? I think it'll be a little while until dinner is ready."

"Whatever you think is best," she replied meekly, and followed him from the room.

"Hey," Emma's mother said.

"What?"

"You handled that really well. You okay?"

Emma nodded. Her grandmother had been diagnosed with dementia nearly a decade earlier, right before they sold the family home in Northern Virginia and moved her out to Seattle. In the beginning she used to blame them for "stealing" her house. Then the medical staff at the assisted living center in Kirkland put her on antidepressants, and while the dementia had continued to worsen, at least she seemed happier. The times Emma found hardest were when her grandmother asked where Roger and Dean were and they had to remind her that her husband and eldest son had been gone for more than two decades. Emma's dad often said that at least his brother had passed away *after* their father died of a heart attack. That way her grandfather could be spared the knowledge of his firstborn son's untimely death.

"Who's Elizabeth again?" Ty asked, grabbing a handful of almonds from the bowl on the kitchen island.

"Wash your hands," their mother said without turning around as she pulled a bottle of sparkling grape juice from the refrigerator. "Elizabeth was one of your grandmother's sisters."

"My hands are clean." Then he snickered. "Sort of."

Emma didn't want to think about where a thirteen-year-old boy's hands might have been. Really, she wasn't going to miss living with her brother now that he'd left cute little boyhood behind. No mixed-floor dorms for her, either. Not that her parents would let her live with guys anyway.

"Tori says most of the girls on the team get apartments

together by sophomore year," she said, heading back to her potato-peeling station at the kitchen sink.

"Tori says," Ty mimicked. "So tell us, Em, does that Jamie girl know she has competition?"

With their mother's back turned, Emma felt that giving her brother the finger was a solid choice.

He didn't agree. "Mom, Emma flipped me off!"

"No I didn't." She made her voice sound bored.

"Yes you did!"

"Well, you have to admit you kind of deserved it, Ty," their mother said.

He stared at them both open-mouthed. "That is so not fair!" And he flounced out of the room.

Her mother closed her eyes briefly. "I shouldn't have said that. I'm supposed to be the grown-up here."

"Then you probably don't want to hear that I did flip him off," Emma admitted, trying not to smile.

"I already knew that." She paused. "Your brother does have a point, though, however crassly stated. You've been talking about this new girl quite a bit. Is there anything you want to share, honey? Anything at all?"

Emma stared at the potato in her hand, drawing the vegetable peeler quickly across its brown, nubby exterior. "Um…"

Her mother wiped her hands on her apron and drifted closer. "Okay. So I'm a peds nurse at a large urban hospital. Do you know what that means?"

Emma leaned against the kitchen counter, facing her. "For the purposes of this conversation? No."

"It means that I see parents on a daily basis faced with the possibility of losing a son or daughter. It means that even when your brother is at his pre-pubescent worst, or when you make it clear you'd rather be anyplace but home on Family Soup

Night, I know how lucky I am because you and your brother are healthy and safe. But most of all, it means that there is nothing either of you could do or say—or be—that would make me stop feeling lucky."

Emma stared down at her hands, knuckles white from her grip on the peeler. "Even if I'm not who everyone thinks I am?"

"Are you more worried that you're not who other people think you are, or that you're different from who *you* thought you'd be?"

She shrugged. "I'm not sure." Then, before she could overthink it, she added, "I like girls. As in, *like* like them." She watched her mother's expression but it didn't change at all. "Why aren't you surprised? I mean, look at me. I wear make-up. I paint my nails! What self-respecting gay girl does that?"

"Do you think you're gay?" her mother asked, head tilted. "Because there are other options."

"I don't know." Emma tossed the peeler into the sink, flinching as metal struck metal. "Seriously, I don't have any idea. I just know it's been there a while and I keep waiting for it to go away and it won't. It effing won't."

"Oh, sweetie." Her mom slipped an arm around her shoulders, tugging her closer. "I'm sorry this is hard for you, but you don't have to have all the answers right now. You're still growing, and who you think you are now might change a dozen times in the next few years."

She groaned. "Change sucks. I want to know what I'm doing."

"I know. Flexibility has never been one of your strong suits. Sorry—you get that one from me."

"Thanks a lot."

"But I promise, the not knowing does get easier. Anyway, you'll figure out what you want eventually. You're your father's daughter in that regard. Once you decide you want something, you don't let anything stand in your way."

Emma leaned her head against her mother's. "So you don't hate me for not being completely straight?"

"Well, now that you mention it…"

"Mom!"

Her mother cupped her cheek and gazed into her eyes. "I told you, Emma, I love you and your brother. That's it. Besides, you've always had a good heart, and that's what matters most in my book."

She released a breath. "Huh."

"Huh what?"

"I totally didn't believe Jamie when she said coming out isn't as hard as you think it's going to be."

"Her parents know about her, don't they?"

"Of course. She's so brave about everything. I wish I had even a miniscule amount of her courage."

"You do. It may not always feel like it, but trust me. I know a brave kid when I see one."

Emma thought about all the nights her mom came home from work exhausted from fighting to repair a child's broken health. Neither of her parents had chosen easy work, but it was necessary work. It was work that had meaning of a sort that playing soccer couldn't. Still, being an athlete only lasted a decade or so, if you were lucky. Assuming she lived to an average age, she would have half a century after soccer to do something truly meaningful. Look at Mia Hamm and Julie Foudy. They hadn't even retired yet and they were already using the fame their soccer careers had garnered to launch altruistic and charitable initiatives.

Not that she was comparing herself to Mia Hamm or Julie Foudy. More like Carla Overbeck.

"What are you smiling about?" her mom asked.

"Soccer. Naturally."

"See? There you go."

"What do you mean?"

"Gay girls are supposed to think about sports a lot, aren't they? Maybe you're not such an odd duck, after all."

Emma pushed her mother away. "Very funny. Now, come on. We better get back to cooking before Ty returns and demolishes half the Thanksgiving meal."

Her mom turned up the radio again. As they moved in tandem around the kitchen, sharing the space comfortably, Emma paused every so often to reflect that she was probably, in fact, the lucky one.

CHAPTER FOUR

For some reason, Jamie had always found it amusing that her therapist had a couch in her office. She had never done anything except sit on it cross-legged, but today, their last session of 2003, she flung herself down on the cushions and pillowed her head on one arm.

"So doc," she said, "what's on the docket today? Get it? *Doc*-ket?"

Shoshanna gazed at her evenly. "That would be humorous if I were, in fact, a doctor."

"Geez, tough crowd. Happy almost New Year, by the way. Oh, and happy Hanukkah."

"Thank you. Now, are you done deflecting?"

"Me, deflect?" Jamie said, placing a hand over her heart as she sat up and crossed her legs. "Why would I ever do such a thing?"

"Perhaps because I suggested we use this session to practice some role-playing exercises for your conversation with Emma?"

"Doh!" Jamie slapped her forehead. "I totally forgot."

Shoshanna finally smiled. "I'm sure you did. Tell me, did

you give it any thought this week?"

"Sure, on my way over."

That was actually where she did some of her best thinking about the "homework" Shoshanna gave her. If she was being honest, she had always been a procrastinator. She worked best under pressure with a deadline looming—except when it came to soccer. The pitch was the one place where she was willing to put in unlimited work for what could only ever be an uncertain outcome.

"All right." Shoshanna nodded. "Let's hear it then."

An hour later, Jamie emerged from the four-story brick building to find her sister waiting for her on a bus bench. Shoshanna's office was above a sandwich shop not far from Cal, and Meg was munching on french fries.

"Yo, sis."

"What's up?" Meg tucked her book into her purse. "How was the head shrinker this week?"

"A little more uptight than usual, I have to say. But we came up with a game plan for me to tell Emma."

Meg stared at her. "You mean...?"

"Yep. It's supposed to be like this big healing step, or whatever."

"You don't have to sell me on the tough guy act. I already know you have more balls than the football team."

"American football," Jamie corrected, elbowing her. "Soccer is the real football."

"So I've heard. Come on. I found a spot a couple of blocks away."

That night over dinner, Jamie announced her plan to tell Emma about France. Her parents exchanged a look, and then her mother said, "That's a big step. Are you sure you're ready?"

She nodded. "I've been thinking about it for a while."

"What does Shoshanna say?"

"She thinks Emma is a good choice for the first time. She's older than I am and has her shit—sorry, I mean, her stuff together. Plus she doesn't live here, so if she freaks out and bails on me, which I don't think she will, but if she does, then at least it's not someone I have to see every day."

"They have a plan," Meg put in. "She practiced on me in the car. Seems pretty well thought-out—for Miss Seat-of-the-Pants here, anyway."

"Hey, now." Jamie tore a piece off her roll and threw it at her sister, who ducked and reached for her peas.

"Don't even think about it," their mother said witheringly.

Both girls froze, and their father snickered, which brought the wrathful glare his way. He winked at Jamie, who hid a laugh. Taking one for the team—that was their dad all right.

"What else do you want to do while Emma is here?" he asked.

They spent the next few minutes discussing the best spots in and around the Bay to take visitors, the locations they had been bringing out-of-town guests to visit for years, from the Pasadena relatives to her mother's Colorado-based clan. In fact, Jamie's maternal grandmother, two sets of aunts and uncles, and five cousins had just left California to return to Denver in time for New Year's. They traded off at Christmas. Every other year, one side of the family flew to spend the holiday with the other.

"I'll probably bring her to practice, too," Jamie added.

"Of course." Her father nodded. "I wouldn't expect anything less."

Prep season had started as soon as club ended—actually try-outs had happened before travel season finished—but Berkeley High Soccer went on hiatus during the winter holiday break. Their last game had been on the Saturday before Christmas and their next one wouldn't be until the Saturday after New Year's. Emma would be in town for two practices and their first game back. Jamie couldn't wait. Even the notion that she would soon be divulging her darkest secret couldn't dampen her happiness at the thought of hanging out with Emma for five whole days.

Besides, it wasn't really a secret if more than a handful of people knew, was it? Her mother had requested permission to talk to her two sisters about Lyon, and Jamie had granted it, specifying that her mom had to wait until the end of the visit, though. That way Jamie wouldn't have to deal with their reactions for long. Her mother had respected her wishes and even invited her to be present for any conversation that might happen, but Jamie declined. She really, really didn't need to be there to hear how her mother would describe what had happened. She was pretty sure her mom was equally as happy not to have her there.

The last day of the family visit, her Aunt Shelly, an older, plumper, and (chemically) blonder version of Jamie's mom, had cornered her after lunch to give her a hug.

"I am so sorry, sweetheart," she said, her voice thick. "If I could, I would track that bastard down and cut off his—"

"Okay, Aunt Shelly." Meg had practically forced her way between them. "I think Jamie gets it. But maybe tone down the vigilante talk. Not sure that's helping anyone."

Jamie, who hadn't realized her sister was watching the interaction, gave Meg a grateful look and patted her distraught aunt on the arm. "Love you, too, Aunt Shelly," she'd said, and backed away.

That conversation had come up in her session with Shoshanna.

"What if Emma responds in a similar manner?" the therapist had asked.

"She won't," Jamie said.

"How do you know?"

"She's more sensitive than that."

"Does that mean you think your aunt is insensitive?"

"Not exactly. I guess I mean Emma listens to me more. Like, she can read me."

"How can you be so certain? You haven't seen her in six months, and then it was only for a few hours."

"I just know. Only being able to talk on the phone and write emails, you get to know someone in a different way. And Emma pays attention. She always has."

"What about you? Do you think you pay attention?"

Jamie had frowned. "I don't know. I hope so."

Now as she and Meg cleaned up the kitchen after dinner, she tried not to worry about Emma's visit. She was so excited to see her, but what if Shoshanna was right? What if she had built up an image of Emma that didn't exist? What if Emma really did respond like her aunt, or worse, pulled away in disgust? Her gut told her that wouldn't happen, but then, her gut didn't have the best track record. Sometimes people reacted to things in ways you least expected, as she well knew. Being an out, dykey tomboy in high school wasn't always safe even in the twenty-first century, even in liberal, progressive Berkeley. She had learned not to travel alone, which, given she was on the soccer team and friends with the skater crowd, was easy enough to arrange most days.

"Penny for your thoughts," Meg said as she rinsed a plate and handed it to Jamie to dry.

She rubbed the old, soft dish towel decorated with faded Christmas wreaths over the Fiestaware plate she still thought of as the "new" set they had bought a few years ago to replace the 1980s table settings their parents had received at their wedding.

"I was thinking about Aunt Shelly. Not sure I ever thanked you for intervening at the best possible moment."

"No problem," Meg said, and elbowed her. "I got your back, kiddo, and don't you forget it."

73

"I've got yours too, you know, if you ever need me."

"No offense, but I kind of hope I don't."

"I feel you, my sister."

"Right here, James." Meg pressed a soapy fist to the front of her Berkeley High Orchestra sweatshirt. "Right here."

As a now nearly sixteen-year-old, Jamie was embarrassed to admit that back in middle school, she had worried about being seen with her sister because she was a self-avowed orchestra geek. It wasn't until she'd gotten to high school and realized how valued the various musical organizations were that she'd relaxed her social biases. The Berkeley Community Theater was located on Berkeley High's campus, and since the late 1960s had hosted music greats like Jimi Hendrix, Van Morrison, The Grateful Dead, Bruce Springsteen, and David Bowie. Not bad for a public high school.

Besides, Meg was super talented. Even Jamie could recognize that, and she could barely hold a tune. But the fact she didn't make music herself, good or otherwise, didn't mean she couldn't appreciate those who did.

They were almost finished with the dishes when their father wandered in. "Hey, kid, feel like shooting baskets?"

"Totally."

"Oh, I see, don't ask me then," Meg said, rolling her eyes.

He paused. "Do you want to join us?"

"No, but it's nice to be asked."

"Drama queen." Jamie flicked her with the end of her dish towel.

Meg whirled around and pointed the sprayer in Jamie's direction. "Go ahead," she intoned, squinting Eastwood-style. "Make my day."

Jamie and their dad both sidled away, giggling. Then they turned and hoofed it toward the front door, yelping as water struck them in the ribs.

"You're going to have to clean that up," Jamie called back to her laughing sister.

"So? It was totally worth it."

"She's crazy," Jamie said to her dad as they pulled on sneakers and headed outside.

"Your mother and I prefer to think of her as *spirited*."

The sun had set hours before, but the street lamp and the spotlight on the side of the house lit up the short driveway where the portable basketball hoop resided. Almost no one in their neighborhood, one of the older residential areas in Berkeley with leafy trees and bungalows galore, had garages. Where one might have stood on their property was, instead, a small shed that her mom had long since converted into an art studio.

They warmed up, tossing the ball to each other for shot after shot while sirens and car horns sounded in the distance. Her dad was pretty good. He'd played in high school in rural Indiana and had harbored dreams of walking on at Cal. While that hadn't happened, he had played intramurals all four years. When she was younger, he'd coached her rec basketball team. Softball, too. But then they'd gone to see Mia Hamm, Michelle Akers, and the rest of the '99ers play a friendly match in LA, and that was it. Jamie knew what she wanted. To become the best of the best, she understood that she would have to focus on soccer and only soccer.

Her dad had taken her defection to a sport about which he knew little incredibly well. He ribbed her occasionally, but if he resented her abandonment of his favorite sport, he didn't let on. In fact, he was the one who drove her to most of her practices and games, the one who took photos and video footage, the one who cheered her on no matter what.

"Horse?" he asked.

"You're on." She tossed him the ball. "Let's see what you got, old man."

He arced his middle-aged body gracefully and swished home a shot from the top of the imaginary key.

"Ooh," Jamie said, "white boy can jump."

He threw the ball to her and they switched spots. "Put up or shut up, kid."

As soon as she let the ball go, she knew it was a brick. Sure enough, it thudded against the backboard. "Whoops."

"That was... close," he offered.

"Do you need to get your prescription checked?"

"Always a possibility at my age."

They played on, bantering as was their habit. Her dad used to kick a ball around their small back yard with her, too, but by the time she was in sixth grade his form was too painful for her to watch and her perfectionist streak was too much for him to endure, so that ended. But basketball was usually a safer outlet. They'd had some of their best conversations out here in the driveway while Meg practiced one or more instruments and Jamie's mom worked in her studio.

"So," her dad said after she'd chased the ball down the driveway for the third time. "About telling Emma."

She passed him the ball, a little surprised. Since the day she got home from France and confessed to her parents what had happened, she and her dad hadn't spoken much about it on their own. "What about it?"

"I want you to know that I'm happy to be there with you when you do it, if that would help. Your mom, too."

"Thanks, but I think it'll go better if I do it on my own," Jamie said, watching as her father sank a ten-footer.

"Can I ask why?"

"Oh." She thought about it as she traded places with him and sized up the shot. "I think I'd be too self-conscious if you guys were there. Like having an audience or something." She let the ball fly, cursing under her breath as it hit the edge of the basket and bounced out. "Besides, Mom makes me nervous."

"What do you mean?" he asked, corralling the ball.

"She's, I don't know, unguarded, I guess." That was the word she and Shoshanna had come up with to describe the way her mom stared at her when she thought she wouldn't notice.

"And that's a bad thing?"

"It can be. Sometimes I wish she would look at me the way you do."

He turned toward her, his face in shadows. "And how is that?"

"Like you're not thinking about what happened. Like I'm still the same me." She squinted into the light, wondering if he would defend her mom.

Sure enough: "She's trying, Jamie. She really is. One of the hardest things for a parent is to see your child hurting and be unable to do anything about it."

She wanted to point out that she was the child in this scenario even if she didn't feel particularly child-like these days; to tell him that she wasn't sure she could manage the weight of her mother's sorrow on top of her own. She didn't even think she should have to. But she couldn't say that, not to him. Instead they stood in silence, watching each other until a car horn sounded somewhere nearby.

As the sound died away, she gestured to the ball on his hip. "Quit stalling, dude. Take your shot already."

"Fine. But if you change your mind about Emma, say the word." He lined up another ten-footer from the other side of the key and sank it easily.

Jamie tried again, and again she missed. "Damn it!" She punched the ball, spiking it off the driveway. "How do you do that?"

"Years of practice, young one. Years and years. Now take a breath."

"You sound like Shoshanna."

"Then there's probably something to it."

"Yeah, yeah." Jamie fired the ball at him.

They didn't mention Emma's visit again as they played on under the spotlight, the air cooling and the neighborhood settling around them.

#

Emma lay quietly on the futon mattress they'd set up on Jamie's floor, staring up at the paneled ceiling. It was dark still on this, her next to last morning in California, and she could hear Jamie snoring lightly nearby. Finally the younger girl rolled over on her twin bed, stretching her arms above her head and kicking off her covers as she had done every morning since Emma had arrived.

"You awake, Blake?" she asked, peering through the dimly lit room.

"Yep."

"What are you doing?"

"Just thinking."

Jamie paused. "You nervous about flying tomorrow?"

"A little."

Jamie was one of the only people in the world who knew that while she wasn't exactly afraid of flying, she didn't entirely trust the process. Not only were images of 9/11 forever burned into her brain, she had inherited a wariness of flight from her father. When her dad was in medical school, his older brother, Dean, had died in a small plane crash during a ski trip. Emma had overheard her mother tell one of her sisters that sometimes he still woke up sweating from a recurring nightmare. It was always the same—the plane's broken windshield letting the water rush in as the damaged craft sank into the cold, dark depths of Lake Michigan. He couldn't get his seat belt undone, couldn't do anything but hold his breath for as long as possible and watch the light overhead fade away.

For the last six or seven years, her father had flown on average something like thirty times a year, sixty if you counted round trips. He had to face his biggest fear routinely in order to save people he didn't know from *their* biggest fear: losing a child. When she thought about it like that, she had to admit, she almost felt sorry for him. How ironic that he worked so hard to keep other families together while his own fell apart.

Except that they hadn't fallen apart, not completely. He was home more now, traveling less, and Emma had to admit that her parents seemed happier together than ever. Maybe the adage her mother liked to repeat was true: *We forgive those who hurt us for our own sake, not theirs.* Nice idea in theory, but in reality forgiveness wasn't that easy. At least, not for Emma.

"I can't believe it's almost time for you to go home," Jamie said, watching her from the bed.

Emma looked away from the adorable picture of Jamie in her boxers and tank top, her hair tousled in yet another new bedhead style. "Me either."

"It's been awesome, hasn't it?"

"Best winter break ever."

Jamie threw her legs over the side of the bed and paused. "What do you want to do on your last full day in town?"

"I don't know. What sights haven't I seen yet?"

"Golden Gate Park?"

"Sounds perfect."

And she was sure it would be. So far she had loved the Bay Area. Her second night there had been New Year's Eve, and Jamie's family had ventured into the city with Becky's to watch the annual fireworks display near the Bay Bridge. After roller skating at a disco rink in the Haight, they'd caught a train to the waterfront where, at precisely midnight, the fireworks began, accompanied by music blasted from loud speakers along the shoreline. The display lasted fifteen minutes, and then, cold and happy, the two families and Emma had caught a train—BART ran late on the last night of the year—back to Berkeley.

Jamie had practice the next couple of afternoons, so Emma went with her to watch from the empty stands. Back home, Emma's school sat on a hillside overlooking Lake Washington, and was bordered by two parks that contained nearly a hundred acres of second growth forest. Berkeley High's campus, meanwhile, occupied two full city blocks. A group of homeless men on the corner near the high school made the sort of comments Emma had only ever been subjected to walking around downtown Seattle. When she asked Jamie if this happened regularly, she'd only shrugged and said, "Yeah, but you get used to it."

Being accosted by strange men wasn't the only hazard to negotiate at Jamie's high school. At the first game of the new year, a handful of boys in the stands had cat-called every time Jamie touched the ball. She was focused on the game and didn't seem to notice the harassment, but Emma, who was sitting a few rows away with Jamie's family, had soon had enough. Midway through the first half, she'd walked over to their row, leaned in, and said, "Keep it up, boys. But you should know that every time you harass her, you're basically telling the world how tiny your dicks are."

And then she'd flipped her hair and sashayed back to her seat, purposely letting her hips sway a little extra in her low-rise Levi's. When the boys left a few minutes later without another word, Meg and Becky turned to her, eyes wide.

"What did you say to them?" Meg asked.

"The truth." She held up her pinky finger where only the two girls could see it. "That only small men harass girls like Jamie."

"Oh my god, I think I love you." As Emma's forehead creased, Meg added, "Not like that. Don't worry, I leave the ladies to my sister."

Emma had felt her face growing warm and turned back to

the game in time to see Jamie rip the ball from the end line across the mouth of the goal. One of her teammates tapped it in and the stands erupted—in a good way, this time.

Now as they got ready to go play tourist, Emma wondered if this was it. Was Jamie finally going to reveal her deep, dark secret? A couple of times, Emma had been sure she would. Her first day in town, they'd driven with Meg and Becky over the Golden Gate Bridge and out to Stinson Beach in Marin County. There, she and Jamie had wandered off on their own, making footprints in the sand and rolling up their jeans to clamber over the rocks at one end of the park. She'd been sure Jamie was going to tell her then as they sat on a rock close together watching the ocean spray ricochet off nearby rocks, but instead they'd talked about the biggest earthquakes they'd survived—a 7.1 in 1989 for Jamie, a 6.8 in 2001 for Emma. Then Meg and Becky caught up with them and the conversation had shifted again.

Another morning, they'd gotten up early and hiked from the Cal soccer fields up through the Redwoods to Grizzly Peak. At the lookout, they'd munched sandwiches and fruit, and as they gazed out over the expansive view of the Berkeley Hills, East Bay, and the city of San Francisco, the Pacific shimmering in the distance, Emma had been sure Jamie was going to open up about her past. Instead the conversation had revolved around 9/11—where they were, what they saw, whether or not they knew anyone personally impacted by the terrorist attacks. Neither had, but Jamie admitted her parents weren't so lucky. It seemed like almost everyone in the Bay Area knew someone who had a friend or relative or neighbor connected to Flight 93, the San Francisco-bound plane that had crashed in Pennsylvania.

At this point, Emma was starting to think she'd misread the situation. Jamie seemed less troubled than when they'd first met, and anyway, there were a million reasons why she could have been distraught that last night at Surf Cup. Maybe she was upset about losing the tournament finals. Maybe she'd gotten in a particularly nasty fight with her mother. Or maybe she was premenstrual. The possibilities were endless.

If Jamie didn't have anything to confess, Emma told herself as they jogged downstairs for breakfast with the rest of the family, then she would take the bull by the horns herself and officially come out. Things had gone so well with her mother at Thanksgiving that she was actually looking forward to telling Jamie. After all, it wasn't like the girl who had come out at thirteen was going to give her a hard time for revealing that she thought she might be bisexual.

The morning started out foggy, but by the time they had finished breakfast and caught the train into the city, the marine layer had burned off. They disembarked near the University of San Francisco and walked a block to the park, set their watches, and started a leisurely run along the park's wooded trails, chatting as they went. This was Jamie's one day off from soccer for the week, but like Emma she didn't like to go a day without exercise. It wasn't an addiction, they assured each other. Then they laughed. Well, maybe it was. But at least it was a healthy addiction.

Their route took them past tennis courts and the picture-perfect Victorian Flower Conservatory.

"Want to check it out?" Jamie asked.

"Definitely."

Inside, they wandered the narrow aisles of blooming tropical plants, pausing to inhale the rich scent of earth and plant life.

"This place is amazing," Emma murmured, lifting her face to the winter sunlight filtering through the greenhouse roof.

"It's always summer in here." Jamie closed her eyes and breathed in deeply. "You wouldn't know to look at it, but this building was almost destroyed by a wind storm a few years back. But then a bunch of people got together and got it named a historic site and raised enough money to remodel. It only reopened a little while ago."

"My mother would love this place."

"That's right, she's a big gardener, isn't she? So is my Aunt Mary."

"The one in Pasadena?"

"That's the one." Jamie glanced at her, eyes narrowed.

"What?" Emma asked expectantly. This would be the perfect place for Jamie to tell her, surrounded by blooming flowers from foreign lands.

"Nothing." She shook her head, and they walked on.

Outside a little while later they resumed their run, following the trail down through a wide courtyard between a pair of museums. They continued past the Japanese Tea Garden and veered off on a path that led to the shore of a small lake. The day was lovely, and Emma kept telling herself it wasn't possible she would be back in gray, rainy Seattle in less than a day. She felt so at home here. No wonder people always said Seattle was a smaller, more provincial version of San Francisco. Both cities had plentiful water, bridges, gardens, and evergreens, not to mention high tech start-ups, Subarus, and yuppies galore. Yet another reason she and Jamie connected so easily.

They ran around the lake, past the polo fields in the center of the park, around the golf course and archery range, and slowed to a walk at the northwest edge of the park. They cooled down a bit before stopping in front of a brewery that sat almost on the beach.

"What do you think?" Jamie asked as Emma checked out the menu.

"Looks good to me. It's my treat, okay?"

"No way. You had to buy a plane ticket to get here, remember?"

"It was a frequent flyer ticket. Besides, my parents gave me spending money and you still haven't let me pay for anything. Let me get lunch at least. Please?"

Jamie rolled her eyes. "Fine. I would hate to offend your

parents."

They were soon seated at a table by the wide front window overlooking the sea. The midday sun hovered unseen somewhere over the city, so they set their sunglasses on the table beside their cell phones. A server came by and Emma watched as the girl, who was about their age, smiled particularly widely at Jamie and leaned over her shoulder to point out an item on the laminated menu, her sizable chest brushing against Jamie's arm.

"She was totally flirting with you," she said when they were alone again.

Jamie glanced up at her. "What?"

"The server. She was flirting with you."

"Really?" Jamie rubbed a hand along the back of her neck, eying Emma doubtfully. Her eyes were the color of the winter sky beyond the window, her cheeks flushed from their run. She was gorgeous in an androgynous, jock girl sort of way, and she clearly didn't know it.

"Really," Emma said, and looked down at her menu.

Throughout her visit, there had been small moments like this where she noticed how attractive Jamie was, or how great she was with her family, or how tough she appeared walking around the Bay Area with her shades on and her Adidas warm-up jacket zipped to the top. At those moments, like now, Emma would realize that her feelings definitely blurred the friendship boundary. But they couldn't. She couldn't. She lived in Seattle and Jamie lived here and soon they would be on opposite coasts. Besides, Jamie was too young for anything to happen between them, and there may or may not be that pesky secret to worry about.

"Does that creep you out or something?"

Emma glanced up to find Jamie frowning at her, and tried to ignore the fact that serious Jamie was almost even cuter than sweaty, pink-cheeked Jamie. "No. Should it?"

"I guess not."

Their eyes held, and Emma's heart rate, which had recovered from their run by now, picked up again. Did Jamie feel it, too? But then the waitress returned, and Jamie locked her eyes on the menu, mumbling that they needed another minute. Shy Jamie was the most adorable incarnation yet, Emma decided. Then she sighed to herself. That kind of thinking was not helpful.

They ordered salmon burgers and french fries and talked five Ks and trail running while they waited for their food to arrive. The restaurant wasn't as busy as Emma would have expected on such a nice weekend day, so it wasn't long before Nadine, the flirty server, was back with their food. She brought Jamie another root beer without asking—"on the house"—and ignored Emma almost entirely. When she walked away this time, Jamie smiled sheepishly.

"Okay, so you may be right."

"Does this happen to you a lot?"

"Free drinks? I thought it happened to everyone."

Emma laughed. "No, it definitely does not. You're going to break a lot of hearts when you get a little older, you know that?" She said it mostly to remind herself, not expecting the comment to have much of an effect on Jamie.

But across the table, she shuddered a little and reached for the ketchup bottle. "God, I hope not," she said, her eyes darkening.

There was that look again, the one Emma had noticed the first time they met, the one that had been missing for most of her visit. Jamie exhaled in an almost but not quite sigh, glanced out at the ocean, and retreated inside herself briefly. Emma wanted to ask what the problem was, wanted to apologize for obviously saying the exact wrong thing. But she only sat still and waited. When Jamie finally looked at her again, she seemed almost back to normal.

"What about you?" she asked. "Are you really swearing off dating until North Carolina?"

Emma took a bite of burger, chewing slowly. An image of Tori popped into her head, followed by Justin Tate, the soccer player who had indeed asked her out. She kept saying no, but he kept asking. And she had to admit, he was cute in a preppy jock sort of way. Sian and Dani couldn't believe she hadn't given in yet. *Yet*—as if going out with him was inevitable. And in the world she came from, it almost seemed that way. In her world, female servers hit on male patrons, not on fellow teenaged girls.

"That guy Justin asked me out again," she admitted, and took a sip of soda.

"The soccer player? I thought you said no."

"I did."

"At least he's persistent."

"I'm not sure that's a plus, really."

Jamie laughed and Emma joined her, and all at once it didn't matter that she couldn't decide who she most wanted to kiss. She and Jamie were here together in this restaurant on a lazy Sunday, sharing a delicious meal with the ocean laid out before them. The Future with all its mysteries and unanswerable questions could wait. For now, she was with one of her best friends and she was happy.

But her runner's high faded, as it always did. And then, as they walked along the beach a little while later, Jamie turned to her and said the words Emma had been waiting days, weeks, months for: "Do you mind if we sit? There's something I've been wanting to talk to you about."

Finally! But then a frisson of fear touched her. What if she wasn't up to the conversation? What if she said the wrong thing again?

"Of course I don't mind," she bluffed.

They sat down together on a massive driftwood log half

buried in the sand, and Jamie looked down, running her fingers over the smooth, bleached wood. The waves were a ways out, and Emma gazed at the ocean, wondering why this felt so familiar. Then she remembered—the night they met they had sat together just like this on a bench at the edge of the Pacific, getting to know each other bit by bit. They had come so far in half a year. As long-distance friends, they had bonded over soccer and high school life and possibilities they both hoped lay in their near future—youth national team call-ups and college soccer at big-time programs and then? And then the big show, whatever that might mean now that WUSA, America's first professional soccer league for women, had folded only days before the start of the World Cup.

Jamie glanced over at her. "I didn't want to do this over the phone. Honestly, I wasn't sure I was going to tell you at all, but you've become one of my closest friends. Even though you live like a thousand miles away."

"Eight hundred. But who's counting?" Emma scooted closer on the log. "You know, you can tell me anything. I'm not going anywhere."

"Technically, that's not true."

"I meant it figuratively." She hesitated as Jamie dangled her hands between her legs and stared down at the sand. Obviously this was not going to be an easy conversation. "Would it help if I told you I think I already know?"

Her brow creased. "What? How? Did my sister tell you?"

"No. No one told me anything. It was more something you said."

"Something...?" She pursed her lips. "When?"

"Right before my birthday. You were telling me about that girl on your team who was pregnant, and I said—"

"That I hadn't ever had to worry about something like that. I remember." She stood up, running a hand over her already mussed hair.

Emma stood too and hesitantly reached for her.

But Jamie stepped back, squinting at her. "Are you serious, Emma? You let me go all this time worrying about how to tell you? Worrying about whether or not you'd still want to be my friend once you found out I snuck out to a bar with some teammates our last night in France and drank too much and this guy who was buying for us waited until my friends weren't paying attention, and then he pulled me into this back room and he—he… I didn't even do anything to stop him. I was so scared I froze." She stopped, blinking against the tears Emma could see hovering on her lashes. "I didn't do anything. I didn't do a thing." As her voice turned to a whisper, all the anger went out of her and she seemed to fold in on herself.

Emma didn't let her fall, though. She caught her and pulled her close, held on tight as Jamie cried, her tears dripping onto Emma's neck.

"It's okay, Jamie," she murmured. "I've got you. I won't let go, I promise."

Her heart hurt at the sound of Jamie's sobs, low and deep in her chest, body racked with every breath, and it was all she could do not to cry herself. She had been expecting this, of course, but she had hoped she was wrong. God, how she had hoped this wasn't the secret Jamie carried. But even knowing something terrible had likely happened hadn't prepared her for the reality of Jamie's confession. This tough, vulnerable girl who loved soccer the same way she did and had parents and a sister and friends who loved her, Jamie, one of her closest friends, had been raped by a strange man in the back of a bar in a foreign country. The knowledge made Emma's heart race uncomfortably, and for a moment she wondered if she might throw up. As she swallowed down the nausea, she remembered again the phone call that had started all of this—the joke she'd made, not realizing how deeply it would sting. Tears stung her eyes as she understood how cruel, however unintentionally, she had been.

But crying wouldn't help Jamie. This wasn't the time to apologize for her own cluelessness or to wallow in horror, however justified. She remembered what the pamphlet her mother had given her said: *Support your friend. Don't make it about your feelings. Let her know you believe her and that you care about her.*

"I'm sorry," Jamie choked out, holding the back of Emma's sweatshirt in her fist. "I'm so sorry."

Emma blinked back her own tears and rubbed soothing circles into Jamie's back. "You don't have to be sorry. It wasn't your fault. You didn't do anything to deserve what happened to you."

She pulled away, swiping at her wet face. "But I shouldn't have had so much to drink. I should have run or fought back or, I don't know, done *something*. All I did was stare at the ceiling telling myself it wasn't happening. That it couldn't really be happening, not to me."

Emma shook her head. "You did the best you could to get through an awful experience. You survived, and I'm so thankful you did. So is everyone else who loves you."

"How can you say that? You know as well as I do that it was stupid to get myself into that situation."

Her hands gentle, Emma squeezed Jamie's shoulders. "Nothing you did could possibly justify what he did to you. Do you understand? It's not your fault that asshole took advantage of you. Would you think it was my fault if the same thing had happened to me?"

Jamie's eyes flickered. "Well, no."

"Then allow yourself that same latitude, okay?"

"I don't think it works that way."

"It can if you let it." Although that was easy enough for her to say. She wasn't the one who'd had her virginity taken by force. Hands still on Jamie's shoulders, she tugged her into another warm hug. If only she could squeeze all the hurt out of her and leave only good feelings behind. If only there was something more she could do to help.

"Why are you being so great?" Jamie asked, her voice muffled against Emma's hoodie.

"Because I'm your friend and I care about you." The declaration didn't feel like nearly enough, but she heard Jamie sigh and felt her rigid muscles soften.

"Promise?"

"I promise. This could never change how I feel about you. I sort of already knew, remember, and I'm still here, aren't I?"

"Yeah." Jamie pulled back to stare at her. "You are."

"What happened that night doesn't define you, at least not in my eyes. You are so much more than that one night. You are smart and funny and a good person, and I'm so glad I met you."

"Funny, or funny-looking?" Jamie joked weakly, trying to smile.

"Definitely not funny-looking, if Nadine is any judge."

"Nadine?"

"Our server," Emma said, secretly pleased that Jamie hadn't taken much notice of the less-than-subtle waitress. She hesitated, trying to gauge where Jamie was at. "Do you want to sit down? Or maybe walk a little?"

"Let's walk. I think I could use some motion right about now."

Emma linked their arms, and the closeness felt just as comfortable as it had the night they met as they strolled down the beach together, strides matching and hips occasionally bumping.

"So obviously your family knows," Emma said after a while.

"Yeah. My therapist says it's important not to let what happened turn into a secret within the family."

"You're talking to someone, then?"

"My parents said I had to or they wouldn't let me play

soccer."

"Good. That's really good. Have you told anyone else what happened?"

She bit her lip and glanced over at Emma before quickly looking away. "No. Outside of my family, you're the first."

"Really?"

"Really."

For some reason, this admission brought Emma's tears back. Blinking them away again, she squeezed Jamie's arm. "Thank you for trusting me. It means so much to me. You mean so much to me."

She smiled back shyly. "Thank you for being so awesome. You mean a lot to me, too, you know."

"You're pretty tough, aren't you?"

"I literally cried all over you not two minutes ago."

"Crying has nothing to do with strength or weakness. You went through this potentially life-altering thing, and instead of destroying you, it made you stronger."

"That is the cliché, isn't it? What doesn't kill you?" She shrugged and kicked at the sand. "Honestly, I'm not sure when I'll be done going through it. Sometimes it feels like I'll always be going through it."

"I can see that," Emma said, even though she couldn't, really. Nothing in her life had happened yet that couldn't be undone. The closest she had come was when her parents nearly split up, but the separation had only lasted a couple of months. Her grandmother's dementia was sad, but older people got sick and died. It was a normal part of the life cycle, to be expected even. Rape, while far too common according to the materials her mother had shared, was not a normal part of life. Not in the least.

She tugged Jamie closer against her side. "You don't have to go through it alone. You've got your family and you've got me, too. I told you, I'm not going anywhere."

Yet.

The word hung between them, unspoken. Emma was sure Jamie felt it too. How could she not? They had rung in the new year together knowing that 2004 would put even more distance between them. Soon she would leave the West Coast, and then who knew what would happen? They might stay in touch, but she had seen older friends come back from college changed, their minds crowded with new teams, new people, new ideas. This day, this visit might be the only time they would ever be in the same place together. She hoped not, but there was no way to predict if the separate arcs of their lives would intersect again.

"I'm going to miss you," Jamie said quietly, leaning into her.

"I'm going to miss you, too."

If this was all they had, then at least they could be there for each other now. Maybe that was why they had been brought together—so that she could help Jamie through the first year after France, the hardest year. And in turn, Jamie had helped Emma see that the label didn't define the person. Even if they grew apart and went in different directions from here, their friendship had made a difference in each of their lives. Whether Jamie knew it or not.

Briefly she thought about sharing her own secret. But it was so small in comparison, and anyway, today wasn't about her. Once more she bit back the words and walked on with Jamie, the winter breeze buffeting them as they kicked through the sand side by side.

CHAPTER FIVE

Two weeks later, Jamie ran down the stairs and almost collided with her father.

"Whoah, there, birthday girl. Where's the fire?"

"Blair's on his way to pick me up."

"And where are you two going, exactly?" her mother asked, emerging from the kitchen in an apron.

"The skate park. If that's okay?" she made herself add, even though it was her *birthday* and she was sixteen, for god's sake, too old to be asking her parents if she could go out for a couple of hours in the middle of a Sunday afternoon.

"It's fine," her dad said. "Have a good time. Just be home in time for dinner, okay?"

"You got it," she said, and offered him a high five. When he swung, she pulled her hand away and ran it over her hair. "Too slow, old man."

"I don't know why I still fall for that," he complained.

That made two of them.

"Be careful," her mom added. "And wear your helmet."

Jamie barely resisted the urge to roll her eyes. "I will. See ya."

On the porch, she pulled on her helmet, tucked her board under her arm, and ran down to the street. Then she hopped on and started down the road. At least her parents no longer insisted she wear pads. Though she caught bigger air when she was decked out in safety gear, going without looked cooler.

"Dude," Blair crowed as he pulled alongside in his Jeep Wrangler. "Happy birthday!"

"Boy-ee!" She laughed and grabbed onto the rollover bar. "Tow me?"

"Hang on!"

He hit the gas and took the next corner fast enough that she gasped and then laughed as she struggled to follow the Jeep's line without getting crushed.

"How's that?" he asked, grinning at her in the rearview mirror.

"Awesome!"

The skate park was located down near the waterfront, only a short distance from the freeway. Blair pulled over a little ways from her house and she climbed in, tossing her board and helmet in back. There were a ton more cops downhill than in Elmwood, and Blair, a year ahead of her at Berkeley High, had already had to go back to driving school once.

As usual, they parked on Fifth Street near the skate park. Jamie was already reaching for her helmet when Blair hopped out and started to put up the Jeep's soft shell top. She glanced back at him in surprise. This neighborhood wasn't the best, admittedly, but they would be less than a hundred feet away.

"Hold on," he said, smirking at her. "I have to give you your birthday present, don't I?"

She smiled slowly and let go of her helmet. "Sweet."

Once the top was locked into place, they fastened all the flaps, put up the windows, and checked the surrounding area one last time. There were a couple of kids on the park's soccer field and a handful of skaters, but other than that the block was pretty dead. The industrial warehouses behind them were closed for the weekend, and the overcast sky was keeping the masses away. Besides, there was an NFL wild card playoff game on. While Jamie didn't mind the NFL, she definitely wouldn't give up an afternoon at the park for a game that didn't involve the Forty-Niners.

Coast unofficially clear, Blair pulled a joint out of his cargo pants while Jamie retrieved a plastic lighter from the glove compartment.

"Ladies first," he said.

She glanced over her shoulder. "Wait, do you have a girl up in here?"

"Hilarious. Light it up, James."

She did, inhaling deeply and holding the sweet smoke in as long as she could. Then she blew it out and handed over the joint. "Mmmm." She exhaled tension she hadn't even known she was holding in. "That shit is smooth."

"Only the best for you, son." He pulled off his knit beanie and tucked his long hair behind one ear before taking a hit. Then he offered her the joint again.

"One more and I'm out." As he stared at her, still holding his breath, she shrugged. "You know I'm in season."

He exhaled finally. "You're always in season."

They'd been friends since they played on their first AYSO team together, but lately Blair had seemed increasingly impatient with the time she reserved for soccer. He'd quit in middle school when he started hanging around the skate park every waking minute. Soon after, he'd moved on to a different social group at school, stoners and skate punks who Jamie liked but didn't have much in common with. Still, they were fun to hang with and good for the medicinal marijuana hook-up. She had managed to wean herself off of the formerly required nighttime toke, but a hit here and there didn't go amiss, especially when the anxiety she'd struggled with ever since

France set up shop in her thoughts again.

Blair handed her a small, clumsily wrapped package, the shape of which revealed its contents even before she tore off the tissue paper.

"Thanks, man," she said, holding up her hand for a high five.

He complied. "De nada. Want to play it?"

"Totally."

They listened to the CD in comfortable silence while he smoked the joint down. Every year he burned a new mix for her birthday. Unfortunately he was still into grunge music even though the 1990s were long gone, as she liked to tease him. But she had to admit, the songs he'd put on this year's mix were good. Maybe she would make Emma a copy. Emma's taste tended toward pop music and hip hop, which Jamie thought was funny given she lived in a suburb of one of the least racially diverse cities in the country. But so far she'd liked all of the CDs Emma had sent, including the one she'd made for her birthday.

That morning, Jamie hadn't even been awake yet when her mother knocked on her door and came in with the phone, yawning. She held it out without a word before disappearing back down the hall.

"Happy birthday!" Emma had shouted as soon as Jamie grunted into the receiver.

She'd slid back down under her covers, adjusting her boxers and tank top more comfortably. "The hell, Blake? It's six o'clock in the morning."

"More like six *thirty*. Was I the first person to wish you a happy birthday? Was I?"

"Yes, for eff's sake." Jamie closed her eyes and smiled. "My mom is totally going to feel shitty when she realizes she forgot."

"Ooh, parental guilt. That should be good for something.

Now come on, open your presents!"

Jamie grumbled good-naturedly as she pulled the package from under her bedside table, but the grouchiness was mostly for show. Emma's excitement was too much to resist, and besides, she loved getting presents almost as much as she loved giving them.

"Open the small one first," Emma commanded.

Accustomed to her bossy ways, Jamie complied. Inside the square box lay a green and black leather bracelet with a silver half cuff shaped like an anchor.

"Oh my god," she murmured, lifting it out. "You remembered."

During Emma's visit they'd explored the Haight with Meg and Blair, and Jamie had come across this very bracelet. But it had been out of her price range so she'd placed it back in the display case, intending to come back in a few weeks with the birthday money assorted relatives could be relied upon to send.

"Meg went back and got it while we were at practice. Check inside the clasp," Emma added, her voice soft.

Jamie turned it over and read in tiny lettering, "JAM - I'll be your anchor if you'll be mine - ELB." She reread the inscription, swallowing against the sudden tightness in her throat. After what Jamie had revealed, she'd half-expected that Emma would go home and never contact her again. But nothing had changed after the visit. Well, that wasn't quite true. They were closer now, easier with each other than before. Shoshanna had seemed pleased that the telling of her back story, as the therapist called it, had gone so well, though she'd cautioned that might not always be the case.

"Well?" Emma had asked. "Do you like it?"

"I love it," Jamie had assured her. "It's perfect." *You're perfect*, she'd thought, but somehow that felt like coming way too close to a line she didn't even want to admit existed between them. "Did Meg tell you my middle name?"

"Yep. You have a very excellent sister."

"True. So what's the L stand for?"

"I had a feeling you were going to ask that."

"Duh. Why, is it really bad?"

She sighed. "It's Louise, okay? For my mom's mom."

"That's not so bad." Jamie tried unsuccessfully to hold back a snicker. "We had a cat named Louise when I was little."

"Thankssss."

As she reached into the box again, Jamie could almost feel Emma's glare through the phone line. "Let's see what else you got me, Blake. Better not be a Man U jersey."

"I'm more original than that, thank you very much," the other girl had said sassily as Jamie opened her next present.

Now as Blair took another puff on the joint beside her, Jamie rubbed the smooth metal anchor. She hadn't taken the bracelet off all day, except to shower. It calmed her somehow to have Emma's words pressed against the vulnerable inside of her wrist.

And dang it, there was that line again. If she wasn't careful, she was going to have to think about what it might mean.

"Isn't that the bracelet you were jonesing for over break?" Blair asked.

"It is."

She would have told him where the bracelet came from, but she wasn't in the mood to hear the comments that information would garner. Her childhood best friend had made no secret that he found Emma hot. His exact words after he met her were, "If you're not going to hit that, can I?"

As if Emma would ever go out with him.

The joint was almost gone when her phone rang. Jamie checked the screen: unknown number from an area code she didn't recognize. She almost let it go to voicemail, but at the last minute she picked up, hoping her voice didn't sound too rough. "Hello?"

"Jamie Maxwell?"

The woman's voice sounded familiar, but she couldn't quite place it. "Yes."

"This is Jolene Nichols. I'm a coach with the US women's national youth team program. How are you doing today?"

"Um, good, thanks," she said, trying to keep her voice steady as her heart threatened to leap out of her chest. Jo Nichols was a former captain of the US women's national team and the current coach of the under-16 side. Was the weed stronger than it'd seemed, or was this actually happening?

"Your mother gave me your number. Is this a good time?"

Jamie glanced over at Blair, who was trying to get the lighter to fire up. "Sure, *Coach Nichols*," she said, shushing him with her free hand.

"All right, then. I think you know from one of your club coaches that we've had our eye on you."

"Yes, ma'am." She tried to breathe normally, also without much luck.

"We've decided we would like to take a closer look. There's an under-16 training camp coming up next month at US Soccer headquarters here in LA, and we would very much like it if you would consider joining us."

"Awesome." Jamie bit her lip, trying to contain her massive grin. "I'll totally be there."

Jo Nichols laughed. "I appreciate your enthusiasm, but why don't you talk it over with your parents first? I'll send you an email with all the details." She confirmed Jamie's email address and then added, "I'm looking forward to meeting you, Jamie. We all are."

"Thank you, ma'am," she said, the grin finally splitting her face. "I can't wait."

"Don't worry, the time will go by faster than you expect.

Oh, and by the way—happy birthday."

The line went dead and Jamie held the phone away from her ear, staring at the screen. *Best. Birthday. Ever.*

She hit recent calls and clicked on a name. "Pick up, pick up, pick up," she muttered as the line rang and rang. She was about to give up when she heard Emma's breathless greeting. "Oh my god!" she yelled by way of hello, and then reined in her voice as Blair flinched and gave her a quizzical look. "Guess who called to wish me a happy birthday?"

"Um, Mia Hamm, judging from your current decibel level?" Emma teased.

"Close. Jo freaking Nichols, that's who!"

"Wait, does this mean you got called up?"

"Totally! There's an under-16 camp next month, and they want me there. Can you believe it?"

Blair finally seemed to grasp the enormity of the phone call and held up his hand for a high five. Jamie complied perhaps a tad over-zealously and winced at the resulting sting.

"Of course I can believe it." Emma's voice was warm. "I told you it would happen, Jamie. The way you see the next play and the play beyond that… I'm serious, that kind of vision isn't very common in someone our age."

Jamie's ears felt warm as she touched the bracelet. Emma thought she had *vision*. This birthday kept getting better.

They talked for a little while longer, and then Emma said she had to go. She was out for the day with her family in Seattle, and her parents were miffed she hadn't turned her phone off earlier when they'd asked her to.

"I must have known you were going to call," she added.

"Right, because you're so psychic." Emma's supposed telepathic powers were a running joke between them. "But I should go too. Assuming you're done, dude?" She wiggled her eyebrows at Blair, who nodded, smiling lazily.

"Who are you talking to?" Emma asked.

"Blair. We took a few minutes to get a little happy in his Jeep, if you know what I mean, before hitting the skate park."

"You were *smoking* when Jo Nichols called?"

"I know. Too funny, huh?"

Emma released a noisy breath. "That's one word for it. Go have fun, birthday girl. And don't get hurt! You have national team camp to prepare for."

Hearing her say it out loud made the excitement come roaring back. "Holy *shit*, Emma! It's really happening, isn't it?"

"It is. Good job, Jamie. I'm so happy for you."

"So am I," she said, and she wasn't even joking.

As soon as they hung up, she dragged Blair out of the Jeep, even though the smoke cloud hadn't quite dissipated. But she didn't care. Nothing could bring her down from the high of getting her first call-up. She was sixteen, and not only would she have her driver's license by this time tomorrow but she would soon be training with Jo Nichols and the rest of the girls' national pool. *A-freakin-mazing.*

Life was sweet, she decided as she and Blair headed into the park, nodding at a couple of other skaters they knew. Even with everything that had happened in the last year, she couldn't help but feel that things were looking up. She pressed the anchor clasp against her chest, right over her heart, and then she stepped onto her board and dropped into the large oval bowl in the middle of the park.

"Woo hooo!" she shouted, and behind her, she heard Blair and the other guys cheer in response.

#

Emma returned her phone to her purse and headed back inside the Pacific Science Center. Skateboarding while high didn't seem like the best plan, but it wasn't like worrying from afar could change anything. Besides, she was too happy about Jamie's call-up to fixate on her dicey decision-making. With both of them on the national team track, their friendship had a much better chance at a future. Obviously any number of things could happen to prevent either of them from playing at the highest level, but at least now they were both officially in the national pool. Too bad Jamie's call-up hadn't come sooner. The under-16s and -17s often had training camp together and scrimmaged each other semi-regularly. Now that Emma was in the under-19 pool, their paths were less likely to cross.

When she reached the science center's NASA exhibit, her brother was suiting up for a spacewalk simulation while her parents looked on indulgently. Her mom was leaning against her dad's chest, his arms loose around her, and the sight only amplified the happiness Emma felt at Jamie's news. Her dad glanced over his shoulder and caught her eye, offering a quick smile and wiggle of eyebrows. He had been away the previous weekend for work, so this was their first real family time since she'd gotten back from Berkeley. Next month it would be her turn to fly away again—the U-19s had camp and a friendly against Mexico coming up in Texas. She was starting to rake up the frequent flyer miles, too. Like father, like daughter.

"Emma," her mom said as she reached them, "I thought we agreed to no phones?"

"It's Jamie's birthday, Mom, you know that."

"I thought you already talked to her this morning."

"I did. But guess who she got a call from? Jolene Nichols."

Both of her parents looked impressed. Probably best that she leave out the part about smoking weed at the skate park.

"Isn't Jo Nichols the under-16 coach?" her dad asked. When Emma stared at him, he shrugged. "What? I pay attention."

She snorted. "Yeah, to your call schedule and the *Journal of Otolaryngology*."

"That's not fair." Her dad's pout reminded her of Ty.

"Let's be honest," her mom put in. "It's pretty fair."

"I see how it is. Girls ganging up against the guys, as usual."

"You said it, not me." Emma held up her hand and her mom slapped it.

"Now will you turn off your phone?" her mother added.

"Fine." But she only turned it to vibrate. If by chance Jamie ended up in the emergency room, she wanted to find out sooner rather than later.

After their science center adventure, Ty and their mom headed to a pizza place on Denny Way while Emma and her dad stopped at the Experience Music Project. The first-floor restaurant there was one of her dad's favorite dinner spots in the city. Like most Seattleites, he claimed to find the exterior of the EMP confounding. But ask him about the interior and he would wax poetically about the curves and high ceilings and gorgeous polished wood and metal, not to mention the tranquil environment he called "a cross between a church and a fish tank." The food was damn good, too.

They ordered their usual: potato pancakes to start, followed by the portabella mushroom napoleon for her and the trout for him. Her dad's pint glass glowed amber in the overhead lights, and when he saw her eying it, he pushed it toward her.

"Go ahead. We can share."

"Really?"

"You're a good kid, Emma. You don't have to pretend you're perfect. At least, not with me."

She took the glass and gulped down a slug of the microbrew, wiping her mouth as she slid it back his way. "You have good taste in beer."

"Apparently so do you. Tell me, what's new in your world? I feel like one of us is always away."

"Probably because we are. Are you and Mom still going to Maui in March?"

"Planning on it. If you'd rather not stay alone with your brother, I'm sure we could make other arrangements."

"I'm okay with it. I bet Mom's nervous, isn't she?"

"Maybe a little. You know how she is."

Cautious bordering on overprotective, for which she routinely blamed her job. For some reason, his work seemed to affect him differently.

"We'll be fine," Emma said. "Ty's almost fourteen, and it's not like we're going to throw a party the second your back is turned."

"Is that a promise?"

"Uh, yeah. Talk about stressful. Why would I do that to myself?"

He laughed. "You are so your mother's daughter."

"She said the same thing recently."

The server brought their latkes, filled with smoked salmon and chives and topped with crème fraiche, and Emma immediately dug in. After her morning run followed by a day of wandering Seattle Center, she was starving.

"Anyway," her dad said, his hazel eyes slightly narrowed behind frameless glasses, "I'm glad we're getting this time together. In a few months you'll be starting what probably feels like your real life."

She nodded, swallowing a bite of salad greens. "It does feel like that. Although with everything going on with the under-19 national team, I kind of think I've already started."

"I can imagine." He paused. "Did I ever tell you about the year I took off before med school?"

"I don't think so." She'd known he took a break after college, but he'd never gone into much detail about his time off.

"I ended up in New Zealand working on an organic farm. Don't look so surprised. Organic farms have been around for a while. Anyway, I was only marking time before med school, but looking back, I wish I had paid more attention. I loved farming."

She could honestly say she had never thought that last sentence would come out of her father's mouth. "You did?"

"Absolutely. I loved getting up early in the morning and working outdoors all day with tractors and hydraulic equipment. There was something so elemental about it. You had to be patient, and a storm or a flood or a drought could destroy all of your work. It was completely different from what I do now. On that farm, I wasn't in control the way I am with surgery. I wasn't responsible for anyone else's life, not directly."

Emma really looked at her dad across the table. His salt-and-pepper hair was perfectly coiffed as usual, his button-down shirt clean and crisp even after a day out, but there were dark creases beneath his eyes. He looked like he hadn't slept in days. Seeing as he had recently crisscrossed the globe, his internal clock was probably all messed up. With his travel schedule, it seemed like he was jet-legged more often than not.

"Are you saying you wish you had become a farmer instead of a surgeon?"

"No, not at all. I only wish I hadn't been so focused on the end point that I ignored the ride. It's like the difference between being a journey hiker and a destination hiker. If you spend too much time thinking about where you're going, you risk missing the side trails and viewpoints along the way."

Was he trying to give her advice about her own life? Because in her case, playing soccer *was* the journey. Or at least, it was what made her happy. On the soccer field she got to be part of something that was greater than just herself.

"Of course," he added, "if I had paid more attention to the journey than the destination, I might not have gone to med school at all. And if I hadn't, I wouldn't have met your mother, and then you and your brother might not exist. So ultimately I'm glad I stayed the course because you and Ty and our family are what I'm most proud of in my life."

It was such an uncharacteristically sentimental statement that Emma stared at him, trying to determine if he was joking or not. But his eyes were earnest, his smile sincere.

"Even more than all of the kids you've saved?" she asked.

"Yes. It's not even a question." After a minute, he added, "And not because you're on the national team. Though for what it's worth, I think you have what it takes to be the next Mia Hamm."

"More like Joy Fawcett or Carla Overbeck," she corrected him. "I'm not a goal-scorer and I never will be."

"You don't know that for sure. You're still young, and people change, Emma. The trick is to follow your heart and not give in to what other people want or expect of you." He paused. "But I don't think you'll fall prey to the same traps I did. You're more like your mother—steady and loyal, and way too smart to let what someone else thinks sway you."

"Thanks. I guess." He was so chatty today. What was the deal? He never talked this much. She could almost sense the wheels turning in his head and waited, wondering what would come out of his mouth next.

The latkes were gone and their entrees half-demolished when he finished off his beer, set his fork down, and said, "Your mother tells me that you and she have had some pretty serious conversations in the past couple of months."

Emma nearly choked on a bite of portabella. She washed the tender meat down with a sip of soda and sat back, gripping her napkin beneath the table. "What exactly did she tell you?"

"She didn't offer up any details, only said I might want to ask you about it."

Well, that explained why he had suggested they grab dinner together. She chewed the inside of her lower lip. "I don't know. They're not the kinds of things you and I usually talk about."

He looked down, toying with his fork. "I'm not going to force the issue, Emma. I only wanted you to know that I'm ready to listen to whatever you might want to tell me."

She couldn't stop the words that came out: "Really? Because the last time we talked about Jamie, you didn't exactly listen. In fact, you've been pretty emphatic right from the start that I shouldn't get too close to her."

His eyes were unreadable. "Is that what this is about, then? You and Jamie?"

The way he said it, she knew he thought she was trying to tell him they were together. She started to deny it, but then she realized that even if it wasn't Jamie, it would be someone else—Tori or another girl from training camp or UNC. Given the world she occupied, it seemed inevitable that at some point in the future she was going to develop feelings for a girl who liked her back. Even if Jamie didn't.

"Would that really be so bad?" she said instead, hating the way her voice trailed off at the end.

He shook his head, and his voice was tired when he spoke. "I don't know, Emma. I want you to be happy, I do, but there's so much you don't understand yet about the world. I can't help but worry about you getting involved with someone like her."

"Someone like *her*?" she repeated, her fork clattering against her plate. "You don't even know her. Jamie is one of the strongest, bravest people I know. And her family? They actually enjoy being around each other. Imagine that."

He leaned away from the table. "You know, I've about had it with that kind of talk from you. I've been hanging in here trying to earn back your trust, but nothing I do is good enough. So you tell me, Emma. What can I do to help us move forward? Because truthfully, I'm running out of ideas."

She blinked at him, and then she looked away, feeling her cheeks flush at the glances their raised voices had drawn from nearby tables. "I don't know," she admitted, wringing her napkin with both hands now.

"Your mother and brother have forgiven me. Why can't

you?"

Her anger rekindled almost immediately. "Seriously? Ty only forgives you because he has no idea what you did."

His eyes narrowed. "What are you talking about?"

"Don't pretend you don't know." She glared at him across the table. Was he really going to make her spell it out?

He gazed back at her, arms folded across his chest.

As the silence lengthened, she felt her pulse begin to race with the same breathless rage that had sent her careening up the Berkeley High stadium stairs to confront the dipshit boys heckling Jamie. As it turned out, her father wasn't all that different from those boys. Her anger wasn't all that different, either, as she finally flung the long-dormant words at him: "I know you cheated on Mom."

He flinched and pushed his chair back from the table, and she knew: He was going to walk away. Once again, he was going to leave when things got tough. But before he could, she threw her napkin into her half-eaten meal, eyes blurring as she rose and tugged on her jacket. He didn't make any move to stop her, only watched in silence as she slipped her purse over her shoulder and started toward the exit.

But as she walked away, she realized she couldn't do it. Leaving definitely was not her style. It wasn't even that satisfactory. Halfway to the door, she turned around and went back, glaring down at her father. "Are you really not going to say anything to me?"

"What do you want me to say?"

"Gee, I don't know, Dad. Maybe start with 'I'm sorry'?"

"God damn it, Emma!" He stood up so quickly that his chair screeched and nearby diners turned to stare again. "I have said I'm sorry until I'm blue in the face. You either decide to forgive me or you don't. That part's up to you."

"Are you serious right now? You didn't have any idea that I knew about that woman."

"I had a pretty good idea." He dropped his napkin onto the table. "You're not exactly subtle."

"You knew I knew, and yet you still had the nerve to tell me that Jamie isn't good enough for me?" She shook her head. "She has more character in her elbow than you have in your entire body."

"That is enough," he ground out. "You may think you're all grown up, but you're still a child and I'm still your father. You *will* treat me with respect as long as you live in my house."

She stared at him, her own anger fading as quickly as it had come. "You don't get it, do you? I'm not a child anymore, something you would know if you were ever home long enough. But don't worry, I won't be living in *your* house much longer. In fact, I think I'll be staying at Dani's tonight," she added, and turned away once again.

"Emma, come back here."

But this time, she didn't go back. Outside she headed toward Aurora Avenue, phone cradled to her cheek. "Please call me when you get this," she said into Dani's voicemail. "I got in a huge fight with my dad and I need a place to crash tonight."

As the wind gusted, she pulled a knit hat from her purse and huddled deeper into her down jacket. The sun had set an hour earlier and even though the sky was overcast, the temperature was dropping fast. If Dani couldn't come get her, she was going to have to call a cab.

God, how had things gotten so fucked up? It was such a cliché. *He* was such a cliché. What was it about men her father's age that made them go looking for younger women? She would have sworn he wasn't capable of such a thing. But then she heard her mother crying one night after he moved out, and while it was completely unintentional, she ended up overhearing her on the phone with her sister. She hadn't wanted to believe it, so she'd gone to the hospital a couple of days later and tracked down the nurse in question, one of her mother's supposed friends. The way the other woman reacted to seeing her was proof enough. They hadn't even spoken. Emma had simply turned and walked out—sort of like she'd done tonight. But how could she stay? And how was she supposed to forgive him?

Before the surgical patent, before the years of incessant travel, he'd been so different. His favorite thing to do, he told anyone who would listen back then, was go hiking and camping with his wife and kids. Once when they were on a trail in North Cascades National Park, a black bear had stalked them. Eventually the bear had charged, and their mother covered Emma and her brother with her body while their father stood tall and strong, screaming at the bear to get the hell away from his family. Emma couldn't see him from the ground but she could feel his ferocity, and so had the bear, apparently. It had veered off and ambled away, leaving them untouched.

That was how she'd always thought of him, first as her hero, and then as a hero to the hundreds of families whose children he treated successfully. Maybe that was why she was struggling to forgive him now. She'd looked up to him for so long that she wasn't sure how to accept that he wasn't heroic after all, but just a man who, like other men, was sometimes fallible.

He was right about one thing, though. Her mother had forgiven him. So why couldn't she?

Her phone buzzed. It wasn't Dani, unfortunately. She hesitated before answering. "Hi, Mom."

"Are you okay?"

"I'm fine."

"What happened?"

"What did he tell you?"

"Not a lot. Except that you're going to Dani's tonight?"

"I need some space. I can't be around him right now."

"Honey, don't stay away. Please come home. You don't

even have to talk to each other."

She sighed, shivering as the winter wind gusted again. "I don't know…"

Her mom played her trump card: "Please? I only have you for a few more months, and half of that you're going to be traveling for soccer."

It may have been a low blow, but what she said was perfectly true. Besides, Emma still hadn't heard from Dani, and she didn't feel like calling Sian. They were more of the fair weather type of friends.

"Fine," she said reluctantly. So much for staying strong in the face of what someone else wanted.

A little while later her mom pulled the Volvo up at the gas station on Taylor Avenue, and Emma slipped into the backseat beside her brother.

"I thought you were with Dad?" he asked.

"Gatorade run," she said, and held up her convenience store purchase for proof.

"Whatever, freak."

"*I'm* the freak? Maybe you should look in the mirror, zit boy."

"Children," her mother said, eyes on Emma in the rearview mirror.

Emma nodded once at her mom—*I'm okay*—and the car pulled out into Seattle traffic. She stared at the back of her father's head as they poked along Mercer. He was looking out the window toward the city skyline, his shoulders slumped, defeated almost. Was that because of her? Did she really have the power to affect him that deeply? Before tonight she would have said no, but now she wasn't sure. He seemed so full of regret, questioning the path that had led him to this moment as if he couldn't quite believe that he wasn't the hero anymore, either.

She remembered what her mother had said on the phone

that night more than a year before: "He says it's over. He says she was the only one, but how can I believe him? Now that he lied, how do I know if I can ever trust him again?"

And yet, she had obviously decided to trust him and move past his *indiscretion*, as Emma had heard people refer to extramarital affairs. But how did someone do that? How did you wake up one morning and decide that the past didn't matter, that only the present and future were important? Maybe her mother wasn't prepared to live without her father and that's why she had chosen to believe him, why she had re-committed herself and trusted him when he said he was doing the same. They had been together for more than twenty years. Maybe the combined weight of those years meant more than the few months he had spent with someone else.

Personally, Emma couldn't imagine forgiving someone who had betrayed her. But she knew she couldn't really understand something as complicated as her parents' marriage. Which was fine. Soon she would be far away from this rain-soaked city, far from the house her mother and father had paid for with their work for other people's children. Soon she would be playing soccer for one of the best-known collegiate programs in the nation, not to mention the under-19s. Her father was right about one thing—she was on the cusp of starting the rest of her life. And, god damn it, it was going to be freaking awesome.

Her phone buzzed. Jamie had sent her a funny text, a hang loose sign drawn in exes, stars, and number signs. Apparently she had survived her skate park adventure unscathed. Emma sighed in relief and texted back, "Goofball."

She was tempted to text more, but she really didn't want to taint Jamie's birthday with her family drama. Instead she put her phone away and slid lower in her seat, watching the other cars race past on the freeway as the brightly lit city faded away behind them.

CHAPTER SIX

One weeknight in early March, Jamie lay on her bed, staring at her phone's small, glowing screen. The text had arrived fifteen minutes earlier, which meant she was well outside the window of a "quick" reply. She could blame it on practice, but in truth she'd been home from practice for a while. Dinner, too, was long since history. There were always the old standbys—dead phone or parental intervention—but one, she didn't want to lie, and two, she didn't want it to seem like she'd gotten into trouble when, except for the occasional escapade with Blair, she was an honors student and practically straight edge.

And yet, she wasn't sure how to handle this development. She wished she could call Shoshanna, but the therapist's cell was for texts and emergency calls only. Besides, she had an appointment set for the following afternoon and this wasn't exactly an issue that couldn't wait.

She clicked on Emma's name and texted, "Call me when you get a chance?" Then she reached for her history textbook and began copying dates and events into her notebook. They had a test next week, and she might as well get some studying done while she waited to hear from Emma.

As time passed and her phone remained silent, focusing

became increasingly difficult. Emma rarely took this long to respond. Was she out with the new guy? She'd been single for so long that it was still strange to picture her dating someone. And yet Jamie hadn't really been that surprised the previous month when, midway through training camp in LA, she'd logged into her email to find a note from Emma that described club soccer, family life, and school in great detail, and then mentioned in an offhand aside at the very end that she had gone out on a date with the highly persistent Justin Tate, captain of the Shorecrest High boys' soccer team.

Seated at the computer in the hotel conference room, Jamie had closed her email and done a quick web search, clicking on a link to a Seattle newspaper article about the previous year's prep season. There he was in a photo with his coach. Justin was a "scoring machine," according to the article, and had set a school record as a junior to prove it. He was good-looking, she had to admit—if you liked the clean-cut jock type. Honestly, she wasn't a fan. They were too often the ones who made cracks about female bodies and their own studly powers over said bodies.

Maybe this Justin guy was different, though. Emma wouldn't go out with a total dick, would she?

"Whatcha doing?" a voice had drawled from her right elbow.

She'd been so caught up in cyber-stalking Justin Tate that she hadn't noticed two girls enter the hotel conference room.

"Cute, but I wouldn't have thought he'd be your type," the smaller of the two commented, squinting at Justin's photo.

"He's not, jackass," Jamie had said, and closed the browser window.

At first glance, Brittany Crawford and Angela Wang were opposites in every way. Where Britt was tall, blonde, and hailed from the Southwest, Angie was short, Asian, and a diehard Jersey girl. But at their first training camp the previous year, the keeper and midfielder had apparently bonded over rap music, wallet chains, and, of course, their mutual interest in kissing girls. The moment Jamie set foot in the hotel in February, they had adopted her as the third member of their self-proclaimed under-16 bro band.

With Britt and Angie at her side, her first camp had flown by, a blur of the double training sessions, team meetings, bonding exercises, and study breaks that Emma had told her about. Training camp participants were closely monitored with a nightly curfew and random bed-checks, but none of the other girls seemed to even consider testing the limits. They were all there for the same reason: to learn from the best, make a good impression on federation staff, and earn a call-back next time around. The under-16 girls' program was still relatively new, and everyone in the pool understood that this team was a stepping stone to further federation involvement. Not to mention a badge of honor that could only help in the college recruitment department.

When her phone finally buzzed, Emma's name flashing across the screen, Jamie set her history textbook aside and grabbed it.

"Sorry, hanging with the family," Emma had texted. "Call you on the land line?"

"OK," she replied, and went to look for the upstairs receiver. As she returned to her room and settled back on her bed, her stomach rumbled uneasily. Would Emma even want to talk about this kind of thing?

The receiver pealed. Too late to back out now.

"What's up?" Emma asked.

"Not much. Sorry to bug you."

"No worries. I was only too happy to escape the love fest. My parents are acting like they're abandoning us in a couple of weeks, my dad especially. You'd think they'd never gone on vacation without us."

"Didn't you say they haven't been to Hawaii since their

honeymoon?"

"Yeah, but they've been to Europe a bunch. Usually my dad has a conference and they bundle it all together, but this time my mom invoked the 'no work allowed' rule."

"That's cool. My parents only ever do date night or an occasional weekend away in wine country. Even that they haven't done in a while." She stopped as she realized how long it had been: nearly a year. Did they think something would happen if they left her for even a few days? Clearly they needed to have a chat. She was doing much better now. Although not well enough to deal with the text she'd received tonight, apparently.

"What's on your mind?" Emma asked. "Because I'm pretty sure you didn't ask me to call so we could talk about our parents' vacation habits."

"Psychic as ever, I see." She hesitated. "Do you remember Amanda?"

"The girl from the Gay-Straight Alliance you thought had a crush on you?"

"That's the one." She paused again. Why did it suddenly feel weird to talk about this with Emma? They were friends, and Emma had said numerous times that she didn't mind talking about Jamie's until now mostly theoretical love life.

"So?" Emma prodded. "Did you finally make a move?"

"No, but she did." Quickly she described the message she'd received asking if she wanted to go out the following night, just the two of them minus the usual GSA hordes.

"That's good, isn't it? You said you liked her."

"I know." Jamie slumped back against her husband pillow, which Meg had taken to calling her "wife" pillow ever since Gavin Newsom, mayor of San Francisco, had declared gay marriage legal a few days before Valentine's Day. "But what if we start hanging out and she kisses me, and I totally freak out?"

Emma was quiet for a moment. "Do you really think that

could happen?"

"The kissing, or the freaking out?"

"You know what I mean."

"Yeah." Jamie pinched the bridge of her nose between her forefinger and thumb, and then stopped when she realized that was her mother's habit. "I'm not sure. I think it's not impossible."

"Look, I know you said you haven't had a boyfriend or a girlfriend before. Don't get mad, but—"

This should be good.

"—well, have you ever kissed anyone?"

She shot up on the bed. "Of course I have!"

"Sorry. I wasn't trying to offend you, honestly."

"I know." Jamie shut her eyes briefly, glad for once that she and Emma weren't in the same room. "It's kind of embarrassing. I've only kissed two people, well, boys really, at a party right before I came out."

"Let me guess. Spin the bottle?"

"You got it. Or, as Mr. Hanson, our GSA advisor, calls it, the classic adolescent heteronormative shakedown."

"Sounds about right." Emma cleared her throat. "Actually, um, speaking of GSA, I've been thinking about checking out a meeting up here."

Jamie almost dropped the phone. *No fucking way.* Then she focused on the second initial: Gay-*Straight*-Alliance. Was Emma considering joining because of their friendship? "That's awesome. What does Justin think?"

"How would I know? I'm not exactly in the habit of asking the people I date for permission to live my life."

"Easy there, champ," Jamie said, laughing at her feistiness. "How about saving it for someone who actually wants to fight you, huh?"

Emma exhaled noisily. "Dork."

"Nerd."

"*Anyway*, back to the reason for this entire conversation. What did you tell Amanda?"

"I haven't answered yet. Hello, I was waiting for advice from my best friend."

There was silence again at the other end. Then: "Am I really your best friend?"

"Who says I was talking about you?"

"Jamie!"

"Kidding." She touched the bracelet Emma had given her. She still hadn't taken it off, not even for national team camp. "Why, do you not want to be?"

"No, I do. I just didn't know you thought of me like that."

They were both quiet, and Jamie remembered how Emma had said she was thinking of joining the GSA; how she didn't ask the "people" she dated for permission to do what she wanted; how she had always seemed cooler about Jamie's queerness than the average straight person. Was Emma trying to tell her something? Wait—was Emma...? Her mouth went dry. *Seriously, no effing way.* She could not handle the possibility that Emma Blakeley might be into girls because... Well, she couldn't. Her brain was physically incapable of processing such a thing.

"I guess the obvious question," Emma said finally, "is do you want to go out with her?"

"Yes," she said, the single syllable markedly more assured than she felt. All at once it seemed vitally important that Emma know she wasn't some immature kid who freaked out at the very idea of a kiss. Even if she'd already admitted that she basically was.

"Then go for it. Text her back and say yes."

"Okay. I will."

"Good. You totally should."

Another silence fell, which was odd for them. They rarely ran out of things to say, as their cell minute usage more than proved. But for some reason, Jamie could feel the tension building, as if neither of them was saying what she really meant. She reached into her bedside table and found the false back, fingers lingering on its cool, solid surface.

"I should probably let you get back to Family Fest '04," she said.

"Probably. My dad is going to give me puppy dog eyes as it is for interrupting the Cranium tournament."

"Cranium's my total fave. Who's winning?"

"My mom and I are kicking their butts."

"Naturally. Girl power and all."

"Exactly." Emma paused. "Good luck on your date. You said it's tomorrow, right?"

"Right. Are you going out with Justin?"

"Dani and I are planning to check out a party, and he'll probably be there too. Everyone is starting to get all, 'It's our last chance to hang out.' As if we aren't sick of each other after going to school together our entire lives."

"Meg's friends are the same way." Meanwhile, she was stuck in Berkeley for the foreseeable future, waiting for the rest of her life to begin... "Anyway, world history is calling. I'll talk to you soon, okay?"

"Okay." Then she added, "Are you okay, Jamie?"

"I'm fine." It came out more strongly than she intended. "Bye, Emma."

"Bye."

She turned off the phone even though something in Emma's voice made her want to stay on the line. What was wrong with her? They had talked about everything, from favorite colors and breakfast foods to the assault and Emma's father's affair. Why was she suddenly uncomfortable talking to

119

her about dating?

"I believe you know exactly why," Shoshanna's reasonable voice intoned inside her head.

"Shut it, doc," Jamie muttered aloud, and pulled the pipe and baggie from her bedside drawer.

But she couldn't exactly say that to Shoshanna's face in their session the following day. So instead of mentioning Emma, she shared her anxiety over her upcoming date.

"First of all, are you sure that it's a date?" Shoshanna asked.

What a straight lady thing to say. "Um, yeah."

"How do you know?"

"Because she asked me if I wanted to go out with her. Besides, she broke up with her boyfriend over winter break and has made a big deal about being single."

"Boyfriend?"

"She's bi. As in, sexual?"

Shoshanna seemed unperturbed by her sarcasm. "All right. I simply wanted to make sure you had all the facts."

Jamie shook her head.

"You seem upset."

"Well, yeah. If a guy had asked me out, you wouldn't be so concerned about 'the facts.' The assumption would just be there, unquestioned."

"Hmm." The therapist turned her head a little. "You know, I believe you're right. Thank you for feeling comfortable enough to point that out. Heterosexism is so pervasive that sometimes I need to check my own privilege. I apologize."

Jamie blinked. "Oh. Well, that's okay."

"If you feel all right continuing, perhaps we could explore the root of your uneasiness over a date with someone whom, by your own admission, you find attractive."

At first, Jamie talked in an elaborate circle around her

feelings as she always did while Shoshanna waited patiently for her to narrow in on the real issue. Eventually the therapist heard something that interested her.

"You said you're afraid she'll figure out that you're damaged." When Jamie nodded, she continued. "Why do you consider yourself damaged?"

"You know why."

"Because of the assault?" Jamie nodded again, and Shoshanna hummed a little. "When I look at you, I see a very capable young woman—a talented athlete, a good student, a loyal daughter, sister, and friend. How exactly are you damaged?"

"He'll always be the first person I slept with. Whenever anyone asks me about my history, I'll have to tell them."

"Why would you have to tell anyone?"

Jamie stared at her. "I thought you wanted me to tell people. Isn't it supposed to be this major sign that I'm, like, moving on with my life?"

"What you're talking about and what I meant are very different things. You were tested after the assault and there were no complications, correct?"

She nodded, remembering the hours she and her mom had spent at the hospital the night they got back from France—the rape kit, STD tests, emergency contraception pill the doctor had prescribed, and follow-up blood tests weeks later to make sure she wasn't HIV positive or, almost as disturbing a possibility, pregnant.

"And you've said the panic attacks have almost entirely ceased, and the flashbacks have significantly reduced as well, correct?"

"Yeah." The tools Shoshanna had given her—meditation, guided imagery, and a focus on rational over "magical" thinking—to combat the psychological aftereffects of the attack had not only helped quell her fears but had also given her better focus at school and on the soccer field.

"Then tell me more about this feeling you have of 'damage.'"

"I can't." She shook her head. "Unless it's happened to you, I don't think there's any way you can understand."

"You may be right. However, I think the cognitive part of the work we're doing together involves separating out *damage* from *hurt*. Are you hurting? Absolutely. Will you carry the pain of what happened for the rest of your life? I suspect you will, and it sounds like you do, too. Most of us have some painful thing—or things—that we carry with us. But ask yourself this. If your sister had been assaulted, would you think she was damaged, or would you see her as someone who was strong enough to survive and keep striving to be happy?"

This sounded so much like what Emma had once said to her that Jamie sighed. "I get your point. But I'm not sure that telling myself I'm not damaged will make the feeling go away."

"How do you know until you try?"

Jamie shrugged. "I feel like such a wuss with all of this. Other people have it so much harder than I do. Look at 9/11. Look at all the girls my age in Asia who are being sold into slavery. Meanwhile I have this awesome family and we have more than enough money and never have to worry about the kinds of things way too many other people do, like food and shelter and clean water."

"None of that changes the fact that you're recovering from a major trauma, Jamie. Let's get back to your date tonight. What worries you the most?"

"I don't know. What if she asks if I've ever had sex?"

"I would be surprised if that subject came up on a first date. But regardless, as we've discussed before, there's a difference between having sex and being raped. If you had contracted an STD or had other physical repercussions from the assault, then the ethical underpinnings would be very different. But your wounds are primarily emotional, and that's what we're working on together. Please don't ever think you have to tell anyone what happened unless you decide you want to."

"But you seemed really psyched for me to tell Emma."

"That's different. Emma is someone with whom you already share a close emotional bond, and telling her was a way to reinforce and deepen those ties." She paused, looking at Jamie over the top of her glasses. "Have you told Emma about your date?"

"Yeah."

"And?"

"She said to go for it."

"Is that all she said?"

"Look, I know what you're getting at with that 'close emotional bond' stuff. Everyone else thinks it, too—Meg, my parents, Blair, even Becky said something. But there is nothing going on between Emma and me."

Shoshanna took off her glasses. "Okay."

"What?"

"If you truly believe you feel nothing but friendship for Emma, then I believe you."

Jamie toyed with her bracelet, aware of the older woman's gaze on her, as unrelenting as ever. "I hate it when you do that."

"Does that mean you don't believe it?"

"No," she grumbled.

When she didn't say anything else, Shoshanna asked, "Do you want to know what I see when you talk about Emma?"

She shrugged again.

"I see a wonderful person who came into your life at the right moment and offered you the kind of caring relationship you needed. But Emma is a safe emotional outlet specifically because she lives so far away. With her in Seattle and you here, there's not much chance of a physical relationship. And while that has helped you in the short term, a long-distance friendship is not going to meet all of your emotional needs in the long run."

Jamie leaned forward, elbows on her knees. In the back of her head, unbeknownst to the front of her head, she had been holding on to the hope that someday, somehow she and Emma might be more than friends. If she was honest with herself, though, what Shoshanna was saying made sense. Emma was going to UNC and she was staying in California, at least for the next couple of years.

"If you're saying I should ditch her, that's not going to happen."

"God, no," Shoshanna said, her usual mask of decorum slipping. "I don't see any reason for you to stop being friends with Emma, do you?"

Jamie shook her head.

"I'm simply suggesting you avoid the temptation to use your relationship with her as an excuse to avoid dating someone who might be a more realistic possibility. Assuming you're ready to date."

"How do I know if I'm ready?"

"Only you can answer that question. Remember, I'm here to help you figure yourself out, not to tell you what to do or how to be. Your life is your own, and granting other people power over what you think or do—even someone like me— can be risky."

The session ended a little while later. Before Jamie left, Shoshanna looked through a shelf on her floor-to-ceiling bookcase until she found the title she wanted.

"I think you might be ready to read this," she said, handing it over. "Hang on to it as long as you need. I can always get my hands on more copies."

Jamie looked at the title: *The Courage to Heal.* She wondered if Shoshanna was trying a little reverse psychology on her, challenging her to be brave because she knew Jamie wouldn't want to back down. Once again, the therapist's strategy was on point.

"Thanks," she said, tucking the book into her backpack alongside her math textbook and *To Kill a Mockingbird*, the novel they were currently reading in American Lit.

And then she hustled down the stairs to meet her sister. They were going to have to hurry if she was going to be on time for her date.

#

On the last Friday of March, Emma stood in the hall outside the classroom, trying to get up the courage to enter. This was the second time in a month she had stood outside a GSA meeting fidgeting with the straps on her messenger bag. Her phone vibrated and she moved off down the hall, hoping no one had noticed her skulking about. Maybe next time she would find the courage to actually walk through the door.

The text was from Justin, asking what time he should come over tonight. Emma's parents had been in Hawaii for the past week and were due to come back on Sunday. With Ty spending the night at his best friend's house, this would be their opportunity to reach teenage relationship Mecca: spending an entire night together without chance of adult intervention. It would also be their first time having sex. They had already messed around a few times at his house, but she had stopped things before they could go too far. His parents seemed much more willing to give them space than her parents, who were liable to knock on her partially closed door—a fully closed door was not allowed—at any time to see how homework was going or if Justin wanted to stay for dinner. This was code, she and Dani had joked, for "Wanted to make sure you're not boning."

Sometimes she insisted they hang out at her house for that very reason. Not that she didn't like what they did together, but he was an eighteen-year-old boy, which meant that was pretty much all they would ever do if he had his way. At her house they could talk and listen to music, do homework or watch a movie, and while they might make out, she never had to worry about losing her bra. Emma had only had sex with one other person. Not Josh, who had been respectful to the point of occasionally seeming uninterested, but with Drew, who'd broken up with her the previous summer because he didn't want to be "tied down" when he left for U-Dub.

He'd been her first and she'd thought she loved him. But looking back now, she wasn't sure what she'd loved more—Drew himself or the idea of having a boyfriend. His parents, Jan and Richard, had been so sweet and supportive through her parents' near split. His mom in particular had helped her to view her mother and father as individuals outside of the family unit, which in turn had allowed her to accept that she and Ty weren't responsible for the marriage's problems, no matter how much it might feel they were. Jan still invited her over to dinner every once in a while, and sometimes Emma even babysat Melissa, Drew's little sister.

In the school parking lot, Emma slid into her car and clicked reply to Justin's text. Then she sat there staring at the phone, unsure what to write. Did she really want to sleep with him? The last time they'd fooled around, she'd kept picturing Tori, the girl from the national team. Justin wasn't exactly the hairiest of guys, and when he kissed his way across her neck she'd closed her eyes and pretended it was Tori's mouth on her skin, Tori's soft hair under her fingers, Tori's hand sliding under her shirt.

National team camp in Texas at the end of February had been short but sweet. The powers that be had assigned Tori as her roommate at the hotel in Dallas, and they had been inseparable all week. The last night of camp, they'd snuggled under the covers in Emma's bed way past lights out supposedly watching a movie. Emma had barely noticed the flickering television screen in the darkened room, too aware of Tori's body next to hers. Nothing had happened, unless you counted some tickling contests and a few longer than average hugs. But she was pretty sure something could have. Still, they hadn't texted or emailed since, so maybe it was one of those camp flirtations that she had heard her school friends who didn't spend their summers playing soccer talk about.

While she was debating how to answer the text, her phone vibrated again. Jamie. She smiled as she pulled up the message, her stress fading.

"Hey, girl," Jamie's text read. "How goes Shoreline?"

"Good. What about Elmtown?"

"It's Elmwood!"

"Ha ha, kidding. When are we watching your team lose?"

It was the knockout stage in Champions League, and both Man U and Arsenal had played for a spot in the quarterfinals earlier in the week. Given school and their conflicting club team schedules, they hadn't found time yet to watch together.

"I'm still getting over this stupid cold," Jamie wrote, "so I was going to suggest we ditch our dates and watch tonight. But maybe I'll watch without you."

"You wouldn't!"

"I might, and then text you the scores…"

"That's totally against the bro code," Emma replied.

"Wait, so now we're bros? Then you definitely have to stay in tonight. You know, in solidarity."

By unspoken agreement, they talked about their current relationships but didn't discuss sex. Jamie had only been dating Amanda for a couple of weeks so they were nowhere near that stage yet, and Emma didn't want to make her uncomfortable by bringing up the things she did with Justin. This meant that while Jamie knew she was going out with Justin tonight, she didn't know about the overnight plan. Could she cancel? She liked Justin. She'd even dreamed about making out with him the other night. Of course, Tori and her light brown eyes had made an appearance, too, and U-19 World Cup qualifying started in a couple of months, which meant they'd be spending even more time together…

Her phone alerted again: "Never mind. Have fun tonight. I promise I won't watch until we're both free."

Emma typed quickly. "Hold your horses, bro. I'm in. Let me text Justin and then we can make a plan, okay?"

"Really? 'Cause I don't need your pity, Blake."

"Are you kidding? I can't wait to watch Arsenal get their asses handed to them."

"Don't you mean watch Man U get walloped?"

"Dream on. I'll text you back."

"Sweet."

She switched back to Justin's message, fingers still hovering over the keyboard. She couldn't really cancel their sex date by text, could she? Sighing, she hit the phone icon by his name.

"So hey," she said as soon as he picked up, "I've got some bad news. I sort of have to cancel."

"What? Are you serious? Why?" He sounded angry. He definitely sounded angry.

"Well, I have this sick friend…"

He didn't even let her finish. "A sick friend? No, really. Are you being totally serious?"

"Yes, I'm being serious." She tried not to be irritated by his tone. They had been planning this night all week; it made sense he would be disappointed. "I'm sorry. I'll make it up to you."

"What about tomorrow night? Can't you get rid of your brother then?"

"No, I can't just 'get rid of' my brother, Justin, even if I wanted to. It takes planning."

"Even if you wanted to?" he repeated. "Nice, Emma."

"That's not what I meant."

"It's what you said." His voice changed as he switched gears. "Come on, your friend doesn't really need you. That's what parents are for."

"Nice, Justin," she threw back at him. "How empathetic of you."

"What friend are you even talking about? I don't remember anyone at school being sick."

"A girl from travel soccer. No one you know."

There was silence for a moment, and then he said, "Tell me it's not that Jamie chick."

Well, damn. She had not seen that coming.

"It is, isn't it? Are you fucking kidding me?" he said, his voice rising. "You'd rather talk to some dyke on the phone than spend the night with your boyfriend?"

"Don't you dare call her that," Emma said, her voice low and dangerous. "And for the record, you're not my boyfriend anymore."

"Emma, come on."

"Fuck off, Justin."

She ended the call and sat in her car, heart pounding loudly in her ears. What an asshole. How had she not realized this sooner? Probably because in addition to being a homophobic twat, he was a liar. Before they were officially hanging out, back when he was still trying to get her to go out with him, she'd mentioned Jamie as a sort of litmus test. She knew he had to have heard the rumors Josh's friends had spread, but he'd only shrugged and said, "My cousin's gay. I don't see what the big deal is."

Had he only said that to get into her pants? To think it had almost worked. At least he'd let the mask slip sooner rather than later. Imagine if she'd found out what he was really like *after* she slept with him.

Her phone rang. Justin. She hit ignore and sent him a quick text: "I'm done. Don't call me."

She waited a second to see if he would call again, but he didn't. A text popped up instead: "I'm sorry. I shouldn't have said that. I was bummed about tonight. Give me another chance?"

As if. She started a new text, but before she got very far gave up and hit the call button. She tapped her fingers against the steering wheel as the line rang and rang. When she heard the voice she was waiting for, she launched in: "Why are high school boys such douchebags?"

"Uh-oh," Dani said. "What did Justin do?"

"He called Jamie a dyke."

"What the hell?"

"I know, right?"

"What a moron. I don't get it. Why would he do that when you guys were about to hook up?"

"Welllll…"

"Emma, what did you do?"

She confessed her role in the disagreement quickly, knowing that Dani wouldn't pull punches. That was one of the things she loved about her—Dani could always be counted on to tell it like it was.

But: "Okay," was all she said when Emma finished, her voice uncharacteristically reserved.

"That's it? That's all you've got?"

"Is that all *I've* got? You're the one who cancelled sex with your boyfriend so you can talk on the phone with the girl who likes girls. To be perfectly honest, it kind of seems like you might have something you need to tell me."

Emma pictured the door to the classroom where the GSA met. "I know, Dan. I'm sorry."

"That's okay. It's just, I'm here or whatever. You know?"

The question was, would she still be after Emma told her the truth?

"I know," Emma repeated, closing her eyes briefly. "Can I come over tonight after Jamie and I watch soccer? I don't really want to stay at my house alone."

"I was about to say the same thing. I mean, I don't think Justin would try anything, but he can be kind of a hothead."

Emma was glad she wasn't the only one who had worried about that. "Can I bring Lucy? I don't want to have to come get her later."

"Of course. Ginger has been missing her buddy."

"Cool. I'll call you later then. And thanks, Dan."

"You don't have to thank me. Duh."

When they hung up, Emma immediately texted Jamie. "Home in ten. First game in fifteen?"

The reply came while she was driving. She pulled up to a stop sign, checked to make sure there wasn't anyone else around, and read, "Yesssssss!!!!!"

God, she was cute even in text. Emma sighed and tossed her phone into the passenger seat. Dani was so going to kill her.

Her cell rang again as she was pulling into the driveway. Better not be Justin. But it wasn't. Instead, her mother's cell number flashed across the screen. That was strange. Weren't they supposed to be out on the ocean all day swimming with dolphins or something? Maybe they'd checked up on her and found out that she'd never planned to stay the night at Dani's house. Briefly she considered not answering, but she knew it would only add to her parents' displeasure. Anyway, now she really would be staying with Dani. Plausible deniability, that was the ticket.

"Hey, Mom," she said, forcing herself to sound cheerful as she parked in the driveway and turned off the engine.

"Emma."

Her neck tingled. From the heaviness in her mother's voice, she knew immediately: Something awful had happened.

"What is it? What's wrong?"

"Where are you?"

"In the driveway. Jamie and I are going to watch soccer before I go over to Dani's."

"Is Ty with the Chandlers?"

"Yeah, he went home with Benji on the bus. What happened? Is it Grandma?"

"No, it's not your grandmother. Emma, I need you to do something for me." But she stopped and didn't continue.

A thought occurred to Emma, but she told herself it couldn't be. Still, she asked: "Where's Dad?"

She heard what sounded like the rustle of fabric against the receiver. Then her mother came back, and this time she lapsed into what Emma and Ty called her "charge nurse" voice. "I need you to get to your brother. I need you to go to the Chandlers' house right now and call me back when you get there. Do you understand?"

Emma's heart raced. Her eyes felt strange, as if there was a pocket of air between her and the rest of the world. "Where's Dad?" she repeated.

Her mother breathed out long and shaky. "Please, honey, can't you just do what I'm asking?"

"Not until you tell me what's going on," Emma said, shaking her head even though her mom couldn't see her. "You have to tell me, Mom. Did something happen to Dad?"

And then her breath caught as she heard her mother's muffled sobbing. What had she done? She should have put the car in reverse and driven the two miles to Benji's house. But she couldn't move. Not until her mother said the words.

"Something happened to him, didn't it?"

"Yes," her mother admitted through her sobs. "Oh, god, Emma, I'm sorry. I'm so sorry. I tried, but we should never have been out on that boat. I should have known. I should have seen it but I didn't and now he's—he's…"

"He's in the hospital?" Emma finished for her, willing the words to be true.

"No, honey. I mean, yes, we're at a hospital, but we didn't make it in time. Your father had a heart attack. We did CPR but by the time we made it back to shore, he had been down for too long."

A heart attack? Didn't make it in time? What did that even mean? But she knew. She had grown up shadowing her parents around the hospital. Better than most people her age, she understood the euphemisms medical professionals used to describe death. Her mother meant that she would never see her father again. Not ever.

She should feel something, shouldn't she? Something other than this profound sense of unreality? The tears kept falling, so she knew that at some level her mind was processing her mother's terrible news. But it was like she was one of those prehistoric creatures who had suddenly been swallowed up in a mountain of ice, flash frozen with the remnants of her most recent meal still in her stomach.

"Emma?" her mother asked. "Honey, are you still there?"

She swallowed past the lump in her throat. "Yes, I'm here."

Her mother breathed out. "I'm sorry, I didn't want to tell you like this. I wish I could be there with you. I wanted you and Ty at least to be together. I didn't want you to be alone for this, Emma."

"I know. I'm sorry. I should have gone over there. I don't know why I didn't."

"No, sweetie, it's my fault. Of course you would want to know what was wrong. I'm not thinking very clearly right now."

Emma stared through her windshield at the basketball hoop that hung on the garage. The night before they left for Hawaii, he had shot baskets with her and Ty even though Ty kept whining about how cold it was outside. "I don't understand. There was nothing wrong with his heart."

Her mother didn't say anything.

"Wait, did you *know* there was something wrong and you didn't tell us?" she asked, her voice climbing.

"There were some warning signs, yes, but no indication that it was this far along. There was no way of knowing, Emma."

"But you said you should have known."

Her mom sighed again. "Maybe I should have. After all, it is my job."

It wasn't her mother's fault; she knew that. And yet the tiny spark of anger felt so much better than the Titanic-sized numbness. She squeezed her eyes closed as hard as she could as if she could blot out the world simply by refusing to see it. This couldn't be happening. She had talked to him a couple of days ago. He was so excited about the hikes they'd taken and the chance to swim with dolphins again. He couldn't actually be gone. She would wake up and this would all be a dream, an incredibly vivid, oddly true-to-life dream and she would lie in her bed in the dark feeling her heart rate slow, thinking how relieved she was that her dad was still around even if it sometimes felt like he had these sharp points that hurt if she got too close. She would wake up and he wouldn't be gone. She would wake up.

"I need to tell your brother," her mother said, "and I'm hoping you can be with him when I do."

"Right." She opened her eyes. "I'll go right now."

"Do you really think you should drive?"

"I'm fine." Emma wiped the tears from her face. Thankfully, they had dried up. Or maybe they were frozen like the rest of her. She turned her key in the ignition, and the car beeped out its seat belt warning even though she hadn't undone the belt yet.

"Emma, I'm serious. If you don't think you can drive, then

don't. I couldn't handle it if…"

"Mom," she said, "I'm fine. I promise. You know I wouldn't drive if I thought I couldn't, not after what happened with Jeff."

Dani's older brother had done three months in County for vehicular assault after nearly killing a ten-year-old kid in another car. His experience had served as a cautionary tale for pretty much all of Shorecrest High.

"All right, then," her mother said. "Call me when you get there. I'll get in touch with Karen and Mark and let them know you're coming."

"Okay. I'll be there in five minutes."

"I love you, Emma, very, very much. I wish we were all together right this second."

All of us somehow now meant only the three of them. She had worried that he would leave again, but in every scenario she'd envisioned he was still in the world, still somewhere he could return from just as he had the last time.

"Me, too, Mom. I love you."

They hung up and she set the car in gear, and then she stopped and put it back in park. She scrolled through her calls and hit send.

"You ready to watch your boys lose?" Jamie asked, her voice hoarse.

Emma had forgotten she was sick. "You sound like crap."

"So do you. Are you sick, too?"

"No. Jamie, actually, I need to tell you something." But like her mother a few minutes earlier, all at once she couldn't find the words. This was it. This was the first time she was going to have to deliver the news she would be retelling for the rest of her life. *My father died. My father is dead.*

"Are you all right?" Jamie asked. "Were you in an accident? Do you need me to call someone?"

"I'm fine. It's—it's my dad." She stopped again. Why was this so hard? But she knew. As soon as she said it out loud, it would be real and nothing could undo it. Was this what her mother had felt on the phone? Was this what Jamie had felt when she told her about the assault? She remembered the way Jamie had seemed to fold in on herself at the beach that day. If only she were here now to keep Emma from falling.

"Is he okay?"

"No. No, he's not. He had a heart attack."

"Oh my god, Emma." Jamie stopped and waited at the other end of the line.

Emma tried to figure out how to say what needed to be said. At last she settled on her mother's phrasing: "He didn't make it." Her voice cracked and she felt the ice threatening to recede. "I have to go find my brother. I can't watch soccer."

"Of course," Jamie said quickly. "I'm so, so sorry. Are you okay? Can I do anything?"

"No. I mean, go ahead and watch the games. I don't know if I will."

"Emma, I don't care about soccer right now. I care about you." It almost sounded like she was crying. "I wish I was there with you."

"You do?"

"I really do. I'm supposed to be your anchor too, remember?"

Tears welled up in her eyes again, and Emma shook her head. She couldn't cry, not now. She had to get it together and be there for Ty. Losing their father was going to be so much harder on him.

"I should go."

"Okay. Yeah." Jamie hesitated. "I'm thinking about you. Sending you lots of love, okay?"

Love? Emma leaned her forehead against the steering wheel.

"Me, too, Jamie."

They sat in silence for a while, even though Emma knew everyone was waiting on her. Finally her text alert sounded. It was her mom, checking to see if she was with her brother yet.

"I really do have to go," she said, rubbing her eyes.

"I know. I miss you."

"I miss you too. I wish you were here." She regretted the words as soon as they escaped. Even though Jamie had already said the same thing, she had been through enough. She didn't need to have all of this dumped on her, too.

"So do I. Call me when you can, please? Anytime. I'll leave my phone on tonight, okay?"

"Okay. I don't know where I'll be, but I'll try to call you," she promised.

"Good. I'll talk to you later, then?"

"Yeah. Later."

After another pause, she forced herself to end the call. Then she shot her mother a quick text—"Sorry, on my way"— started the car again, and headed across town. At her neck lay the silver pendant Jamie had given her for Christmas: a spiral sun meant to keep her warm, she'd said, through the chill gloom of a Seattle winter. Emma held onto the pendant now as she drove through the gray afternoon, trying to wring from it every last bit of imagined warmth she could.

CHAPTER SEVEN

Jamie held the phone in her hand, the Man U-Porto kick-off frozen on the TV screen before her. Meg had orchestra rehearsal on Fridays so she was alone in the house. Brushing her tears away, she left the den and headed into the living room to wait for her parents, who worked at the same software company in the city. While her dad was usually at work at least an hour before her mom, they commuted home together most evenings.

When she heard the key turn in the front door, she jumped up from the couch and ambushed them before her mom could even put her purse on the dining room table.

"I need to talk to you guys," she said, rubbing the soft, shaved hairs at the back of her neck.

"What's wrong?" her mother asked, and stepped toward her. "Have you been crying?"

"It's not me. Emma called a little while ago. Her father had a heart attack in Hawaii and, well, I guess he didn't make it."

"Oh my god," her dad said, gripping the back of a chair with both hands.

"That poor family." Her mom moved to give her a hug. Soon her dad joined in, and they stood together quietly under the arch that separated the dining area from the living room.

While their initial meeting at Surf Cup had been a bit bumpy, Emma had worked hard to win Jamie's mom—and dad—over. Her visit in January had cemented their adoration of her, especially after Jamie told her parents the way Emma had responded to her revelation. Then again, everyone who met Emma loved her. You'd have to be crazy not to.

Jamie pulled out of the hug and folded her arms across her chest. "I want to go to Seattle. I want to be there for her the way she's been there for me."

"Have they set a date for a service?" her dad asked.

"I don't know. Her mom is still in Hawaii. They hadn't even told her brother yet. I told her to call me tonight anytime. If that's okay."

"It's fine," her mom said as her dad nodded. "I'm not sure about you going up there, though, honey. I know you and Emma are close, but they may want this to be a private, family-only time."

"I don't think so. Emma says she wants me there." As her parents exchanged a look, Jamie snorted. "I can see you, you know. And I'm not an idiot, despite the general family consensus."

"No one thinks you're an idiot," her father said. "But your mom is right. This is an extremely difficult time for Emma and her family. Even she may not know what she needs right now."

Jamie swallowed hard and straightened her shoulders. "Well, I'm going, whether you like it or not."

"Excuse me?" Her mother's eyes narrowed as her chin jutted forward incrementally.

"That look doesn't scare me," Jamie lied. "I'm serious. You guys should get on board with this because I'm going to Seattle, with or without your permission."

Her hands were shaking as she jogged up to her room, and she honestly felt like she might throw up. Out and out rebellion wasn't usually her thing. She much preferred to slide under the radar and let her sister and mother duke it out. But this was different. This was Emma, and Emma needed her.

Upstairs she paced her room, the muffled sounds of her parents' voices rising through the floorboards. What if she ended up phone-less and grounded for the near future? Or what if they took away soccer? Obviously she had not thought this through, but it was hard to think rationally when she knew that Emma's heart had been broken and she was too far away to even give her a hug. Not that a hug would fix anything. But the day she'd told Emma about France, Emma had held her and soothed her tears, and something about that moment had made her feel as if maybe someday she might actually be happy again, the way she hadn't even known she was before a stranger in a bar changed everything.

She was sitting on her bed wondering if she should text her sister when a knock sounded at the door.

"Come in." Her voice sounded a little hoarse, but she told herself it was from her leftover cold, not from the dread curling through her belly. As the door opened, she pulled her knees up to her chest. How bad was this going to be?

Her parents stood together near the door, faces molded into serious masks. As in past conflicts, her dad was the parental spokesperson. Jamie and Meg had decided that he did most of the talking because he was more even-tempered and therefore less likely to get all pissed off and have to apologize later for yelling—something that *might* have happened a few times with their mom.

"Your mother and I have talked," he began, arms folded across the front of his button-down shirt, "and first of all, we want you to know that it's not all right to make threats."

"But Dad—" she started.

"Let me finish, okay?" After a second she nodded, and he continued. "That said, we also recognize that you've experienced a big shock today. So while the way you spoke to us was disrespectful, to say the least, it did make us take note because that type of behavior is pretty far out of the norm for you."

Reminding them that she had sneaked out of the hotel in Lyon would probably hurt rather than help her case right now, so she stayed quiet.

"You're a good kid," her dad added, his voice softening. "We know how much you care about Emma and how upset you are to be so far away when she just lost her father. It's really quite generous of you to offer to go to Seattle for her, especially when it sounds like she asked. Given that fact, and given how strongly you obviously feel about all of this, your mother and I are willing to discuss the possibility of you going up there. We're not saying okay yet, but we are willing to consider the idea."

"Oh my god, thank you!" she exclaimed, relief lending extra volume to her gravelly voice.

Her dad held up a hand. "That is, on two conditions. One, that you miss as little school as possible, and two, that Emma's mother agrees."

She nodded quickly. "Of course. Seriously, thank you guys. I don't think you understand what this means to me."

Her mom was frowning, but the look managed to come off as more troubled than terrifying. "Do you understand why it means so much, honey?"

"I think so." She leaned back against her pillows, trying to find the right words. "One of the things Shoshanna and I are working on is not letting what happened make me a victim in the rest of my life. But it's hard when I still depend on other people so much. Meg ditches her own plans to come get me anytime I ask, and you guys haven't gone out much in the past year. It's like you're afraid to leave me alone for more than a few hours."

"It's not that we don't trust you," her mom said, moving closer to the bed, "but we could have lost you, Jamie. Things could have turned out even worse than they did, and knowing that, it's hard to be away from you. Letting you go to training camp by yourself last month was one of the most difficult things we—okay, *I*," she conceded, "have ever done."

"Then the thought of letting me go to Seattle must be hard, too."

Her mother nodded. "It is. Incredibly."

"I feel like this is my chance to do something for someone else finally, after a year of like, non-stop taking. You know?"

Her dad came closer, slipping his arm around her mom's shoulders. "I take it back. You're not a good kid. You're a good person."

Somehow Jamie resisted the urge to roll her eyes at her dad's schmaltziness. "I don't know about that, but it turns out Shoshanna is pretty incredible at what she does."

"And to think we had to blackmail you into going to see her," her mom said.

"I know, right?" She hesitated. "In case I've never said it, thank you."

"You're welcome," her parents said in unison.

"Now come give us a hug," her mom added with the scowl that really did frighten Jamie and pretty much everyone else she knew.

She jumped off the bed and went to them, and as they hugged again, all three of them, she noticed for the first time that she was taller than her mom. The thought startled her, and she closed her eyes, blocking out her mother's slightness, her father's receding hairline, the lines at the corners of their eyes. If she wasn't a little kid anymore, that meant they were aging, too. Emma's dad was—had been, she corrected mentally—only a year older than hers.

"Is this what you guys do when I'm not at home?" her sister said from the hallway.

Jamie turned sideways and peered at her. As soon as Meg

saw her face, she set her clarinet case down and stepped into the room. "What's wrong?"

"Emma's dad died," Jamie said.

"Oh, shit. I mean, crap. Sorry, Mom."

"That's okay. It is a shitty deal. Family hug?"

Meg sighed as if terribly put upon, but she joined in anyway. "How did it happen?"

"Heart attack."

"Poor Emma. You're going up there, aren't you?"

"Totally. We just have to figure out when."

"Good. She's going to need you."

"I know." Jamie refrained from giving her parents a *told-you-so* look, seeing as they had already agreed to (maybe) let her go.

Normally family hugs made her feel safe, protected, loved. But today, there was something missing. Or rather, someone. Today her heart was split between her own family and Emma's, and no amount of hugging could ease the ache.

Her cell rang after dinner, and she hurried to grab it from the kitchen counter, almost ignoring it when she saw it wasn't Emma. At the last second she hit answer.

"Hey, we're doing dishes, so I can't really talk."

"That's all right," Amanda said. "I wanted to see how you were feeling."

"A little better."

"Good. Will you text me later?"

"Yeah, maybe. Although I think I'm probably going to do some homework and go to bed."

"Oh." Amanda hesitated. "Well, are you going to your game tomorrow?"

"Well, yeah."

"I thought you were sick?"

"Not that sick," she said before she thought about it.

Jamie could almost hear the other girl thinking: *Sick enough to cancel our date but not enough to miss soccer?* And the thing is, she would have had a point.

"Look, I gotta go," Jamie said quickly. "I'll call you tomorrow, okay?"

"Fine," Amanda said, and hung up without another word.

Jamie returned her phone to the counter and went back to drying dishes. She probably could have handled that better, but she had enough on her mind right now without having to worry about Amanda's feelings. They'd only been going out for a few weeks and already the girl had "passed Needytown on the way to Clingsville," as Angie, her U-16 teammate, had said in an email the other day.

"Was that Amanda?" Meg asked, retrieving a large wooden spoon from the soapy side of the sink.

"Yeah."

"Huh."

Jamie didn't respond as she tucked a colander away in a cupboard.

"I said, *huh*," Meg repeated a little louder.

"Huh, what?"

"You didn't tell her about Emma's dad?"

"No. Why would I?"

"You guys are dating, aren't you?"

"We're hanging out. It isn't serious."

"Have you not seen the way that girl looks at you?"

"It isn't serious." Jamie shot her sister a look. "Let it go."

Meg held up her soapy hands. "Okay, okay. No need to hit me with game face. Usually it's eerie how much you look like Dad, but then you make that face and you're like Mom's twin all of a sudden."

Before France, Jamie had always believed she was more like

their dad. But in the last year of working with Shoshanna, she had come to realize that she, like their mother, was made of sterner stuff. That was one good thing about surviving the assault and moving on with her life: She knew now that she would always be okay. Emma, on the other hand, was still in the early stages of loss, and it probably felt like a nightmare she couldn't escape. That was why Jamie wanted to be in Seattle. Emma needed people around her who could help her recognize that even though she felt awful now, she wouldn't always feel that way.

People around her—all at once Jamie wondered: Had Emma told Justin about her father before or after she called Jamie? She hadn't mentioned him when they talked, but that didn't mean anything. Jamie dropped her towel, frowning. Maybe Emma didn't need her there, after all.

"Hello," her sister said, flicking a few drops of water at her. "Did you hear anything I said?"

"No, sorry. Just thinking about Emma."

"Are you going up for the funeral?"

"I think so, assuming they have one. I don't really know yet."

"Aren't you supposed to be in Portland over spring break for a tournament?"

"That's right. I could combine the trips. You're a genius!"

"Naturally. But will your coach let you play if you miss practice?"

"I don't think he would bench me for going to a funeral. Besides, would you risk the wrath of Mom if you were Pete?"

"Good point."

Later, Jamie closed herself in her room and tried to do homework. Next week was mid-terms, and then it would be spring break, which was when her travel team was headed to Oregon. Portland was only a few hours from Seattle. Emma always called the city "Seattle's mini-me." Jamie leaned back against her pillows and closed her eyes, wondering what Emma was doing. The fact she couldn't text or call her was driving her crazy. Patience had never been one of her stronger suits.

Sleep, on the other hand, she could do. An insistent vibration under her right elbow eventually woke her up. Groggy, she blinked at her bedside clock. A little past midnight. Why was her cell...? *Emma.* She scrambled to answer.

"Hi," she breathed into the phone.

"Hi," Emma murmured back. And then she began to cry.

Jamie hugged one arm across her chest. It literally hurt to listen to Emma crying. "Hey," she said softly, "it's okay. You're okay, Em. I'm here."

"I'm sorry," Emma managed through her sobs. "I haven't cried at all, but then I heard your voice..."

"Em," she repeated, "you don't have to be sorry. I wish I could be there with you."

"I do, too," Emma choked out. "You have no idea how much."

Her heart seemed to rise in her chest, even though she knew Emma's admission was more about her dad than it was about her. "I guess it's a good thing my parents said I can come, then."

"What?"

As Emma's sobs abated, Jamie told her about her confrontation with her parents. "I thought they would ground me but instead they gave in. On one condition: that it's okay with your mom."

"I'll ask her tomorrow. They—I mean, she caught a red-eye out tonight, so she'll be home in the morning."

"What about...?"

"He's coming with her. There's something called an escort fare, I guess. So that's what they're doing." She paused. "I have to stop saying 'they,' don't I?"

"Not yet. Not with me."

"Are you really coming up here?"

"Of course. Remember, I was prepared to run away if I had to."

"Your parents must love me about now."

"They always love you, you know that. Especially now—that's why they're letting me come see you."

It wasn't only her parents who loved Emma. But she couldn't exactly tell her that, could she? Though she supposed she'd already come perilously close to doing so on the phone earlier. Her heart swooped again as she remembered Emma's response: *Me, too, Jamie.*

"Still," Emma said, "I can't believe you did that for me."

"Why not? You'd do the same for me, wouldn't you?"

"I don't think it would come to that in my family."

"Why? Because you're the princess and everyone bows to your wishes?"

"I was going to say because I have my own frequent flyer miles. Anyway, why be a princess when you can be a queen, right?"

It was an old joke between them, and for a moment Jamie thought she heard Emma laugh. The sound morphed almost immediately into a sigh.

"How're you doing, really?" Jamie asked, staring up at the familiar shadows her bedside lamp cast across the ceiling.

Emma told her about her night—how she called her mom so that they could give Tyler the news, how Ty took off crying and Emma had to chase him down the street, how they sat through a painful, awkward dinner with the Chandlers who had known them since Emma was eight and Ty was four and yet seemed at a loss as to how to handle this particular crisis. After dinner, Dani and Sian came over for a little while, and then their mom called again to let them know she was about to get on a plane. Emma's aunt, her mom's older sister, would be flying in from Minnesota the following morning, too. Emma had volunteered to pick them up—she needed something to keep her busy other than babysitting her brother.

"Did your mom mention a service of any kind?" Jamie asked. "My parents were thinking maybe I could be there for that."

"She said something about next weekend."

An entire week? She didn't want to wait that long to see Emma.

"He wanted to be cremated," Emma went on. "He donated his organs, too. Mom says his corneas and kidneys already went to people who could use them, so that's good. Obviously not his heart, though."

How could she be so matter-of-fact about the redistribution of her father's organs? But then again her parents were both medical professionals, and she'd said she and Ty practically grew up at the hospital where they worked together.

"Did you know there was anything wrong with him?" As soon as the question was out, Jamie recognized how ridiculous it sounded. Emma would have told her if she knew.

"No, but I guess he and my mom were aware there were some issues. I don't know all the details. I'm not sure I want to, either."

"I don't blame you."

Emma's breath whistled into the phone. "This all feels so surreal, like it's a dream, or maybe a movie—I can practically hear the soundtrack. Do you know what I mean?"

"I do."

For a while the previous summer, Jamie had listened to a song called "Damaged" over and over again, the dark melody and scarily apt words offering the perfect accompaniment to her frame of mind. When Shoshanna learned of this habit, she'd suggested Jamie burn a CD of songs more along the lines of Gloria Gaynor's "I Will Survive" and Christina Aguilera's "Can't Hold us Down."

Maybe she should burn a copy for Emma. A little girl power never hurt anyone. And speaking of girl power…

"Did you end up seeing Justin tonight?" Jamie asked.

Emma hesitated. "Well, no. I haven't actually told him what happened."

"What?" Jamie rolled over on her side so fast she bonked her elbow on her math textbook. "Ow."

"Are you okay?"

"Fine. Surprisingly, my math book doesn't make a very good pillow."

"Crap, I woke you up and you're still sick. I should let you go."

"No, really, I'm fine. Why haven't you told Justin?"

"Um… We sort of broke up?"

"You what? When?"

"Earlier," she said vaguely. "Don't worry, it was my call. I don't want to get into it right now except to say he showed his true colors, and they were ugly. Like, really fucking ugly."

She sounded even more pissed than she had a few months earlier when they were watching Man U play Arsenal in the match the press had nicknamed the Battle of Old Trafford.

"Christ," Jamie said. "I'm sorry."

"Don't be. It's not your fault he's an asshole."

Talk about a shit-storm—Emma had lost her dad and broken up with her boyfriend all on the same day. And yet part of Jamie was relieved she wouldn't have to share Emma with Justin. Most of her, actually. Which she knew was uncool, but as Shoshanna had said often enough, you couldn't help how you felt.

Actions, however, were a different story.

"I know it's not my fault," she said, "but I'm still sorry he picked today to be a dick."

"To be honest, his timing was perfect."

She didn't elaborate, and Jamie let it pass. When Emma was ready, she would tell her more. Or not. Either way, Justin was out of the picture and she, for one, hoped he would remain that way.

They stayed on the phone a little while longer, and then Emma finally said she should head to bed. Her brother was sharing his best friend's bunk bed, as he'd done a thousand times before, and they had rigged a futon on the floor for her so that she would be at hand if he woke up. She told Jamie she'd expected her brother to protest the arrangement, but he'd seemed almost relieved.

"Poor kid. He doesn't have a dad anymore," Emma said.

"What about you?"

"I'm a girl so it's different for me. Plus I'm supposed to be leaving for college in the fall."

"Supposed to?"

"No, I'm sure I will. It's just hard to picture what's going to happen right now."

Jamie understood. When your axis shifted the way Emma's had, none of your plans for the future felt quite as secure.

"I should go," Emma murmured again. "I have to be up early."

Assuming she would sleep at all. Jamie wished she could share her medicinal marijuana supply with Emma, but she doubted the other girl would accept even if they were in the same city. As a self-proclaimed control freak, Emma claimed to prefer alcohol, the devil she knew, to drugs any day. Then again, this wasn't any day.

"All right," Jamie said reluctantly. "Let me know what your mom says about me coming up there."

"I will." She hesitated. "And thanks, Jamie. Seriously."

"You're welcome." Another few seconds ticked past before she brought herself to say softly, "Love you, Emma."

The silence lasted so long that Jamie thought Emma had hung up. But then she heard her whisper, "Love you, too."

Jamie ended the call and set her phone next to the alarm clock. Then she turned on her side and hugged her pillow, swallowing against the pain in her throat. She wasn't sure if it came more from her lingering cold or from her certainty that Emma's words held a completely different meaning from her own.

#

Emma and Ty huddled together on the couch in the den, Lucy snuggling between them. Dani had offered to take care of the dog the night before, which was fortunate because Emma had completely forgotten about her. Now she kept one hand on the dog's silky fur as she and her brother watched sports, flipping back and forth between March Madness, early MLS match-ups, and Champions League on DVR. Anytime a commercial showed a father and son or a happy family, Ty would look away until Emma changed channels. For once, there was no battle over the remote.

Their mother's flight had arrived on time that morning, followed by Aunt June's a couple of hours later. Emma and her mom had killed time in a restaurant outside security, picking unenthusiastically at their breakfast sandwiches and talking mostly about Tyler and logistics for the coming week. Her mom had readily agreed to Jamie's visit and had even offered to help cover her fare, if necessary. Other relatives were planning to come for the service the following weekend, but Emma wouldn't mind sharing her room with Jamie, would she? No, she'd assured her mother as she texted Jamie the good news. She wouldn't mind sharing her room at all.

They were almost back to baggage claim when her phone buzzed—Jamie would arrive Thursday night and stay for close to a week, assuming that worked at their end. Her mom had approved the plan, and Emma wrote back, "See you in five days... Can't wait."

"Me too. XOXO," Jamie replied.

Emma had traced her fingers over the glowing characters. Five days seemed like too long, but they had gone for months at a time without seeing each other. What was another week, really?

Back at home, Aunt June had quickly taken charge. After a run to the grocery store she'd started cooking. At first Emma, her mom, and Ty sat at the kitchen bar watching her move like a whirlwind through the too-still house. She hadn't let them linger long, though. Soon she was banishing Emma and Ty to the den and leading her "baby sister" upstairs with a Valium from her own stash. She was going through menopause, she let them all know, and those hot flashes certainly could keep you up at night if you weren't prepared.

Emma thought she could probably use a sedative herself right about now. Despite her exhaustion, she couldn't seem to get her mind to shut off. Everything reminded her of her dad, especially in this room. The dog—Lucy was technically his, and sometimes Emma and Ty joked that he missed her more than anyone else when he was out of town; his favorite recliner with his slippers and a pair of reading glasses close by; the many basketball and hockey games destined to remain forever unwatched on the DVR; even the television itself, a wide-screen plasma model with matching sound system that he had brought home at Christmas. The set was sweet, Emma had to admit, but the price tag had been, frankly, embarrassing. Not that they couldn't afford it. Her dad's surgical patent raked in millions each year, and his appearance and seminar fees were substantial. If they'd wanted, her parents could have retired years earlier. But their work was so much a part of each of them that they'd never even considered stopping, as far as she knew.

Now he wouldn't ever have the chance. Instead of an

awkward retirement party at the hospital to celebrate his career, he would have a memorial service where colleagues and people from the community could pay their respects. He was going to miss so much, she realized, and then stopped the thought before it could go any further. She wasn't ready to picture the multitude of future events—graduations, holidays, family vacations—that wouldn't be the same without him. Better to pretend nothing had changed, to tell herself that he was at work or on a trip, anywhere but stuck in the casket her mother had had to pick out before flying all night across the ocean, his body somewhere below her in the plane's cargo hold.

The surreal quality she'd described to Jamie the night before shadowed Emma throughout the afternoon, which seemed almost to slip away when she wasn't paying attention even as it dragged interminably. Ty clung to her the way he used to when he was little and in the grip of a cold or fever. Even at dinner, he pulled his chair close to hers. Aunt June had baked a cheese and potato casserole, or "hot dish" as they called it back in Minnesota. No one seemed to have much of an appetite though, and the dining room remained so quiet that Emma could hear the grandfather clock ticking in the next room.

Afterward, they left the dishes soaking in the sink, piled into the Volvo, and drove a handful of miles up I-5 to retrieve Emma's grandmother. Then they backtracked to Shoreline, their intended destination a funeral home on the east side of I-5 not far from the high school. As usual, her grandmother didn't seem to understand what was going on around her, which, given the circumstances, was probably for the best.

At the funeral home, Emma and her brother waited in the front hall while their mom and aunt spoke with the director. Their grandmother leaned against her cane nearby, looking lost, and Emma closed her eyes briefly. The numb feeling was back. Her heart and mind felt heavy, encased in ice. This couldn't really be happening, could it? He couldn't really be gone. He wasn't even fifty yet. How did a forty-nine year old surgeon die of a heart attack?

Suddenly Ty grabbed her hand. "I don't want to see him," he said, voice breaking more than usual.

"I don't either." She squeezed his fingers. "But I think we owe it to ourselves, Ty-Ty. If we don't say goodbye, we might always regret it."

"But what's he going to look like?"

She had asked their mother the same question, worried that organ donation may have left him disfigured, and had been assured that he wouldn't look all that different from the last time they'd seen him. Because their parents were opposed to embalming, his body had been preserved with dry ice and refrigeration rather than formaldehyde. In the morning he would be cremated, which was why they were here now.

"I think he's going to look like himself, only sort of empty," she said. "His body is still here, but his soul, the thing that made him Dad, is gone."

She bit her lip as Ty stared at her, his chin trembling. She hadn't cried since she'd talked to Jamie, not even when she met her mother at baggage claim and stood in her arms for a good five minutes. But now looking into her little brother's eyes, she could feel her own tears threatening again. She couldn't cry, though. She had to be strong for Ty, who was looking at her as if he thought death might have turned their father into a zombie. Understandable, really—they had never seen a dead person before, and now they were expected to visit their father's body only twenty-four hours after they'd learned he was gone? It was harsh, but the lack of embalming fluid meant they only had a short window to work with.

Between basketball games that afternoon, she'd made the mistake of doing a web search on what happens to the body after death. While she hadn't read much, it had been enough to convince her that immediate cremation really was the way to go. Still, she couldn't shake the sense that things were moving too fast. The night before, after hanging up with Jamie, she'd been unable to sleep until she told herself it wasn't true. Her father wasn't dead; he would come home on Sunday as planned and she would see him then. Though she hadn't truly believed the lie, the temporary feeling of normalcy the fantasy had engendered allowed her heart rate to slow, her eyes to close. Beyond drained, she had finally fallen asleep.

Now here she was in a hallway outside of a private viewing room at the funeral home she had passed a hundred or maybe a thousand times in her life, never realizing that someday their father would be lying on a table here waiting for her and Ty to say goodbye. Not that he would know. Seeing him like this wasn't about him; it was supposed to help them accept that he was really gone. Or so their mother had said.

"Ready?" Aunt June asked, offering Emma and her brother a sympathetic smile while their mother stood at her side fidgeting with her wedding ring.

The funeral home had transported the casket from the airport, so Emma knew her mother hadn't seen him since leaving Maui. She reached out and touched her arm. "You okay?"

Startled, her mom looked up, and Emma realized how far away she had been. Reliving the moments of his death, maybe? Castigating herself for not saving him? Or was she too thinking of all the times she had driven past this building without suspecting the circumstances that would leave her a widow at forty-seven?

"Fine, honey," her mom said, and wove her fingers between Emma's. She offered her other hand to Ty and the three of them walked through the door the funeral director opened for them. For the moment, their aunt stayed behind with their grandmother.

Even though their mom had prepared them, Emma couldn't help but feel light-headed when she saw her father laid out on a table under the window at the opposite end of the small room, dressed not in a suit and tie but in his favorite weekend outfit—a Shorecrest High Women's Soccer crew neck sweatshirt layered over a tie-dye T-shirt that her brother had made him in elementary school.

She swallowed against the bile rising in her throat and closed her eyes again. She didn't want to be here. She couldn't be here. This wasn't happening, her mind insisted. He couldn't really be dead, could he? But when she opened her eyes, he was still lying on the table, unmoving.

His head rested on a pillow and a blanket covered his lower half. His face and hands looked ashen, but he seemed more like himself than she'd expected. He didn't look like he was sleeping, though. He looked absent; that was the only word she could think of. Her heart fell, and she didn't bother to blink back her tears this time. Some part of her had wanted desperately to believe the lie she'd told herself the night before. Seeing him like this now, she couldn't pretend there was a chance he would ever come home again.

They walked toward him side by side. When they were only a few feet away, Emma heard a noise and felt her mother's fingers release. Ty had turned and was running toward the door. Emma started to turn, too, but her mom shook her head.

"I'll go," she murmured. "You stay with your dad."

No! Emma wanted to shout. But before she could say anything, her mother slipped out, leaving her alone. Well, almost alone.

At first she stood where she was on the Oriental rug, trying to get used to the sight before her. The back of the sweatshirt was embroidered with "Blake #8," she knew, and it was strange to think that he would be going to the crematorium wearing her nickname and soccer number. But her mother had explained that he'd chosen the outfit himself a few years ago when they'd made end-of-life arrangements. He'd been so proud of Emma. Even when he was living at the hotel and she'd told him she hated him, her mother said he would brag about her to anyone he could trap in conversation long enough.

"I think you have what it takes to be the next Mia Hamm," he'd said on Jamie's birthday, right before she walked out on him.

Only a truly committed parent could delude themselves into believing that their daughter could be her generation's entry in the perennial greatest of all time competition. Then again, he'd pioneered a revolutionary surgical technique. If he could be world famous, why couldn't his kid? And in return for his faith, she had thrown his love back in his face. All he had wanted was to be closer to her and all she had done was push him away. If she'd known he would be gone, really gone, she would have done things differently. But she couldn't have known and there was no going back. No changing what had already happened, despite how much she wished she could.

She sniffed, wiping at the tears dripping from her chin onto her ratty old club sweatshirt from eighth grade select. She'd pulled it out of the back of her closet and paired it with jeans she hadn't worn in years because she knew that she wouldn't want to wear today's clothing ever again. Even the scrunchie she'd picked came from the inside pocket of one of her old soccer duffels. She wanted nothing to remind her of this day—not that she was likely ever to forget.

Slowly she stepped forward and reached for his hand. The skin was cold, and she tried not to picture the refrigerated container she imagined he had been stored in before they arrived. Cold now, but by tomorrow he would lie in flames that would reduce his body to ashes. She winced at the thought. She knew he was dead and gone—there was no response to her touch, and she could see herself that there was nothing left to animate his tissues and bones. But he was still her dad, and the idea of what was left of him being burned up was awful. Not as awful as what would happen if he wasn't cremated, but terrible all the same.

There was no good end, she realized. None except for him

to sit up and say that it was all a mistake, that he hadn't really died, that he was ready to come home with them.

"Hi, Daddy," she murmured, her hand still on his. She thought about hugging him, but the most she could bring herself to do was lean down and kiss his hair. It smelled like salt water and sunshine, and she realized he would be cremated with the scent of the ocean on his skin.

All at once, a hundred memories surged back—building sand castles and body surfing at Richmond Beach; playing soccer at Golden Gardens; watching beach volleyball at Alki; snorkeling off the coast of Mexico; sailing in Puget Sound; windsurfing off the Gulf Coast; riding the green Washington State Ferries to San Juan and Orcas and Lopez and Shaw. They had done all of these things when she was younger, back before his career and her soccer commitments overshadowed everything else. Once he began traveling for work and she started traveling for soccer, finding beach or ocean time had become increasingly difficult.

She was just like him, wasn't she? Her dedication to soccer was almost as unswerving as his to surgery. She had missed family reunions, friends' birthday parties, even weddings for soccer tournaments. Family vacations had to be planned around her schedule and her dad's, and in recent years they'd almost always ended up piggy-backing family time onto existing trips. Whatever they did had to be scheduled around a conference or a tournament, and she hadn't even thought to question this practice. It was simply what they had to do to make everything work.

What that meant was that he had missed her growing up, and she had missed the final years of his life. Always assuming there would be more time, more opportunities, more chances to be together, they had missed each other, and now it was too late. He wouldn't be able to schedule a presentation in North Carolina this fall to coincide with one of her games. He wouldn't see her play at the U-19 World Cup or the College Cup finals. If she one day made the senior national team and played in a World Cup or the Olympics, he wouldn't be there in the stands wearing her number and cheering her on. He wouldn't be there.

"I'm so sorry, Dad," she said, her voice breaking. "I didn't hate you. I hope you know that. I love you. I'm so, so sorry I didn't tell you that."

"Oh, sweetie, you didn't have to say it," a voice said behind her. "He knew. He always knew."

And then her mother and Ty were there beside her again and they were all hugging each other and crying, and she knew she would have to say a final goodbye to her dad soon but not yet. For now they could stand together beside him and they could still be the family she had always known, even if he wasn't really there.

"He knew you both loved him," her mom said, brushing her own tears away. "And he loved you both so much. You know what? His last words were about the two of you. The last thing he said to me was to tell you that he loved you. So I'm telling you, okay? And when you start to feel guilty, and you will because everyone does when they lose somebody, remember this: His last thoughts were of the two of you, and he knew you loved him. He knew it every single day of your lives."

Emma tried to hold back the sobs but she couldn't. Finally she turned her face into her mother's hair and let herself cry. As she sobbed, she remembered the day Jamie had told her about France. She had cried just like this. At the time, Emma had had no way to truly understand the pain Jamie had dealt with. But now she knew, and knowing how hurt Jamie had been by what had happened made her cry that much harder. The world was not a safe place, or easy. Girls could be brutally attacked, and parents could die before you had a chance to forgive them. There was nothing to do but keep going, to move forward even if you had no true idea of how to do so.

At that moment, soccer seemed like a silly thing to love as

intensely she did. But then she thought about what she really loved about the game—sunshine and the smell of freshly mown grass; the rush of adrenaline that took her out of her head and rooted her firmly inside her body; the feeling of power and near invincibility when she made a goal-saving slide tackle or game-saving clear; the bonds she shared with girls she had played with all her life and girls she had only just met. Soccer had taken her places she wouldn't otherwise have gone, and soon, if her luck held, it would take her places she couldn't imagine. Soccer had made her feel strong and fierce. Soccer had given her Dani and Sian and the rest of her closest friends. It had brought her Jamie. And soccer had made her dad proud of her in a tangible way even as it gave them something uncomplicated to share.

After a little while, Aunt June brought Emma's grandmother in. She still didn't seem to understand what was going on, but she sat down in a row of chairs with the rest of them and listened quietly as Emma's mother told them about the trip to Maui and how happy they had been there. And even though in the beginning Emma hadn't wanted to enter this room, now she couldn't imagine leaving.

When the funeral director opened the door and walked slowly into the room, Emma had to bite her lip to keep from telling him to leave them alone. Beside her, Ty shook his head, glaring at the interloper. Glad to have something else to focus on, Emma reached behind their mother's chair and set her hand on her brother's shoulder, squeezing hard. He looked at her quickly, his eyes filling with tears.

"It's okay, Ty," she said. Even though they both knew it wasn't.

A line from a recent song by the Indigo Girls, one of her mother's favorite bands, came back to her—how there are some things in life that can never be made right. Her mother had listened non-stop to the new album all spring, and while before when she heard this particular song Emma had thought of Jamie, now it fit her own family, too.

The funeral director gave them another few minutes, and then there were no more delays. Emma clung to her mother and brother as they left the room, turning back for one last look at her father lying motionless on the table. This was it. This was the last time she would ever see him. But he wasn't here. He was already long gone, and the truth was that she hadn't had a chance to say goodbye.

The car was quiet again save for the sounds of her brother's sniffles. She offered him her hand and he held tight all the way home. Familiar landmarks along the way somehow seemed darker and more sinister than they normally did. Back at the house, they put her grandmother to bed in the guest bedroom and then sat around the kitchen for hours, drinking tea and hot cocoa and retelling favorite family stories. By midnight Emma was completely cried out, and it was all she could do to send a simple text to Jamie: "Sat with my dad's body tonight. Can't wait to see you next week. Love you."

There was that phrase again, the one Jamie had introduced to their interactions: *Love you*. And she did. Only she wasn't prepared to consider how much or in what way.

She wasn't as successful in preventing her mind from dwelling on other difficult topics as she lay in bed trying to fall asleep. This time she didn't have the luxury of telling herself he wasn't really gone. This time she couldn't forget the image of his body, cold and motionless, her soccer sweatshirt covering a heart that no longer beat, veins full of blood that no longer flowed. In the morning he would be fed into an incinerator, his muscles and tissues consumed by fire and everything else ground into powder that the crematorium would return to them. As if having his pulverized bones back to keep in a closet or on a shelf or on the mantle would help them deal any better with his absence. They wouldn't keep his remains for long, though. He had requested that his ashes be scattered in a wildflower meadow on the flanks of Mt. Rainier along a trail they had hiked as a family at least once each hiking season. That meant that either this summer or the next, she, her mom, and Ty would be hiking the old familiar trail and releasing what remained of her dad into the wind, there in the shadow of the mountain he had always loved.

When she did finally sleep, she dreamed of her dad. She was sitting on a beach on Puget Sound thinking how much she missed him, and then suddenly he was there, standing above her, holding out his hand. After a moment of shock—"But you can't be here, you're dead!"—she took his hand and they ran together into the water, and even though in the dream she was the age she was now, her dad was a much younger man, laughing and carefree beside her. They splashed in the shallows for a while, and then they went back to the beach and kicked a ball around. They talked, too, but she couldn't remember afterward what they said. Eventually her dad held out his hand and she took it, and they went for a walk as the sun set. Right before the dream ended, her dad slipped his arm around her shoulders and hugged her to his side, and she heard him whisper, "I will always be with you, Emma."

When she woke early in the morning and remembered that he was gone, she waited for the crushing pain to return. And it did, briefly. But then something else happened. As the picture of his body lying still and inanimate on the funeral home viewing table started to take hold, memories of the dream flooded her mind, and she smiled, tears filling her eyes as she remembered her father's youth and happiness, her own joy at the unexpected extra time they'd been given. In that moment with the sky still dark beyond her window and her comforter creating a warm cocoon around her, she understood: Her dad had visited her in her dreams so that she would remember him as he had been in life, not as his body appeared in death. He had come to say goodbye the only way he could. He had come back to her, after all.

Emma closed her eyes. "Thank you, Dad," she murmured. But the only answer she heard was the wind blowing through nearby trees and the creak of the house settling around her.

CHAPTER EIGHT

Jamie glanced around baggage claim, keeping an eye out for Emma. This was her first time flying into Seattle, and the airport was significantly larger than Oakland. She'd had to check a bag with all her gear for the Portland tournament, and now as she looked around the baggage area, she hoped a sign would point her toward the correct carousel. But all she saw were milling passengers and the people who were waiting for them.

Then the fluorescent lights caught on a white US Soccer baseball cap, and she did a double take—Emma, scanning the crowd, too. With her hair tucked under the cap and a navy fleece hiding her curves, she didn't look like her usual fashionably girlie self.

"Emma," Jamie called, willing away the butterflies that had taken flight in her gut. The way Emma's eyes lit up the moment she saw her didn't help a bit.

Quickly they crossed the short distance, and then Emma was flinging herself at Jamie. She dropped her carryon and stumbled back a bit, absorbing the other girl's weight. She was taller but Emma was broader—good Scandinavian peasant stock, she'd joked more than once—not to mention curvier. Jamie grasped her tightly and lifted her off her feet briefly, hugging her as hard as she dared.

"You're here," Emma murmured against her shoulder, and Jamie could feel the hitch in her breathing.

"Good thing. Clearly you need someone to look after you." Emma laughed a little, at least Jamie thought it was a laugh. But then she felt tears on her neck and squeezed Emma tighter again, murmuring softly, "Shh, I've got you. I'm right here."

The whole last week, Jamie had wanted nothing other than to be in Seattle. As it was, she'd had to content herself with the usual phone calls, emails, and text messages in between studying for mid-terms. It was almost unreal to finally be here holding Emma in her arms instead of listening to her cry over the phone.

Not that there had been much crying since the previous weekend. The day after Emma had texted about viewing her father's body, visitors had begun to descend upon the Blakeley house—first a plethora of local friends with flowers and casseroles followed shortly by the first of the relatives and friends from Minnesota, Virginia, and Boston. Emma and her brother had stayed home from school all week, but she told Jamie school would probably have been better than being stuck at home with the influx of hospital staff and family friends with their sorrowful expressions and protestations of shock. The visitors didn't seem to realize that rather than offering comfort, mostly they were reminding the family of what they'd lost.

"Honestly," she'd told Jamie the night before her flight, "it's not that different not having him here. But every time someone comes by to check on us, I remember he's not just away. It's starting to feel like people want to gawk at the bloody aftermath. You know, like rubbernecking? Only in this case my mom and brother and I are the smashed cars in the median."

"Is this your way of telling me you'd rather I not come see you?" Jamie had asked, only half-joking.

"Of course not! Unless—do you not want to come?"

She'd sounded so nervous that Jamie had rushed to assure

her that the opposite was true. If anything, she'd wanted to get there sooner and stay longer. Five and a half days in Seattle didn't seem like nearly enough time.

At least she was here now. Finally.

"I'm sorry," Emma mumbled, rubbing her face against Jamie's jacket. Then she froze.

"Did you wipe snot on me?" Jamie pulled away to peer down at her.

Emma bit her lip. "I think it was mostly tears?"

"We're even then, since I'm pretty sure I ruined your sweatshirt at Golden Gate Park."

"No, you didn't. Turns out snot doesn't stain."

Her voice was so earnest that Jamie cracked up. Pretty soon Emma was laughing, too, but it didn't last long.

"Come on," she said, wiping her cheeks and marshaling her features into a stoic mask. "Let's find your bag."

The mask remained in place as they followed the freeway north past the glittering nighttime skyline of Seattle, chatting about Jamie's flight, the city's geography, and soccer. At her mother's insistence, Emma was taking a break from her travel team.

"I'm not really sure why, though," she grumbled as she guided the Volvo wagon across an impressive bridge, city lights slipping away behind them. She pointed to one side of the freeway. "That's the University District, by the way."

"Cool. So you would rather be playing?"

"Totally. Soccer has always been great at taking my mind off things."

"Same. When I came back from France last year, my concentration at school was crap. Same with my moods. But on the soccer field I could stop being me, you know?"

"Exactly," Emma said, glancing over at her as speeding cars jockeyed for position in the three lanes around them. She started to lift her hand from the steering wheel, and for a moment Jamie thought she was going to reach for her. But then she glanced back at the road, tucked a loose strand of brown-blonde hair behind her ear, and gripped the wheel again.

They didn't speak much the rest of the way. Jamie kept thinking about the way they had been ending their emails and texts for the past week. "See you later" had been replaced by, "Love you." Not "I love you," but also not a casual "love ya" that could be more easily dismissed. Jamie wanted to ask Emma what she meant when she said "love." She wanted to ask why Emma was thinking of joining the GSA. She wanted to know if Emma felt like there might be something more between them, too. But Emma's dad had just died and Jamie was there to support her, not browbeat her about what was going on between them.

She stared out the window as the freeway wound through the outskirts of the city. Such an inopportune time to realize she had a crush on her presumably straight best friend. But really, was there ever a good time for such a realization?

Ten minutes out of downtown, Emma guided the Volvo off the freeway. In a few minutes they reached a busy intersection bordered by used car lots—"Aurora," Emma told her—and then they were leaving behind the industrial area. The transition to leafy residential neighborhood happened faster than Jamie expected, and soon they were turning at a stop sign onto a dark, wooded drive with two signs. One advertised sharp curves and the other a dead end.

"*This* is your street?" she asked as they passed a secluded, gated property lit up against the night sky.

"Yeah, we're a little ways down."

As they wound downhill along the twisty road, Jamie caught glimpses of large homes on even larger lots. In Berkeley, even the uber sophisticated homes in Claremont Hills were built practically on top of each other. But here, landscape lights revealed long driveways, extensive gardens, and wide lawns. Some houses were built into the trees, security lights shining on giant evergreens. Others offered panoramic views of a dark, open expanse that she knew must be Puget Sound. If she hadn't known better, she would have sworn they were hundreds of miles from any city.

When they turned onto a long driveway that led to a two-story cedar shake cape overlooking the Sound, Jamie shook her head a little.

"What?" Emma asked.

"This neighborhood is unreal."

"My parents have stressful jobs. They bought this place to make sure they had a retreat from the hospital."

It looked like they'd gotten their wish. But Jamie didn't comment further. She knew Emma wasn't entirely comfortable with her family's privileged status.

Once they'd parked, Emma insisted on carrying her bags from the attached garage into the house. Jamie followed, trying to convince herself she wasn't nervous about meeting Emma's mother. As she recalled, her father hadn't seemed thrilled to make her acquaintance the summer before, and though Emma had never said as much, Jamie was pretty sure he had made his opposition to their friendship clear. It wasn't like it was the first time someone had looked at her the way Emma's dad had. Parents tended to react in one of three ways to her unapologetic baby dyke ways: Either they commented on how impressed they were to see someone so young dancing to a different drummer (she had heard that phrase easily a hundred times since chopping off her hair), stared her down the way the late Mr. Blakeley had, or pasted on a fake smile and pretended to be fine with her gender expression.

Emma's mom was in the kitchen when they walked in, seated on a stool talking to another woman at the sink. When she saw them, she set down her nearly full glass of wine and slid off the stool. She looked like she had in the pictures Emma had shared: an older version of her daughter, still trim in middle age with a kind smile in spite of the sadness lurking in her tired eyes.

"Jamie," she said, and held out her arms. "It's so nice to finally meet you in person."

Jamie stepped into the hug. "Thanks," she murmured, glad she had practiced this meeting in her head during the flight. "It's nice to meet you too, Mrs. Blakeley. I wish it could have been under different circumstances." Emma had told her how sick she was of hearing people say they were sorry for their loss, so she had tried to come up with a suitable alternative.

"So do I, sweetie. And call me Pam." Keeping one arm around her shoulders, Emma's mom turned toward the other woman. "June, this is Jamie, Emma's friend from California. Jamie, this is my sister June."

The aunt stared at her. Jamie recognized the look—clearly she was trying to decide between a glare and a fake smile. In the end, her Midwestern training won out. "Nice to see you."

"You, too," Jamie said equally politely.

"How was your flight?" Emma's mom asked. Then, before Jamie could answer, she added, "Are you hungry? You're probably hungry. They don't do food on airplanes anymore. Except on the way to Hawaii. We had quite a nice meal in first class. Frequent flyer miles certainly do come in handy, don't they?"

At the mention of Hawaii, everyone else froze. Jamie glanced at Emma, seeing her eyes glaze over at the reference.

"I could eat," she said quickly.

"Why don't you get settled upstairs and June and I will see what we can rustle up. Are you a vegetarian?"

She shook her head. "No, I eat pretty much everything. Except baby animals." As Emma rolled her eyes, Jamie mock glared at her. "What? Have to draw the line somewhere."

Emma's mom was watching their interaction with a gentle,

almost sad smile. "Emma, could you ask your brother if he'd like a snack before bedtime?"

"Sure, Mom," Emma said, and leaned in to kiss her cheek as she passed.

It was such a sweet gesture, such an Emma gesture, that Jamie couldn't breathe for a second. She felt Emma's mom's eyes on her again and wondered if she imagined the understanding in them.

"Thank you for dropping everything to fly up here," she said, squeezing Jamie's shoulder before releasing her. "It means so much."

Emma's cheeks were a little pink as she elbowed Jamie. "Come on."

"Yes ma'am," she said, figuring the response worked for both Blakeley women.

"Hope you don't mind staying in my room," Emma said as they climbed a wide set of carpeted stairs.

"Of course not."

"My uncle and cousins arrive tomorrow, and I think the boys are staying in the den. Which means," Emma added as she reached the top of the stairs and headed down the hallway, "we'll have to share my bed, if that's okay with you. Or you could always sleep on the couch in the living room."

At the end of the hall, she led the way through a partially open door. Jamie paused in the doorway to take in the large bedroom with its attached bath and wide windows overlooking the Sound. They would be sharing a bed? As in, the narrow double bed in the middle of the room with the white lace ruffle and the pink and gray quilt?

Emma set her bags on the floor near a white desk. "What do you think? Will this be okay?"

"Sure," Jamie said, hoping she sounded casual. In reality she was trying not to hyperventilate as she reminded herself that her train to Portland didn't leave until Wednesday. That meant she'd be staying here five whole days and six whole nights. *Crap.* She walked to the wall of windows and pretended to gaze out across the dark water. What had she gotten herself into?

Downstairs, Emma's brother barely even looked at Jamie as they shared a pre-bedtime snack of granola and hot chocolate. Emma chatted with her mom and aunt about her new year's trip to Berkeley, and occasionally Jamie stopped shoveling food into her mouth long enough to answer a question. She asked for seconds, which seemed to make both of the older women happy. Apparently Minnesotans liked to feed people.

They stayed up for a little while comparing California, Washington, and Minnesota weather and politics. June still lived in their hometown, Rochester, where the Mayo Clinic had its headquarters. While Rochester had a population under a hundred thousand, June insisted it wasn't a typical small city. Because of the world-class medical facilities, Rochester residents were used to visitors from all over the world and therefore were a more cosmopolitan bunch than you would find in the average comparably sized Midwestern city.

"Is that why you became a nurse?" Jamie asked Emma's mom. "Because of the Mayo Clinic?"

"Probably."

"It definitely was," June said. "Most of the women in our family are nurses, except for the occasional teacher."

"Some of the men are nurses, too," Emma's mom said, giving her sister a look.

June pursed her lips disapprovingly.

"One of their cousins is a male nurse," Emma said, wiggling her eyebrows subtly at Jamie.

So being gay did run in her family. Interesting.

Jamie asked where Emma's mom had done her training, and with a little more probing got her to open up about going to the U in the Twin Cities and then leaving the Midwest to intern at Boston Children's Hospital.

"That's where she met Dad," Emma told Jamie. "He was doing his residency at Children's. It was love at first sight, wasn't it, Mom?"

"Maybe for him." The older woman smiled, and for the first time, Jamie noticed that it appeared genuine. "I took a little more convincing."

"How long did you live in Boston?"

"Six years. Emma was born there right before we moved to Seattle."

Jamie glanced at her, surprised. "I didn't know that."

"There are plenty of things you still don't know about me," Emma said.

"Doubtful. You are like the least mysterious person ever."

"Am not."

"Are too."

"What are you guys, like ten?" Tyler asked, his tone superior.

"You should talk," his sister said, "Mr. I-hate-showers."

"I don't hate showers. I just don't like taking them every day. I mean, I'm only going to get all dirty again anyway."

"Don't let Jamie hear you say that," Emma said. "If she could, she would take three a day. Wouldn't you?"

Jamie shrugged. One could never have too many showers, in her opinion. Her mom and sister were always getting after her for wasting water, but she couldn't help it. The Bay Area frequently suffered from a damp chill, and a shower was the fastest way to warm up. For a few weeks the previous spring, though, her shower urge had taken on an obsessive quality. Fortunately Shoshanna had helped her curb most of the OCD tendencies that arose in the wake of the assault.

They stayed up talking about Boston and Emma's parents' life there for another half hour. Then Jamie yawned one too many times and Emma's mom sent them off to bed.

"Are you tired from staying up to study?" Emma asked as they climbed the stairs.

"That's part of it. But mostly I've been up late worrying about you."

For a second Emma's step faltered. Then she recovered and flashed Jamie a shy smile over her shoulder. "Sorry."

"Don't be." Jamie smiled back at her. Emma in person in Seattle was different from Emma in California or even on the phone. Face to face at home she was quieter, less certain of herself. Maybe her reserve was related to the fact that she'd lost her dad less than a week earlier.

They took turns getting ready for bed same as they'd done in Berkeley a few months earlier. Then they stood next to the bed, facing each other. Jamie was wearing a tank top and boxers while Emma had pulled on a worn, soft-looking UNC T-shirt and cotton pajama shorts. Jamie tried not to stare at her bare legs, tanned except where the soccer player's nemesis, the shin guard strap, had left a semi-permanent mark.

"Which side is yours?" she asked, hoping her nervousness didn't show. She'd slept in hotel beds with teammates plenty of times before, but she hadn't had massive crushes on any of those girls.

"This one," Emma said, pointing to the near side.

"Cool." Jamie dropped onto the bed and arranged herself on Emma's side, pillowing her head on her upraised arms. "Comfy," she added, grinning up at Emma.

"My brother's right, you are ten."

Quickly she flopped to the other side and crawled under the sheet. "Kidding. Geez, Blake."

"So was I. Geez, James." Emma slid in beside her and reached for the bedside lamp. "Ready?"

As I'll ever be. Jamie nodded.

The light went out, plunging the room into darkness. A digital clock sat on the bedside table, and as her eyes adjusted,

Jamie could see Emma's face partially lit by the green glow. Somehow it was easier in the dark to ask her the question she'd been holding in all evening: "So how are you really?"

"Okay."

"You don't have to pretend with me."

"I know. You've been through so much, though, I don't want to burden you."

"It's not a burden. I want to help."

Emma sighed. "You make it sound easy, but we weren't all raised by California hippie types, you know."

Jamie laughed. "Believe me, before Shoshanna got her hands on me, I was at least as repressed as the next person."

"Huh." In the dark, she felt Emma fidget beside her. Then: "I've been dreaming about my dad dying—or, at least, I think that's what the dream is about."

She sounded so matter of fact, but Jamie reached out anyway and found her hand, squeezing her fingers. That was easier to do in the dark, too.

"He used to have this recurring nightmare about his brother's death, and in the last week it's like my brain has adopted it. Sometimes it's still in my mind when I wake up, replaying over and over—broken windshield, water rushing in, the airplane sinking—only I'm the one who can't breathe, the one watching the light overhead fade away."

"It doesn't help to tell your mind to stop the movie either, does it?" Jamie smoothed her thumb over the back of Emma's hand. "Once your brain grabs hold of a picture like that, it's hard to redirect."

"Tell me about it. I've tried reading, listening to music, even watching TV. But you know the only thing that works?"

"Kicking the crap out of a soccer ball?"

She turned her palm up to meet Jamie's. "Exactly. You said it was like that for you after France, didn't you?"

"Yeah. To be honest, sometimes it still is."

She held on to Emma's hand, telling herself that it didn't have to mean anything. Emma was the girl who had made her feel less alone during the worst year of her life, and she loved her as a friend. Or, you know, whatever.

"It was sweet of you to ask my mom about how she became a nurse," Emma said softly, turning on her side to face Jamie.

Now all she could see was Emma's light-colored hair silhouetting her darkened features. "Oh. Well, my dad said when he lost his father, the one thing that made him feel better was thinking about all the good times they'd had. I guess I thought talking about the beginning might help your mom forget about the end."

In the dark, Emma shook her head. "You're amazing, you know that?"

"No, I'm not."

"Yes, you are." Emma squeezed her hand.

Jamie's cheeks burned, and for the first time in her life, she realized she wanted to kiss someone. In a bed. With no one else around. Her heart started beating so fast she worried she might have an anxiety attack, but the sensation remained on the pleasurable side. Mostly.

Out of the blue she felt a touch on her cheek and jumped a little.

"I'm sorry," Emma said quickly, pulling back.

"No, I was surprised is all. It's okay, really." She stopped, willing herself not to sound too desperate. It wasn't like anything could happen. Or should, for that matter.

"Thanks for coming to visit me," Emma said.

"You don't have to thank me. Whatever you need while I'm here, all you have to do is ask."

She hesitated. Then her voice dropped almost to a whisper. "Could you hold me? Or would that be too weird?"

In response, Jamie opened her arms. Emma flipped onto her opposite side and backed into her. Soon they were spooning and Jamie's arms were around Emma, her lips mere centimeters from her hair. *Weird* was so the wrong word. *Amazing* was good, *fantastic* even better, or maybe *astonishingly perfect* was the ticket. As was the girl in her arms. She thought of how Emma had held her on the beach in San Francisco, how she'd seemed more worried about her brother than herself the night their dad died, how she'd kissed her mother's cheek on the way out of the kitchen earlier. Emma was so good, and Jamie was so lucky to have her in her life.

"Is this okay?" Emma asked, her voice uncertain.

"Of course," Jamie said. "You don't always have to be the one who takes care of everyone else, you know. Not with me."

And then she wondered if she'd said the wrong thing as Emma started to shake. She was crying again, quietly this time, breath rushing in and out in great, nearly silent gasps, and Jamie's heart ached as much as it had the night Emma's dad died and Jamie listened to her sob over the phone line.

That night she hadn't been able to do anything. Now she held Emma closer, murmuring soothingly, "You're all right. I've got you. It'll be okay."

But they both knew it wouldn't. Emma's dad wouldn't be there to her graduate this spring, he wouldn't fly out with her to North Carolina to get her settled at college next fall, he wouldn't see a single match she played at UNC or for the national team. He wouldn't meet her future boyfriends or walk her down the aisle one day or hold his grandchildren in his arms. It wouldn't be okay because his story had ended just as his daughter's was getting started.

Eventually Emma stopped trembling. "I told him I hated him," she said, her voice thick with tears. "He asked me about my life and I refused to tell him anything. I let him think that I didn't love him."

Jamie rubbed Emma's arm. "I'm sorry. That must feel

terrible."

"It does. It really does. There's no way to take it back, either. I thought we would have more time. I didn't know this would happen."

"Of course you didn't. There was no way of knowing." Jamie paused and tried to channel Shoshanna. "Do you think he knew you loved him?"

Emma didn't answer for a minute. Finally: "Yes."

"Did you know that he loved you?"

The answer came more quickly this time. "Yes."

"Good. I'm glad."

They didn't say anything else. Jamie just kept holding on, one arm gradually going numb as Emma's breathing slowed and steadied. She knew Emma hadn't slept much all week and wasn't surprised that she would drop off so quickly after her crying jag. But damn, was it hard to hold her without feeling certain things. Her hair smelled of cucumber and strawberry, and her bare skin felt soft and smooth beneath Jamie's fingertips. This was simultaneously the best and worst feeling she could ever remember, lying this close to Emma and not being able to do anything about the thoughts wending through her brain. Finally she gave in and pressed her face into Emma's hair, kissing her softly. That wasn't creepy at all, was it?

Emma stirred and Jamie froze, praying the other girl was asleep. Soon enough Emma settled back against her, and Jamie closed her eyes in relief. She was here as a friend, she reminded herself, not to make a move of any kind. Then again, even if she hadn't, Emma would be perfectly safe. Jamie wouldn't know how to make a move if it hit her upside the head.

When her fingers started to tingle painfully, she slowly, incrementally pulled her arm out from under Emma.

"Wait," Emma mumbled sleepily. She caught Jamie's other hand and wove their fingers together, holding their intertwined hands against her chest. "Mm, better."

Or worse? Jamie was pretty sure she could feel the soft swell of Emma's breast rising and falling beneath her palm. Yep, no doubt about it: definitely the best and worst feeling ever. She closed her eyes and tried to focus on anything and everything else as her heart thrummed seemingly in time to a distant rhythmic rush that sounded like—and probably was—the ocean.

#

In the morning, as light leaked into the room around the wooden slats of the window shades, Emma awoke to find that Jamie had slipped away sometime during the night and was now sleeping on the other pillow facing her, short hair standing up all over, face relaxed and even younger looking than usual. Emma watched her sleep, moved by a depth of feeling that soon had her backing out of bed to put some space between them. Jamie had flinched at her touch the night before. That as much as thinking about her father had triggered Emma's crying jag, because that involuntary reaction had reminded her how badly Jamie had been hurt, how untouchable she still was. And all at once, that knowledge combined with the pain of losing her dad had felt like too much to bear.

Somehow, though, with Jamie's arms around her, the hurt had melted away with her tears. She didn't even remember falling asleep. All she knew was that with Jamie beside her, she had slept better than she had all week. For once, she couldn't remember any of her dreams.

In the bathroom she peed and brushed her teeth and stared at herself in the mirror. The UNC T-shirt, which she had snagged from Tori at the last camp, was supposed to remind her to stay away from Jamie. Obviously that plan had worked really well. At least she hadn't kissed her—and after the way Jamie had reacted to her merely touching her cheek, she probably never would. Her head might not be in the best place right now, but there was no way she was going to risk hurting the one person who had, as her mom pointed out, dropped everything to make sure she was okay.

At the airport, Jamie had repeated back to her one of the first things Emma had ever said to her: "Clearly you need someone to look after you." And it was true. As much as she hated to admit it, she did need someone. But it was okay somehow to need Jamie because they had already shared so much. That was also precisely the reason she needed to be careful around Jamie. The younger girl was still recovering from what had happened to her, and Emma wasn't about to cause her any more pain if she could help it.

*You **can** help it*, she told her reflection. Hormones weren't remotely worth risking their friendship over even if they were an excellent distraction from everything else currently transpiring.

When she left the bathroom, the first thing she noticed was the empty bed. Then she saw Jamie standing at the picture window with the shades drawn up, hands on her slim hips, face lifted to the sunlight leaking into the room. Her eyes were closed, and despite her crazy bedhead, she was easily one of the most beautiful people Emma had ever seen.

She cleared her throat. "Good morning."

Jamie's eyes flew open and she turned away from the window. "Oh, hi."

She looked worried, and Emma was tempted to tell her not to be. She had no intention of bringing up anything that had happened after they'd turned out the lights. She came from a long line of Minnesotans whose motto, according to her mother, was, "Why talk about something if you could just ignore it?" That, and, "Could be worse." Because, usually, it could be.

From downstairs she heard a chorus of voices rising and falling. "Great," she said, crossing to the dresser to pull a baseball cap from the stack on top. "More people with sad eyes and hushed voices. I need a break from all the effing sorrow. Do you think we could run away?"

Jamie's head tilted. "Probably not. But we might be able to

get away with going for a run. What do you think?"

"I think you're a genius."

"Well, duh." Jamie smirked at her, the effect ruined only a little by the patch of hair sticking up on one side of her head.

Fifteen minutes later they were guzzling Gatorade and munching Power bars in the hand-me-down Volvo Emma's parents had given her for her sixteenth birthday—not a new car, Emma had pointed out when Jamie alluded to her perhaps being a tad spoiled—on their way to Carkeek Park, her favorite local running spot. They parked in the lot and warmed up with a jog, pausing to stretch at a viewpoint overlooking the Sound before ratcheting up their pace. From her New Year's visit, Emma knew they made good running partners, with similar strides and paces. They chatted about favorite trails and personal records as they ran, then compared the U-16 and U-19 national team training regimens. Every coach seemed to think he or she had The Answer to maximizing fitness and improving technical skills when in fact, they agreed, most of the programs were so similar it was difficult to see much difference between them. What mattered more was fitting the right people into the right spots. That, and team cohesion. The team that gets along wins.

Thirty-five minutes and five miles later, they returned to the car to grab their cleats and a soccer ball from the Volvo's back seat. Then they walked down to the lawn area near the kids' playground and started passing and juggling. For as thoughtful as she could be off the field, Jamie was a goofball on it. At least today she was. She seemed determined to make Emma laugh, balancing the ball on all sorts of body parts, pretending to trip herself as she did tricks, falling dramatically and grinning up at her from the ground. Emma couldn't help laughing, even though she felt guilty every time she did. Her dad had only just died. She wasn't supposed to even smile, was she? But soccer and Jamie were two things that could be relied upon to make her feel good, so she supposed it made sense.

After their workout, Emma drove them to her favorite brunch spot, a tiny restaurant that, from the outside, looked like someone's house—mainly because it had in fact been someone's house at one point.

The server, a girl in a Shoreline Community College T-shirt, greeted them with a sympathetic smile. "I was so sorry to hear about your dad, Emma. How are you holding up?"

"Fine," Emma said, pretending to smile back. "Got any cinnamon rolls left?"

"You're in luck. I think there might be a couple."

She led them to a mosaic-topped table in one corner of the smaller of the two dining rooms and left with promises to return shortly with rolls and hot beverages.

"Is that okay?" Emma asked as they settled in kiddy corner to each other. "I didn't even check if you like cinnamon rolls."

"Of course." Jamie gazed at her as if she was crazy for thinking such a thing. Then she sipped from her Gatorade bottle and glanced around the restaurant. "This is like the cutest place I've ever seen."

Jamie's cheeks were flushed from their run and her backwards baseball cap ably hid her bed head, and Emma found herself thinking that she might be the cutest girl she'd ever seen. "We used to come here on weekends when Ty and I were younger. Before the craziness of life took over."

"I know what you mean. My dad and I must spend at least ten hours a week in the car for my travel team, and his job isn't nearly as intense as your dad's is—or was, I guess."

Emma ignored her slight stumble as the server returned with the promised rolls and coffee for her (she was a Seattle native, after all, Jamie teased) and herbal tea for Jamie (typical California hippie, Emma teased back). They ordered eggs benedict and potato pancakes, both of which the little restaurant was known for, and the server left again.

As Emma added cream to her coffee, she remembered that

she'd ordered potato pancakes the last time she and her dad had gone out, the weekend of Jamie's birthday. She'd had no idea it would be their last dinner out together, no clue that in a matter of months he would be gone. A week ago at this time her father had been dying, or had possibly already passed, and she hadn't known it yet. The first minutes had ticked past without him in the world, and then the first hour, followed by the first day. And now, somehow, it had been an entire week.

"You okay?" Jamie asked around an oversized bite of cinnamon roll.

"Yes," she said automatically. Then she looked up into Jamie's eyes. "Well, no. Not really."

"Do you want to talk about it?"

She shrugged. "I was pondering the nature of time."

"Oh, is that all?" Jamie's eyebrows rose.

"That's right, sophomores aren't allowed to take physics, are you?"

She didn't often tease Jamie about her age, but she figured it wouldn't hurt to remind herself of the manifold reasons she couldn't reach across the table and weave their fingers together the way she'd done the night before in the darkness of her bedroom.

"Ha ha," Jamie said, making a face.

The conversation drifted to school. Both agreed that it felt like they were playing hooky, knowing that all their friends were in class today without them.

"Do you think this is what it's like to be an adult?" Jamie asked. "Like, going for a run and out to breakfast any time you want?"

"Yeah, and not having any homework ever?"

"I guess there *is* the job thing standing in the way of Friday morning brunch."

"True. What do you think you'll do after college?" Emma

asked.

"Play professional soccer. Assuming there's another women's league by then."

"Right. But after that, I mean."

Jamie shrugged. "I'm not sure. What about you?"

"I don't know. I kick around the whole non-profit management thing sometimes. My dad always says that if you have a little, you should give a little. And, well, we'll have even more now."

"You will?"

"They were planners. Besides, it's not like the technique he patented is going anywhere. There will always be sick kids."

They were both quiet, munching cinnamon rolls and sipping warm beverages. Emma tried to find something less depressing to talk about. What came out was the question that had been bouncing around her brain all morning: "How are things going with Amanda?"

Jamie didn't look up from her plate. "Fine."

"Have you been hanging out much?"

"Not really. Not with soccer and mid-terms." She glanced up. "What about Justin? Have you seen him since you broke up?"

Emma snorted. "No, and I don't plan to, no matter how many times he asks."

"He's been asking, then?"

"Unfortunately."

"At least his persistence is consistent."

"By now I'm pretty sure that's not a good thing."

Jamie toyed with her fork. "So what happened with him, anyway? You still seem pretty pissed."

Telling Jamie the truth felt too much like confessing she may or may not have feelings for her, and that was not a road

182

Emma wanted to go down right now. Or, like, possibly ever.

"Turns out he's an asshole and I should have listened to my instincts to begin with. Hey, did I tell you I was thinking of taking a couple of community college classes?"

Jamie blinked but didn't comment on the abrupt subject change. "No. Why would you do that?"

"So I'd be ahead credit-wise at UNC in case I ever need to take time off for the national team."

"Talk about being a planner…"

"I have camp and World Cup qualifiers at the end of May, though, so I don't think I can take on anything extra this semester."

"This might not be the best time to take on extra things, anyway," Jamie said.

Emma glanced up at her, trying to read her meaning in the serious lines of her face. Was she including herself in the category of "extra things," or was that in Emma's mind only?

"You might be right," she agreed, and reached for her coffee mug.

Afterward, Emma couldn't help but feel that brunch had passed too quickly. By the time they finished she was enjoying Jamie's company so much, her stomach full and her limbs heavy from the almost pleasant exhaustion that comes after a good workout, that she'd almost forgotten why Jamie was there. But as much as she wanted to stay away from home, more relatives were due to arrive shortly. Probably they should get back.

At least their generation was cool, she thought later that afternoon, watching her Minnesota cousins greet Jamie with easy acceptance. Maybe someday when she came out to them… *Gagh.* That was the last thing she wanted to think about right now.

Compared to her morning with Jamie, the rest of the day dragged. But finally, somehow, night was falling, and after another exhausting round of remembering her dad with the extended clan, she couldn't wait to go upstairs with Jamie and close her door on the rest of the world. The second night went much like the first—they got ready for bed and turned out the lights, and only then did the words they'd been holding in come trickling out, a little at a time.

"Is it hard hearing your mom tell the story over and over again?" Jamie asked. They were lying on their sides again facing each other, and her features were barely visible in the greenish glow from the alarm clock.

Emma shrugged. "Not really. I think she needs to tell it. Obviously it can't have been easy."

"Obviously. But is it something you and Ty need to keep hearing?"

"I don't know," she admitted, frowning. "I wasn't there, so no matter how many times she describes it, I can't actually imagine what it was like."

This was what she had told herself numerous times this week, but was it really true? Her mother had shared the details of her father's final hours with so many friends and family members that by now Emma knew the story by heart. How her father wasn't feeling well the morning of the boat ride, but he thought he had indigestion so he popped some Tums and they decided to go on the charter trip anyway because he loved the ocean and they'd done a similar trip on their honeymoon.

"Might as well be sick on the ocean as sick in the hotel room," he'd apparently joked.

Her mom kept checking in throughout the morning, but he kept insisting he was fine. They'd already snorkeled with one pod of Spinners and were on their way to the next site when he reached for her hands.

"Something isn't right, Pam," he'd said. "I can't seem to catch my breath."

"What do you mean?" she'd asked, noticing how cold his

hands felt, how pale his face was. Then she realized that even his lips were pale, and she knew before he said it.

"I think I'm having a heart attack." Her mom reported that the last intelligible thing he said was, "I love you. Tell Emma and Ty I love them too."

He'd rambled then, stuttering out a few sentences that didn't make sense, and then he turned gray and slid off the seat onto the floor of the boat even as Emma's mom shouted for help. The boat turned around immediately and the crew radioed the Coast Guard for assistance. Another passenger that day happened to be a trauma surgeon, and between the two of them they'd confirmed his heart wasn't beating. The boat's defibrillator had been taken off a week earlier by a cleaning crew, so Emma's mom and the doctor had administered CPR for the entire twenty minutes it took to get to shore, checking frequently to see if his heart had restarted. It never did.

A helicopter was waiting to take him to the nearest hospital, but even there he couldn't be successfully resuscitated. Too much time had passed without blood or oxygen to the brain, and his advanced directive clearly stated that he didn't want extraordinary measures to be taken. The ER doctors had officially declared him dead, Emma's mom had had his organs donated, and the hospital had helped her arrange transport home to Seattle. She'd changed her ticket to be an escort ticket because, "We came to Hawaii together, and we were damn well going to leave together," her mother had said each time to signal the end of the story.

Now Emma closed her eyes and sighed. "Do you really think he said he loved us? I mean, honestly, what are the odds those would be his last words?"

"Pretty strong odds, I'd say."

And then she felt it—Jamie's touch on her cheek, slow and tentative. And before she could stop herself, she moved closer, pressing her body against Jamie's. She needed her. She needed what only Jamie could provide—the feeling that everything might someday, maybe, possibly be all right.

This time, Jamie didn't flinch away. She wrapped her arms around Emma and tugged her closer, their bare legs slipping together as they hugged under the covers. This was how it had felt to be close to Tori, too, only that was different because while Tori was attractive and exciting to be around, she wasn't her best friend who would do anything for her and vice versa. She wasn't a friend at all, really.

Emma felt Jamie's breathing quicken, and she pulled away. She'd done it again. She'd freaked her out. She had to stop doing that.

"I'm sorry," she said miserably. "I didn't mean—"

But Jamie was shaking her head, squinting at her in the dark. "No, I wanted to. It's okay, really. I want to."

Wanted to what? But she knew. She'd seen the way Jamie looked at her, recognized her own feelings reflected in her eyes. All at once she understood that the multitude of reasons she'd come up with for why she and Jamie couldn't be more than friends was utter crap. The only reason that mattered was that Emma had seen the way other girls looked at Jamie, and she knew that one day soon Jamie really was going to start breaking hearts. And in all honesty, Emma couldn't bear the thought of hers being the first.

She turned her back to Jamie and scooted closer, feeling the other girl stiffen for a moment before her arms came slowly, almost reluctantly around her.

"Can you hold me?" she whispered, hating her own need. But she did need Jamie. She needed her touch and her comfort, and most of all she needed her friendship for as long as Jamie was willing to offer it.

"Of course," Jamie said, her voice quiet.

Emma relaxed into her arms, holding tight to Jamie's hand. She remembered their conversation over brunch about being adults with jobs and lives of their own. In reality, though, they weren't on the same timeline. Even if something happened between them now, how would they ever hope to make it work?

Really, she told herself, blinking back seemingly ever-present tears, having Jamie as a friend was better than not having her at all. Because right now, she didn't think she could take losing one more person she loved.

CHAPTER NINE

Jamie leaned against a stone pillar inside Seattle Center's Fisher Pavilion, watching as Emma stood with her mother and brother greeting people streaming in from the grassy lawn just outside. It was another sunny day in Seattle, and the flowers along nearby pathways waved gently in the summer-like breeze. Even the weather seemed determined to celebrate Emma's dad that afternoon.

She couldn't believe how many people were here. The inside seating reserved for family, friends, and hospital colleagues was filling up fast while the lawn was still packed with well-wishers. They stood in small groups talking over the classical music playing softly on the speakers set up both inside and outside of the glass-walled pavilion built into the hillside near the Seattle Science Center. Behind the crowd in the near distance she could see the arced jets of the International Fountain rising and falling in time to some pre-determined choreography.

As Jamie watched, Emma glanced over her shoulder and caught her eye for a moment before turning back to smile at yet another well-dressed adult who pressed her hand. Emma looked like an adult herself, clad in an LBD, as she had called it—a little black dress that still managed to retain a slightly conservative air with its high collar and knee-length skirt. Jamie, meanwhile, was feeling distinctly out of place in her dressiest black pants and a dark gray dress shirt paired with black Doc Marten wing tips. She'd considered bringing along her favorite clip-on tie but had decided ultimately that an open shirt collar might be the more respectful choice.

And yet when she had emerged from Emma's bathroom a couple of hours earlier, her hair freshly pomaded into a slightly neater version of its usual fauxhawk, Emma had turned from the window to stare at her.

Jamie thought she recognized the look. "I'm sorry. Maybe I should borrow something of yours?"

But Emma shook her head. "No, you don't have to change."

"Are you sure? I thought maybe I looked too…" She trailed off, unwilling to say the word out loud: *queer*.

Emma moved closer and took hold of her arm. "Don't worry. You look great. You look beautiful, okay?"

"So do you." Jamie's gaze swept over Emma's black dress, gray tights, and chunky heels, focusing at last on the spiral sun pendant at her throat. "You're wearing that?"

"I always wear it."

Jamie became aware of the warmth of Emma's hand on her arm, the slight hesitation in her hazel eyes that today looked more gray than green. "Me too," she said, nodding at her wrist where the leather bracelet Emma had given her was clasped.

Unfortunately, Emma's brother had picked that moment to bang on the bedroom door. "Yo, ladies, you better not be naked in there!"

Emma had scowled and stalked to the door. "What the hell, Ty?" she'd demanded, throwing it open.

He was leering at them from the hallway, but when he saw Jamie, he started laughing. "Dude, we look like twins." And they did, except that Ty was wearing the clip-on she'd omitted.

As he held up his fist, Jamie stepped around Emma and bumped it with her own, smiling back at him. "Totally twinning it."

Ty was okay for a kid his age. They'd bonded over skateboarding the previous day, practicing ollies and kickflips in the driveway while Emma was otherwise occupied. As they'd kicked back afterward playing with the dog and watching the older cousins shoot baskets, Ty had told her she was cooler than he'd expected. "You know, for a girl."

Now as he stood with his mom and sister in the receiving line near the entrance, he looked like he wished he could be anywhere but here. Honestly, she couldn't blame him.

"This crowd is wild, huh?"

The voice came from behind her, and Jamie glanced back to see Emma's closest friends, Dani and Sian. Their outfits matched Emma's almost perfectly down to the ankle boots and subdued jewelry. They were giving her the same slightly doubtful look they'd worn the day before when they came over to the house after breakfast. That look was why she'd asked Ty if she could borrow a skateboard. Hanging out with him had suddenly seemed more attractive than being a fourth wheel with Emma and her ultra hetero school friends.

"Wild," she agreed, trying not to fidget under their gazes. "Who are all these people?"

Dani pointed out the family friends, mostly neighbors, hospital staff, and fellow soccer families. Several clusters of teenaged girls and guys dotted the room, Emma and Ty's friends from school and sports. The people they didn't know were likely either non-profit connections—Emma's dad had served on the boards of several area foundations—or the families of former patients.

"I heard Pam say almost a hundred patients and their families were planning to attend," Sian said.

"A hundred?"

"Yeah, and that's like only a fraction of the people he treated."

Jamie liked Sian. She was the quieter of the two and seemed less judgmental than Dani, who was as filterless as Emma had described. But that wasn't entirely true. The way Dani looked at her told Jamie that she was holding something back in their interactions. Did she sense Jamie's crush on her best friend? Was she worried Jamie would try to make a move on Emma now when she was at her most vulnerable? As if.

But she couldn't exactly tell Dani that, so instead she asked questions about Emma's dad that soon had Dani and Sian recalling memories of the elder Blakeley cheering them on from the sidelines, grilling "the best ever" salmon at family get-togethers, and teaching them how to sail during one rare, lazy staycation. He'd been a good dad, they agreed—when he was around. Unfortunately, his work had taken him away more than Emma and her brother—and he?—wanted.

The receiving line finally slowed, and soon Emma came over to tell them the service was about to start. Her eyes were dark gray, her lips unsmiling. Jamie wondered if she was nervous. Her mother had asked her to say a few words at the service, so she'd spent half the morning in her room polishing her speech while Jamie and Ty threw a football with a couple of the Minnesota cousins on the wide lawn that overlooked the Sound. These cousins were college-aged but not actually in college, and they seemed almost as impressed by the panoramic view as she was. Only Ty appeared not to notice the distant snow-capped mountains gleaming in the spring sunshine.

As they made their way to the reserved seating area near the stage, the Seattle mayor stepped up to the mic and asked if everyone could take their seats. Jamie would have recognized him even if she hadn't already known he would be emceeing the event. He'd made national news a few weeks earlier by issuing an executive order that required Seattle city government to recognize the same-sex marriages of municipal employees. With Massachusetts expected to start offering legal same-sex marriages in the next month or so, assuming Governor Romney and the legislature didn't somehow complete an end around the state's Supreme Court decision, the Seattle order was more than symbolic.

At Emma's direction, Jamie sat between her and Dani, only realizing belatedly that she had scored the "best friend" seat. Emma's leg pressed against hers, and Jamie started to move away. But then she realized the contact was purposeful and stayed where she was. Emma leaned into her shoulder too, and Jamie suppressed the desire to take Emma's hand. What happened in Emma's bedroom at night was one thing, but she doubted Emma would want to hold hands in front of the hundreds of people seated behind them.

The crowd noise quieted to a low rustle as the service began. It quickly became clear that the theme of the day was Emma's father's legacy. There were representatives from the causes he'd championed, from civic engagement and the arts to open spaces for all; patients whose lives he had saved and the families whose lives he had changed; and colleagues and friends who had come to bear witness to the important role he had played in their professional and personal development—interns he had mentored, surgeons he had trained, friends he had alternately entertained and been entertained by. Men and women young and old spoke for more than an hour and a half about the impact David Blakeley had had on them individually and on the world at large.

At last the best man from Emma's parents' wedding stood up to talk about growing up in Northern Virginia with David and heading off to college at Dartmouth together, just a couple of DC boys who had hated the snow but thrived on the intellectual challenge of the Ivy League institution. They had stayed close all of these years, meeting nearly every spring for some type of outdoor adventure. Last year they'd achieved a lifelong dream: rafting the Colorado River through the Grand Canyon. The best man choked up as he described a conversation about love and death that they'd had beside a campfire under the narrow swath of night sky visible from the floor of the canyon.

"The thing is, David wasn't afraid to die," the best man said. "He was only afraid of not seeing his children grow into the amazing people he knew they would be."

He paused and glanced at Emma and Ty, who both stared down at their feet. Jamie felt Emma tense beside her. Without thinking she started to reach for Emma's hand, but she stopped as Emma shifted away. *Idiot*, she castigated herself, training her gaze back on stage as the best man read a passage from John Wesley Powell's journal of the 1869 raft expedition along the Colorado River: "We have an unknown distance yet to run, an unknown river to explore. What falls there are, we know not; what rocks beset the channel, we know not; what walls ride over the river, we know not. Ah, well! We may conjecture many things."

He paused and looked out at the crowd. "We may conjecture many things about where David Blakeley is now, but what isn't open for speculation is the kind of man he was. Those of us who loved him know that he was a man of great intellectual capacity, a man of great empathetic powers, a man of great reverence for the natural world, and most importantly, a man of deep and abiding love for his family. Davie, wherever you are, the world has lost one of its stars, and we will never be quite the same without you. Love you, man."

Emma's turn came next. She rose from her seat and walked to the stage, and if Jamie hadn't known better, she would have believed the calm, stoic facade Emma projected. But even from a distance, she could feel the restless energy radiating off of the older girl.

Up on stage, the best man kissed Emma's cheek and retreated as she unfolded a piece of printer paper and set it on the podium. She looked up at the crowd, and for a moment her mask slipped and Jamie's heart leapt in matching panic. But then Emma's gaze fell on her. Jamie nodded at her—*You can do this*—and Emma nodded back almost imperceptibly.

"My father was not a perfect man," she started, her voice shaking a little, and the crowd rumbled uneasily. This was not the opening they had expected from the good doctor's good daughter. On the other side of Ty, Jamie saw Emma's mom's gaze sharpen as she stared intently at her eldest child.

"He was a study in contradiction. He loved his family, and yet he spent half of each year on the road. He loved what he called the 'beautiful precision' of surgery, and yet he spent what would be the last years of his life teaching others how to operate more efficiently. He loved forests and mountains, but he spent more time in airplanes and sterile operating rooms than he did outdoors. For a long time, I believed these inconsistencies signaled a failing on his part. I believed he wasn't living an authentic life. But in the past week, as I've thought about his legacy, I've come to realize that he was actually one of the most selfless people I know. He set aside everything he loved best because he understood that he had a different purpose. And that purpose was to bring health and a chance at happiness to the people who needed him the most.

"My father was not a perfect man, and yet he was a great man. But his greatness doesn't lie in all the lives he saved or the surgical techniques he invented. His greatness lies in the example he set. His greatness lies in his willingness to give his time and energy to people he didn't know and, in many cases, would never meet. As one of his heroes, Robert Ingersoll, once wrote, 'Character is made of duty and love and sympathy, and, above all, of living and working for others.'"

Emma paused and looked down, blinking rapidly, and now Jamie's heart ached for her. She stayed that way for twenty or thirty seconds while the audience shifted again. Jamie glared out across the crowd. What the hell? Why couldn't they sit still and be present for Emma's pain? It was a memorial service, for Christ's sake. What had they expected?

When Emma spoke again, her voice was only a little shaky.

"As you've heard, my father loved the outdoors. One of his favorite books was John Muir's *The Mountains of California*. I thought I'd share with you one of his favorite passages. Muir has just reached the glacier beneath the summit of Mt. Ritter, and even though he knows he doesn't have the right equipment and that it isn't the right time of the year, still, as he says, 'We little know until tried how much of the uncontrollable there is in us, urging across glaciers and torrents, and up dangerous heights, let the judgment forbid as it may.'

"Against the odds, Muir makes it across the glacier to the peak where he starts free-climbing the rock face. But soon he finds himself stuck, unable to move up or down, certain that he's about to fall to his death. As he later wrote,

When this final danger flashed upon me, I became nerve-shaken for the first time since setting foot on the mountain, and my mind seemed to fill with a stifling smoke. But this terrible eclipse lasted only a moment, when life blazed forth again with preternatural clearness. I seemed suddenly to become possessed of a new sense. The other self, bygone experiences, instinct, or guardian angel—call it what you will—came forward and assumed control. Then my trembling muscles became firm again, every rift and flaw in the rock was seen as through a microscope, and my limbs moved with a positiveness and precision with which I seemed to have nothing at all to do. Had I been borne aloft upon wings, my deliverance could not have been more complete... [T]he strange influx of strength I had received seemed inexhaustible. I found a way without effort, and soon stood upon the topmost crag in the blessed light.

"My father studied this passage before almost every surgery to remind himself that even when he felt stuck, there was always a way through. This, I believe, may be his greatest legacy: the conviction that if you are faced with a seemingly insurmountable cliff, you have only to open yourself to experience or instinct, to your other self, and you will find your way to what Muir called 'the noble summit.' That is the lesson I will take from my father's life, the legacy I will try to carry forward in my own."

She looked at the large color photo of her dad on an easel to the right of the podium and stared at it for a minute. "We miss you, Dad. Love you."

Jamie blinked back tears. God, Emma was incredible. She really was.

The crowd seemed to exhale in unison as she collected her speech and stepped down from the stage. Her mom was waiting for her in the aisle, and they hugged for longer than a beat. Then Emma continued back to her seat while her mom made her way onto the stage.

"Good job," Dani whispered, reaching across Jamie to grasp and squeeze Emma's hand. Jamie watched the gesture enviously. How much easier everything would be if only she looked like Dani.

"Thanks," Emma said, and glanced at Jamie, her eyes a little glassy, a little lost.

"You were amazing," she murmured. "Doing okay?"

Emma shook her head no and leaned into Jamie again, and this time when Jamie reached for her hand she didn't pull away. As she let Jamie weave their fingers together, she placed her other hand over her brother's. Ty glanced over at them, his eyes red, and Jamie gave him a sympathetic nod. He nodded back, trying to look tough, and the three of them sat together, hands linked as Emma and Ty's mother spoke about their father—the type of man he had been, the people and things he had loved, the massive hole his passing had left in her heart and in the hearts of so many others.

Like Emma, she ended with a passage from Muir:

The rugged old Norsemen spoke of death as *Heimgang*—"home-going." So the snow-flowers go home when they melt and flow to the sea, and the rock-ferns, after unrolling their fronds to the light and beautifying the rocks, roll them up close again in the autumn and blend with the soil. Myriads of rejoicing living creatures, daily, hourly, perhaps every moment sink into death's arms, dust to dust, spirit to spirit—waited on, watched over, noticed only by their Maker, each arriving at its own Heaven-dealt destiny. All the merry dwellers of the trees and streams, and the myriad swarms of the air, called into life by the sunbeam of a summer morning, go home through death, wings folded perhaps in the last red rays of sunset of the day they were first tried. Trees towering in the sky, braving storms of centuries, flowers turning faces to the light for a single day or hour, having enjoyed their share of life's feast—all alike pass on and away under the law of death and love. Yet all are our brothers and they enjoy life as we do, share Heaven's blessings with us, die and are buried in hallowed ground, come with us out of eternity and return into eternity. Our lives are rounded with a sleep.

"Our lives are rounded with a sleep," she repeated. Then, like her daughter had done, she glanced at the photo on the easel. "Sleep well, my love. Until we meet again."

Jamie couldn't stop the tears from spilling over as Emma's mom found her way back to her seat. Beside her, Emma and Ty were crying, too, and she was pretty sure most of the crowd was as well. *All alike pass on and away under the law of death and love*—that phrase, along with the image of a flower that lived for a single hour, was burned into her mind. The entire passage had evoked a sensation of insignificance that reminded her of flying home from France, when she'd looked down on the vast ocean and even vaster planet and realized how small in the scheme of things her life was. Except instead of feeling even more alone as she had on the plane, Muir's words made her feel like part of something beautiful, something immense and, ultimately, immensely outside her control.

Emma held tight to her hand as a video montage began to play across the screen at the back of the stage, photos of her dad from every stage of his life accompanied by some of his favorite music, starting with "Blackbird" by the Beatles and ending with "No Expectations" by the Rolling Stones. She held on as the last chords of music faded away and the final family photo they'd taken at the top of the Space Needle that winter—on Jamie's birthday, Emma had told her—remained on the screen. She didn't let go during the mayor's closing remarks or even when her mother asked her and Ty to go back to their position by the door. She simply pulled Jamie along with her as she walked arm in arm with her mother toward the wall of windows at the opposite side of the pavilion.

They were almost there when Emma faltered. Jamie glanced at her, noting the way her eyes narrowed at a dark-haired woman who was slipping out ahead of their arrival. The woman hurried away, and Jamie watched Emma look at her mom. She was talking to Ty, her eyes trained on his face, and didn't appear to notice the woman who melted quickly into the crowd outside the pavilion.

"She has some nerve," Emma whispered to Jamie.

"Wait. Was that…?"

Emma nodded. And then they were reaching the entrance where, already, a group of people waited to say their farewells. Jamie let go of Emma's hand and backed away, leaving her to do the family thing. Emma looked at her quickly, brow creased, but Jamie only shook her head and turned away. Emma may think she wanted her there, but her presence would only raise more questions. Besides, she didn't want to take advantage of Emma's grief to push her into something she might later regret.

As Jamie returned to the same pillar she'd leaned against earlier, she noticed a group of guys their age in suits lingering near the stage with Dani and Sian. One of the guys said something and nodded at Jamie, and the entire group shifted to stare at her. Dani replied, but the guy who'd asked the question kept his gaze trained on Jamie. She stared back, realizing why he looked so familiar as he started across the room toward her, his face hard. Justin Tate, Emma's ex.

What was his deal? She and Emma had been friends long before he convinced Emma to go out with him. If anyone should be pissed it should be her since apparently he'd been a dick to someone she cared about. She folded her arms and watched him approach, feigning casual indifference. Despite the coiled tightness of his approach, she couldn't believe he would actually cause a scene at a funeral.

Justin stopped in front of her, his eyes narrowed. But before he could say anything, she felt an arm at her waist. Startled, she glanced over as Emma slipped in against her side. While part of her melted at the feeling of Emma's arm around her, another part flinched. For whatever reason, Justin was already pissed off. Did Emma not realize she was basically waving a red flag in his face?

"Everything okay over here?" Emma asked, her eyes as cold as her voice.

"I was about to introduce myself to your 'friend,'" Justin said, emphasizing the last word. "I'm sorry about your dad, by the way."

"Thanks. And thanks for coming." Her tone held a note of finality that was difficult to miss.

"That's it?" Justin asked, staring at her. "That's all you have to say to me?"

"I told you before, Justin, I'm done. Why are you even here?"

"Come on, Emma. Don't be like that." He stepped closer and reached for her arm, but right before he made contact, Jamie's hands on his chest pushed him back.

"She said she's done," Jamie growled, her voice nearly unrecognizable even to herself. "Maybe you should try listening for a change."

His face darkened, and for a second Jamie thought he might shove her back—or worse. But then he laughed, the sound low and harsh. "You know, it must suck to be born into a chick's body when all you really want is to be a dude."

Despite the rage bubbling beneath her skin, Jamie forced a matching smirk. "It must suck even more to realize a 'chick' is more secure in her masculinity than you are in yours." She couldn't resist adding under her breath, "Asshole."

"What did you call me?" His mocking smile fell away and he surged toward her, slamming her into the pillar.

"Justin, stop it," Emma hissed, grabbing his shoulder. But he shook her off easily.

"Fucking dyke," he bit out, pinning Jamie against the hard stone. "You don't belong here and you never will."

She blinked, feeling herself freeze as his face loomed over hers. Before she could convince her body to react, she glimpsed a flash of dark hair over his shoulder.

"Back off, Justin," Dani said, her voice low and threatening. "Otherwise my brothers here might lose their tempers, and I don't think you want that."

Beside her hulked a pair of scruffy guys who looked like they could pick Justin up with one hand if they wanted. Apparently he thought so too. He let her go and took a step back, raising his hands in mock surrender.

"That's cool. I was just on my way out. Emma," he added with a nod. Then he glared at Jamie again. "*Freak.*" And he went off to join his boys, most of whom were milling around uncertainly a little ways away.

As he retreated, Jamie clenched and unclenched her fists, her breath coming in short gasps. It wasn't too late. She could still hit him. Her mind seized on the nearest object—a folding chair in the back row—and she cycled through the possibilities in less than a millisecond: grabbing the chair and breaking it over his head; watching Justin be strapped to a stretcher and carried away in an ambulance; and finally, being arrested and hauled off in handcuffs herself for assaulting Emma's ex-boyfriend at her father's memorial service.

Yeah, Justin Tate definitely wasn't worth it.

Tears of reaction stung her eyes as she forced herself to stay where she was. The last time someone had put their hands on her like that...

"Are you okay?" Emma asked softly, touching her arm.

Jamie flinched away from the contact. "Fine," she muttered, and looked away from the hurt in Emma's eyes. "I'll be right back." She stalked off without waiting for an answer.

In the women's restroom she headed straight for a sink, ignoring the older woman who did a double-take at her appearance. Jaw clenched, she dunked her hands under the cold spray and closed her eyes, trying to focus on her breathing. When she heard the other woman leave she relaxed a little, relieved that she hadn't had to argue that no, she wasn't a teenaged boy, and yes, she belonged in the women's room. She didn't think she could handle another confrontation so soon.

The icy water soon shocked her brain out of fight or flight mode, so she moved on to reciting her mantra. The familiar refrain helped but she still felt jittery, as if her bones wanted to escape the confines of her skin. She and Shoshanna were going to have plenty to discuss at her next session. For one thing, she had never felt so close to bludgeoning another person. The rage had ignited suddenly, and her blood pressure must have risen with it because her vision had actually seemed to narrow and darken. Apparently "seeing red" wasn't only a figure of speech.

Behind her she heard the door open, and she leaned over the sink, splashing her face while checking the mirror surreptitiously. Not that she really thought Justin would come after her again, but stranger things had happened.

Dani stopped inside the door. "Are you okay?"

"Yeah. Fine."

"Emma sent me to check on you. She had to get back to her mom and Ty."

"Of course." Jamie turned the water off. She didn't look at Dani as she pulled a paper towel from a dispenser and dried her face. "I guess it's a good thing my mascara's waterproof."

"What?" Dani looked at her blankly.

Jamie tossed the paper towel. "Just kidding."

"Oh." After a moment, Dani's features relaxed into a slight smile.

"Thanks," Jamie added, "for showing up when you did."

Dani shrugged. "No problem. It looked you and Emma could use some back-up."

"You could say that."

They studied each other in the dimly lit bathroom, and Jamie wondered if she was imagining the change she thought she sensed in the other girl. Dani's earlier doubt seemed to have vanished, almost as if she had decided at some point in the past couple of hours to accept Jamie's place in Emma's life—whatever that might be.

"Come on," Dani said, nodding at the door. "I'll walk you back out there. Blake's orders."

"In that case, we better get going," Jamie said, and followed her out into the bright lights of the pavilion.

#

Emma barely made eye contact with the people who came to say goodbye to her family. She kept glancing toward the far side of the massive room looking for Jamie and Dani, and only relaxed when they finally reemerged from the hallway. They hadn't been gone all that long and everything appeared fine, but Emma was still on edge. Justin could have hurt Jamie—in fact, it was possible he had—and it was all her fault. If she had responded to any of his overtures instead of completely freezing him out, he might not have gone after Jamie like that. Or maybe he still would have. Thank god Dani and her brothers had been there. Otherwise, Justin might have...

She stopped the thought and tried to focus as another man she didn't know stopped to offer his condolences. While her mother thanked him for coming, Emma forced herself to smile politely yet again. It was almost over. All week they had been planning the service, and now that it was nearly done she wasn't sure what came next. She'd known people would show up; she just hadn't realized how many.

At first she'd hated the idea of their family's pain being on display in front of such a large crowd. But then so many friends and acquaintances had shared stories of her dad's impact on their lives that in the end, the service had turned out far better than she'd anticipated—even if she'd felt dishonest painting him in her eulogy as a selfless saint and herself as the good daughter. The reality was far more complex than most of the people present could have imagined.

Beside her Ty fidgeted, his eyes on Jamie and Dani where they stood with the Minnesota cousins.

"Do you want to go hang out with them?" Emma asked her brother.

"Can I?" He looked surprised.

Emma nodded. "Go ahead. Mom and I have this."

He offered her a grateful smile. "Thanks, Em." And then he almost sprinted over to the small group, a bigger smile on his face than she'd expected to see today. Jamie held up her fist and they cycled through some elaborate greeting she must have taught him over the weekend while Emma had been occupied with her friends and working on the eulogy. It was so sweet how Jamie had taken it upon herself to look after Ty. She was like a big sister and a big brother all rolled into one. Ty was going to be bummed when she left.

Who was she kidding? *She* was the one who was going to be bummed. At least they had a few more days together before she would have to face that particular loss.

The pavilion finally emptied out a little while later. While family and close friends wandered off to enjoy the next few hours before the evening reception, Emma, her mom, Ty, and Jamie carried the mounted photo and a box of leftover programs to a nearby parking garage. As they stood next to the Volvo, her mom said, "It's such a nice night and I don't want to go home yet. What about a quick walk in the arboretum?"

Everyone agreed and the plan was settled. As she'd done on the way into town, Emma let her brother have the front seat so that she and Jamie could share the back. Once the car was headed crosstown, she leaned over and said softly, "We always take a walk in the arboretum during the first week of April."

Jamie only nodded, gazing out the window at the city as they sped along Denny Way. Her jaw seemed squarer than usual somehow, and she still hadn't really looked at Emma since the scene with Justin.

Hesitantly, Emma covered Jamie's hand with her own. "Hey," she said, keeping her voice low.

Jamie's eyes remained fixed on the skyline, but at least she didn't pull her hand away. "What?"

"I'm sorry about Justin."

That got her attention. "Why are you sorry? He's the asshole."

"I know, but it feels like it's my fault he came after you."

"Why would it be your fault?"

She thought again about telling Jamie why she'd broken up with him, but it still felt too much like an invitation to have The Talk. She couldn't risk losing Jamie, not now.

"I guess because he was only there because of me," she said.

"Oh." Jamie looked out the window again, her jaw still tight.

Emma knew she should say something. It was her ex-boyfriend after all who had threatened Jamie, her… what? Her best friend? Her girlfriend? Neither title quite fit. But what else did you call the girl you loved and who you were pretty sure loved you back, if not your girlfriend? Jamie had dropped everything to come be with her and hold her through the night so she wouldn't have nightmares, and how did Emma repay her? With violence and fear, mixed messages and cowardice. Jamie deserved so much more than she was able—or willing?—to give.

She closed her eyes and leaned her head back against the seat. A memory flashed into her mind, that night at the EMP when her dad warned her away from Jamie for what would be the last time. What he thought about Jamie didn't matter now, if it ever had. He was gone and Jamie was here, though not for long. Soon she would be gone too. And then so would Emma.

Again Emma had the sense of time slipping away too quickly, carrying her away from everyone and everything she thought she knew. She wished there was a pause button she could hit, a giant do-over button that everyone got to use one time in their lives.

But who would she choose to save, Jamie or her father?

The arboretum was crowded. Ty ran ahead to climb trees like he usually did, leaving Emma to walk behind flanked by their mom and Jamie. She slipped her arms through each of theirs, relieved when, after a tense moment, Jamie's eyes finally softened and she relaxed into Emma's side. She had wanted Jamie to be in Seattle so badly the previous weekend, but now she was glad that if she was here for anything, it was this—the day they started the rest of their lives without him. The service had signaled a shift from handling the details surrounding his passing to beginning to adjust to life without him. He really was gone, and this was where the actual mourning started: here in this beautiful park he'd loved, with tulips blooming in colorful waves and cherry blossom petals floating on the breeze.

She remembered her mother's reading—insects that opened their wings for the first time to morning sunlight and succumbed to death at sundown on the same day; flowers that bloomed for a single hour before passing away to, what was it? *Return to eternity.* She had read that passage before more than once. Both of her parents were obsessed with John Muir, so she'd grown up with his collected works the way kids in other families grew up reading the Bible. Still, she'd never really stopped to think about the constant flow from birth to death of the creatures—insects, flowers, leaves, trees—all around her. At least, not that she remembered.

Another memory sparked then, and she nudged her mother. "Tell Jamie about the first time you brought me here."

Her mom smiled, glancing across her to focus on Jamie. "Emma was a year old when we moved out from Massachusetts and already running around like crazy, of course. That fall, when we came around a curve in the path and saw a pile of leaves the gardeners had raked together, Emma stopped running and started to cry. We couldn't figure out what was wrong until she took a handful of leaves and tried to put them back on one of the trees."

"Aw," Jamie said, smiling over at Emma. "That's so cute."

"She was. Still is, actually," her mom added.

Emma rolled her eyes, but secretly, she felt better at that moment than she would have thought possible. They walked on, reciting familiar stories about long-past family outings, and in the warm sunshine filtering through trees bursting with new growth, Emma could almost convince herself that everything would be all right.

But then night fell, as it always did, and her fragile sense of well-being faded. By the time the informal reception they'd held back at the house began to wind down, Emma more than needed a break. She loved her extended family, but she could only take so much rehashing of the service and retelling of yet more stories.

"Lucy," she called, grabbing the extension leash from the hook with one hand and her fleece with the other. As the old dog lumbered over, Emma caught Jamie's eye where she was drying dishes. *Coming?* Jamie nodded and tossed her towel to Kent, the oldest cousin.

They pulled on jackets, stepped into sneakers, and slipped out of the warm, brightly lit house. The sun was still setting over the Peninsula. Overhead the clouds were dark gray, barely tinged with pink. Emma thought of all the times she and her father had taken this walk down the long driveway together, Lucy trotting along between them. He had been worried about the old dog's health lately, concerned that he would go away and something would happen to her in his absence. Instead, the opposite had come to pass.

How did you tell a dog that the person they loved most in the world wasn't ever coming home?

"You hanging in there?" Jamie asked.

Emma reached over and slipped her arm through Jamie's. "I am now." She had never been a touchy feely person, not even with Drew, her first boyfriend. But somehow she felt better when she and Jamie were close, calmer, more at peace with herself and the world. It was selfish, she knew, but she had felt the connection ever since the night they met, and she didn't have it in her to resist its pull right now, not after the day she had just lived through.

Gently Jamie tugged her closer, and Emma was glad she didn't seem to need to talk either. They simply walked the dog and looked at the light fading from the sky and listened to the sound of the waves coming and going somewhere below them.

They didn't get another chance to talk until bedtime. Then, as soon as they were snuggled up together as usual with Jamie's arms around her and the darkness pressing in, Emma said, "Thank you for being here."

"You're welcome."

"I almost lost it up on stage, but then I saw you looking at me and I knew I could do it."

"Yeah? 'Cause I totally thought you were going to freak out and pull a Ty."

Emma smiled a little. "So did I, to be honest."

"You did an amazing job, though, you know?"

"Thanks." The truth was, she did know. To her surprise, once she'd gotten going—and in spite of the occasion—she had actually enjoyed being up there in front of all those people. Another way she was like her father, apparently. He'd always liked public speaking.

"So was that woman who left at the end the one your dad…?"

Emma exhaled. "Yeah. I still can't believe she had the nerve to show up."

"I don't know. I kind of feel sorry for her. You can't help who you fall in love with."

"True. But you can help who you fall in bed with." As soon as the words were out, she realized her timing could have been better, given the fact they were currently lying wrapped around each other in her bed. "Anyway, who would have thought a memorial service would have so much drama? I'm sorry again about Justin."

"I told you, you don't have to be sorry. You're not responsible for his actions."

She knew she wasn't, but Jamie might feel differently if she could see the big picture. Wouldn't telling her only send more mixed signals, though? More mixed than, say, cuddling with her in bed every night and then pretending each morning that it hadn't happened? She burrowed deeper into Jamie's arms, seeking the sense of safety she provided so easily, so willingly. So selflessly.

Selfless. Emma shivered a little, and Jamie hugged her tighter.

"What?"

"You know how I read that quote from Robert Ingersoll about character?"

"Yeah."

"I told my dad a couple of months ago that he was pretty much completely lacking in character because I knew how much it would hurt him."

She didn't mention they'd been arguing about her. What was it about Jamie that provoked the people in her life? No, the *men* in her life. Her mother had shown Jamie nothing but kindness, as had Ty. But her brother was still a boy, really.

"Were you talking about the affair?" Emma nodded, and Jamie added, "Well, he did lie and cheat, so…"

"I know, but that's not the sum of who he was. It's funny, today I actually felt like I was the one lying. I get that his purpose was greater than being my father, but I wish I could have said the truth."

"Which is?"

"That being his daughter hurt. But those people today didn't want to hear that I don't think he was a saint. They don't want to know that I think he thrived on the power of being a surgeon, that he liked having control over other people's lives."

"Couldn't he be all those things and still be what you said he was? Selfless and like, overall a good person?"

"Yeah, I think he is. Was," she corrected herself. "My mom is one of the smartest people I know, and she was able to take him back and trust him again. I guess it's that today I felt like I had to focus solely on the good, and that feels dishonest because of where he and I are. *Were.* You know?"

"I think so."

Emma paused. Then: "Jamie."

"What?"

"You don't have to tell me what I want to hear just because it was my father's funeral today."

"Actually, that's exactly why I have to tell you what you want to hear."

She smiled in the dark. "You're a good egg."

"A good egg?"

"It's something this girl on the national team always says. She's from New York though, so…"

"Those right coasters are weird."

"Aren't they?"

Emma pictured Tori, born and bred in upstate New York, and realized she hadn't thought much about her in the last few days, not even when she pulled on her pilfered T-shirt at night. Which was strange—when she was with Jamie, she barely thought about Tori, while at camp, Jamie was always on her mind, even when she flirted with Tori. Maybe especially then.

Jamie's breath tickled her neck. "You know, it does get easier. Right now it's probably hard to imagine, but the pain lessens. It's almost like you get used to it, or like a callus grows over the bruise. If you press hard enough, you can still feel the pain. But normal, everyday use? You don't even notice after a while."

Emma found Jamie's hand. "Justin pressed hard enough, didn't he?"

She was quiet for so long Emma thought she might not answer. Then: "Yeah, I guess so. But mostly I think I was worried about you."

Emma closed her eyes. Here Jamie was putting herself in potential bodily harm for her, and she was thinking about hooking up with Tori. Maybe she was more like her dad than she wanted to believe. "Well, thanks for having my back."

"Thanks for having mine."

She wanted to tell Jamie she always would, but she didn't trust herself to keep such a promise. So she didn't say anything at all, just tried to live in the present moment where Jamie made her feel safe while outside the wind picked up, roaring off the

water and across the shore, bending already stooped
evergreens a little more with every passing minute.

CHAPTER TEN

The train station was in a "not so great" part of the city, Emma told her as they trolled the streets at the edge of Seattle's downtown district looking for parking. Jamie knew she should help look for a spot, but she couldn't concentrate on meters or the flow of pedestrians in the blocks immediately south of Seattle's skyscrapers. She was leaving in less than an hour, and she wasn't sure when—if?—she would see Emma again.

Without any help from her, Emma soon had the car parked and was leading the way to the train station, Jamie's duffle over her shoulder.

"I can get it," Jamie said again, trying to take the bag.

Emma swatted her hand. "Stop it. I'm bigger than you, remember?"

"I'm taller."

"Barely. And you, my beanpole friend, are still filling out."

Beanpole? Did Emma really think of her like that? Jamie frowned and walked along the street block, the arc of the new Seahawks stadium visible beyond the old train station's tall, thin clock tower. A clock, incidentally, that most definitely did not reflect the correct time, unless she had somehow missed her train by more than a little.

"Don't worry," Emma said before she could check her watch. "That clock has been frozen forever. The other side is stuck on a different time, if you can believe it."

Jamie shrugged, still smarting from the beanpole comment. You didn't call someone that if you were remotely interested in them. Her shoulders dipped slightly. She had been convinced she was reading the signs correctly since arriving in Seattle. Emma almost had to like her as much as she liked Emma, didn't she? Why else would they snuggle at night and hold hands when they walked the dog after dinner? That morning she'd awakened to find Emma holding her from behind, and she'd been sure Emma was awake. She'd almost rolled over to ask her what was going on, to demand an explanation for all of the contradictory signals she'd been sending all week. But she'd chickened out, just as she'd done the day before and the day before that, and now any hope she'd had of Emma returning her feelings had collapsed under the weight of a single word.

As they approached the station, Jamie straightened her shoulders. For the last twenty-four hours, she'd fixated on their imminent goodbyes, dreading the moment she would have to leave Emma. Now, though, she was almost relieved that she was going. A few hours on the train and she would be back with her club team friends, not one of whom inspired even a smidgeon of the angst Emma generated with every look and touch. Even better, she would be back on the soccer field where feelings didn't matter and the only time someone held your hand was either to wish you luck before the match or to congratulate you on a game well played.

Inside the station, they double-checked the departure board—still on time—and found an empty bench in the waiting room.

"So," Emma said, toying with the zipper on Jamie's duffle, "did you remember the book?"

The night before, Emma had given her a copy of John

Muir's *The Mountains of California.*

"I thought you said your father gave you this?" Jamie had protested, smoothing her palm across the well-worn cover.

Emma had waved her off. "I know you'll take good care of it. Besides, we have other copies."

Now Jamie nodded. "Do you want it back? It's okay if you changed your mind."

"No. I told you, I want you to have it."

At Emma's throat, Jamie caught a glimpse of the sun pendant she'd given her peeking out from under the collar of her crewneck sweatshirt. *I always wear it,* she'd said the morning of her father's funeral. What did that mean? What did any of it mean?

She squinted as the loud speaker crackled. This was it. Her train was boarding. Before she could think it through, she blurted, "Can I ask you something?" just as Emma said, "I have to tell you something."

They both stopped. It wasn't the first time they'd talked over each other. Especially when they were debating soccer tactics or referee calls, their words sometimes collided. But this was different. Jamie remembered the passage Emma had quoted from the book tucked away in her backpack, something about not knowing how much of the "uncontrollable" we have inside, urging us up dangerous heights. That was how she felt right now—like she was climbing without a rope and one slip would send her crashing down the mountain.

"You first," she said.

Emma shook her head. "No, you go."

"That's okay."

"Jamie, I'm serious. What did you want to ask?"

She stared at Emma, questions cycling through her mind: *What are we doing? How do you feel about me? Will I ever see you again?* Then she reminded herself for easily the tenth time in half as many days that now was not the time to ask those questions, no matter how much she might want answers. She settled for a less messy one: "Are you going to be okay?"

Emma closed her eyes for a moment, her shoulders slumping. "I don't know," she admitted. And when she opened her eyes, she was crying again, the tears slipping soundlessly across her cheeks.

Jamie tugged Emma to her feet and hugged her, closing her eyes against the curious stares of the people around them. This was how the visit had begun, her holding Emma and comforting her.

"I'm going to miss you so much," Emma whispered.

"I'm going to miss you, too. But we'll see each other again," she said, trying to sound more positive than she felt.

"When?" Emma pushed away slightly, clenched fists resting against Jamie's chest. "We both have school and club and the national team, and I leave for North Carolina the first week of August."

"August? But school doesn't start until September."

"Pre-season, Jamie. Soccer starts early."

She stared at Emma. "Are you saying this is it? I'm not going to see you again before you leave?"

"I don't know. Maybe." She smoothed her hands across the front of Jamie's fleece. "But that's not what I want."

"What do you want? Because honestly, Emma, I have no idea." Jamie held her breath. She hadn't meant to ask. She wasn't even sure she wanted to know the answer.

Emma looked up at her, hazel eyes dark. "I don't know," she admitted.

And there it was. Jamie reached for her hands, holding them briefly before stepping away. "Then maybe it's time you figure it out." It came out more harshly than she'd intended, but she didn't have time to fix this. Her train was being called again. She reached for her bags.

"Wait," Emma said, gripping her sleeve. "Don't leave like this. Please, Jamie. You can't be mad at me."

Actually, she could. But then she remembered that Emma had been angry with her father when he died and now they would never have a chance to make up. God, what was she doing? Emma had been nothing but good to her practically since the moment they met. She was supposed to be returning that goodness, not punishing her for how she felt. Or, more accurately, how she didn't feel.

You can't help who you fall in love with, she remembered saying to Emma. What was equally true was that you couldn't help not falling in love with someone, either.

"Come on then." As Emma gazed at her uncertainly, she added, "Walk me to my train?" And she held out her duffel bag.

Nodding quickly, Emma took the bag and followed her from the waiting room down the stairs to the track number printed on her ticket, where a shiny Amtrak train idled. As they reached the platform, Jamie turned and took the duffel, dropping it beside her backpack. Then she pulled Emma into her arms and hugged her tightly again, stroking her hair the way her own mom used to do when she was younger. Emma sighed, hiding her face in her fleece.

They stood together while people streamed around them until finally Jamie said, "No snot this time, okay? This one's not waterproof."

Emma squeezed her waist and pulled away a little. "Jerk."

"For future reference, I'm not mad at you."

Emma's brow furrowed. "Are you sure?"

"Completely. I'm mad at this." She waved between them. "I'm mad that you live so far away. I'm mad that you're graduating and I'm not. I'm mad that I might never see you again."

"You'll see me again," Emma said, her voice soft. "You're

my anchor, remember? And I'm yours."

Jamie nodded, gazing down at her. "I hope so. Emma, I…" But she stopped. There were so many reasons she couldn't tell her. So many really good and really awful reasons.

"I know," Emma said, reaching up to touch her cheek. "Me, too."

And then before Jamie could guess her intent, Emma leaned up and pressed their lips together, her thumb sliding gently across her cheek.

What the… The thought trailed off as her eyes closed against a rush of sensations. Emma's lips were soft against hers, their touch as gentle as the hand at Jamie's waist. She could almost feel the care emanating off of Emma, the tenderness in the way she cradled Jamie's body lightly against her own as if she were something delicate to be treasured. No one had ever touched her the way Emma did, which shouldn't have been a surprise because Emma was the only person who had ever looked at her like she actually saw—and appreciated—all of her. And somehow it didn't really matter that she didn't know what she was doing or that her hands were resting uncertainly on Emma's shoulders or…

All at once, Emma backed away. "Oh my god, I shouldn't have—I'm so sorry." And then she turned and rushed away, taking the steps back up to the station two at a time.

At first Jamie only stared after her, too stunned to do anything else. Then her brain kicked into gear and she called, "Emma, wait! *Emma!*"

She wasn't sure if Emma heard her. If she did, it didn't stop her from pushing through the station doors and vanishing from sight. Jamie watched the doors as if they might magically re-open and spit Emma back out. What the hell had just happened?

"Final boarding call for Amtrak Cascades with service to Portland, now departing from track two," the loud speaker crackled. At least, that was what she thought it said. She was still in shock. Emma had *kissed* her. Emma Blakeley had kissed *her*—and then promptly run away. How was that even possible? The kissing part, that is. The running away part seemed all too conceivable. Jamie wanted to go after her so badly that she actually took a step toward the stairs. But then she stopped. The night train to Portland was sold out, which was why she'd promised her parents she would be on this one. The tournament started in the morning and there was no way she could miss the first game. She had promised her coach, too.

Reluctantly she shouldered her bags and stepped onto the train, soon settling in a window seat in an empty row. The trip would take close to five hours, but the train hadn't even made it out of the station before she was on her phone dialing Emma. After three rings the call went to voicemail, which meant Emma was either on the phone freaking out to Dani or she'd hit "ignore" when she saw who was calling.

Crap. Jamie leaned her forehead against the window and ended the call. She couldn't leave a voicemail. What would she say? "Um, hey, I know you kissed me and pulled a Ty, but I'd really love to talk to you right now and I'm hoping the feeling is mutual."

Yeah, no thanks.

And yet, she couldn't go to Portland without knowing where they stood, either. She typed a quick text: "Call me? Please?"

After she hit send, she stared at her phone, chewing on her lower lip. She waited five full minutes, touching the power button every time it started to shut off automatically. Five minutes was a lifetime when you had nothing to occupy your brain. Why wasn't Emma answering? Maybe she wasn't near her phone. But the three-rings-to-voicemail situation suggested otherwise.

To distract herself from the soap opera twilight zone her life had entered, Jamie dug into her backpack and pulled out

The Mountains of California. Might as well give Muir a whirl. But after a few minutes of reading the first page of the first chapter ("The Sierra Nevada") with little to no reading comprehension, she closed the book and looked out the window again, watching as the train traveled farther from the industrial heart of the city.

Emma had kissed her. She touched her mouth, remembering the feel of the other girl's lips on hers, soft and warm and tasting of Emma's vanilla lip balm. She hadn't known a kiss could be so sweet. Then again, the only thing she had to compare it to was that atrocious spin-the-bottle experience in eighth grade. Michael Henley's braces had ensured a semi-painful experience, while Trey Renshaw's kiss had been so fleeting that she didn't think it counted. And, of course, there was France. But that definitely didn't count.

"Come on, Emma," she murmured, checking her phone again. "Where are you?"

There was still no response, so she pulled out her iPod and tuned it to the playlist Emma had made her for her birthday, humming along to Pearl Jam's "Wishlist" while she stared out at gray clouds flitting over the gray-green landscape. *I know*, Emma had said. And, *Me too*. What did that mean? Why had she freaked out so badly? It wasn't like Jamie had put the moves on her.

And yet now that she was on the train to Portland, she almost wished she had. In bed that morning, she could have turned to Emma and kissed her. She had heard Emma breathing, heard what sounded like the flutter of eyelashes against the pillow they shared. But neither of them had moved until Ty banged on the door and told them they better be decent because he was coming in. At that, Emma had leapt out of bed, run to the door, and thrown it open. The only sign of her brother, though, was his laughter echoing up the stairs.

"Little bastard," Emma had muttered as she closed the door.

By then Jamie's feet were on the floor, arms stretched over her head as she yawned. She'd thought she caught Emma's eyes on the strip of skin her raised tank top revealed, but the other girl had turned away quickly and headed for the bathroom. And that was that.

Now she wished she could have the moment back. Wished she could rewind the clock and wake up all over again in the still-dark room with Emma's arms around her, their heads resting on the same pillow. She had felt so safe in Emma's bed, enveloped by her warmth, surrounded by her. Safer than any other moment she could remember in the past year, in fact.

Nirvana came on, Kurt Cobain singing his famous, unintelligible lyrics about teen spirit, and the memory of feeling safe evaporated. She skipped to the next song, but it wasn't much better—STP's "Interstate Love Song," with lyrics that were a little too close for comfort: leaving on a southbound train, someone lied, time to say goodbye. She paused the music and returned to the main menu, looking for something that wouldn't make her feel quite so hopeless. Tracy Chapman. That was the ticket. She sang sad songs, but somehow Jamie still managed to feel quasi-optimistic after listening to her.

She closed her eyes against the Western Washington scenery and hummed along with "Fast Car," wishing she was back in Emma's car beside her heading anywhere Emma wanted to take her.

By the time she reached Portland, Jamie was starting to feel more than a little pissed that she hadn't heard from Emma. Her friend Amy and her mom met her and brought her to the hotel where the team was staying, and still Jamie's phone stayed silent. All through dinner in downtown Portland with a couple of other families—pasta, for the ultimate in carbo loading— the only texts she got were from people other than Emma. She kept her phone next to her as she and Amy and a couple of other girls watched television and played cards after dinner, but nothing. Finally, right before she went to sleep in a hotel bed next to a girl who was most certainly the wrong girl, she let her anger flare and texted: "Seriously, Emma?" But there was no quick reply, no answer at all before she shut off her phone.

Soccer did what it always did—took her out of her head and located her inside her body, where she became the action required of her in any given situation: sprinting, tackling, resting, passing, crossing, shooting. She had played with these girls for two years now and knew them better than some of her high school teammates. On the field they were aggressive, all hard tackles and harder goals, while off the field they were goofy. Someone was usually playing a prank on someone else, or telling a joke, or wearing pre-wrap or pony tail holders in unusual, amusing ways. There were teasing remarks about flub-ups on the field, snarky comments about significant others, elaborate jokes about bodily functions, and Jamie joined in as she always did because what was she going to do, allow Emma to ruin the tournament? Not even.

At breaks in the action, though, she couldn't help checking her phone, surprised a little less each time by Emma's continued lack of contact. Jamie didn't text her again, didn't call her either. Emma knew how to get in touch if she wanted to. Clearly she didn't want to. *Asshole*, she found herself thinking at the end of the second full day of silence. Clearly Emma Blakeley and Justin Tate deserved each other. But thoughts of Justin felt sticky, precarious somehow, so she pushed them away, trying to live in the present moment of rainy soccer fields and uncomplicated team friendships.

The weekend arrived and so did her parents, and Seattle receded further until it seemed like an episode completely removed from normal time and space. In a way, maybe it was. Her parents tried to talk to her about Emma and the memorial service, but she dodged their questions, telling them she needed to stay focused on soccer for now. And she did. But it was easier said than done, especially at night in the darkened hotel room she shared with three other girls, none of whom seemed to have any problem whatsoever falling asleep after a long day of soccer.

On the field she channeled her frustration into the game, and it seemed to work—except for the yellow card she received near the end of one match for talking back to the referee. Pete benched her for the last ten minutes, and she sat on the grass glaring at the field while Shoshanna's voice droned in the back of her head. And she knew her inner therapist was right, fully recognized that while anger might seem easier to process than hurt, at some point she would need to stop fuming and deal. Just, not yet.

When her team won the final match on Sunday morning, her first thought was to text Emma, which only pissed her off more. After a brief celebration with her teammates and their families, they started the long drive back to California. She alternately slept in the back seat and stared out the window at the passing scenery, trying not to think about her silent phone. Without soccer to throw herself into, it was harder to avoid the hurt lurking beneath the surface. Her parents weren't helping, either. They kept asking about her time in Seattle, trying to draw her into conversation, but when she still only replied in monosyllables and the occasional short sentence, they finally stopped pushing.

When they got home late that night, she helped her parents unload the car, and it was almost like she'd never been away at all. Except that instead of texting Emma to let her know she was home, she set about unpacking sweaty soccer gear and getting her school stuff ready for the next morning. It was after eleven when she heard it: her phone's text alert. She tried not to, but she couldn't help it—she dropped the shin guard she was holding and practically leapt across her bedroom to the dresser where her phone was recharging.

"Are you home?" Amanda had written.

Amanda. Jamie's shoulders fell. To be honest, she'd all but

forgotten about her. She stared at the message, and then the text notification went off again, startling her so much that she actually jumped a little, her eyes widening as Emma's name flashed across the small screen. Finally. Only now that Emma had reached out to her, she wasn't sure she wanted to know what the message said. What if Emma told her to stop calling and texting? What if she never wanted to hear from her again?

She paced the room a couple of times before stopping near the dresser. This was ridiculous. She was being a chicken. She had survived worse things than a potential brush-off from Emma Blakeley. She sat down on the edge of her bed, took a deep breath, and opened the message.

"I'm sorry."

She was sorry? For what, exactly? For generally being a dick, or for specifically freaking out and vanishing off the face of the earth? Jamie shook her head, glaring at the glowing words. What the hell was wrong with her? You couldn't kiss someone and then not to talk to them for four effing days and then text a cryptic, two-word apology. It wasn't okay, not any of it.

Her fingers hovered over the keys as her mind cycled through potential responses: "Go to hell." Okay, maybe a tad too harsh. "I don't care." Obviously untrue. "Are you fucking kidding me?" Better, but too similar to her last message, which stared out at her above the majorly belated apology: "Seriously, Emma?"

She thought about how it had felt to wait all weekend to receive even those two measly words from Emma. Well, now it was *her* turn to wait.

As the phone shut down, Jamie considered smoking up and crashing into a dreamless sleep. The idea was tempting, but she had come so far from her toke-and-sleep days and didn't want to slide backwards now. Instead, she headed down the hall and knocked on her sister's door.

"Come in," Meg called.

Walking into Meg's room always felt like entering a

different world. Whereas her own room was decorated with posters that featured female athletes in beautiful outdoor locations accompanied by captions like, "The task ahead of you is never greater than the strength within you," each of her sister's bedroom walls was painted a different primary color barely visible beneath the multitude of band posters.

Meg was seated at her desk, laptop open in front of her. When she saw Jamie in the doorway, she turned sideways in her chair. "What up, little chick?"

Jamie ignored the old nickname that used to drive her crazy. It absolutely didn't remind her of homo- and transphobic Justin Tate. "Are you busy?"

"Working on physics homework I left for the last minute. But by all means, distract me if you so choose." And she waved at the bed.

Jamie dropped onto her sister's bed and leaned against the headboard, hugging her knees to her chest. "Emma and I held hands all week and she kissed me at the train station and now we're apparently not talking."

Meg stared at her. "Holy hell, James. I thought you were going to a funeral, not guest-starring on *The L Word*."

"I know." Jamie groaned, hiding her face against the top of her knees. Then she grimaced. She'd forgotten about the already purpling bruise on her right kneecap, a memento from that morning's game.

"So I guess this means you're breaking up with Amanda," Meg commented.

"Dude, I've never broken up with anyone before. How does it even work?"

Her sister looked at the ceiling briefly before glancing back at her. "Well, typically you would figure out what you want to say ahead of time, and then you would meet her someplace neutral and have the conversation."

"So you're saying I can't text her?" Jamie asked, even

though she was pretty sure she already knew the answer.

"Um, you can if you want to be a TOTAL DICK. Jesus, Jamie. Now start at the beginning. What the hell happened up there?"

It took a while to summarize the past ten days. Meg listened quietly to her less-than-linear recap, making sympathetic comments here and there and doing a generally good job of not rolling her eyes. Only at the end did she finally lose it.

"She kisses you and takes off?" she sputtered. "What the fuck? Who does that?"

"I know, right? I called and texted a couple of times, but she's been doing the radio silence thing since I left. At least, up until about fifteen minutes ago."

"What happened fifteen minutes ago?"

"She sent me a text that says, 'I'm sorry.'"

"That's it?" Meg snorted. "Speaking of being a total dick..."

Jamie squinted at her sister. Hearing Meg call Emma names didn't feel the same as thinking them herself. "I don't know that she's being a total dick. Her dad did just die."

"That doesn't mean she gets to screw with your head."

"Yeah, but this whole thing is partially my fault, too."

"What? How?"

Jamie hesitated. "I might have told her on the phone that I loved her." She winced pre-emptively, waiting for her sister's reaction.

Meg frowned. "Before or after the kiss?"

"Before. The night her dad died, actually."

"As in love, love?"

"I don't know. We didn't talk about it." She paused. "Though she did kind of say it back."

Meg came over to the bed and sat down next to her. "Wow. Okay. That changes things."

They were both quiet. Then Jamie said, "She's so messed up about her dad. I wanted to take all of the hurt away, you know? But I think maybe I made things worse."

"I doubt that."

"No, I did. I mean, I got in a fight with her ex at her dad's funeral. Who does that?"

"Someone on *The L Word*?"

"That was rhetorical, you ass."

"Right. Sorry. Anyway, that sounded more like his deal than yours."

"Maybe. She did defend me against him. She was pretty fierce, to be honest." Not as fierce as Justin, but still, Jamie had appreciated Emma's protectiveness even if it had only ended up antagonizing the future frat boy further.

"I could see that." Meg took a breath. "As your big sister, can I just say that it sucks that you have to be collateral damage in her existential crisis?"

Jamie rested her chin on her uninjured knee. "I know. And I know what I would say if you told me a guy was acting like this, but this is different. Emma is different. She's been so good to me. She genuinely cares about me, Meg."

"In what capacity, though?"

Jamie hugged her legs tighter. "I don't know. I'm not even sure she knows."

"And is that good enough for you?"

"Of course not. But no one forced me to figure myself out. I don't want to be the one who tries to force her."

"But—"

Jamie held up a hand. "Emma is going through the worst period of her entire life. I can't begin to know what it feels like to be her right now. Can you?"

Meg shook her head reluctantly. "No. But if she hurts you…"

"She already has and she's probably going to again. Not because she wants to but because she leaves for UNC in a few months. And you know what? Even knowing that, I still wouldn't trade our friendship. Not for anything."

As she said it, she realized she was revealing a truth she hadn't recognized herself until that very moment. This was why she had come to talk to her sister. At some level, she'd known it would help her figure out what was going on inside her own head.

"Maybe I should go see Shoshanna," Meg said, slipping her arm around Jamie's shoulders. "Because damn, girl, you seem like you have your shit together these days."

"It's mostly an act. Which isn't to say that Shoshanna isn't awesome."

A little while later, Jamie got ready for bed, pausing in her parents' doorway to say goodnight.

"Everything okay with you, honey?" her mother asked from where she sat in bed beside Jamie's dad, a library book open on her lap. She adored historical mysteries, and this week's cover featured yet another queen (or was it a princess this time?) in rich reds and golds, her clothes and jewelry painted in vivid detail.

"Not exactly," Jamie admitted. "But I talked to Meg and it will be, I think."

Her dad smiled at her over the top of his laptop. "Good. Don't forget you see Shoshanna on Wednesday this week instead of Friday."

"I won't. Goodnight. Love you guys."

"Love you," they said in unison.

In her room, Jamie grabbed her phone and crawled into bed, yawning as she waited for the screen to flicker back to life. While brushing her teeth, she'd decided it would be petty to punish Emma for the days upon days of silence. Besides, she wasn't sure she could get to sleep knowing that Emma might be lying awake waiting for her reply.

"Okay," she typed. "But what does that actually mean?"

Emma answered right away. "It means I'm an asshole."

"No argument here." She almost sent an emoji to soften it. Almost. "What are you sorry for?"

"For kissing you like that. Given your history and all."

Her history? Oh. *Oh.* "I was fine with the kiss," she typed, briefly reflecting on the severity of that understatement. "It was the running away that was less fine. And being blown off. That wasn't so great either."

"I know. I freaked out. I'm really sorry."

"So you've said."

There was a pause before Emma's next text arrived: "I miss you."

What was she supposed to say to that? Despite what she'd told her sister about giving Emma time to process, she wasn't sure she could—or even should—if Emma was going to say things like that. Besides, it had been four days. That was enough time, wasn't it?

"Why did you kiss me?" she typed, and then let her finger hover over the send button for a good thirty seconds before launching the message out into the cellular universe.

Radio silence, more than a half minute's worth, ensued. She waited, trying to ignore the pessimistic little voice at the back of her head. Emma was most certainly not going to disappear on her again so soon. She had started this conversation. She wouldn't skip out in the middle.

Her phone vibrated at last. "Because I'd been wanting to for a while."

Jamie's heart rate speeded up. So she hadn't been misreading the signals. "*So had I,*" she typed, but then deleted the admission and wrote, "Why did you freak out?"

The answer came faster this time. "Because I was scared of

hurting you. I don't want to lose you."

"*I don't want to lose you either...*" Delete. She tried again. "*I'm scared too...*" Delete, delete. Finally, she settled on a different kind of truth: "I don't think we get to keep each other, though. Do you?"

Her reply took a while again. "No. I guess not."

Jamie read the words over again, her throat tightening. She could almost see Emma in her bedroom with the wide windows overlooking the Sound, could practically feel the firmness of the mattress and the smooth wood of her headboard and the warmth of Emma's body pressed against hers. But even though she knew exactly what it felt like to be there with her, even though they had slept night after night with their arms around each other in the dark, Emma wasn't hers. Probably she never would be.

Another message arrived: "I have to go. My mom is being a hard-ass about school tomorrow. She says hi, by the way, and congrats on winning."

"How did she know?"

"We kept track online."

Knowing that Emma and her mom and probably Ty, too, had been following her team's progress all weekend made Jamie's throat tighten even more.

"Thanks," she replied lamely. "Tell her hi back. Ty too. Talk to you soon?"

"I hope so. And Jamie, just because we don't get to keep each other doesn't mean I don't wish we could."

It took her a second to translate the double negatives. When she did, her eyes blurred and she bit her lip hard. *Damn it.*

"Same here," she finally admitted. "Sweet dreams."

"Sweet dreams to you too. Miss you."

"Miss you too." *I love you.* She didn't write it, though. Neither, she noticed, did Emma.

She turned her phone off and lay back in her bed, the soft murmur of her parents' voices audible from down the hall. Emma had feelings for her and didn't want to lose her, either. Jamie knew this realization should have had her floating on a haze of happiness, but she couldn't shake the not-so-niggling feeling that all was not rainbows and sunshine. Because if Emma had wanted to kiss her for a while, why hadn't she done it sooner? Was it Jamie's "history" that had stopped her? Could she not stand the idea of being with someone who was damaged?

A thud from her sister's room distracted her. Jamie had apparently inherited all of the athletic genes their parents had to offer because Meg was a klutz, always dropping her music cases and tripping over assorted furniture. Maybe they got along so well because they were opposites, or maybe she'd just gotten lucky when it came to the family she'd been born into.

Luckier than Emma, that was for sure. Even though the world believed David Blakeley had been a great man, Jamie would never see him that way. It wasn't that he had looked at her the one time they'd met as if he didn't want her anywhere near his daughter. It was more that he had made his daughter feel like *he* didn't want to be anywhere near *her*. Great that he'd saved the lives of hundreds if not thousands of children. Fantastic that he'd donated time and money to deserving causes around his community. Awesome that his politics were progressive and enlightened. None of that altered the fact that he'd allowed his own children to think that they weren't good enough. He'd made them question his love for them, and she didn't think she would ever forgive him for that.

Not that he had cared what she thought. If anyone had been happy that she and Emma were headed in different directions, it would have been Emma's father. She had no doubt about that.

Tiny glowing words appeared against her closed eyelids: *I don't want to lose you.* And she had responded by telling Emma that they didn't get to keep each other. God, she was such an idiot. Emma had answered her questions bravely and honestly. Why couldn't she have been brave, too?

Except she knew why. The last few days of not knowing if Emma would ever talk to her again had been awful. As in, legitimately distressing. She would rather live in the same old limbo than risk freaking Emma out again. At least this way they could stay friends. Couldn't they?

#

"It looks like we have a new face." Mr. Eckhart, Shorecrest's journalism teacher, smiled encouragingly at Emma. "It's been a while, so why don't we all introduce ourselves? Please say your name, why you're here, and an interesting fact people may or may not know about you. Preferred gender pronouns are helpful, and of course, if you'd like, you can share how you identify. But there's no pressure to do so."

Emma sat at a desk at the fringe of the circle in the Graphic Arts classroom watching as each of the twenty or so members of her high school's Gay-Straight Alliance introduced themselves. She recognized many of them but not all. In a school of eighteen hundred, there were bound to be people she didn't know. Most offered a silly fact that made everyone laugh, many willingly shared how they identified—what was *pan*, she wondered after the third person invoked it—and everyone said which gender pronouns they preferred.

It had only been a few weeks since she spoke to a crowd of hundreds at her father's memorial service, and yet as her turn came closer, she could feel her hands trembling. She sat on them to keep herself from fidgeting, planning out her words and practicing them in her head. It was ridiculous to be this nervous. No one had even looked surprised when she entered the classroom before the meeting. Why would they? In the two weeks since spring break had ended, more than one of her friends had reported that Josh and Justin were both telling anyone who would listen—in person, online, anywhere, really—that she was a lesbian, although that wasn't the term they preferred.

Yet despite all the rumors, somehow attending this meeting felt like a dangerous act. Which, again, was silly. She'd spent a week flirting shamelessly with Tori and another week actually sharing a bed with Jamie. Still, hanging out in private with self-avowed lesbians—and even kissing one—wasn't the same as publicly declaring your otherness. Dani had offered to come to the meeting with her for moral support, but she'd insisted she wanted to do this on her own, at least the first time. What the hell had she been thinking?

When it was her turn, she cleared her throat and said, "I'm Emma. I've actually wanted to check out a meeting for a while. My preferred pronouns are she and hers, um, I can name all fifty states in alphabetical order, and I-I don't really label myself."

"Welcome, Emma," the group responded, many smiling in her direction, and she nodded back.

A girl she recognized from the volleyball team went last, and then Mr. Eckhart turned the meeting over to the student leader, Ricky Gonzalez, who she was pretty sure she remembered from middle school as a girl with long hair but who now had next to no hair, a pierced eyebrow, and preferred male gender pronouns.

Ricky went over the agenda. First was reading the club's mission, which basically stated that their club had three main purposes: (1) to create a fun and safe space for LGBTQ students and their allies to socialize; (2) to provide a safe space for LGBTQ students to address feelings and issues they faced on a day-to-day basis both at school and at home; and (3) to create a safer and more accepting school for LGBTQ students by educating teachers, administrators, fellow students, and others, changing school policies, and working to stop harassment and discrimination.

That was all. Was it even possible for a group this size to

effect such change? There were more people on the soccer team than in this room. And yet, she had to admit that GSA events—National Coming Out day in the fall, the GLSEN Day of Silence in the spring, and the monthly Queer Movie Night— were well publicized and well regarded by the rest of the school, for the most part. Apparently they were doing something right.

With the mission out of the way, they broke up into small discussion groups to talk about home life and any other relevant issues. This meant that Emma mainly listened to three kids she didn't know chat about people and places they obviously knew well. They were friendly, but blabbing to strangers wasn't her thing. Hell, she wasn't even that good at talking to people she cared about. Except maybe Jamie.

Once they'd rejoined the larger group again, Ricky made some announcements about the upcoming Day of Silence, the next movie night, and the annual queer prom in June on Capitol Hill. There were brief discussions on each of these topics before Ricky opened the floor.

Ashley, the girl Emma recognized from the volleyball team, raised her hand. "I was planning to bring up a bullying situation, but the person it impacts is here, so now I'm not sure if it's appropriate or not."

All eyes shifted to Emma, and she sat up straighter at her desk. This was definitely not how she'd seen her first GSA meeting going.

Mr. Eckhart frowned. "Does it affect other people in the school?"

Ashley nodded. "Not directly, but I think so."

Ricky spoke up. "Ash, I'm not sure talking about it in front of the entire group creates the safe space we're aiming for. Maybe you and I can meet afterward to brainstorm another approach."

"Is this about me?" Emma asked, her voice steadier than she expected.

Ashley nodded again. "I'm sorry, but it's starting to get out of hand."

Emma felt her face flush, and suddenly she wished she had never come. Who was she kidding? She didn't belong here. She stood up, slipping her purse strap over her shoulder. "It's fine. I can go."

"Wait, Emma, please," Ricky said. "If you're being bullied, we can do something about it. You wouldn't exactly be the first person in this room to be a target. Am I right, guys?"

Emma stopped, glancing around at the nodding, mostly supportive faces turned her way. Of course she wasn't the first person there to be harassed. Ricky was trans; Ashley and her girlfriend, a volleyball player who had already graduated, had gone to prom together the previous year; and other LGBTQ students openly wore their gender fluidity and homo- or bisexuality like armor as they navigated classes, hallways, and playing fields. Like Jamie, they were far braver than she had ever had to be.

"Okay," she said, and sat back down. "I'll stay."

"Good." Ricky smiled at her encouragingly. "Do you feel comfortable talking about what's going on, or would you rather Ashley go first?"

His calm, competent demeanor reminded her of Jamie. Maybe once you'd found your way to accepting yourself for being so profoundly different from the masses, it took more than name-calling to upset you.

"I can talk about it. I assume this is about my ex-boyfriend calling me a dyke?" she asked Ashley, stumbling only slightly over the epithet.

"Among other things. My little brother is on the soccer team, and he told me that there's a group of guys who are spreading some nasty rumors about you."

"What kind of rumors?" Emma's stomach churned, and all at once she wished she hadn't snarfed down that granola bar right before the meeting.

"I guess Justin told everyone that you begged him to take you back after spring break once your 'experiment' was over. Stuff like that."

Stuff like that—she could imagine the details of that particular fiction. God, why had she ever let him talk her into dating him? His "persistence" should have been a red flag; a guy who wouldn't take no for an answer was probably not someone you should go out with. But they'd grown up in each other's periphery, and he'd played the sweet, hot guy role almost perfectly—until he hadn't.

"I'm sorry," Ashley repeated. "I thought someone should do something, you know? He shouldn't be able to get away with it."

Emma nodded at her. "It's fine. I get it."

"Does anyone else have information to share about this situation?" Mr. Eckhart asked, but the room stayed quiet. "All right, then. Emma, Ashley, and Ricky, why don't we stay after and talk about this more in depth. In the meantime, let's open the floor back up."

A boy she recognized as the head of the debate club raised his hand. "I won my gay marriage arguments at our meet last weekend."

The group clapped and whistled appreciatively, and Emma could almost feel the relief in the room as the mood shifted. She joined in the applause, trying to tamp down the queasiness Ashley's revelation had caused. How did Jamie do this day in and day out? Maybe being out in an urban high school near San Francisco, queer capital of the entire freaking world, was easier than trying to do it in the Seattle suburbs. What would UNC be like? Was it even worth the fight? Dating guys was simpler in some ways, but if she let Justin and his buddies bully her back into the closet—assuming she had ever left it— wouldn't she be letting them win?

She remembered how Justin had called Jamie a freak, how

he had actually put his hands on her. Emma had tried to intervene but she had been powerless to stop him. And now here she was, tacitly letting him get away with bullying not only her but Jamie, too. She hadn't told her mom or anyone else what he'd done because of the unwritten jock code: Athletes don't rat out other athletes. If Ashley hadn't brought it up, Emma probably would have continued to stay silent, especially with graduation so close.

When the meeting adjourned, she and Ashley stayed behind to meet with Ricky and Mr. Eckhart. As it turned out, there was a system in place to deal with issues of this nature, one that Mr. Eckhart said had been used successfully in the school's recent past. If Justin had done what Ashley's brother said he had, then he would have to apologize, at the least.

"There's something else," Emma said. And then she told them about Justin's comments about Jamie's gender identity, about the way he had shoved her up against the pillar and would likely have done more given the chance.

"I'm sorry you and your friend had to go through that," the teacher said, shaking his head. "Were there other witnesses?"

Emma nodded.

"That's helpful. The incident might not have happened on school grounds, but you and Justin are both members of the campus community." He reached into the folder on his desk and pulled out a sheet of paper. "This outlines your options, Emma. Are you able to speak with your parents—sorry, you said you lost your father. Is your mother supportive?"

"She is, but I'd rather not bother her with this." She paused. "I don't have to pursue it if I don't want to, right?"

"Technically, no. But I wouldn't advise letting it go. Things like this contribute to a hostile environment for other LGBTQ students. You may be graduating, but most of the GSA members are coming back next year. Students like Justin need to know there are consequences for their behavior."

"Exactly," Ashley said. "We have to stand up to the bullies

if we ever want it to change."

Beside her, Ricky nodded. "I know it may not seem like it, Emma, but this isn't only about you and your girlfriend. It's about everyone in the GSA and all the kids out there who might not ever feel comfortable joining this group."

"Jamie's not—" she started. But then she realized it didn't matter how she defined their relationship. Justin had gone after them because he sensed they were more than friends, label or no label. "Can I have the weekend to think about it?"

"Of course," Mr. Eckhart said. "Stop by on Monday and we'll figure everything out."

Ashley walked out with her. As they headed for an exit at the back of the building, she touched Emma's shoulder. "Are you all right? I know that was a lot for your first meeting."

"No kidding. But yeah, I'll be fine."

"Do you think he'll retaliate?"

She pictured Justin. He had seemed so great in the beginning, smart and funny and nice even to her little brother, though Ty had told her after the first time he came over that he thought Justin seemed fake. She had attributed the comment to Ty's low-key skater vibe bumping up against the more assertive, preppy soccer player energy that Justin emanated. Now, though, she realized her brother had pegged her would-be boyfriend accurately on the first try.

What was he going to say when he heard about all of this? What would her mother say? Not like they didn't already have enough to deal with.

"Emma?" Ashley prodded.

"Oh, sorry." She shook her head as they neared the student parking lot. "I don't know if he'll retaliate or not. I didn't expect him to do any of this."

"People can definitely surprise you. And not always in a good way."

When they reached Emma's car, they discovered Dani

perched on a folding chair Emma knew came from her parents'
stash of soccer mom accessories.

"How's it going, Ashley?" Dani asked.

"Not bad. But it would be better if Justin Tate weren't such
an asshole."

"Sounds about right."

Dani waited until Ashley had said goodbye and walked off
to her own car to ask, "How did it go? Did you actually talk
about you and Jamie?"

"God, no."

Dani rolled her eyes as she stowed the camp chair in the
back of her Subaru. "That's right, the Ice Princess doesn't
share. How did Ashley know about Justin, then?"

"Her little brother plays soccer. And don't call me that."

"Sure thing, Princess. Are you doing the family thing for
dinner tonight?"

"Nope. Ty's at Benji's again and my mom's picking up
another double." As Dani's eyebrows rose, Emma added, "I
mean, it's not like she ever sleeps anyway."

"Which, to be honest, is a decent argument for not pulling
another double. Sushi?"

"Heck yeah. I can always do sushi."

An hour later, over dinner at the same restaurant where
they'd celebrated her birthday—ah, fall, before her father died
and Justin turned into an asshole and Emma basically accosted
Jamie—she relayed what had happened at the GSA meeting.

"Jesus," Dani said when she'd finished. "What are you
going to do?"

"I haven't decided yet. Any thoughts?"

"If it were me, I would go after him." Her tone was decisive.
"I would totally make him pay. What's the downside? We
graduate soon, and then you never have to see the phony
bastard again."

"One could only hope." She popped a few edamame beans out of their pod and into her mouth. "I don't know, though. Would it be too much for my mom? And Ty starts at Shorecrest next year. Is he going to get shit for being my little brother if I rat Justin out?"

Dani paused. "I hadn't actually thought of that."

"He would, wouldn't he?"

"Maybe. You know who you should talk to about all of this?" Dani wiggled her eyebrows.

"Who?" Emma tried to stare her down.

"You haven't called her yet, have you?"

"No." She and Jamie had texted or emailed nearly every day since spring break, but they hadn't spoken on the phone even once. Emma knew the ball was in her court mainly because she had received an email from Jamie that indicated as much.

"Em, you can't freeze her out the way you did Josh and Justin. She doesn't deserve it."

"I'm not freezing her out. I'm just, you know, taking a little space."

"You're the one who freaked out on her. Isn't she the one entitled to take space?"

Emma hadn't given Dani all of the details of her near split and tentative reconciliation with Jamie. For example, her best friend didn't know that Jamie was the one who had said they couldn't be together.

"Whatever. Can we change the subject? I'm sick of talking about my big, fat, gay life."

"I thought you didn't do labels?"

"Bite me."

"Kinky. But no thanks."

Emma threw an edamame shell at her, trying not to laugh. God, she loved Dani. But not in a gay way; in the way you loved your best friend since kindergarten who, though she didn't understand why or how you could be attracted to both sexes, accepted who you were because she loved you, too. Though not in a gay way, either.

After dinner they went to the indoor mall on Sixth Avenue, where they rode escalators and traipsed in and out of their favorite shops. On a whim they decided to see what movies were playing, and ended up going to see *Scooby Doo 2: Monsters Unleashed* even though "the first one was sooo bad!" The sequel was equally as atrocious, but they made the most of the nearly empty theater by keeping up a running commentary. On the way home, they stopped for ice cream on Capitol Hill and people-watched from a table near the window at Ben & Jerry's. Emma tried not to remember that the last time she'd been there had been with Jamie, the day before she kissed her and ruined everything.

"You're not going home by yourself tonight, are you?" Dani asked as they reached the ends of their cones.

She shrugged, picturing her house all dark and empty except for the dog.

"Come stay over," Dani said. "We never got to have that sleepover."

Because her dad had gone and died and Jamie had come to the rescue. Why did everything seem to come back to her?

"Okay. Let me text my mom."

And that was how a couple of hours later she ended up lying awake in Dani's bed while the other girl snored away, Lucy curled up on her dog pillow beside the bed. This room, with its cream walls and Pottery Barn furniture, was almost as familiar to her as her own. Strange to think that soon they would be in entirely different places. Dani had opted for the SoCal urban experience at UCLA, while she was headed to the unknown—the Southeast, where pickup trucks with Confederate flags adorning their hoods weren't all that unusual. Soccer had taken her to Texas and Florida fairly often, but during her visit last year, North Carolina had felt more foreign than Canada ever had. Fortunately, Chapel Hill was a university town. Like Atlanta, it was a liberal outpost in a conservative region. Or, as one of her future teammates had joked, "A progressive island floating in a sea of rednecks."

She'd shared that gem with her dad in the car on the way home from Sea-Tac after her visit, and he'd agreed wholeheartedly. He had spent time over the years in and around the "Research Triangle," as the Raleigh-Durham-Cary region was known, demonstrating his technique at area hospitals.

"You're going to love it there," he'd assured her as they drove toward home. "With Duke, UNC, and NC State all within a short distance of each other, there's always something going on. Just think about March Madness! I'll have to come out to see UNC versus Duke."

"And to see me play, of course," she'd said pointedly.

"Of course." He'd frowned. "That goes without saying, Emma."

With him so much had gone without saying, and now it was too late to ask. She hadn't known he worried about not seeing her grow up. When her mother said he was afraid of flying, she had assumed that meant he was scared of his own mortality. But at the memorial service Mike had said he wasn't afraid to die. He was afraid of missing his children's futures.

Jamie had reached for her hand at that point in the service, she remembered now, and she had moved out of reach. God, she'd been so selfish. She'd used Jamie to make herself feel better, pulling her close when she needed her and pushing her away when she didn't. And through it all, Jamie had been there for her, holding her hand when she let her and melting into the background at precisely the right moment. Well, the right moment if Emma wanted to stay in the closet, anyway. But after her eulogy, while her mother was up on stage, Emma had needed Jamie more than she'd worried about what everyone else thought. She'd leaned into her and held on tightly then, drawing on the strength that Jamie offered up so easily.

But was it easy? It definitely came at a price—Dani and Sian treating her like an interloper they hoped wouldn't linger long; Justin, assaulting her verbally and physically; Emma, kissing her and then, as Dani had said, freezing her out.

Unable to sleep, she slipped out of bed and grabbed her phone from the dresser. She carried it to the papa san chair near the window and turned it on, waiting impatiently for it to load. When it finally did she typed out a quick text: "Are you around at all this weekend? DC plays LA, and I was thinking maybe we could tape it and watch together at some point. Let me know. Sweet dreams."

She hit send and sat looking out the window. Dani lived in a neighborhood with street lamps and sidewalks and other houses within sight, only a few blocks from where her own family had lived before her father got famous. Residential, that was what her mother called it, while their current neighborhood was made up of private estates. What would life have been like if her father had never invented his technique? Would he have stayed healthier longer without the stress of constant travel to wear him down? Would they have lived here among other families with kids her and Ty's ages, instead of in that huge house on the side of a hill with mountains, water, and sky as far as you could see? That house didn't feel like home anymore, not without her dad.

And yet, she could still see Jamie stretching in the sunlight angling in her bedroom window, her bedhead adorable, her eyes shut tightly against the light. Even after her father died, the house had felt like home—as long as Jamie was in it.

She closed her eyes as a tear squeezed out. Only she wasn't sure who she was crying over: her dad or Jamie. Probably both. Because without either of them to anchor her in place, she didn't know where home was.

CHAPTER ELEVEN

"Pass the tape, will you?"

Jamie handed Meg the tape and watched her secure either end of the package, wrapping paper drawn up in perfectly square, even flaps. Then Meg added a ribbon and used the scissors blade to curl each strand.

"Crap." Jamie gazed down at her own slightly askew, ribbon-less wrapping job. "I think I'm missing a straight girl gene."

"Or two or three." Meg ducked as Jamie tossed a spare strip of wrapping paper at her. "Hey, it's the thought that counts, right?"

"Are you done yet?" Becky asked from the bed where she was reading *Rolling Stone* and critiquing their wrapping skills.

Their mom's birthday was the following day. Tonight, Saturday, they had come over to Becky's house, where they'd stashed their presents earlier in the week.

"Yes, oh patient one."

Becky ignored Meg's sarcasm. "Let's go then. I don't want to miss the first set."

A band Meg and Becky liked was playing an all-ages show

at a club in San Francisco, and Jamie was planning to check it out with a girl from her Spanish class. A week earlier, Faith had approached her at her locker and asked her out. The show would be their second date.

On the train into the city, she checked her reflection in the opposite window. She was wearing a black and white bowling shirt (her favorite thrift shop purchase ever) over a black tank top paired with close-fitting olive cargo pants and her usual Doc Marten's. She looked good, she thought, checking her profile.

"Easy, lady-killer," Becky said, elbowing her.

"Whatever. You're just jealous."

"Of you, or of her?"

Jamie looked at her quickly and saw the challenge in Becky's eyes. *Wait.* Becky was straight, wasn't she? Could Jamie really have missed something that important about her sister's best friend? Before she could decide what the look meant, Meg said something from Becky's other side and the moment passed.

Her phone buzzed and Jamie's heart leapt a little. But it was only Faith making sure the plan hadn't changed. She texted back and tucked her phone away. Emma was currently away at U-19 World Cup qualifying in Canada, and just like every other national team camp had only texted and emailed a few times. Even though Jamie understood why, it was hard not to worry when Emma stopped calling. No matter how temporary, the hiatus reminded her of the break they'd taken after her Seattle visit. They'd eventually started talking again, but things had never been quite the same as they were before Emma's dad died.

In a way, she was almost relieved that Emma was away at qualifiers right now. Dating was stressful enough without having to worry about how to talk to Emma about it. The last time she'd gone out with a girl, she'd ended up making her cry. Honestly, she would prefer to avoid repeating that experience if at all possible.

As Meg had suggested, Jamie had ended things with Amanda right after she got back from Portland. Only instead of simply accepting Jamie's declaration that she thought they'd be better off as friends, Amanda had asked if she was ending things because of Emma.

"I knew you had feelings for her. You slept with her, didn't you?" Amanda had demanded, brushing away a tear as they sat in her car outside Jamie's house.

Jamie had hesitated, trying to determine the line between sleeping with and *sleeping with* someone. "No, I didn't. I just realized while I was gone that I'm not sure I see a future with you." Which was completely true. So she might have told Emma she loved her and Emma might have kissed her. Amanda didn't really need to know those details, did she?

As Amanda turned her head away, her breath catching, Jamie had sat motionless, trying to resist the urge to open the car door and bolt away. She had never made anyone cry before, and she was tempted to take it all back, to tell Amanda never mind, they could keep hanging out after all. But then she remembered her sister threatening to tell Amanda what had happened in Seattle herself, and she tamped down on her decidedly unhelpful fix-it tendencies.

Faith was different, though. Jamie had liked her on and off for a while now. Maybe she would be exactly what she needed to finally move past her feelings for Emma.

As the train slowed for their stop, Jamie's phone buzzed again and she grabbed it, heart all aflutter for all the wrong reasons.

"Stop thinking about Emma," the text read.

Jamie leaned forward and flipped off her sister. Unlike Shoshanna, Meg wasn't oath-bound not to hit her over the head with how she believed she should be managing her life.

Meg did have a point, though, Jamie had to admit as she followed her sister and Becky from the train. She didn't want to be thinking about Emma tonight. Earlier in the day she'd scored a goal and assisted another at her club match, and now she was headed out on a date with a girl she actually thought she might want to kiss. Or not. Asexuality was a thing, wasn't it? *God.* Why had she agreed to come to the city tonight when she could have been getting high with Blair and watching *Independence Day* or *Lord of the Rings* for easily the hundredth time?

Faith was waiting for them on the corner with her own trio of girls decked out in ripped jeans and skater hoodies. She smiled when she saw Jamie, and Jamie's heart fluttered, this time for the right reasons. Faith had left her wavy brown hair down and flipped over one shoulder, and her hoodie hugged her curves nicely.

Okay, so maybe dating wasn't so bad, after all.

"Hey," Jamie said, giving Faith a casual nod. Blair and a couple of their skate park buddies had coached her up on how to play it cool with girls. Supposedly being stand-offish made them like you more.

Faith's smile dimmed a little, and she stayed with her friends as they made their way to the club.

"What are you doing?" Becky hissed.

"What do you mean?"

"Quit acting like a stupid boy and hold her hand."

"Are you sure?"

"Trust me," Becky said, and pushed her forward.

Faith's friends made room for her, and after a moment, Jamie worked up her nerve and reached for Faith's hand. The smaller girl glanced up at her, surprised, and then gave her a slow smile that set the butterflies to afluttering like crazy. She glanced over her shoulder at Becky, who winked at her.

Huh. Who would have thought Meg's BFF would be some kind of girl-whisperer?

At the club, Jamie bought Faith a soda and followed her to a table away from the others. The warm-up band was still getting set up, and it was quiet enough that they could talk.

"You had a game today, didn't you?" Faith asked, sipping her soda.

"Yeah, in Oakland." Jamie watched her lips close around the straw and wondered what it would be like to kiss her. Emma was still the only girl she had ever kissed, and she'd been too surprised to do much other than close her eyes and—*stop it*, she ordered herself, pushing the memory away.

"How did your team do?"

"We won," Jamie said. "What about you? How did you spend the day?"

"Visiting family in the city, which involves a lot of cooking, eating, and playing mahjong."

"On the computer or in real life?"

"In real life, of course," Faith said, laughing.

Jamie knew she hailed from a close-knit Filipino family with relatives spread throughout the Bay Area, including a ninety-one year old grandmother who lived in Excelsior not far from this club. Faith was out to her two sisters and a handful of cousins, but no one in the older generations knew she was gay.

They talked about their families and final exams—with only two weeks left in spring semester, their classes were down to the wire—until the music started, and then they drifted back to their group, standing near the center of the crowd. Faith slipped her hand into Jamie's and she relaxed into the other girl's touch, smiling as the lights went down, the crowd cheered, and the bass thudded through the small room. She could be happy with someone who wasn't Emma. This was proof, right?

During the third song, when Faith got bumped by a tall guy for the umpteenth time, she stepped in front of Jamie and leaned back into her. For a moment, Jamie stilled, remembering how it had felt to hold Emma at night, her face pressed into Emma's hair, arms around Emma's strong body that fit hers perfectly. Faith was smaller and rounder, and her hair smelled spicy rather than sweet. Tentatively, Jamie slipped her arms around Faith and was promptly rewarded with another dazzling smile.

In the darkness they swayed together, and when Faith reached back and palmed Jamie's hips, she managed not to flinch. No one had touched her there since France, and her attacker's grip hadn't exactly been a caress. Fortunately, this wasn't even remotely similar, she realized, relieved by the discovery. Faith's touch was light and tantalizing and made her long for—something. She wasn't sure what, but the fact that she wanted more and not less seemed like a good sign.

Between bands, Faith went outside with her friends for a smoke.

"She smokes?" Meg asked, watching the younger girls go with a frown.

"I think it's her friends," Jamie said. "She doesn't smell like it, anyway."

"Have you kissed her yet?" Becky asked.

"Not yet."

"Ew," Meg said. "And on that note, I'm going to the restroom."

"I thought you wanted me to go out with her?"

"I do. I just don't want to hear details."

Becky waited until Meg was out of earshot to say, "Don't take this the wrong way, but do you want some advice on how to kiss?"

"Why would I need advice?"

"Come on. I know you haven't exactly been little Miss Lothario." She held up a hand. "No judgment, only a word to the wise. Do you want to hear it or not?"

"Fine," Jamie muttered, because she knew Becky had dated more than a few orchestra geeks in the past couple of years.

Turned out that while they tended to be on the homely side, musicians were a horny-ass bunch.

"When you kiss her, don't go all in like you're trying to stick your tongue down her throat. Kiss her softly and wait for her to make the next move."

"Why would I try to stick my tongue down her throat?"

"It's called French kissing, idiot." And then her face changed. "Oh. Sorry."

Jamie's gaze narrowed. "Why are you sorry?"

Becky shrugged, watching the club workers tow an amp across the stage. "No reason."

"There must be a reason." Becky still wouldn't look at her, and all at once Jamie figured it out. "Meg told you, didn't she?" Her eyes scanned the club. She was going to kill her sister.

"Don't be mad," Becky said, her hand on Jamie's arm. "She was really upset and I'm her best friend. I'm your friend, too, Jamie. You know that, right?"

She glanced at the girl she had known for as long as she could remember. In the past decade, she had watched Meg and Becky go from jump ropes and braces to electric guitars and lipstick, and they had watched her go from roller skates and pony tails to bowling shirts and, well, girls.

"I know," she said finally, nodding. "I just wish she'd told me you knew. I mean, it makes sense. It didn't happen only to me. Nothing like that ever does."

Becky slipped an arm around her shoulders and tugged her against her side, eyes on the stage. "I get that I'm not supposed to say this, but if I could, I would find that man and make sure that he couldn't do anything like that ever again. Like, *ever.*"

In that moment, Jamie believed her. Musicians were a skinny lot, but they were tough, too.

Out of the corner of her eye, she saw Faith and her friends approaching. Quickly she pushed Becky away. "Dude, don't cramp my style."

"As if. Remember—keep your lips soft. Most teenage boys don't realize how much better soft kisses are than pulverizing ones. Oh, and touch her cheek softly with your thumb when you kiss her. Girls love that. Got it?"

Jamie wanted to remind her that she wasn't actually a teenage boy, but she was too busy remembering Emma's hand on her cheek at the train station. Even the gay girls liked that move. "Got it."

Faith came right up and leaned against her. She smelled like clove cigarettes, which wasn't as good as weed but was significantly better than regular cigarettes.

"Did you miss me?" Faith murmured into her ear.

"Um, yeah." Jamie winced at her own awkwardness.

"Come with me to the bathroom?"

She swallowed hard. "Okay."

Faith slipped her hand into Jamie's and tugged her toward the hallway. They passed Meg on the way, who lifted her eyebrows at her sister. Jamie shrugged back and followed her date across the club.

They were barely out of sight of the main room when Faith turned and pushed Jamie against the wall, cupped one hand around the back of her neck, and pulled Jamie's lips down to hers. Jamie was so surprised that she stood woodenly for a second. *Soft lips*, she reminded herself, closing her eyes and trying to relax as she pressed her mouth against the other girl's. She tasted of cloves—and something else. Wait, was that rum? Jamie pushed away her aversion to the taste and focused instead on keeping her lips relaxed as she smoothed her thumb across Faith's cheek. Her skin was so soft, just like—she banished the name before it could form. And then Faith's lips parted and her tongue flicked against Jamie's mouth, and all of a sudden she was dizzy, her head spinning, and she couldn't breathe because it wasn't Faith kissing her but someone else entirely, someone tall and rough and who also tasted of alcohol—

Her eyes flew open and she pulled her head back so fast it hit the wall behind her with a dull thud.

"Jamie," Faith said, her eyes widening. "Are you okay?"

"Yeah," she said quickly, trying catch her breath. Her heart was racing so fast she felt like her vision was darkening. Or maybe that was only the lighting in the hallway. "I, uh, I thought I heard someone coming."

"Aw, are you shy?" Faith asked, smiling up at her.

"Don't tell anyone," Jamie said, faking a smile as she swallowed down the bile that had risen in her throat. She caught the bottom of her shirt in one fist, twisting the cloth nervously.

"Your rep is safe with me, Maxwell. Besides, I think it's cute."

"Good, because I think you're cute. Now I hate to say it, but I really have to pee."

"Me, too." Faith grabbed her hand again and tugged her down the hallway.

When they returned to the main room, Becky lifted an eyebrow and Jamie gave her a weak smile and a thumbs-up behind Faith's back.

"What was that for?" she heard Meg ask.

"You don't want to know," Becky answered.

The lights fell as the first chords rang through the bar, and Faith took up her position in front of her again. Jamie draped her arms around the other girl, her eyes unseeing on the stage. All she could think of was how Emma had asked her if she might freak out when Amanda kissed her. Now that she had her answer, she wished she could call Emma and talk to her about it, tell her how it had felt and hear Emma tell her that her reaction was normal, that Faith and the French guy were nothing alike but it was still okay to feel what she was feeling. Because she knew that Emma would say all of those things— at least, the old Emma would have. But would post-Seattle

Emma be upset with her for making out with someone else? They hadn't talked about The Kiss again since that first text exchange. But if Emma told her *she* had kissed someone else—make that *when*—how would she feel? Shitty, that was how. Which in and of itself was pretty shitty—she'd already told Emma they couldn't be together. Now she didn't want anyone else to have her, either? *Really cool, Maxwell.* And yet, accurate.

Seriously, she shouldn't even be thinking about Emma at all when there was an available girl who liked her back dancing in the loose circle of her arms. Sighing, she closed her eyes and swayed to the music, trying to meditate until the memories of Seattle and Lyon receded back beneath their separate calluses.

#

Emma asked Dani to meet her at Sea-Tac the Sunday night after World Cup qualifying. Ty was at Benji's house, as usual, and her mother was at the hospital. Since returning to work, she'd been there more than she'd been home, which was partly why Ty was at the Chandlers' house so often. Emma thought he also might be actively avoiding home. She didn't blame him. The two weeks in Canada had given her a break from the cloud of sorrow that seemed permanently camped out over their house. In her mind, Seattle was dark and ominous while Montreal and Ottawa were shiny and new. And how new they had proven to be.

"How was it?" Dani asked as they headed out to short-term parking.

"Good," Emma said, "even though we lost to effing Canada today."

"I saw that. But you still qualified for the World Cup, so that doesn't really matter, does it?"

"No, but I wasn't on my game. It wasn't my player who scored, but still, maybe if I'd played better we would have won."

"Soccer is a team sport, remember?"

"Easy for you to say. You're a striker. If you don't score, your team doesn't necessarily lose. But if a defender or keeper screws up, it usually means a goal."

"Give yourself a break. You've had a lot on your mind, in case you hadn't noticed."

Emma bit her lip, trying to hold back a smile.

Dani glanced over. "Oh my god, you totally hooked up with that Tori chick, didn't you?"

"I did. Like, a bunch of times."

"Damn, girl." Dani laughed. "No wonder you don't seem as pissed as you usually do when you lose a big game. I figured it couldn't just be two weeks of soccer and summer sun."

"Oh, it was sunny all right. In my bed."

"How does that even work? Tell me you didn't do anything with other people in the room."

"Of course not. Although I've heard that happens a lot in college."

"Yeah, not sure I'm down with that."

"Me either. Especially after we were interrupted once."

Emma paused her story as they reached Dani's Forester. Her parents had given it to her as a reward for earning a nearly full ride to UCLA. She'd wanted something sportier, but they'd liked the Subaru's height, stability, and mileage. Not to mention the price tag. You could take the Italian-American out of Jersey, Dani liked to say, but you couldn't take the cheapness out of the Italian-American.

Bags and seat belts secured, Dani pulled out of the spot and headed for the parking gate. "Details," she prodded. "Now."

Emma gave her the abbreviated version of the last couple of weeks. She and Tori weren't roommates this time, but on the second day of training in Montreal, Tori invited her to go for a walk to a nearby coffee shop where they'd stayed almost until curfew. Tori had kissed her in the elevator on the way up to their floor, and while it hadn't compared to her kiss with Jamie, Emma had still found the clandestine nature of the exchange thrilling. The next day, they spent their afternoon free period riding scooters to the top of Mount Royal, where they'd explored the park holding hands and making out behind trees and assorted sculptures.

On the fourth day of camp, Emma's roommate, a girl from Texas, invited her shopping with a group of other girls. When Emma said she was tired and wanted a nap, her roommate gave her a knowing look on her way out and told her to "have fun, girl."

Emma had texted Tori and then taken a quick shower. She was brushing her hair when Tori knocked on the door, and Emma had opened it, trying not to feel nervous. Unlike Jamie she had kissed her fair share of people. Not that she was thinking of Jamie, because she definitely wasn't.

"Come in," Emma said, smiling at Tori. She looked cute and freshly showered in a tank top and board shorts, the tribal tattoo on her shoulder lending her a slightly edgy air.

"Are you sure about this?" Tori had asked, and for once her eyes were deadly serious.

"Positive." Emma had glanced up and down the hallway, slipped a "Do Not Disturb" sign on the door, and pulled Tori into the room by her tank top. Then she kissed her, trying not to remember kissing Jamie.

Tori's surprise gave way to intensity. She stroked her tongue across Emma's lips—

"Stop," Dani said, checking in her rearview mirror before switching lanes.

"You said details."

"Maybe not quite so many. But how was it? You said you were interrupted?"

"Not that time. And it was, I don't know, surprising. I think maybe she's really good at everything because honestly, it was never like that with Drew."

"Oh, that's right, he's your only, isn't he?" Dani asked.

"Sorry, we can't all lose our virginity at thirteen."

"Ouch."

"What? You always make it sound like I'm the cutest little near-virgin you know."

"You are. You're also the only ambisextrous near-virgin I know."

Emma rolled her eyes. "You've been saving that one, haven't you?"

"Totally." Dani smiled smugly.

She certainly had come a long way in the past couple of months. When Emma first told her she liked girls, Dani had been unsurprised but also uncharacteristically quiet. Then the thing with Justin had happened, and her best friend had taken her side without hesitation. Dani's encouragement was one of the reasons Emma had decided to report Justin to the administration, an action that had led to his temporary suspension and an official apology in front of her mom and his parents in the school principal's office. Now here Dani was making jokes about Emma's sexuality as if she was even more comfortable with it than Emma was. Which might be the case. Emma still couldn't quite believe that she'd kissed Jamie and slept with Tori. Grief really did interfere with impulse control.

As they drove home, she filled Dani in on the rest of the trip and answered her plethora of questions. No, it wasn't serious, she and Tori had both agreed. Yes, it was even better the second, third, and fourth times, except in Ottawa when Tori's roommate came in and Emma had to hide, giggling, under the sheet until the other girl found her purse and fled. Yes, she had "reciprocated." And yes, sex with a girl was different than it was with a guy.

"How?" Dani asked, guiding the car off the freeway.

"For one, girls are softer and smoother and not as hairy. It's also more intimate. You know how guys can sort of close their eyes and plug away as if you're not even there?"

Dani pulled up at a red light and gave her a pitying look. "Oh, honey, Drew was definitely not doing it right if that's how it was with him."

"Really?"

"Really. Did you ever, you know, with him?"

Emma shook her head.

"What about with her?"

She nodded, feeling her cheeks redden. "Like, a bunch of times."

"Now she blushes," Dani said to the air as the light changed. "But good for you. What are you now officially, gay?"

"I'm definitely gay for her."

"What about Jamie? You were gay for her first, weren't you?"

Emma winced. "Doesn't matter. I told you, she's not an option."

"Maybe not, but she's still your friend last I checked. You slept with someone who's not only on the national team but is also your future college teammate. How do you think Jamie is going to feel when she finds out?"

"Who says she has to find out?" Emma said, only half-joking.

"Dude, you're all in the national team pool. It's only a matter of time."

"Oh my god, you're right." Emma groaned and slid down her seat. "I'm an awful, terrible, horrible person."

"You forgot 'drama queen.' Seriously, maybe you could, I don't know, try not to act like a hormonal teenager who can't keep it in her pants?"

"I know I've said I appreciate your unfailing honesty, but I think I'd like to take that statement back."

"Way too late for that," Dani said as she guided the Subaru into Emma's driveway. "Now are you feeding me or what? My brothers are at home this weekend, and I cleared out midway through Sunday dinner when the fireworks started."

"What's up with Jeff these days, anyway?" Emma asked as they unloaded her bags, only too happy to shift the conversation away from her own disaster of a life. It had honestly never occurred to her that Tori and Jamie could meet. Apparently, as one of her mother's nursing school friends liked to say, denial wasn't just a river in Africa.

Dani stayed and helped her polish off the chicken casserole her mom had left in the fridge, catching her up on the last two weeks of school as they ate at the kitchen bar. Then she finally said she should get home so she wouldn't be too tired for her last final in AP US History the following day.

"Don't worry. The actual AP test was harder," Emma said. "You'll do fine."

"I can't believe you got to take your exams with you."

"That's one thing about the national team. They make sure you get your homework done."

"School stuff they're good with. Preventing underage girls from getting it on in hotel rooms, not so much."

"Zip it." Emma shoved her sideways as they walked out into the cool night. Montreal and Ottawa had been hot and muggy most of the time, with the occasional thunderstorm to break the humidity. That was one of the things she loved about Seattle—there weren't many big cities she could think of that were as comfortable during the summer. Except, maybe, San Francisco…

Almost as if she had sensed it coming, her phone vibrated. She paused beside Dani's car to check the text: Jamie. Normally Emma texted her as soon as she got home from national team camp. But tonight, as had increasingly been the case, she wasn't sure what to say.

"Was that her?" Dani asked.

"No, it's Jamie."

"That's who I meant." Dani squeezed her shoulder. "You're going to call her, aren't you?"

"I don't know."

"Em, you have to talk to her. She's your best friend. I should know because that used to be my job."

"Dan..." Emma stared at her, stunned.

"No, it's okay. When I was with Nick, I was the same way. He and I connected on a level that I've never experienced with anyone. But you're my oldest friend and I'm yours, and I love you. Though I am definitely not gay for you, hon."

"Ditto, pal." Emma pulled Dani in for a hug. "I promise, I'll talk to her. I'm not sure I'm going to tell her about Canada, though. It didn't mean anything. I barely know Tori."

"Which is why she was your perfect first girl?"

"Exactly."

They slapped hands and Dani paused to admire her nails—some of the girls at camp had had a spa afternoon in their room—and then it really was time to say goodnight.

As the Subaru disappeared down the long driveway, Emma went back inside and turned on the alarm. She'd rarely stayed alone in the house at night, and it wasn't a very comfortable feeling. Their neighbors were so far away that no one would hear her scream. But the alarm made her feel better as she settled in the living room with the land line, Lucy snuggled up against her.

Jamie picked up on the third ring. "Hey, Shoreditch."

"That's Shorecrest to you, Maxwell," Emma said automatically in a snotty British accent. She was tired, really tired, but now that they were actually talking, it was almost a relief to hear Jamie's voice. She'd missed her. Nothing new—she always missed her.

"I heard about Canada. Sorry, dude."

"Me, too. But at least we qualified."

"I know. Congrats! By the way, have you seen MLS scores?"

"I actually saw a lot of the games the past couple of weeks. You know, as part of our training."

"I figured." She hesitated. "I watched without you. Hope that was okay."

"Oh. I mean, of course." Emma had set the DVR before she left so that they could watch together like they usually did. But finding time could be difficult, so it made sense.

"How was the tournament?"

Emma told her about her experience in Canada, leaving out the part about any girl-on-girl action. She would rather stick a hot poker in her eye than admit to Jamie that she'd had same-sex sex. Instead she relayed the interesting and amusing bits, hoping she was the only psychic one in this relationship. Friendship. *Whatever.*

"What about you? Anything new?" she asked eventually.

"Actually, yeah," Jamie said, and suddenly she sounded nervous. "I, um, started dating someone."

Emma sat straight up on the couch, blinking. Outside a ferry boat was passing, and she focused on the familiar sight, trying to catch her breath. It was ridiculous to be this upset about Jamie going out with someone else when she'd had her hand up Tori's shirt less than twenty-four hours before.

"Emma?"

"Sorry, Dani was texting me. What were you saying? You went out on a date?"

"Yeah." She sounded wary. "Two dates, actually."

"Congratulations." Emma forced her voice to sound cheerful. "Who's the lucky girl?"

"Faith."

"As in, Spanish class Faith?"

"Yeah. She asked me out last week."

Emma leaned back against a throw pillow, rubbing her temples to ease the headache beginning to form there. The girl Jamie had liked on and off all year apparently liked her back. She should be happy for her, right? Right. Totally.

"Wow," she managed. "That—that's great. Good for you."

Jamie hesitated. Then she said, her voice soft, "You know, if it's too weird, we don't have to talk about this."

Emma slid her fingers through Lucy's silky fur. "It's fine. We're friends, right? This is what friends do."

There was silence at the other end. A long silence, in which Emma could almost hear Jamie thinking: *But are we? Friends?* Which of course they were. Because if they weren't, then what were they?

She tried again. "Tell me about Faith. You've had a crush on her forever, haven't you?"

"I guess so," Jamie said after a moment. "She's pretty cool. We went out for ice cream a few days ago and then to a show last night with Meg and Becky."

As Jamie described her second date with Faith, Emma closed her eyes, trying not to picture her in a dark club in San Francisco, some girl pressed up against her as a band played a few feet away. When Jamie said they'd kissed, Emma felt numb. Not quite like the day her dad died, but similar. And that's when she realized: What she had feared all along had happened. Jamie had managed to break her heart anyway, possibly without even knowing it.

She sat up and reached for her cell, opened it and made it beep just as Jamie was saying something about a conversation they'd had about Amanda a while ago; did Emma remember?

"I'm sorry," she said, the lies coming easily now, "my mom needs me to call her. Can we talk later in the week?"

"Oh. Yeah. Text me, okay?"

"I will." Emma hesitated. "Good luck with Faith. I hope

she knows how lucky she is."

Then she hung up before Jamie could say anything else. She lay back on the couch and pressed her face against the soft fleece pillow they'd had for as long as she could remember. The scent of her father's aftershave lingered on it still, and she took a deep, shaky breath, unsurprised when it turned into a half-sob. None of the girls at camp had known anything about her dad, and she hadn't mentioned it to anyone, not even Tori. The coaching staff knew and made sure to check in regularly to see how she was holding up. But Surf Cup aside, he hadn't been a very involved soccer parent in years, and no one else's parents showed up at the U-19 camp. U-17s was one thing, but most of the girls in Canada were already in college or, like her, about to start. From now on, national team camps and competitions would be mostly parent-free, which meant no one would have to know about her dad unless she wanted them to.

The same went for Tori. And right now, other than Dani, she was pretty sure she didn't want anyone to know about their hook-up. If one of Dani's first comments had been to ask about Jamie, she could only imagine her mother's reaction. Her mom already thought she and Jamie were a couple, as did Ty. She was pretty sure they'd be pissed at her for "cheating" on Jamie with another girl.

Had she cheated? No, of course not. Jamie was the one who had put the brakes on after her visit—not that Emma hadn't given her ample cause with her temporary disappearing act. Why did it feel like she had betrayed Jamie then? *You can help who you fall in bed with*, she had told her the night of the memorial service. Nice theory, but it was proving less black and white in practice.

Beside her, Lucy moaned in her sleep, feet twitching as if she were chasing—or being chased by—something in her dreams. Emma rubbed the dog's neck and whispered, "It's okay, Luce. I'm right here. You're okay."

Hadn't Jamie whispered those same things to her as they lay in bed together, nearly as close as two people could get? She'd sworn she wasn't going anywhere, just as Emma had. But even as they'd made those promises, Emma had known they couldn't possibly keep them. Still, how she'd wished they could.

A Nancy Griffith song her mom loved popped into her head. If wishes were changes, Jamie would have been the one she met at U-19 camp, the one who would be her teammate for the next few years. But wishes weren't changes, and so Jamie would remain in Berkeley with Faith for the foreseeable future while Emma joined Tori at UNC. Life was unfolding in the only direction it could: forward, inexorably carrying them away from each other.

She couldn't pretend she hadn't known that this split, this break was coming. But just because something was inevitable didn't mean it hurt any less. She sucked in a sharp breath, her lungs tight as if there wasn't enough air in the room. Beside her, Lucy's tail hit the couch rhythmically, comfortingly. Emma closed her eyes as she tried to breathe, fingers entwined in the warm fur of her father's dog.

This wasn't how her senior year was supposed to go. How had everything gotten so messed up? And, more to the point, how was she possibly going to fix it?

CHAPTER TWELVE

Jamie lay on her stomach on the hotel room bed, clutching the extra pillow over her ears. She had only been in LA for a few hours and already national team camp was not living up to her expectations. She'd been psyched about this opportunity ever since she'd received the call the week after school let out. For the first—and possibly only—time all year, the U-16s, -17s and -19s would spend a week training together at US Soccer headquarters in Carson before another round of friendlies with the Mexican and Canadian youth teams. This meant that not only would she get to experience an awesome week of high-level soccer, but she and Emma would actually be at national team camp together. Even though things had been strained between them recently, she couldn't pretend she wasn't looking forward to seeing Emma before she left for North Carolina.

Her parents had been excited, too, because LA was close enough that they could come see her and Emma play. Instead of taking their usual time off around the Fourth, they put in for a week's vacation to coincide with camp later in July. Even Meg was taking a week off from her job at a music store in the Mission to come down and spend time with the Pasadena relatives.

Jamie's excitement had taken its first hit midway through the car ride down to LA, when a text popped up from Emma:

"Hey. Are you on your way?"

"Yes," she'd texted back, frowning as she looked at her watch. "Wait. Aren't you supposed to be on a plane?"

"About that... Call me?"

"I'm in the car with my family."

"Oh. Right."

Jamie waited, chewing on her lip, and then she typed the question she was pretty sure she didn't want to know the answer to: "Are you still coming?"

"No. I pulled a hamstring and my coach thinks I should rest it."

Jamie looked out the window at the passing scenery. People who had never been to California were always surprised when they visited and discovered that most of the state was desert. "What about the redwoods?" tourists from the East Coast inevitably asked. "And the palm trees?" As if the presence of trees in a few coastal stretches signaled the existence of an abundant groundwater supply. In fact, California piped in most of its water from other states. What genius had come up with the idea to concentrate the nation's food production in a state that was chronically short of water?

Emma texted again: "Jamie? Are you there?"

Instead of replying, she hit the call button beside Emma's name. They weren't that far from Bakersfield. Maybe the reception wouldn't be too bad.

"I thought I'd lost you," Emma said.

Jamie kept her face turned toward the window, her voice low. "Are you really not coming?"

"I'm sorry. I can't risk it. There's too much on the line."

She didn't sound that sorry, but then again, Jamie actually hadn't talked to her much lately. It was summer, so they were both busy playing travel league, hanging out with friends, and, in Jamie's case, working. She'd landed a job at Ben & Jerry's and had already made a few friends among the mostly college-aged workers. Who knew that scooping ice cream would turn out to be the queerest of queer jobs in an already mightily queer town? With everything going on in their lives, she'd been hoping this camp might offer a chance to close some of the distance that had opened up between them.

"I'm sorry," Emma repeated when Jamie didn't say anything. "I really wanted to see you before—"

"Before you leave the West Coast and I never see you again?"

So much for being quiet. Out of the corner of her eye, she saw Meg pull her headphones off and stare at her, frowning.

"Of course you'll see me again. It's not like I'm moving to another country. Besides, there's always the national team pool."

"We both know there's no guarantee for me."

"That's not true, Jamie! You're so talented."

"I'm also inconsistent and easily distracted, and my work ethic is sometimes a little iffy."

"Who told you that?"

"Jolene Nichols at the last camp." The U-16 coach had also told her she had a rare gift for the game and that none of those issues were unusual in someone so young. With time and dedication, Jo had said, she was sure Jamie could be one of the best midfielders in the country in her age group.

"Those don't exactly sound like unfixable problems," Emma pointed out.

Maybe she really was psychic. Which, honestly, was an alarming thought on so many levels.

"Look," Emma added, "I would be there if I could. But preseason starts in less than a month and I have the World Cup to think about. You know how tricky hamstrings can be."

She did. Only she had been looking forward to seeing

Emma so much that now, somehow, training camp didn't seem quite as appealing. She pinched the bridge of her nose. She was lucky even to have a shot at the national pool. It would be colossally stupid to let a girl get in the way of everything she'd worked for.

The reception blanked out for a few seconds. "I think I'm losing you," Jamie said, and then winced at her word choice. Nothing like your subconscious mind to mess with you.

Emma's voice dropped. "Will you call me when you get back from camp?"

"Yeah, okay."

"Geez, don't sound so excited."

Jamie dropped her chin to her chest, picking at a scab on one of her knees. "What do you want me to say, Emma? This was our last chance to hang out before you leave."

"Maybe not."

Jamie's head lifted. "What do you mean?"

"I mean I have a bunch of frequent flyer miles, and it's not like Seattle and San Francisco are that far apart…"

"Are you serious?" She stared out the window again, trying to bite back the enormous grin trying to hijack her face.

"Completely," Emma said, her voice soft. "I want to see you too, you know."

She hadn't known, actually. But the handful of words helped make the pain of Emma's absence recede a little.

They'd hung up a few minutes later with promises to talk soon, and Jamie had stared out the window, picturing a weekend in San Francisco with Emma. They would walk on the beach and talk, and maybe this time Jamie wouldn't be so afraid. Maybe this time she would tell her how she really felt. Because whether they were together or not, her feelings for Emma hadn't changed. She was beginning to think they never would.

"You're smiling way too much for that call to mean what I think it did," Meg said.

"Emma got injured and isn't coming," Jamie told her, keeping her voice down so their parents wouldn't hear her over the sound of Yo-Yo Ma's greatest hits. "But... she might come to visit before she leaves for North Carolina."

Meg sighed. "Jesus, James. What am I going to do with you?"

"Maybe let me be happy for as long as possible before reality comes crashing back in?"

"Sure," her sister had said, nodding. "You let me know how that works out."

Now Jamie clutched her pillow tighter, trying to drown out Britt's snoring. The keeper had a deviated septum, as everyone on the team knew. Of all the girls in camp to land as her hotel buddy... Somehow she must have slept, though, because the alarm woke her the next morning at seven. Yawning, she stumbled around the room looking for her baseball cap. It wouldn't be fair to inflict her bedhead on anyone.

"Did I keep you up?" Britt asked guiltily as they brushed their teeth side by side. At least, that was what Jamie thought she said.

"No." She smiled reassuringly around her toothbrush.

"Oh." Britt brightened and spat her toothpaste into the sink. "Sweet."

They stopped by Angie's room to pick her up for breakfast. Downstairs in the hotel conference room they went through the buffet line together, choosing from a smorgasbord of high-protein, low-refined sugar options. Jamie piled fresh pineapple on her plate next to eggs, toast, and bacon, and then paused at the coffee machine. Normally she was a tea girl, but with Britt as her roommate, the hard stuff might be in order.

Coffee, naturally, made her think of Seattle, which made her think of Emma, and she smiled as she remembered the text

Emma had sent that morning: "Good luck at camp! Kick ass, and don't do anything I wouldn't do." She wasn't sure what that last part meant, but the fact that Emma had been up early this morning thinking about her was enough.

"Okay, who's got you looking so sprung this morning?" Angie asked as Jamie approached the table.

She frowned. "I don't look sprung."

"I don't know." Britt glanced at Angie. "There was some major cheesy smiling going on upstairs over the first text of the day."

"Ooh, is it that girl from school?" Angie asked. "Faith?"

"No. We broke up last week."

"But that picture you sent of the two of you was adorable," Angie said, and Britt nodded in agreement. "What happened?"

"I don't know. She wasn't out to her parents and it got kind of old sneaking around."

That part was true. It just wasn't the reason Jamie had ended things. Only Shoshanna knew the real reason—Faith liked to party and wanted to move faster than Jamie was comfortable with, and rather than ask if she would be okay cutting back on the drinking and possibly slowing things down, Jamie had bailed. It was possible the decision might also have had something to do with the fact that she'd thought she'd be seeing Emma at camp. You know, maybe.

"Seriously?" Angie shook her head. "You have some high standards, Max. Almost no one I know is out to their parents."

"Same here," Britt agreed.

Just then a tall girl slid her tray across the table and into Britt's, spilling her orange juice.

"What the hell?" Britt jumped up, whirling around with a glare that turned into a grin as she saw the other girl. "Dude! I didn't know you'd be here!"

"Ditto," the new girl said, and gave Britt a boisterous bro

hug.

The tall girl turned out to be Samantha Sullivan, AKA Sully, from the club team Britt had played on in Tucson before moving to Phoenix. Sully had been called up to the U-19s in the fall, though she hadn't made the roster for qualifiers. There was still hope she might make the World Cup team, though.

"Slim to none, but it's better than nothing," Sully said as she claimed the seat next to Britt.

The Arizona girls were chattering away about people from home when another U-19 girl walked by and nodded at Sully. She paused mid-sentence and returned the nod as the other player kept walking and slid in next to a couple of older girls at the next table.

"Damn. Who's that?" Angie asked.

Jamie knew what she meant. The older girl was beautiful in an androgynous way, with light brown eyes and shoulder-length blonde hair that curled out from under her backwards baseball cap. Her entire being exuded confidence, unmistakable in the way she slid her arm around one of the girl's shoulders and smiled down at her.

Sully rolled her eyes. "Tori Parker, our resident playuh. You know how they say sailors have a girl in every port? Well, Tori has a girl at every camp. The last couple of times she was into this girl from Seattle, but I heard she didn't come this week because of an injury."

Jamie almost spit out her pineapple. "Wait, you're not talking about Emma Blakeley, are you?"

"Totally. You know Blake?"

Jamie stared at her, feeling heat rush up her throat. "Yeah, I do, and there's no way she would hook up with someone like *her*."

"She did, though. They were glued at the hip in Canada, and Tori's roommate in Ottawa even walked in on them. As in, naked."

That couldn't be right. Emma wouldn't hook up with some random lesbian on the national team, would she? And yet, it made sense in a horribly rational, gut-wrenching sort of way.

"Did you say the last two camps?" Jamie asked, unable to help herself.

"Yeah. Sorry if you didn't know," Sully said.

"It's not a big deal." She forced a shrug. "I was surprised, that's all."

"You and everyone else. But straight girls are Tori's jam, so…"

Jamie picked at her breakfast as the conversation moved on, chiming in here and there to keep up the illusion that her heart hadn't in fact been ripped into a thousand bloody bits of torn muscle. But it had, and the last thing she wanted to do was go outside into the hot California sun and play soccer with the girl who had supposedly been caught in bed with Emma.

Fortunately, they stuck to their own age groups that day so Jamie didn't have to encounter Tori on the field. They practiced outdoors early and late to beat the heat. Inside the rest of the day, they kept busy studying tactics and game film, except for an hour before dinner when they were all encouraged to drink lots of fluids and rest. Jamie lay on her bed drafting one text after another to Emma, but she didn't send any of them. What could she say? "So did you really hook up with a girl whose main goal in life other than playing for the national team is to convert as many straight girls as possible?" This approach seemed a bit harsh, even if it was true.

But maybe it wasn't true. Rumors were tricky at camp. Maybe Sully had it wrong. Maybe Tori only wanted everyone to think she had hooked up with Emma. What self-respecting lesbian wouldn't want the world to think Emma Blakeley was into her?

After night practice under the lights, Angie came to their room and they watched a movie until curfew. Then Jamie and Britt got ready for bed and chatted sleepily until Jamie's phone buzzed.

"Go get her, tiger," Britt said, smirking, and rolled over onto her side.

Jamie stared at Emma's text: "How was your first day of camp?"

She hesitated, and then wrote, "Interesting. It would be better if you were here."

"Aw, that's sweet. I miss you, too."

"Were you serious about a plane ticket?"

"I looked at flights today. Want me to send you some dates?"

Jamie hesitated. Then she typed, "That depends."

"On what?"

"I heard a rumor today. Want to hear it?"

She waited, but Emma didn't respond.

"Are you there?"

"Yes. What rumor?"

"I'll give you a hint. It involves Tori Parker."

Again the reply took a while. Finally Emma wrote, "Can I call you? I don't want to do this over text."

Jamie blinked, rereading the message. She'd almost managed to convince herself that the rumor was sour grapes or random gossip. But Emma's text left no room for doubt.

She typed quickly: "Are you serious? You actually hooked up with her?"

"I'm calling you right now."

Her phone vibrated, and even though she knew she shouldn't, she answered.

"I can't talk," she whispered. "It's after curfew."

"Please?" Emma asked, her voice nearly as quiet. "Please, Jamie?"

She hesitated, and then she said, "I'll call you back." Without waiting for an answer, she threw her phone on the bed. Then she pulled on sweats and soccer sandals and crept from the room, heading down to the first floor. She should not be doing this. She should not be breaking curfew at national team camp to hear about Emma's training camp hook-up. But her whispered *please* had sounded almost broken, and honestly, Jamie's body was vibrating so badly with equal parts anger and hurt that she was pretty sure she wouldn't be able to sleep anytime soon anyway.

In the lobby, she dropped onto a cushy chair away from the front desk and slouched down, hood up, one hand over her face. She took a few deep breaths and recited her mantra, but it didn't help. Finally she gave up and called Emma back.

"I'm so sorry I didn't tell you," Emma said, her voice thick.

Why was *she* the one crying? What complete crap.

"Did you sleep with her?" She held her breath, waiting.

"Jamie…"

"Did you?"

Emma sighed. "Yes."

Fuck, fuck, fuck. Jamie squeezed her eyes shut and shook her head at the ache blossoming in her chest. "When?"

"In Canada."

"I heard it was going on before that."

"It wasn't. Honestly."

As if she had any right to use that word. "So you're what, bi?"

"I don't like labels. I'm just me."

"Apparently being you involves hooking up with total skanks."

Emma didn't answer for a moment. Then: "She's not a skank."

"I think I know more about girls like her than you do. Did

you know she's already moved on to someone else in the pool?" As silence greeted her, she felt a glimmer of satisfaction. "Yeah, I didn't think so."

"It's not like we're dating. She's free to do whatever she wants."

"Don't you mean *who*ever?"

"Don't be an ass."

"Oh, I'm the ass in this situation?"

"That's not what I meant and you know it."

Silence lengthened between them again. How had this happened? She'd known Emma was questioning her sexuality. Not only was there the kiss and Emma's ensuing confession, but she'd attended a handful of GSA meetings that semester and had even participated in the annual GLSEN Day of Silence. Plus, no straight girl could like Giada De Laurentiis *that* much. And yet, Jamie had assumed Emma would open up when she was ready, would tell her about anyone who came into the picture, girl or guy, same as they'd always done. What did it mean that she hadn't?

"Are you even injured?" she asked.

Emma's pause told her all she needed to know.

Jamie expelled a noisy breath, trying to focus on her anger rather than the pain seizing at her lungs. "So you would rather not ever see me again than deal with me and your girlfriend in the same place."

"I do want to see you. That's why I was looking at flights. I wanted to tell you all of this in person."

"Right."

"I'm serious. And she's not my girlfriend. It didn't even mean anything."

"That makes it so much better."

Emma made a frustrated sound. "God, Jamie. You're the one who said we don't get to keep each other."

"That's why you kept this a secret? To get back at me?"

"No, of course not. I did try to tell you once."

She stopped, thinking. "Are you talking about at the train station? This was the thing you had to tell me."

Emma hesitated again. "Yes."

"So it was going on before qualifiers." Jamie rubbed her eyes, willing the tears to recede. They were angry tears, that was all. She was angry.

"I had a crush on her, but nothing happened before Canada. I swear."

"That's the thing about lying, Emma. Once you've done it, the other person doesn't know if they can ever trust you again."

As soon as she said it, Jamie knew she'd crossed a line—Emma had told her she'd heard her mother say that very thing about her father.

"Wow," Emma said after a moment, her voice cracking. "I didn't realize you had a mean streak. I guess I wasn't the only one hiding things."

They sat in silence, breathing into their phones. Jamie pictured Emma in her bedroom, curled up on her bed with the white lace ruffle that matched the curtains on the windows. Then she remembered that Emma liked to sleep in a soft, worn UNC Soccer T-shirt. UNC—where Emma was headed in a matter of weeks. Where Tori Parker, according to the camp roster, was a rising sophomore.

"Oh my god. That shirt was hers, wasn't it?"

Emma didn't ask which shirt. "Jamie, wait…"

"I have to go."

She didn't wait for an answer. Hands shaking, she ended the call and turned her phone all the way off, still trying to hold back her tears. All this time, Emma had had feelings for someone else. The nights they'd spent pressed together in Emma's bed—had she been thinking about Tori? Had she been pretending Jamie was someone else that entire time? The thought made her feel hot all over, as if she couldn't stay inside her own skin another moment.

She almost made it back to her room undetected. Almost. But as she passed the alcove that housed the ice and soda machines, she glanced up to see one of the assistant coaches watching her. *Fuck.* She lowered her head and hurried down the hallway, expecting the coach to come after her at any moment. She was so busted. Would they kick her out of the pool for breaking curfew? Had she destroyed her soccer future over a girl? Except Emma wasn't just a girl. She was Emma, and even though she'd lied, Jamie couldn't help how she felt about her.

You can't help who you fall in love with, she'd told Emma. Had she known then that she was in love with Emma? Or had she still believed it was only a crush? A crush didn't make you feel safe and cherished, cared for and protected. A crush didn't have the power to make you feel so lost that you weren't sure you'd ever be found again.

Back in her room, she lay in the dark listening to Britt snore while tears slipped across her cheeks and dripped into her ears. She had cried over Emma plenty of times, but never quite like this. Before, it was because the distance between them had seemed insurmountable. Now she cried because the ridiculous hope that she had still stupidly carried, the absurd belief that someday, somehow, they might end up together, had been wrecked not by fate or bad timing but instead by Emma herself. She had lied to Jamie all these months. Even worse, she had slept with a girl who wasn't her. And yes, Jamie had told her that they didn't get to keep each other. But Emma had said she wished they could. Emma had kissed her and told her she loved her too. Emma had offered to come see her before she left for college—except it turned out she only wanted to visit so that she could tell her she'd hooked up with Tori. Tori, who was already in college and presumably as experienced as Jamie was clueless.

Was that why Emma didn't want to be with her, because she had barely even kissed a girl? Or was it that she didn't want to be with someone who was damaged? *Given your history,* she had written when she apologized for the kiss. Honestly, Jamie couldn't blame her. If she was Emma, she wouldn't want to be with her, either.

Shoshanna's voice sounded at the back of her mind, something about boundaries and healthy relationships and how forgiving someone involves letting go of the idea that they or their actions have any power over you. But she ignored the voice and fixated instead on Emma's face in the moment before they kissed. Her eyes had been wide and luminous in the light filtering down to the train platform, and she had looked so serious as she touched Jamie's cheek.

That might be the last time they ever saw each other, Jamie realized, pressing her palms against her closed eyes. She couldn't think how to get past this, not with Emma leaving for UNC so soon. She couldn't go back to playing the supportive friend, not now. She needed to find a way to move past this place she seemed trapped in, to get over Emma once and for all. But if they really were breaking up, or whatever you called it when friends stopped being friends, then that meant she would never again talk to Emma on the phone, never text her first thing in the morning, never call her at the end of the day to say goodnight. Emma's name wouldn't show in her recent calls list or in her messages or emails.

But maybe it still could. Maybe they could get past this. Emma could fly down after camp like she'd offered and they could talk everything through, and maybe they could salvage a friendship, at least. They had been through so much together, and there was no guarantee that they wouldn't end up playing together in the future, either for the US or for a pro side somewhere here or in Europe.

Then she pictured Tori slipping her arm around Emma's shoulders the way she had that girl at breakfast, and her stomach clenched. Tori and Emma would be in Chapel Hill together in a few weeks, not to mention Thailand this fall for the U-19 World Cup. They would be around each other almost constantly, and where would Jamie be? In high school playing for the U-16s, if she was lucky—assuming that sneaking out of her room hadn't gotten her kicked out of the pool for good.

At some point she gave into exhaustion and slept, dreaming vivid dreams she didn't remember later. In the morning she awoke before the alarm went off and lay in bed worrying through one negative emotion after another. At last she rolled over and turned her phone on. Nothing. Emma hadn't called her back after she hung up or even sent a text. Jamie sucked in a breath. It hadn't occurred to her that maybe Emma would be done. But she was the one who had started pulling away first, the one who had occasionally failed to call or text back for more than a day or two at a time. Jamie had given her the benefit of the doubt, assuming that she was just having a tough few months after her dad died. Now that she knew about Tori, though, everything looked different.

Britt was still asleep, so Jamie closed herself in the bathroom and dialed a familiar number, waiting as it rang through to voicemail. "Can you call me when you get this?"

Then she got ready for the day, showering and shaving her legs quickly and smearing her skin afterward with lotion that contained SPF 45. You could never be too careful when it came to skin cancer.

Britt was sitting up in bed when Jamie reemerged.

"Sheesh," she said, yawning. "You're up early, especially for someone who did a runner last night."

"Sorry—hope I didn't wake you up coming back in."

"No problem." Britt hesitated. "Is everything okay?"

Jamie shrugged and didn't look at her.

"I mean, it's none of my business, but you seemed upset about that Tori chick hooking up with your friend. Emma's the one whose dad died, isn't she?"

She wished now she'd never told Britt and Angie about her trip to Seattle. But they'd been texting while Jamie was there, and it hadn't occurred to her to hide her friendship with Emma.

"Yeah, but we haven't been as close since spring break."

"Oh." Britt frowned. "What happened?"

"Her ex-boyfriend and I got into it a little, and ever since then it's been weird. Plus she's leaving for UNC in a few weeks so we're headed in different directions. That's probably why she didn't say anything."

"Right." Britt nodded like what she was saying made perfect sense, and then slid out of bed. "Wait for me to go down for breakfast?"

"Sure."

Britt paused and squeezed Jamie's shoulder. "I'm here if you want to talk, bro. Just so you know."

Jamie nodded, staring straight ahead. Admit to anyone else that Emma had broken her heart? Not effing likely.

Her phone rang while Britt was in the bathroom, and she held it for a second, eyes closed. Then she checked the name and pressed talk.

"Yo, sis," Meg said, yawning. "Got your message. Where's the fire?"

"Can you come get me during free-time this afternoon? We have two hours before dinner, and I have to get out of here."

"Of course. Text me when and where."

"Okay," Jamie said, relieved. "Thanks, Meg."

"You got it. But give me a hint—is this about soccer or Emma?"

"Both, I guess."

She managed to hang on through morning fitness even though not sleeping well two nights in a row had her dragging. At the end of the session, Jo Nichols asked her to stay after, and she almost threw up the Gatorade she'd been pounding.

"Yeah, Coach?" she asked, keeping her eye on the older woman's shirt collar as other players filed out of the weight room.

"I understand you were out of your room after curfew last night."

"Um, yeah. Sorry about that." As the coach gazed at her, she added, "I had a phone call and I didn't want to keep my roommate up."

"As thoughtful as that is, there's a curfew for a reason, Jamie. You're a minor and you're our responsibility. I'm sure you can appreciate the difficult position you put us in by being out of your room last night."

"Yes, ma'am," she said quickly. "It won't happen again. I promise."

"All right, then," Jo said. "I'll let it go with a warning. But I expect better from you. Now go get cleaned up for lunch."

"Yes, ma'am. Thank you, ma'am."

Jamie hurried out of the room, nearly tripping over Britt and Angie in the hallway.

"Dude, are you in trouble?" Britt asked, chewing a cuticle anxiously.

"Nah, just a warning. Let's go eat. I'm starving."

"Me, too."

Angie rolled her eyes. "You guys are always starving. I swear you're like a couple of teenaged boys."

At afternoon free-time, Jamie said goodbye to her friends and went outside the hotel to wait for Meg. She checked her phone for the hundredth time that day, but Emma was still laying low. At this time on Sunday they'd been making plans to see each other; now, two days later, they weren't speaking. How could that be? How could Emma suddenly be gone? But that's what Jamie had done to both Amanda and Faith. Maybe this was karma coming back around to knock her on her ass.

Meg pulled up right on time and they drove to the ocean. Hermosa Beach wasn't quite ten miles away, but it took them almost half an hour to get there and find a parking spot. By the time they were walking on the paved boardwalk that ran for miles at the edge of the beach, Jamie had filled her sister in.

"I'm so sorry, kiddo," Meg said, slipping her arm around her waist and giving her a sideways hug. "But you know, they say that a relationship doesn't end if it doesn't end badly."

Jamie choked out something that was half-laugh, half-sob. "In that case, Emma and I are definitely done. I haven't heard from her at all since last night."

"Do you want to, though? Remember how Amanda blew up your phone after you guys broke up?"

"Yeah, but this is different. We've been best friends for the last year, you know?"

"You could always get in touch with her."

"She slept with a girl, Meg, and then she let me come here and find out about it from other people. She's not even really injured. She just didn't bother to show up."

"Are you more upset about the girl or the fact she didn't tell you?"

"I don't know." She shook her head, and the words that came out next even surprised her a little: "Is anyone ever going to love me?"

Meg stopped and put her hands on Jamie's shoulders. "Don't do that. You're amazing, and anyone would be lucky to have you. Anyway, what about Amanda? Or Faith?"

"That wasn't love. They didn't know me, not like Emma does. She gets me. Or she did, anyway. And she still picked Tori."

"That doesn't mean she doesn't care about you."

She didn't want Emma to only care about her. She wanted

her to look at her the way she had that day at the train station—like Jamie was the only person in the world she wanted.

Then something else occurred to her: "I'm Amanda in this scenario, aren't I?"

"What are you talking about?" Meg asked.

"I'm the girl who didn't even know she'd been dumped for someone else."

"You can't be dumped unless you're actually going out with someone, and you and Emma weren't, were you?"

"Maybe not," she conceded. "But it felt like we were."

They started walking again, and she watched Meg out of the corner of her eye. "Do you think she picked Tori over me because of the..?"

"No," her sister said quickly. "Don't even think that."

"How do you know?"

"I just do, okay?"

"Okay." But pretending to agree with her sister did nothing to lessen the ache in her chest that had taken up residence the night before and refused as yet to budge.

They strolled along the boardwalk, eyes and heads shaded from the incessant SoCal sunshine. Jamie knew she should be somewhere quiet and dark resting, but she'd thought it would help to be out in the world rather than lying on her bed waiting for a text that might never come. Normally she would have enjoyed the throngs of fine-looking people roller blading and playing volleyball and laying out in the sun, but today she kept thinking she saw Emma everywhere. That girl sitting on a blanket wore her hair the same way; another further along the boardwalk had a dimple like hers. As a girl on roller blades passed them, tanned legs reminding her of Emma's, Jamie groaned a little.

"What?" Meg asked.

"Do you think I should try dating guys instead?" But even

as she said it, she couldn't help making a face at the idea.

"Judging from your expression, I would say no. You really are the gayest of the gays, kiddo." But she was smiling as she crushed Jamie in another brief, sidelong hug.

"Yeah, bad idea. By the way, thanks for not saying you told me so."

"I wish I'd been wrong, I really do. But you're going to be okay. You're only sixteen, and in a couple of years you'll go off to college and meet someone who is even more awesome than Emma."

"What if I don't want anyone else?"

"You will, someday. The game must go on, after all."

"Not necessarily. Games get canceled or rescheduled all the time."

Meg rolled her eyes. "I'm going to miss your literal mind next year, you know that?"

"And I'm going to miss your bossiness."

"Good thing I'll be less than an hour away. By the way, I hear Stanford has a stellar soccer program…"

Jamie's eyes widened. "Can you imagine if we both defected to Cal's biggest rival? It's kind of surprising Mom and Dad haven't kicked you out as it is."

"They're happy I'm going to a good school. And you know they would be thrilled if you stuck around for college, Miss World Soccer Traveler."

Jamie thought she would probably be pretty happy to have a few more years at home with the family, too. Or close to home, anyway.

"We'll see," she said. "I have to graduate from high school first."

As they wandered the sandy walkway surrounded by beautiful beach people, the sun shifting overhead on its slow circuit of the sky, Jamie recalled a morning run she and Emma had taken in Seattle. Emma had said she felt like she'd stopped moving when her mom told her about her dad, just completely stopped. Meanwhile everything else around her had continued on and now she was a pace behind and didn't know for sure if she would ever catch up.

"I'll wait for you," Jamie had said as they paused at an overlook, Puget Sound spread out before them. "I'm not going anywhere."

Emma had looked at her then with an odd look, hope and fear and guilt all rolled into one. Now, of course, that look made perfect sense. Emma had already been crushing on Tori by then. Maybe they'd even hooked up, despite her insistence to the contrary. Would she really flat out lie to Jamie? Possibly. Like father like daughter.

She reached for the bracelet Emma had given her and rubbed the familiar engraving. Only this time, instead of calming her like it normally did, the feel of the metal warmed by her skin only made the ache in her chest spread until she thought she might choke. Blinking back tears, she undid the clasp and veered off the boardwalk toward a trash can. Before she could second-guess the decision, she dropped the bracelet into the receptacle where it landed on top of a pizza box.

"Didn't Emma give you that?" Meg asked, frowning.

"Yep."

"Are you sure you want to throw it away?"

"Positive," Jamie said, already feeling lighter.

In her most recent session with Shoshanna, after Jamie had admitted she'd broken up with Faith and was looking forward to seeing Emma in LA, the therapist had asked if her relationship with Emma was still more positive than negative. At the time, Jamie hadn't quite known how to answer, but now she did. She and Emma may have anchored each other through painful experiences, but somewhere along the way they had begun to weigh each other down.

On one wall of Shoshanna's office was a framed Einstein quote: "Life is like riding a bicycle. To keep your balance, you must keep moving." So that was what they would do. They would keep moving and they would both be fine. Maybe, someday, they would even find their way back to each other. But for now, it was time to move on.

Apparently Emma realized that, too.

Slipping her arm through Meg's, Jamie leaned into her sister's side as they rambled on along the boardwalk, the sound of the ocean thrumming in her ears.

#

"I know it hurts, but what did you expect?" Dani asked.

Emma gripped her hand tightly. "Do you think there's any way to stop it?"

"That's not a question I can answer. Only she can."

The woman bending over Emma's hip sat up and raised the magnifying lenses on her glasses. "We'll be done soon. You're doing fine. You should see some of the whiners I get in here. Grown men are the absolute worst."

Emma took a breath and peeked at the tattoo taking shape on her hip. It was actually really nice—clean, simple lines and small enough that no one would ever know it was there unless they saw her naked. Some of her regret faded. Maybe this wasn't the stupidest thing she'd ever done. Probably, she already knew what that was. And like the tattoo, there was no erasing it now.

"Ready to continue?" the tattoo artist asked.

She nodded. "Go for it."

The woman winked at her and went back to work.

"Have you heard from Jamie at all?" Dani asked.

"No."

"Did you email her?"

"Not yet. I don't want to bug her at camp. She'll be home

Sunday."

Dani tapped her fingers against the chair she was sitting on. "Are you sure an email is the best way to handle this?"

"No, but I doubt she'd answer her phone, and I don't want to send her a thousand texts like her ex did."

She wasn't sure Jamie would read an email either, but she couldn't leave for North Carolina without reaching out somehow. Otherwise the next time they met—and she had a feeling they would meet again—it might be too difficult to get past what had happened.

"Okay, but can I point out that this is what you did last time?"

"What do you mean?"

"You screwed up and then you blew her off. Do you really think she's going to forgive that a second time?"

Emma closed her eyes. "It doesn't matter. I'm pretty sure she isn't going to forgive me either way. I wouldn't if I was her."

"Neither would I," Dani admitted.

"I really fucked up this time, didn't I?"

"Yep. But I still love you."

Emma was almost certain the same couldn't be said for Jamie.

The tattoo artist had lied. They were nowhere near to being done. The torture had to end eventually, though, and when it did, Emma found herself blinking back tears that had nothing to do with her damaged skin.

"What do you think?" the woman asked as they all stared at the completed tattoo.

"It's perfect."

Dani nodded. "It really is."

"Can I see the necklace again?"

Emma pulled the spiral sun out from under her T-shirt and waited while the woman briefly compared the pendant to the tattoo.

"I think that's it," the tattoo artist said, nodding.

They went over care instructions as Emma pulled her shorts up, and then Dani and Emma were leaving the cramped shop and walking back to Dani's car.

"Aren't you glad I talked you out of the song idea?" Dani asked, nudging her shoulder as they strolled along Broadway.

For half a second, Emma had kicked around getting a line from Pearl Jam's "Wishlist"—the one about being the verb to trust and never letting someone down—tattooed at the base of her spine. Fortunately, Dani had convinced her that this was not the phrase she wanted to share with future significant others—or with her future children, for that matter.

"I mean, is 'Mommy is a lying liar' really the aesthetic you're going for?" Dani had intoned, eyebrows raised.

Now Emma smiled sideways at her. "Glad doesn't begin to cover it."

Her smile slipped at Dani's next words: "Are you going to tell her about it?"

She knew which "her" Dani meant. "I don't think so. It's not for her, you know. It's for me. Besides, it's more of a compass than a sun."

"Whatever you say, Princess."

Emma resisted the urge to smack her best friend. After all, they didn't have much time left together before they both headed off to college. She couldn't believe it was almost August already. Her post-high school life had seemed so far away for so long, and now it was suddenly, painfully close.

Dani dropped her off at home and she wandered from room to room, looking for her mom or Ty. But no one was home as usual, not even the dog. It was as if her dad had been the sun they revolved around, and without his light and warmth to ground them, without his gravitational pull they were drifting away from each other. What a year. If someone had told her when it started that her father would be gone and she and Jamie would no longer be speaking, she wouldn't have believed it. But here she was alone in the house on a beautiful summer day waiting for her new life to start without two of the people who had been so integral to the old one.

By the time Sunday came, she had revised her letter to Jamie more times than her college application and senior honors essays, combined. After breakfast with her mom and brother, she went into the den and opened the text file to read through it again:

Dear Jamie,

I'm sitting here at my father's desk writing this letter to you, and I can't quite figure out how we got to this place. I know I'm responsible for what happened and that you probably hate me by now. You were my anchor when I was at my lowest, and I repaid you by using you to make myself feel better and then lying to you about what was really going on with me. But you know all of that. What I hope you also know is how much I care about you. You have been an amazing friend this past year, and I am changed because of you.

Please believe me when I say that I truly regret how I handled everything. I don't have any excuse, except to say that I am descended from multiple generations of Minnesotans, a people not known for our ability to process difficult emotional situations. Chop down a forest and tame a river, yes, but deal with our emotions? Oh, hell no. I'm only sorry I couldn't figure myself out better before I hurt you.

My offer to visit still stands, but I also understand if I've botched things beyond repair. Just please know I'm thinking about you. No matter what, I will always be grateful that I went for that first walk with you.

Good luck with school and soccer. Our paths may be diverging now, but I still hope we might meet again someday down the road, and when we do, that we can be friends.

Miss you. All my love, always,

Emma

She copied and pasted the text into an email, read it over one last time, and finally forced herself to send it. There. Now she had to wait to see if Jamie would respond.

Too antsy to be by herself, she went back into the kitchen where her mom was cleaning up the breakfast mess. Wordlessly she picked up a dishrag and set to work on the detached bar while her mom washed the cast iron skillet she'd used for pancakes. Emma was wiping down the individual rungs of each bar stool when she felt her mother's eyes on her.

"What?"

"Now I know something is wrong. Like mother like daughter."

Whenever her mom was upset about a dying patient or a bureaucratic administrator, their house became the cleanest place on Earth. She'd always said that scrubbing the bejesus out of things made her feel better, an impulse Emma had grown to understand better over the past few months. She may not be able to control her feelings—or even her own actions, apparently—but she sure as hell could control how clean the backsplash in her bathroom got.

When Emma didn't answer, her mother pressed. "Want to talk about it?"

Emma balled the dishrag in her fist. "I don't know."

"Might be more beneficial than destroying household cleaning items…"

"Fine. But remember, you asked." She hopped up on one of the stools and rested her elbows on the bar. "It's Jamie."

Her mom came and sat next to her. "I remember the last time you said that to me. I hope it's not as serious this time?"

"No." She hesitated. Her mother had barely been home all summer, pulling double shift after double shift in a transparent attempt to literally work through her grief. She had lost weight, and her formerly fit figure now seemed gaunt. Emma wasn't sure how or if she should tell her that. She couldn't remember the last time they had talked about anything deeper than work, school, or soccer schedules.

"I know I haven't exactly been knocking the parent thing out of the park lately," her mom said, drawing circles on the bar tiles with her pointer finger, "but I would really like to listen, if you feel like talking."

"You've been doing fine," Emma assured her.

"You don't have to say that. We both know I've barely been getting by. I'm sorry your last summer at home had to be like this. I envisioned it going very differently. So did your dad."

"So did I," she admitted.

"What do you think? Do you want to throw your old mom a bone here?"

"Again, pointing out that you asked for it." And she launched into an abridged version of the past few months, starting with the kiss at the train station and ending with the email she'd sent out into cyberspace, uncertain if it would even be read let alone answered.

When she finished, her mom steepled her hands and regarded her. "Did you really hurt your hamstring, or were you trying to avoid camp?"

"It's been nagging me, for sure. But I probably would have gone if the sixteens weren't there."

"I wish I'd known that. I probably would have made you go."

"In the spirit of 'you made your bed and now you have to lie in it'?"

"Precisely. Although, I don't know, maybe it's better this way. If nothing else, you saved Jamie the pain of seeing you and Tori together. You do know why that would have hurt her, don't you?"

Emma bowed her head. "Of course."

"And you? How do you feel about her?"

"The same way. But it can't happen. Even before I messed everything up, it was an impossible situation."

"I'm going to ask you something and I want you to think about it. Is it possible you did all of this so that it would be easier to leave Jamie behind at the end of the summer?"

Emma covered her face with one hand. "God, you sound like Dani."

"Dani knows about all of this?"

"Well, yeah."

Her mom blinked. "You're serious about dating women, aren't you? This isn't about having a crush or trying something out."

"Yes, I'm serious. I thought you knew that."

Slowly her mom shook her head. "You told me, but I'm not sure I fully comprehended. I had crushes on girls when I was younger, too. I think most of us do. But you're talking about something else entirely."

Crap. Emma bit her lip. Technically she was still a minor while Tori wasn't. Would her mom cause problems with the federation? Could Tori get in actual trouble, as in legal trouble, for having sex with an underage teammate? Her mother hadn't interfered when she told her she was planning to have sex with Drew her junior year. In fact, she'd taken her to Planned Parenthood herself and made sure she knew all of her options when it came to protection. But sex with a girl, apparently, was different.

Her mom touched her arm. "Don't worry, sweetheart, I'm glad you told me. Genuinely. Actually, I'm thankful you felt you could after the way I've been missing in action lately."

"Oh," Emma said, breathing a little easier. "Well, good."

"It's apparent that you recognize your mistakes and you're taking responsibility for your actions, so that's a good sign. Now I guess you have to wait and see what Jamie wants to do."

"That's why I suddenly felt the urge to clean," she said, holding up the wrinkled dishrag.

"I could think of some other work around the house…"

Emma smiled. "That's okay. I should probably start packing for school. Only fourteen shopping days left."

"Good point." She paused. "What do you think about making a dorm room list and running to Fred Meyer later?"

"Sounds good to me," Emma said, and hugged her.

Cleaning, working, or shopping therapy—in her family, staying busy had always been the prescription for a broken heart.

For the next couple of days, Emma checked her email almost hourly, trying to distract herself with packing her room and planning for college while the email she was hoping for remained elusive. Finally, on Wednesday night after dinner when Emma checked her email for the hundred and thirty-second time since Sunday, Jamie's name leapt out at her from the sender column. She had replied. Jamie had written back.

Emma pushed back from her father's desk and paced around the den, nearly slamming her shin against the awkwardly situated printer table. She'd heard her dad yelp and curse in here a hundred times, but whenever her mom suggested moving the printer, he insisted he liked it where it was. Now Emma paused to push it closer to the wall, sending her dad a silent apology. She knew her mother would never move the table herself.

Distraction exhausted, she went back to the desk chair and sat down, staring at the screen. Then she clicked on Jamie's reply.

Dear Emma,

I don't hate you. You are one of the closest friends I've ever had, but for whatever reason, you did what you did and neither of us can change it. I've been tempted to rethink the entire past year, but I know that you cared about me, and you were an incredible support at a time when I really needed it. I'll always be grateful to you for that.

The thing is, though, I can't be your friend anymore. At least not right now. Do you remember how I asked you what you wanted and you said you didn't know? And I said maybe it was time you figured it out? Well, you obviously made your choice. I get why you picked her. I really do. I probably would have done the same thing in your position. I only wish I had found out from you instead of from a girl I didn't even know.

You said you still have hope that we might end up as friends one day. I'm honestly not sure how I feel about that. I guess we'll have to wait and see where we're at if and when the soccer gods decide to bring us back together.

In the meantime, I hope you know that I wish you all the best on your path.

See you-

Jamie

Emma scrolled down, hoping for a postscript or an attachment, but that was it. She read through it again, inwardly protesting Jamie's version of events. She hadn't chosen Tori over her. It wasn't like that at all. In reality Jamie wasn't available and Tori was. The older girl was attractive and confident and she didn't even know Emma's father had died. They didn't know each other well at all, which was why, as Dani had said, she made the perfect first girl. Meanwhile Jamie had shared herself with Emma and Emma had opened up to her in return in a way she could honestly say she had never experienced with another human being. In the way that mattered most, Jamie was the true first—no, the *only* girl.

Not that she would ever get the chance to tell her that now. The email was entirely unambiguous in both voice and content. At least if Jamie had still been angry with her she would have had something to work with. But Jamie wasn't mad, and she wasn't willing to try to fix what Emma had broken. She didn't even want to try to stay friends.

"Fuck," she whispered. "Fuck, fuck, *fuck*."

She pictured Jamie at home with her adorable family in their adorable house in adorable Berkeley, and the urge to pick up the phone and call her like she had a hundred or more times in the year since they'd met nearly overwhelmed her. It would be so easy. Jamie wouldn't really hang up on her, would she? Then she remembered how Jamie had told her that once she broke up with Amanda, her feelings for the other girl had shut off as if they had never even existed. Besides, her email was clear. She didn't want phone calls, texts, visits. She didn't want contact with Emma of any kind, possibly not ever.

In the living room, her mother glanced up from her book as Emma entered. "Any word?"

Emma nodded and opened her mouth, but nothing came out. She stared at her mother, eyes blurring.

"Oh, honey," her mom said, and opened her arms.

Emma fell onto the couch beside her, burying her face in her shoulder. She was too old to be doing this, she knew, but she couldn't help it. Jamie had closed the door on their past, present, and possibly their future, too. She knew it was unrealistic, but at some level Emma had still hoped Jamie would care too much to walk away.

When she eventually managed to say as much, her mom stroked her hair and sighed. "That's probably why she *is* walking away, honey. You said yourself it's an impossible situation. Even if she wanted to try, how could you rebuild your relationship when you're going so far away?"

"I know," Emma said, tears rolling down her cheeks. She wasn't only crying for Jamie. She was also crying for her dad and her mom and Ty, for Dani and the other people she was getting ready to leave behind all so that she could do what? Chase a ball across a field? How could a sport mean more to her than everyone she loved and who loved her?

But being a soccer player wasn't, for her, only about playing the game. On her dad's desk was a framed quote from Roger G. Ingersoll that read, "Reason, observation and experience—the holy trinity of science—have taught us that happiness is the only good; that the time to be happy is now, and the way to be happy is to make others so."

The happiest moment in her life so far was still the day years earlier when she had sat beside her father in the hot Pasadena sun watching Mia Hamm, Brianna Scurry, and the rest of the 1999 World Cup champion team inspire a nation, possibly even the world. She had already known that soccer was her life's passion. But on that day, she'd realized it could also be her path to one day making others as happy and inspired as she had felt watching that amazing group of women achieve everything they'd set out to do.

For a little while, she had thought she and Jamie might share that path. Maybe they still would someday in the near or far future. But in the meantime, in just under two weeks, she would fly across the country to the place where her collegiate soccer career would begin. And after that, who knows? Being an athlete is a precarious endeavor. You can never be sure if your body—or mind, for that matter—will hold up under the pressure.

For now, though, national championship berths and World Cup victories and Olympic gold medals were still only dreams that she may or may not achieve. For now, she thought she wouldn't mind resting in the circle of her mother's arms a little longer as the summer sun set over the Olympic Peninsula and a ferry boat cruised across water that rippled orange and pink, reflecting the last light of day from clouds gathering overhead.

BOOK TWO EXCERPT

Thank you for reading the first book in the Girls of Summer series. To read an excerpt of book two, *Game Time*, visit http://www.katejchristie.com/game_time.html.

ABOUT THE AUTHOR

Kate Christie lives with her family near Seattle. A graduate of Smith College and Western Washington University, she has played soccer most of her life and counts attending the 2015 World Cup finals game in Vancouver as one of her top five Favorite Days Ever.

To find out more about Kate, or to read excerpts from her other titles from Second Growth Books and Bella Books, please visit her author website at www.katejchristie.com. Or check out her blog, *Homodramatica* (katechristie.wordpress.com), where she occasionally finds time to wax unpoetically about lesbian life, fiction, and motherhood.

Printed in Great Britain
by Amazon